AMBUSHED

by

Wil Tustin

authorHOUSE®

AuthorHouse™
1663 Liberty Drive
Bloomington, IN 47403
www.authorhouse.com
Phone: 1-800-839-8640

Published by AuthorHouse 11/19/2012

ISBN: 978-1-4772-6301-3 (sc)
ISBN: 978-1-4772-6300-6 (hc)
ISBN: 978-1-4772-6299-3 (e)

Cover painting by Mark Miller
Library of Congress Control Number: 2012915223

Any people depicted in stock imagery provided by Thinkstock are models, and such images are being used for illustrative purposes only. Certain stock imagery © Thinkstock.

This book is printed on acid-free paper.

Because of the dynamic nature of the Internet, any web addresses or links contained in this book may have changed since publication and may no longer be valid. The views expressed in this work are solely those of the author and do not necessarily reflect the views of the publisher, and the publisher hereby disclaims any responsibility for them.

Table of Contents

Chapter One
A Time to Grow Up

"There is a time for everything and a season
for every activity under heaven."
Solomon

My first recollection of the battle between good and evil happened a week after my tenth birthday. I was playing hide and seek with five cousins in the Tarsus Marketplace. Partially hidden behind a perfume vendor's stand, a Macedonian businesswoman and family acquaintance saw me and shouted, "Saul, your father is looking for you. You better get to his shop, now!"

"Yes, ma'am," I politely replied over the growing sounds of commerce spoken in numerous languages.

"Our uncle found out you fell into the Cydnus River," my oldest cousin teased. "You're in big trouble, Saul."

"No, I'm not!" I shouted, promptly leaving the marketplace.

Our house was in the Jewish quarter of Tarsus, an oasis of morality amidst a desert of depravity. The other neighborhoods were filled with harlots, hustlers, and heathen temples. I took a shortcut home and passed through one of them, dodging intoxicated bodies and ignoring vulgar behavior.

When I entered our house my mother said in Aramaic, "Your tunic and mantle are soaking wet. Change them, and then go see your abba. He's waiting for you in his shop."

After changing clothes, I ran out the side door. Father's tent shop was attached to our house, common venue in the Jewish quarter. "Where have you been?" he asked in Hebrew, as I slid open the pocket door. Abba always spoke to me in Hebrew when we were alone. He was proud of his Jewish heritage.

I nervously answered, "Playing in the marketplace with my cousins."

"Foolishness," Abba said, waving his hand in the air, dismissing my childish games.

"What did you want me for, Abba?" I inquired after breathing a sigh of relief.

"The nomads have yet to come down from the mountains. The snow melted in the mountain passes weeks ago. We need their wool for a large, Roman army order of tents and saddles."

"They usually descend the mountain trails weeks before my birthday," I agreed.

"Would you like to hike into the mountains with me to buy some goat hair?"

Our tents were made of cilicium, tightly woven wool. My father's black, goat-hair tents were works of art. They were the preferred tents among the Roman army, traveling merchants, and nomads. He had a unique stitch that enhanced the tent's durability and kept out rainwater.

"Yes, Ab!" I roared with excitement, causing my mother, or ima, to look out the side door window. This was my first trip into the Tarsus Mountains, a strategical and natural fortress for Tarsus.

"Normally, by this time of year I've already finished several tents." Father groaned, hiding his money bag under one of the donkey's packs.

"When do we leave?" I asked while patting my favorite donkey, Festus. He was blind, born without pupils, and small in stature.

"We're leaving now," Abba informed me tying our donkeys to separate lead lines. "We're taking twelve donkeys into the mountains. I'll ride one and guide eight. You can ride Festus and guide two."

"Will all twelve donkeys be loaded with wool on the way home? And will we have to walk all the way home?"

"Yes, can you handle it?" Abba asked, leading the donkeys outside.

"No problem!"

"Then, go give your ima a kiss goodbye."

I met her at the side door and she hugged me so tight my tongue popped out. She cried and said, "I'll miss you, Saul. Be careful in those mountains." The pleasant odor of her geranium perfume stayed in my nostrils for awhile.

Ima hugged Abba goodbye and instructed, "Bring my son back home without any scratches. Also, load up those donkeys with a lot of black wool." Father waved goodbye to my younger brothers with his huge hands, the hands of Tarsus' finest craftsman.

~~

Abba and I rode our donkeys across the fertile plains of Cilicia Pedias to the Tarsus foothills. "Saul, you and the donkeys still seem to have some energy. How about if we go into the hill country and make camp there?"

"That's fine with me. I can stay awake if you can," I boasted, pulling two tethered donkeys. Thirty minutes later I barely caught myself by the reins before falling off Festus. Abba noticed it and made camp. We had a restful night beneath a bank of dark clouds.

The next morning we rose at sunrise, fed the donkeys, and ate breakfast. Then we trekked toward the Tarsus Mountains. When we reached the mountain trails, our enthusiasm and sense of duty kept us moving upward.

After we climbed a steep mountain trail for what seemed like forever, my father pointed and said, "There's the Cilician Gate! It's only a short distance away. We'll take a long rest once we get through the gate."

"Good," I groaned.

Exhausted, we passed through the Cilician Gate. Startled, we were ambushed by eight bandits. Within seconds we were surrounded by evil and its cloud of dust. Apparently, the bandits had been pursuing us for awhile from behind stone boulders like lionesses stalking their prey in tall grass.

They wildly waved their arms and shouted, "You're dead, you stinking Jews!" Their scurrilous insults and frightful screams echoed off the massive boulders they'd jumped from behind.

My father grabbed the first bandit to attack us by the scuff of his mantle. He drove the bandit's nose into his right knee and bellowed, "How does that smell, you stinking thief?"

He turned to confront the next assailant, but three bandits simultaneously jumped him. The bandits threw their fists in frenzy, while my father took calculated punches. He landed twice as many blows as they did.

Abba shouted, "Not as easy as you thought!"

Meanwhile, another bandit grabbed me by the back of the neck and pulled me off Festus. When the bandit leaned over to beat me Festus kicked him. It was as if Festus could see. He kicked the bandit in his groin.

I got up and kicked the bandit, who was rolling all over the ground.

I screamed, "Leave us alone! Leave us alone!" Meanwhile, the last three bandits, much larger in size, finally decided to partake in the skirmish. Two of them swung clubs longer than me and the third waved a small dagger.

Abba held his own, until one of the club-carrying bandits sneaked up behind him. The bandit swung with all his might and connected with the back of abba's skull. He instantly collapsed on the mountain trail. The other bandits kicked, clubbed, mocked, and spat on him. The bandit with the dagger stabbed him twice.

"You murderers. You murderers!" I shrieked, trying to kick free from my thief's ankle tight grip. The pain of my bandit's throbbing testicles abated as he stood up. Once erect, he threw an upper cut with all his might that landed on my lower jaw. The blow lifted me a cubit off the ground, and I fell unconscious on the mountain trail.

When I awoke, my father was holding his chest and moaned, "Saul, help me. Help me." I slowly got up, stumbled over to him, and wept as I gazed upon his beaten, bloody body. Our empty money bag laid on Abba's chest being filled with his blood.

"You've got to get me back to Tarsus. Get me on a donkey," Abba faintly uttered before he passed out from the pain. I looked around for our donkeys, but discovered everything had been taken except for the bandits' two wooden clubs, my wool saddle blanket, and Festus.

I made a travois, using my blanket as netting and the bandits' wood clubs as trailing poles. I whispered into Abba's ear, "I'm going to roll you onto a homemade travois. Then Festus and I are going to take you home." With every ounce of energy left, I shouldered Ab's body onto the travois.

When I stood up, I noticed Abba's sewing kit. The tool of his trade, he always carried it with him. It lay in a pool of blood on the ground. I grabbed the kit and more out of instinct than know how I sewed up Abba's chest wounds. He gained consciousness on the last stitch and screamed, "Jehovah, help us!"

"Good thing you're headstrong." I joked, hoping to bring some levity to our crisis.

I rested my fatigued body for a moment, then tied the travois' poles to Festus and began the arduous task of pulling Abba back to Tarsus. My father slipped in and out of consciousness every ten minutes and wrenched in pain every time he regained awareness.

Several hundred paces from the Cilician Gate I passed out from exhaustion and fell off Festus. I banged my forehead on a large rock and lost consciousness for several minutes. With a pounding headache and blood dripping down my face, I eventually managed to get back up.

"Now, who has the hard head?" Abba groaned in jocularity amidst his excruciating pain.

Festus and I labored for hours, dragging my father down the mountain trail. On the last steep incline Festus lost his footing. Abba and I fell and bounced about twenty paces down the rocky mountain path. My father screamed in anguish. We both lay helpless on the rugged mountain trail for awhile. Then Abba prayed, "Jehovah, please help my son persevere amidst overwhelming odds."

Within minutes, I regained some strength. My weary childhood frame stood up and felt slightly renewed. I managed to get father back on the travois. Festus pulled and carried us down the rest of that lengthy mountain trail. I stopped several times to rest our pain-racked bodies and rewrapped bleeding wounds.

Chapter Two
A Time to be a Grown-up

"All mankind is divided into three classes: Those who are
immovable, those who are movable and those who move."
Arabian Proverb

I lost track of time. We finally reached the stony, green foothills beneath
the glow of an ascending moon. After untying Festus from the travois, I
collapsed and fell asleep on a grassy knoll. Suddenly, my ears were filled
with the sound of howling beasts. Groggy, I jumped to my feet and realized
we were being ambushed by wild dogs. Six of them already had Festus on
the ground and were tearing at his flesh.

One wild dog was licking my unconscious father's chest wounds,
which had reopened. I slowly pulled one of the poles out of Abba's travois
and knocked that wild dog off its feet. It and the rest of the wild beasts ran
back into the mountains. I tried to retrieve Festus's carcass, but the dogs
had already dragged it away.

My father regained consciousness as I cleaned his chest wounds. In a
state of hysteria, I told him, "Ab, wild dogs just killed and ate Festus!"

"Don't worry, we are in good hands. Just do what you can do," his lips
barely uttered.

"Okay," I said, regaining my composure. "I can't pull you over all these
foothills. I'm going to build a large fire with the travois' poles and whatever
firewood I can gather. Then, I'm going for help!"

Father tried to murmur, but he couldn't. Instead, he shook his head and
bumped the avocado size lump on his head against a rock. He screamed
in pain and passed out.

My chilled fingers started a bonfire. I split off a piece of the burning travois pole and cauterized Abba's wounds. His body flinched numerous times, but he never regained consciousness as the red hot twig closed his bleeding vessels. Then I kissed his forehead and whispered, "Abba, I promise I'll be back before the wild dogs or bandits. Jehovah will watch over you while I'm gone."

I jogged over the Tarsus foothills, but found myself crawling across the plains of Cilicia Pedias. It was then, I faintly heard a voice say, "Earthly outcomes are in My hands, but you have to make the effort."

Half way home, a fruit vendor headed to the Tarsus Marketplace, saw me passed out on the stone road amidst the weeds and wild, red poppies. He pushed aside some boxes of figs and placed me in his cart. The vendor gently awoke me at the city gate. I thanked him and sprinted home as light began to overcome darkness.

I collapsed on our kitchen floor, crying and screaming for Ima. She jumped out of bed and began weeping when she saw me. Within seconds, she regained her poise and ordered my brothers, "Go get the doctor and your uncles. Now!"

Five minutes later, a Jewish doctor and Ima's five brothers arrived. The doctor cleaned and stitched up my wounds. My closest and dearest uncle said, "Saul, we need you to show us where your Abba is."

"He's not going back out there!" Ima avowed. "He's exhausted and near death."

"It's our only hope to find your husband before he dies. We'll put Saul on a donkey, and he can sleep on it," Ima's tallest brother stated with firmness.

Ima reluctantly agreed. She hugged me goodbye and wailed, "I won't stop praying till you come back home." The doctor, my uncles, and I were out of the house within seconds.

We traveled as fast as the donkeys could go across the plains of Cilicia Pedias and into the hill country. Once again, while slipping in and out of sleep, I heard a faint voice say, "Occasionally, I shape and mold my flock through hardships, which draws them near to Me. And I will never leave or forsake any who follow me."

When we reached the bonfire, it was out and so was abba. The doctor worked on my father for more than an hour, then said, "Good sewing job, Saul. Your tent maker's stitch saved your abba's life. Plus, cauterizing his wounds diminished his possibilities for infections. Maybe you should be a doctor instead of a lawyer."

"Thank you, sir, but I'm going to be a Pharisee like Abba and these hands are going to make tents for a living like Abba," I proudly claimed.

Three uncles put my father on a donkey, and we headed across the hill country. We stopped numerous times to tend to his near-fatal wounds. When we arrived at our house, they put him in bed, and he stayed there for three weeks. He slowly recovered during the next two months, but he never fully recuperated from the knife wounds and beating. Abba had to walk with a cane, because the bandits broke his right leg in three places and left leg in two places.

~~

Three months after Abba's beating, he half-heartily returned to the tent shop. He displayed a lot more patience with me at the loom. Furthermore, his main interests no longer seemed to reside in the shop, but in his sons' academic achievements.

All Jewish boys from three to thirteen years old were educated six days a week at their local synagogue's House of Books. It prevented us from being defiled by our gentile peers' schools. Our main textbooks were the *Torah, Pentateuch, Writings (Psalms and Proverbs),* and *Books of the Prophets.*

Two mornings every week, Abba showed up at our synagogues' House of Books to assist our teachers. Also, he met me four days a week in the marketplace after school; he accompanied me two days a week to Latin language school and two days to Greek language school.

My scholastic achievements were unprecedented within the Tarsus synagogue and Cilician province. Under Abba's tutelage and the synagogue teachers' auspices I memorized the Mosaic Law, Hebrew rituals, and the rabbinic oral laws by age eleven.

By twelve, I could recite a sixth of the *Psalms* and half the *Talmud* from memory. Also, I excelled in other academic endeavors; languages, mathematics, literature, writing, and poetry.

I occasionally sneaked out of my parents' house after dark to expand my knowledge of Hellenistic rhetoric. The Cynic and Stoic philosophers debated nightly in the Tarsus Marketplace. The Cynic philosophized one should abandon all life's comforts, while the Stoic professed the doctrine of natural law. Both schools used and taught me the diatribe technique, debating through questions.

~~

Two days before my thirteenth birthday and the Jewish Passover, Abba's brother from Jerusalem showed up in Tarsus. Uncle Elisha was a dealer in precious stones and claimed to be in town on business. After he hugged me, I teased, "You really came to Tarsus to attend my bar mitzvah, didn't you?"

"You got me," he bantered. That night we were entertained by Abba and Uncle Elisha reminiscing childhood stories.

The next day Uncle Elisha and I went shopping for my birthday present in the marketplace. He inquired beneath the hot afternoon sun, "Saul, I hear you're an outstanding student with scholastic promise. Are you going to continue your education in Jerusalem at one of our Houses of Study?"

"No, I plan to stay in Tarsus! It's the third largest academic center in the Roman Empire after Athens and Alexandria. The Roman senate just gave us the status of a *libera civitas* because of our academic institutions. This means we can govern ourselves within Rome's civil and criminal laws. You can't say that of Jerusalem!" I boasted of my hometown.

"Tarsus is no Jerusalem," Uncle Elisha declared. "Tarsus' academic institutions are rooted in Greco-Roman culture. Jerusalem's Houses of Study are based on Hebrew ethos."

"I never thought about continuing my education in Jerusalem," I responded, looking at different vendors' clothing items. "My parents want me to stay in Tarsus."

"Saul, you're a smart boy. I mean, man. You need to talk your father into letting you continue your education in Jerusalem at Gamaliel's House of Study," Abba's oldest brother suggested. "You're blessed with extraordinary scholastic abilities. You speak the languages of Jerusalem, Hebrew and Aramaic, as well as I do."

"Uncle Elisha, it would be a dream come true to be under the tutelage of someone like Rabbi Gamaliel, but you really want me to study in Jerusalem so you can spend more time with your favorite nephew," I joshed, while admiring a red Egyptian cotton mantel and green Oriental silk tunic.

"Your bar mitzvah is tomorrow night. You're now a man in the Jewish culture! You have decisions to make as a man. The first one is, will you choose academic pursuits or a chosen craft?"

"Uncle Elisha, that's my dichotomy. Abba and Grandfather say I have what it takes to be an outstanding tent maker. But I want to go to school and become a member of the Sanhedrin, the highest ruling, judicial group in Jerusalem."

"Then, you must decide which city and university will prepare you for the Sanhedrin," Uncle Elisha said as we left the marketplace empty-handed.

Before we entered my parents' house, Uncle Elisha reached deep into the leather bag hanging over his shoulder. He looked me in the eye and said, "Your Aunt Helah couldn't be here because of your cousin Rachel's birth. However, we want you to have this ruby ring as a gift to acknowledge your step into manhood. It's the most precious of all jewels, and you are the most precious of all my nephews. May God bless you and help you find your direction in life."

I embraced my uncle with a huge hug and said, "Thank you," at least ten times.

~~

I felt I'd found my direction in life the day before my thirteenth birthday. So, every night after dinner, for the next three weeks, I pleaded with my parents.

On our twenty-first night's discussion I said: "Abba, I don't have an aversion to your skill, but I'd rather spend my life interpreting the law than making tents. Please permit me to continue my academic studies at one of Jerusalem's Houses of Study. I would love to study under Rabbi Gamaliel, but I will study under Rabbi Shammai or whoever we can afford. Uncle Elisha said, 'Jerusalem is where I belong as a young scholar.'"

"I should've known it was Elisha's idea!" Abba remarked, looking at Ima.

Abba turned toward me and said, "You picked the two leading, as well as most expensive, teachers in Jerusalem." Father folded his napkin and got up from the dinner table.

"I think you should go to school closer to home, in case we need you," Ima remarked, closing the curtain into our dining area so my younger brothers couldn't see us.

"She is right. Saul doesn't need to continue his education at the other end of the empire," my patriarchal grandfather barked from behind a lengthy, snow white beard. His facial hair was so long, one could have weaved a rug from it. "He belongs here making tents! Not in Jerusalem with some maladroit teacher filling his mind with useless knowledge."

Abba had been indecisive for three weeks about sending me to school in Jerusalem; however, he seemed determined to make up his mind. He returned to the table and said, "My son possesses an innate ability to recite our holy scrolls in Hebrew from memory. His scholastic abilities are unmatched in the Jewish and gentile community."

"Granted, Saul is a bright child. He knows more about science, arts, linguistics, Greek philosophies, and Mosaic Laws than any child his age in Cilicia. But a real man feeds his family with his hands!" Grandfather growled, proudly showing us his callous hands. Meanwhile, I silently sat at the table and buried my chin in both palms, praying God would send me to Jerusalem.

Abba remarked, "We are all given a divine purpose on earth before we are even conceived in our mother's wombs. The challenge in life is: pausing and listening to Jehovah, to find our purpose and place in life, and then acting on it."

"You're a Jewish tentmaker, like the other men in this family," snarled my patriarchal grandfather without grace. "This is where your identity and honor lies. Not trying to differentiate yourself in some pious city."

"Yes, Saul's place is here. Tarsus is an outstanding center for higher education," Ima responded, fighting back tears. "Our alumni are among the Roman Empire's intelligentsia."

"Tarsus universities teach in Greek and Latin. I want my son to be educated in Hebrew. Tarsus' schools adhere to pagan laws. We follow the Mosaic Law. Furthermore, as a Pharisee, I'm offended by the Tarsus universities' lack of morals and values." My father paused to catch his breath. "I've decided to send Saul to Palestine where brilliant Jewish boys continue their academic studies. He will continue his education in Jewish law at Jerusalem."

"Hallelujah, Hallelujah!" I joyfully shouted as tears of sorrow flowed from Ima's eyes. I jumped out of my chair, ran over and hugged my parents, along with my incensed grandfather.

"Most young men seek wealth in shekels. I will seek wealth in spiritual truths," I promised them.

"Even Pharisees, rabbis, and religious teachers are required to earn their own keep through a trade. I taught you the art of tent making. Use it to support yourself," instructed father.

Grandfather yowled, "If you don't practice your trade, you're a useless man and a burden to our race." He didn't mince words, and he didn't agree with the decision.

"Mazel tov," Ima cried, getting up from the table to clean the dinner dishes. Everyone else got up from the table in silence. They glumly went about their evening activities, but I spent the night in a blissful state with joy rushing through my veins. Before I went to bed that night, I drew the enclosed map and gave it to Abba to remind him of his geographical impact on me and others.

TARSUS TENTMAKER'S TERRAIN

CILICIA ▲▲ Tarsus Mts.

Perga

Tarsus

• Antioch

• Tyre

• Damascus

CYPRUS

• Ptolemais

MEDITERRANEAN
SEA

• Nazareth

Sea of
Galilee

• Caesarea

▲ Mt. Tabor

• Samaria

Jordan
River

• Antipatris

• Jerusalem

Dead
Sea

• Bethlehem

• Alexandria

Sinai
Peninsula

EGYPT

ARABIAN
DESERT

Nile
River

Red
Sea

Chapter Three
A Time to Begin

"Dare to be wise; begin! He who postpones the hour of living rightly is like the rustic who waits for the river to run out before he crosses."
Horace

Four weeks after my bar mitzvah; Ima, Abba and I left our house for Tarsus' harbor. Upon arriving at the dock, our coastal vessel's captain instructed a sailor to blow the boarding trumpet, for the winds had become favorable. Ima hugged me goodbye, squeezing the breath from my body. She tried but failed to hold back her tears. She sniffed, "May you walk in Jehovah's footprints. And I will miss you every second of every day."

I kissed Ima farewell, then Abba and I boarded the crowded pilgrim ship. This was my first trip to the Holy City; however, my father had been there several times on business trips and religious pilgrimages. We were scheduled to arrive in Jerusalem just before Pentecost, the festival celebrating the conclusion of the spring harvest.

"Release the mooring ropes," the first mate yelled. The dockhands threw the mooring lines to crewmembers on the fore and aft deck then he shouted, "Boats Oars."

"Abba, it seems every Jew in Asia Minor is going to Jerusalem for the festival," I observed, searching the deck for a vacant place to sit and lay our belongings.

"But, we have something most don't," he replied with a tone of arrogance. Buried in each of our belongings was a diptych, small wooden tablet that contained our registration as Roman citizens and birth certificates. Roman citizenship gave individuals special benefits and immunities in their personal lives; one was the ability to travel freely throughout the empire.

"What was your most memorable trip on the Mediterranean Sea?" I inquired over the sound of oars splashing in unison through the still, harbor water.

"The fall your uncles and I accepted a Roman army tent order. We had to deliver the tents to Alexandria in the middle of winter. They paid us twice our fee. We took a large Egyptian grain ship to Alexandria. We were robbed twice by pirates. Fortunately, they had no interest in tents. Our vessel nearly sank four times on that journey in the Great Sea's violent waters."

Abba told me numerous sea tales during our voyage. The first couple of days the winds were fickle. The captain stopped for a day in Tyre, as well as in Ptolemais, to pick up food supplies, additional pilgrims, and cargo.

It took ten days to reach Caesarea. Palm trees gently swayed in the cool sea breezes when our coastal ship rowed past Caesarea's empty beaches and into its crowded harbor. The captain weighted the fore and aft anchor next to King Herod's Palace at sunrise.

As we walked down the gang plank Ab said, "We'll rent three donkeys in the marketplace, two for us and one for your belongings." Before the sun had barely moved above the horizon we'd successfully bartered for three donkeys, joined a pilgrim caravan, and departed Caesarea for the two-day uphill journey to Jerusalem.

~~

At high noon on the second day, after hiking up an incline most of the morning, we beheld the Holy City in the distant Judean hills. I exclaimed beneath the parching Palestinian sun, "Now I know why Jerusalem is the capital of Palestine. It's a natural fortress, built on two triangular ridges."

Four hours later, we entered Jerusalem through the northern gate, a newer section of the city. Abba said, "The city is less than several thousand square paces in size, but home to approximately one hundred thousand people. Furthermore, during our festivals there are up to four hundred thousand people in Jerusalem."

"They pack us pilgrims in like sardines," I chortled.

There were only a couple hours of sunlight left when we passed through the new section. Several hundred workers and slaves were building a foundational wall, the city's third wall. Abba shielded his eyes from the sun reflecting off the temple's white marble and gold inlay and said, "A few years from now this will be a towering fortress wall. It will reach from the Palace of Herod's western wall to Jerusalem Temple's northeastern wall."

I noticed several architects drawing blueprints for villas and asked, "Abba, who are they going to build houses for in new section?"

"They're going to build villas for wealthy Greek and Roman gentiles who don't want to be part of our Jewish neighborhoods," father said. "Little do they know social snobbery runs in two directions."

Just past the slaves and laborers camp we walked through a tent community filled with Pentecost pilgrims. I mentioned to Abba, "Several of those tents looked like our hand work."

"Only the ones that stayed dry inside during last night's rainstorm," jokingly boasted Abba.

We walked through an open gate in the city's second wall. To our left was a tall tower. I inquired, "What's that tower for?"

"It's the Tower of Light," replied Abba. "A priest stands at the top of that tower on Friday afternoon watching the sun's position in the sky. He will light a torch at sunset on Friday night for a priest standing on the Holy Temple's Portico. Then that priest will blow a trumpet announcing the beginning of our Sabbath. They will do the same on Saturday night when the sun sets to declare the Sabbath is over."

Within minutes, we found ourselves strolling past the temple's Western Wall. This section housed the city's busiest streets and marketplace. Since it was the day before Pentecost pedestrian traffic and commerce were all about us. I silently observed the hectic atmosphere from vendors hawking their goods to pompous priests strolling by beneath the late day sun.

Abba brought me two papyrus maps from a temple vendor. "This will help you find your way around Jerusalem and the Holy Temple," he said. The ancient, translated cartographies are enclosed at the end of chapter three and four.

~~

Jerusalem had just received the news of Augustus Caesar's death, Rome's emperor. The news filled the city with thoughts and acts of insurrection. Abba stopped beneath a fruit vendor's sackcloth awning and purchased some figs then appraised the setting. Meanwhile, I watched a group of musicians headed toward the Holy Temple practicing their trumpets, harps, and flutes.

When we passed the Hippodrome I overheard a young Jewish insurgent about five years my senior, whose named I gathered was Barabbas, angrily shouted, "The Roman soldiers have already killed four pilgrims, and the festival hasn't even started. How much longer must we wait? Their leader is dead. Let's take back our land!" His voice pounded in my ears like a door being slammed.

"Be cautious of such talk." an elderly Jewish man yelled. "The Roman guard has been tripled for the Pentecost festival." As he spoke, eleven Roman soldiers on horseback galloped into our crowd. Abba grabbed me by the mantle and plucked me from the horses' path just in the nick of time. The horses' slobber and dust covered my lower body.

"Father, things seem a little rowdy today. I guess Rome gets upset if Jerusalem Jews don't mourn the death of their gentile leader and adhere to the Greco-Roman culture," I said, while we dashed into the Lower City onto the Street of Potters with our three donkeys.

"Jerusalem will never forsake its Jewish heritage! Gentiles have tried countless times. The Greek leader Antiochus IV Epiphanes was the worst! He attacked Jerusalem one Sabbath morning with over twenty thousand soldiers. He killed hundreds of our children, women, and elderly. Still, we resisted his murderous attempts to eliminate our Hebrew culture. So he occupied and defiled our Holy Temple." Father summarized the hundred and eighty year old tragedy.

A crowd of anarchists standing beside us began throwing large rocks at three Roman soldiers and yelled, "Romans are pigs!" Both groups swung swords above their heads. Abba grabbed my elbow, and we hastened toward the Lane of Candle Makers.

I proudly finished abba's story as we round the corner, "Rebel forces led by Judas Maccabeus recaptured and restored the Holy Temple from Antiochus three years later. The Maccabees reinstated our political and religious freedoms."

"Till Pompey conquered Judea and claimed Jerusalem as part of the Roman Empire." Abba said, recalling Pompey's bloody invasion seventy-six years ago, as my eyes beheld a squad of Roman soldiers ransacking several candle makers' shops and homes.

"Looks like we need a Judas Maccabeus, today!" I declared, dashing back onto the marketplace's main thoroughfare.

"We do," agreed Abba. Our bodies were now part of a raging sea of people being frantically tossed in numerous directions. Abba pushed the donkeys and me back toward the Hippodrome wall, then into the City of David.

Both of us weaved through its crowded streets as I asked, "Isn't this part of Jerusalem the original city? And where King David's palace was located?"

"Yes," replied Abba. "Now, close your eyes!"

"Whatever you wish."

He put his arm around my shoulders, and we took a sudden right turn through a gate. This neighborhood seemed peaceful and quiet compared to the activities on the other side of the wall. Thirty seconds later, he said, "Open your eyes!"

I nearly fainted when I opened my eyes. We stood before the academic desire of every Jewish boy in the Mediterranean world, the School of Gamaliel.

"Abba, I can't believe it! Gamaliel is the most highly regarded Rabbi of our race! He's the grandson of Hillel and teaches his principles. He's the most revered member of the Sanhedrin! He's the preeminent scholar of our Mosaic Law!" I shouted in uncontrollable joy.

"Yes to all, my son. Ima and I are thankful Jehovah has provided us with the ability to continue your education under Gamaliel. His teachings will eradicate the Hellenistic influences you possess from growing up in Tarsus."

The university was closed for Pentecost holiday, but a new academic semester began after the festival. "I will remain in Jerusalem till tomorrow morning, and then I have to return home for business," Abba informed me as we walked three blocks south to my boarding house.

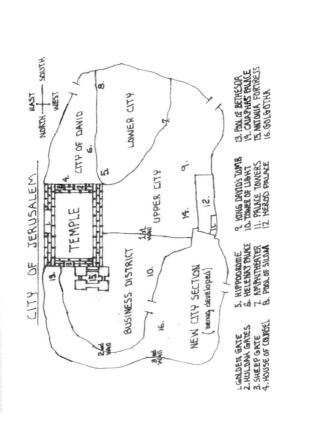

CITY OF JERUSALEM

NORTH · SOUTH
EAST · WEST

TEMPLE

CITY OF DAVID

LOWER CITY

UPPER CITY

BUSINESS DISTRICT

NEW CITY SECTION
(being developed)

1. GOLDEN GATE
2. HULDAH GATES
3. SHEEP GATE
4. HOUSE OF COUNCIL

5. HIPPODROME
6. HELENA'S PALACE
7. AMPHITHEATER
8. POOL OF SILOAM

9. KING DAVID'S TOMB
10. TOWER OF LIGHT
11. PALACE TOWERS
12. HEROD PALACE

13. POOL OF BETHESDA
14. CAIAPHAS PALACE
15. ANTONIA FORTRESS
16. GOLGOTHA

Chapter Four
A Time to Plant

"He will be like a tree planted by the water that
sends out its roots by the stream."
Jeremiah

We moved my personal belongings into an upper room boarding house within a movement of the sundial. After we unpacked the last donkey, Abba sold our pack animals to the boarding house proprietor's brother, owner of a caravan company.

Then Abba suggested, "Let's see if we can catch the twilight service at the Holy Temple. But, first I want to go to the Pool of Bethesda to dip my aching legs in its healing waters."

We left the boarding house and walked past the temple's western retaining wall. We quickly realized that during our brief absence the Roman legion had taken control of the marketplace. Pools of blood filled the main thoroughfare like rain puddles after a springtime storm.

"Maybe we should take the Business District's back alleys to the temple. It might be safer," Abba said, turning the corner onto a steep, sloping alley. The Jerusalem Temple was masterfully constructed atop Mount Moriah. The narrow alleys were bursting at the seams with Pentecost pilgrims.

"What is the name of this building?" I asked my father while passing the backside of an architectural masterpiece.

"It's Antonia Fortress. It was named after Marcus Antony, the great Roman general. It's where the Roman garrison resides in Jerusalem." Father informed as two Roman soldiers in ceremonial armor came out of the fortress's back alley gate.

One of them purposely bumped into me and nearly knocked me off my feet. Abba stopped and stared them in the eyes. He bit his tongue and held back his clenched fists but his look revealed his fury.

"Excuse us!" I politely said in Latin, which caused them to laugh and walk away. Latin was the language of the Roman Empire. The Roman soldiers who frequently visited our Tarsus tent shop had taught me their tongue, and most secular textbooks I read were written in Latin.

Abba whispered, "One day, Jehovah will send our race the Messiah to free our race from these officious Romans."

~~

We stopped at the Pool of Bethesda on the northern side of the city and Abba soaked his legs in its water. When we got up to leave he said, "My legs feel great!"

Then we stopped at a mikvah, purification pool or ritual bath house, one block from the temple. We were covered with dust and sins from the communities we had passed through on our way to Jerusalem. Abba and I needed to cleanse our bodies before entering the Holy Temple where God resided. So, we took a tepid bath and put on clean garments carried with us from the boarding house.

A minute after leaving the mikvah we reached the Sheep Gate, northeast entrance into the temple's white stone foundation. Abba gave alms to a crippled, old beggar without any teeth before we entered the gate. We walked through the spacious gate, down the noisy tunnel, and ascended the numerous marble steps to the temple mount.

Halfway up the stairs, Ab said, "Son, let's check your knowledge on Jerusalem's Temples. How many have been built?"

"Three! But, don't forget Abraham built an altar on Mount Moriah, this very mountain, to sacrifice Isaac." My response echoed off the enclosed stairwell's stone walls.

"You did listen to your abba and teachers in school," Abba snickered.

"The first temple was built by Solomon nine hundred and seventy-four years ago. The second temple was built five hundred and fifty years ago under King Cyrus of Persia. We're climbing the steps of the third temple, built nineteen years ago but still under construction."

"Very good! Who is building this temple? Plus, a bonus question: what is the size of the temple mount?" My father inquired, climbing the last set of steps. He loved to challenge my knowledge of Jewish facts.

"The builder is Herod the Great from Idumean, a man of questionable character. The temple mount is about eight hundred cubits long and five hundred and thirty-three cubits wide," I answered, beholding the Court of Gentiles through the stairwell opening. When we walked through the temple mount's threshold at the northern end of the Court of Gentiles, its size made the people at the southern end look like ants.

Abba put his arm around my shoulder and said, "Good job."

"Look at that marble and gold. And all those Portico columns surrounding the temple mount," I exclaimed, thrilled at seeing the inside of the temple.

The Court of Gentiles was packed with thousands and thousands of Jewish pilgrims from all over the Roman Empire. Some donned worn-out burlap sacks while others were dressed in white silk robes with forearms covered in gold jewelry.

Abba noticed I was overwhelmed by all the merchandising being done in the Court of Gentiles. He explained, "Annas, an influential member of the Sanhedrin, and his family are responsible for this environment. They take advantage of pilgrims who can't bring animal sacrifices to Jerusalem."

"I should have known."

"Annas' vendors exploit the pilgrims by selling sacrificial offerings at two to three times what they are worth. Also, he requires all purchases to be made in shekels, so pilgrims have to convert their country's currency into shekels. Annas charges a sizeable fee for the conversion."

"So, the Court of Gentiles is a court of greed." I said, disappointed. "I thought this court would be a gathering place for mission work to gentiles. It's merely a place to rip off our Jewish brethren seeking to make sacrifices to Jehovah!"

"Yes! Unfortunately, we have come to tolerate these acts in this court."

I noticed Jewish temple guards rather than Roman soldiers were patrolling the temple mount. Ab sensed and addressed my curiosity. "Herod gave the Sanhedrin authority to monitor the temple mount. The temple guards are appointed by the Sanhedrin. However, they're ultimately accountable to Rome's Judean governor."

"At least, they seem less hostile than the Roman legion in the marketplace."

"Sometimes," Abba responded.

We heard thousands of pilgrims praying, chanting psalms, and playing harps unto God throughout the Court of Gentiles. Several hundred pilgrims and residents spoke of rebellion in the Porticos. Moneychangers were obnoxiously shouting for attention and business throughout the Court of Gentiles. I was overwhelmed by the number of merchants selling blemished turtle doves, goats, sheep, and lambs. Abba stopped at a lamb vendor's booth and purchased a beautiful, flawless sheep to sacrifice on the Holy Altar.

"Are you ready to enter the Holy Temple as a man?" My father shouted above the raucous crowd. He had to repeat his question twice; because I was captivated by a young lad. Some mentioned he was from Nazareth. He seemed about my age; furthermore, he was instructing the elders and Pharisees on the ways of God. Everyone appeared in awe of his understanding and knowledge of God's word at such a young age.

"Yes!" I finally responded to my father. We passed through one of several openings in the limestone balustrades surrounding the Holy Temple. I stopped at the Sacred Enclosure, then read aloud one of the many bronze signs in Latin and Greek on the Wall of Hostility: "ON PENALTY OF DEATH, LET NO GENTILE DEFILE OUR HOLY TEMPLE."

"The Gentiles can't enter this part of the temple. Plus, the Romans have given us the power to enforce it," my father proudly stated as we passed through a balustrade opening.

Meanwhile, I was admiring the Holy Temple's three different types of marble. We climbed some steps and entered the sacred terrain through the forty-five cubits wide Beautiful Gate, the outer eastern gate. The Beautiful Gate was overlaid with hand-carved plates of Corinthian brass.

~~

We strolled into the Court of Women just after the conclusion of the twilight worship service. My eyes beheld men as well as women standing or prostrate in prayer throughout the court. Those standing with their arms raised toward heaven looked like glowing candles. Those lying face down on the Temple's marble floor resembled decorative rugs.

"This is as far as your ima or any woman has ever been in the temple," Abba affirmed. I shook my head in acknowledgement.

"Wait here with the sheep. I'll be back," Abba instructed then marched over to one of the thirteen large collection boxes, in the Court of Women, to make a contribution. Meanwhile, I decided to look inside the four smaller, corner courts in the Court of Women.

First, I peeked inside the Court of Lepers to see if lepers were actually inside it. A temple guard saw me and yelled, "Boy, get away from there! Do you want to become one of them?" My head shook eastward and westward.

So I ambled over toward the Court of Oils and cherished the aroma of incenses mixing in the twilight breezes.

Next, I slipped into the Court of Nazirites and beheld pilgrims taking their Nazirite vow. Jews that took this vow separated themselves for thirty days from the secular world and other Jewish people to focus solely on God.

I was walking toward the Court of Wood, where they kept the firewood for sacrificial fires, when Abba shouted, "Saul, it's time for our sacrifice on the Holy Altar. Are you ready?" I shook my head toward heaven and hell. We headed for the Eastern Inner Gate beneath a setting sun painting the horizon in pastel colors.

We climbed the fifteen steps to the Eastern Inner Gate. My ears were filled with the sound of Levites plucking wooden harps and melodiously singing the Ascent Psalms, one psalm for each step they climbed.

When we reached the Court of Israel my abba walked right in. He gave the temple priest's assistant our sacrificial lamb. The long, gray-bearded priest signaled with his eyes that it would be a couple minutes. He was wringing the neck of a turtledove for a Jewish gentleman from Rome. The priest then placed the dead turtledove on the altar's fire. The altar looked like it was well over thirty cubits long and wide.

I pulled at my father's mantle and asked, "Have you ever been in the Court of Priests?" He nodded yes. "Have you ever been in the Holy Place? Or been behind the veil, inside the Holy of Holies? " I inquired. He shook his head no, then motioned with his finger and lips to be quiet.

The priest finally approached us and said, "Lay your hands upon this lamb and let your sins pass from you into this animal." We both prayerfully placed our hands upon the frightened lamb.

The priest in his white linen robe and ivory turban wrestled our unblemished lamb unto the Altar. His bloody right hand held a long butcher knife while his left hand grappled with the lamb. He took his sharp knife and slit our lamb's throat over the Altar's bronze basin. Blood squirted all over him as well as us and flowed into the basin.

I was overwhelmed by the scene as the priest spoke of our duties and blessings. The priest poured the lamb's blood on the Holy Altar's stones and said, "You have been forgiven of your sins through this blood sacrifice!"

~~

Thirty minutes later, we exited the temple mount and headed down the southern wall's stairwell. "How do they place such huge stones atop each other without chipping them?" I asked Ab.

"Lead. They use bars of lead between the stones." He answered as we exited the Huldah Gates. The gates were named after a prophetess who had consulted King Josiah centuries ago.

I turned around and my brown eyes embraced the inimitable features of the Jerusalem Temple. My infatuation caused me to walk backwards and look up at the temple's one hundred and thirty-three cubits, southern retaining wall. "Saul, watch where you're walking!" Abba yelled before I nearly knocked down an elderly lady.

We ambled back into the Lower City where most houses were made of wood. Abba informed me, "This is where the Jewish working class lives, about fifty thousand people. This part of Jerusalem houses the Cilician Synagogue where you will worship. Also, over there is Herod's Hippodrome, and I don't want you skipping classes to watch chariot races!"

After a slight nod, I cherished all the neighborhood activities before we walked through another city gate. When we entered the Upper City father said, "The aristocrats, temple priests, and the wealthy live in the Upper City. Also, Herod's enormous palace is in this part of the city." Then Abba walked up to a large villa's door and started knocking on it.

Uncle Elisha answered the door. "Erev Tov!" He bellowed, giving us both a big hug.

"Erev Tov! Your wish came true!" I joked from the threshold.

"It sure has!" he teased. "Come on in! It's getting dark out there."

"You're just in time for dinner!" Aunt Helah exclaimed, embracing us.

Abba and I took off our leather sandals before we entered their huge multi-terrace house. My uncle's beautiful estate had its own wine cellar, mikvah, room-size Persian rugs with images woven into them, marble floors, linen cloth over the windows, stoneware table, mosaic floors, flower gardens, closets full of jewelry, and four guest rooms.

We washed our hands in their mikvah then joined Aunt Helah, Uncle Elisha, and their baby daughter Rachel for dinner. Aunt Helah had prepared a wonderful meal of lentil soup, lamb, and an olive salad. We filled our empty bellies till they were ready to pop.

After dinner we sat in their spacious courtyard. It seemed like noon with three hundred thousand pilgrims' torches, lanterns, and campfires lighting up the cloudy evening sky. We laughed and stayed up till midnight, listening to Uncle Elisha and Ab reminiscing childhood tales. Abba and I stayed with my aunt and uncle that night.

The next morning, My father and I walked back to my collegiate residence. Abba handed me a new, leather money bag full of silver coins and an old blanket, the blanket I used three years ago to drag him down the Tarsus Mountains. My eyes filled with tears while hugging him goodbye. I sniffed, "Thanks for all the sacrifices Ima and you are making to educate me in Jerusalem. I will do my very best for both of you."

Ab wiped a tear from the corner of his eye and shared a parental maxim. "When chicks are hatching from their eggs, it does more harm then good to help them out of their shells. By breaking out of their shells they strengthen their wings so they can fly. Your Ima and I are pleased to see you breaking out of your shell and about to soar above Jerusalem's skyline. I will miss you and pray for you every day. Shalom!" He shook my hand and dolefully departed for Caesarea.

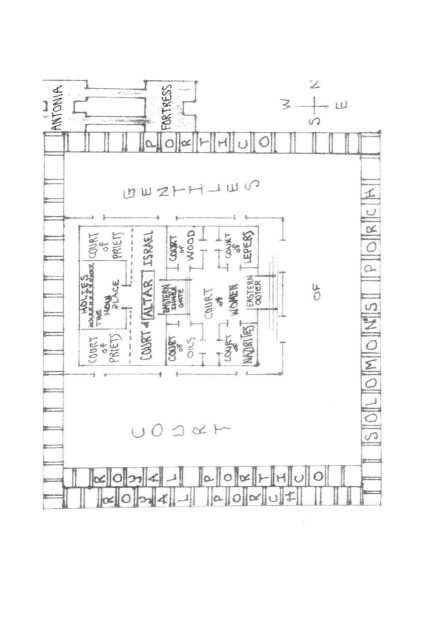

Chapter Five
A Time for Education

"The roots of education are bitter, but the fruit is sweet."
Aristotle

Rabbi Gamaliel only accepted a handful of new students every year. Gamaliel believed in and focused on individualized instruction. His syllabi ranged from Mosaic Law to Judaic Theology to Early Prophets. He was known for his in-depth and comprehensive lectures. Gamaliel's graduates were the gems of Jerusalem and the Jewish world.

His campus was similar to other universities in the Roman Empire, one building with a couple classrooms. We were scheduled to attended classes six days a week all year long except for Jewish holidays. Our academic days started at sunrise and ended at sunset, with a two hour break when the sundial indicated the sixth hour, noon.

Our first week was devoted to getting to know each other and developing relationships. I quickly realized Gamaliel's academy had wealthy, cerebral Jewish teens from all over Judea and Samaria. However, I noticed there weren't any boys my age from Bethlehem, a city near Jerusalem.

I asked a fellow classmate, Philip, from Jerusalem, "Why are there no students here, our age, from Bethlehem?"

"King Herod gave an order to kill all the boys in Bethlehem and its vicinity about the time we were born," Philip replied.

"Why?" I inquired in a state of shock as we walked back into the classroom.

"Three Magi or wise men from the orient saw a celestial sign, fourteen years ago, revealing the king of the Jews was born in Judah."

"I sure hope he was," I exclaimed as we connected as friends.

"The Magi came here to worship him. Herod found out and was disturbed along with all of Jerusalem. A priest told Herod, Christ would be born in Bethlehem. So Herod ordered all the boys in Bethlehem and its vicinity who were two years old and under to be killed," Phillip said, walking into our classroom on the second afternoon of school.

"That man is insane!" I claimed as Gamaliel entered our classroom.

Phillip sat down in his chair and whispered, "The whole family is mentally deranged."

~~

The second week of school we began our numerous expositories on Old Testament scrolls at Gamaliel's feet. He endlessly drilled us on debating techniques in his court of study. By year end, his potter-like techniques shaped our clay minds into analytical vessels.

Toward the end of my second year, Gamaliel told me, "Saul, most of my younger students get stuck in the labyrinth of knowledge, but you walk a direct path to erudition. I'm impressed with your intellectual stature. You've mastered the Pharisaic ability to dispute the major points of grammar in Jewish theology faster than any student I've ever instructed."

The third year we spent hours listening, reading, and reciting Old Testament scrolls in Hebrew, Greek, Aramaic and Latin. We were thoroughly trained in the law of our fathers. Also, Gamaliel had guest lecturers every quarter. They exposed us to secular cultures and philosophies.

My fellow classmates and I really enjoyed our fourth, fifth, and sixth year of college in Jerusalem. We'd spend our mid-afternoon breaks and early evening hours at the temple's Royal Porch reading classroom scrolls. We frequently relaxed on Solomon's Porch and listened to our religious leaders, the Pharisees and Sadducees. The Sadducees would eventually call the Pharisees "Persianizers," and it always sparked an entertaining debated.

Occasionally, we'd act out a play mocking the Herodians flaunting their political power granted by Rome. The Herodian dynasty was the ruling party in Palestine, but the Pharisees were the people's party. The Pharisees possessed vast political clout and were involved in all Jewish decisions.

At least once a week, we harassed the greedy moneychangers and helped the pilgrims get a better price for their currency conversions into shekels, the Jerusalem Temple's legal tender. Also, we called out the perspiring temple merchants that overcharged pilgrims for blemished turtledoves, lambs, or sheep beneath the stifling Mid-East sun. Every time I looked at them, it brought back memories of my childhood when Ab and I were robbed in the Tarsus Mountains.

The days were long, but the nights were even longer. Many a night I studied till dawn. My knowledge of the scripture and aptitude blossomed under Gamaliel's diligent teaching. Over those six years he enhanced my sense of logic, spiritual expositions, debating skills, aphorisms, and teaching abilities.

~~

The day before my 19th birthday, I graduated from college. Gamaliel invited my parents and Uncle Elisha's family to the commencement ceremony. We meet at Gamaliel's residence in the Upper City since the Business District, City of David, and Lower City were in a state of turmoil; moreover, riots were breaking out in nearly every corner of the city.

"Thank you for your devotion, guidance, and influence upon my life," I expressed with gratitude after Gamaliel's abbreviated commencement speech.

"Yes, thanks for watching over our son during the last six years," Ima said.

All of a sudden, the noise of Jerusalem citizens' weeping and Passover pilgrims' screaming filled the room. Aunt Helah peeked out the third floor window and whispered to Uncle Elisha, "Roman soldiers are setting the terraces of small, white houses ablaze in the Lower City. Fire and smoke fill the city's skyline as Roman soldiers search for insurgents."

Gamaliel signed my graduation diploma and scroll of recommendation with his silver stylus and said, "You feverishly outpaced all my students in academic enthusiasm, ancestral traditions, legal customs, and zeal for the Jewish law. I believe God has a unique plan for your life." He stopped and tensed up when he heard a Roman garrison marching onto his street.

"That's because I followed in the footsteps of my grandfather and father. We are Hebrew of Hebrews zealous in regard to the law and its legalistic righteousness." I boasted, oblivious of the events taking place outside the window.

Gamaliel nervously wriggled in his seat like a freshman and asked, "What are your short term goals?"

"I plan on being a Pharisee. And your teaching will help distinguish me from the six thousand other Pharisees in the Roman Empire," I bragged.

"I wish you the best in your Pharisaic and legalistic endeavors," he remarked. Pharisees created a religious hedge of oral laws to protect and preserve the Torah. These oral decrees were focused on behavior regarding the Jewish Sabbath, titling, customs, and meticulous adherence to the Mosaic Law. They are not the laws, Ten Commandments, given by God to Moses but decrees or laws established by man.

Meanwhile, nearly everyone at the graduation ceremony heard fifty Roman soldiers stop in front of Gamaliel's house and accost innocent Passover pilgrims. The soldiers were drinking vino from wineskins, but their real thirst was for bloodshed. They took all the pilgrims' tithes and personal belongings as an act of martial law, and then viciously beat them.

"What are your long-term ambitions?" Gamaliel asked. He began fretting and twisting his thinning, snow-white beard as we heard a small band of Jewish freedom fighters enter his street.

I was myopically focused on myself at this point in life unlike Gamaliel, who was concerned about the pilgrims and freedom fighters outside his house. I declared, "My long-term goal is to be one of the seventy-one members of the Sanhedrin whose decisions are adhered to by Jews throughout the Roman Empire."

"I would be delighted to be one of your sponsors for the Sanhedrin. May God use you as an instrument to stop this hatred and senseless killing," Gamaliel replied as sweat beads formed on his wrinkled face.

"The freedom fighters are preparing to battle those drunken Roman soldiers," Aunt Helah updated the room, peeping through a knot hole in the wooden shutters.

Everyone ran over to the closed windows and peeked through the shutters' slats. We watched the Roman soldiers form a testudo. They marched forward with their bronze spears and iron swords pointed toward the Jewish rebels. The Roman centurion kept his men in a tight formation.

The anarchists were only armed with slingshots and small swords. Their stones and lead shot bounced off the Roman soldiers' overviewed rectangular shields. The insurgents revealed they had more heart than training as the two forces clashed on the street. It quickly became a military disaster for the freedom fighters. The Roman soldiers mercilessly slew them with their experience, spears, and swords. When the conflict was over, the Roman soldiers disfigured the insurrectionists' faces beyond recognition with their daggers.

Ima and the rest of our family were in a state of shock as we beheld the sights from Gamaliel's third floor windows. Everyone, but me had lost their excitement for my graduation ceremony. Meanwhile, the victorious Roman soldiers ransacked the house across the street from Gamaliel's abode.

"I'm sorry to conclude this ceremony but for our safety we had better hide, now!" Gamaliel's words rushed from his lips at a speed I'd never heard before.

He herded everyone downstairs and through the courtyard into a narrow tunnel beneath his house. He closed the tunnel door just as the drunken Roman soldiers burst through his courtyard gate. They sought bloodshed and valuable items.

"Too many of our festivals over the last six years have been filled with Roman violence and bloodshed," I whispered to Abba, while soldiers slaughtered Gamaliel's goats.

Then our nostrils were filled with smoke as the soldiers set fire to his courtyard's arbor. We listened to Roman soldiers ransack Gamaliel's house for precious stones, gold and silver. Thankfully, the Roman trumpets sounded for the changing of the Roman guard before they discovered the tunnel door.

The soldiers obediently left Gamaliel's ransacked residence, to either check in for changing of the guard or to enforce the city-wide curfew. I whispered to Ima, "Rome's imperial justice, heavy taxation, and senseless brutality are draining our race."

"They are," cried Ima. "May our Messiah come soon."

Gamaliel escorted everyone out of the tunnel to his front gate after the soldiers departed. He said, "Saul, you are graduating from school at a time when the empire is full of bitterness, hopelessness, and lawlessness. Focus on God's grace and don't let the evil events that surround you harden your heart."

"I'm only hardened by those who don't hold themselves accountable to the written and oral laws," I remarked, closing his bronze gate.

Gamaliel waved farewell, and then shouted one last professorial credo, "Remember, the way you live your life sets the course of your character."

Chapter Six
A Time to be Concern

"Concern should drive us into action and not into depression."
Anonymous

Two weeks after graduating from Gamaliel's school, I accepted a position as an attorney at the House of Counsel, where I persecuted Israelites who violated the Pentateuch or Mosaic code. Also, I guest lectured or preached in nearly every Jerusalem synagogue within a couple months of graduation.

I was advancing in Judaism's ranks beyond any Jews my own age or older. Numerous synagogues throughout Judea made lucrative offers for me to join their staffs. I chose to stay in Jerusalem where I could expand my religious and political stature.

Unfortunately, three years after my graduation several family issues arose in Cilicia, so I moved back to Tarsus. I returned home a slightly bowlegged man, still under four cubits in height. Fortunately, the Tarsus synagogue I grew up in offered me a position. It was a treat to be back with old neighbors, long-time friends, and family members.

I spent the next eleven years in Tarsus, nurturing family and synagogue members. Under my teaching; the congregants grew in their legalistic behavior, good deeds, and faithful tithing. My sermons and reasoning cut through the congregation's consciousness like an axe through dry, brittle wood. When I wasn't teaching at the synagogue or helping congregational members, I was working at Abba's tent shop because of his failing health.

This young Pharisee daily observed the Mosaic Laws and obeyed the hundreds of oral laws established by the scribes. My scribal traditions, tithing, and ritual fasting surpassed all other Pharisees. I believed my faithful adherence to these decrees placed me above others. I looked down on all sinners, tax collectors, and prostitutes. For example, I wouldn't think of eating at a gentile's house.

I was the most outspoken Pharisee and Jewish lawyer in the Cilician Province. The Cilician synagogues appointed me their province representative to the Sanhedrin. It was a non-Sanhedrin member position, but I voted and wrote the rationale for all our decisions. The position didn't require me to travel to Jerusalem; however, my letters were highly regarded and very influential in the Sanhedrin council meetings.

In the spring and summer of my thirty-first year on earth, we began to hear troubling news about Jerusalem's religious affairs. Pilgrims and travelers who returned from Jerusalem spoke of a charismatic teacher. Some said, "He's a prophet." Others said, "He's is the Son of God."

My eleven-year-old sister, Sarah, and mother were going to Jerusalem for six months early that fall. They were going to stay with Uncle Elisha and Aunt Helah. My sister had been chosen by the High Priest's wife, thanks to my help, to weave the thick, holy veil that separated The Holy Place from The Holy of Holies. Eighty-four young girls throughout the Jewish world were selected for this special task.

Abba was nervous about them traveling alone to Jerusalem. The Sabbath before they departed, Ruth and Jeremiah Bar-Jonah, a couple from our congregation, told my father, "We are going to make a pilgrimage to Jerusalem for the Feast of Tabernacles. We'll keep an eye on your two loved ones during the long journey." Abba was very thankful for their offer.

After that Sabbath service, Jeremiah whispered in my ear, "While we're in Jerusalem celebrating the autumn harvest and making our animal sacrifices, we'll investigate the stories about this prophet from Nazareth."

~~

Ruth and Jeremiah returned to Tarsus in early November. They immediately visited me upon their return, even though it was late.

"Saul, it was unbelievable!" Ruth exclaimed, entering my house. "The prophet from Nazareth heals the sick, walks on water, turns water into wine, speaks in mind-provoking parables and raises the dead."

"What do they call him?" I inquired amidst her new found ebullience.

"His name is Jesus. He is a holy man, full of godly wisdom and love," Ruth spoke with uncontrollable excitement. "The crowds around him grow daily."

"He is the talk of Jerusalem, Judea, Samaria, and all the surrounding areas," Jeremiah interjected with less enthusiasm.

"Does he have disciples?" I inquired with a winsome smile.

"Yes, twelve of them," Jeremiah responded then shook his head with skepticism.

"One of them is our nephew, Simon Bar-Jonah. Jesus calls him Peter," Ruth exclaimed.

Jeremiah seemed embarrassed by his nephew's affiliation and added, "He recruited my brother's son, Simon while he was repairing the family's fishing nets by the Sea of Galilee. He's a bit of an impetuous person."

"Do people in Jerusalem think Jesus is the Messiah?" I inquired.

"Simon, or should I say, Peter, believes he's the Messiah," Jeremiah sheepishly replied.

"Our nephew said two-and-a-half years ago Jesus was baptized in the Jordan River. When he came up out of the water, a voice resounded from Heaven: 'You are my beloved son; in you I am well pleased,'" Ruth spoke with exhilaration.

"He befriends social outcasts, the lame, and those with leprosy. But he challenges Jerusalem's religious establishment, debates ours scribes, and chastises our Jewish leaders," Jeremiah remarked as concern consumed his tone.

We spoke for hours about this one called Jesus. When they departed around midnight, I had mixed feelings about this teacher.

Stories continued trickling into Tarsus about the Rabbi from Galilee during the winter months. News traveled slower and less frequently in the winter months since sea travel shut down every year from early November to late February

~~

In early March Jeremiah, Ruth, and ten others from our congregation made the pilgrimage to Jerusalem for the Passover festival. They all returned seven weeks later, along with Ima and Sarah, on a Sabbath morning.

Three pilgrims were chosen on Tarsus's dock to give an account of Jerusalem's events to our synagogue leaders. The three pilgrims chosen were Ruth, Jeremiah, and Pekah Ben-Amni, nephew of Caiaphas the High Priest. All the others, including Ima and Sarah, went home to bed. The three exhausted pilgrims waited inside the synagogue's foyer till our morning service was over. They were all eager to share their experiences with us.

A half hour after our worship service concluded, the rabbi, head elder and I finally made it to the synagogue foyer. The three pilgrims spoke at the same time. I suggested, "Ruth, please go first."

"This Passover was all about the one they call Jesus," she exclaimed.

"Tell me what happened," I demanded.

"Jesus of Nazareth cleansed the Holy Temple of moneychangers and merchants. He upset their tables and shouted, 'My house will be called a house of prayer, and you are making it a den of robbers,'" Jeremiah informed us as if he was an attaché.

"The Court of Gentiles is a den of thieves. The temple mount should be a place of prayer and praise for all nations, not a flea market." I unexpectedly found myself agreeing with this Galilean prophet.

"My uncle, Caiaphas, the chief priest of Jerusalem," boasted Pekah.

The rabbi interrupted him and said, "He's your uncle five times removed."

"Regardless, he is my uncle," asserted Pekah. "Uncle Caiaphas held a meeting and called for Jesus' death, since he claimed to be the Son of God. The story unfolds with one of his twelve disciples, the temple guards, Pharisees, and my uncle's officials arresting this false prophet in the Garden of Gethsemane."

"They showed up with torches, clubs, and swords to arrested Jesus," remarked Ruth. "His other disciples were frightened to the point where our nephew, Simon Peter, pulled a sword from a temple soldier's scab and struck the high priest servant."

"He cut off his right ear," shouted Pekah. "Your nephew is a hot head."

Ruth ignored him and continued, "Jesus told Peter, 'Put your sword away! Shall I not drink the cup the Father has given me.' Then Jesus healed the high priest's servant's ear."

"Then your fickle nephew denied your savior three times that night," chuckled Pekah.

"He was scared, tried, and confused," cried Ruth. "Jesus was tried that night before Annas, Caiaphas, Pilate, Herod, and Pilate again. He had five trials in one night!"

"Pilate was left with the task of making the final decision on Jesus," said Jeremiah. "When the crowd arrived at Pilate's palace the second time with the chief priest and elders it was early morning. To avoid ceremonial uncleanness the Jewish crowd did not enter the palace. They wanted to be able to eat the Passover meal."

Pekah interrupted Jeremiah and bragged, "Pilate came out to us and asked, 'What charges are you bringing against this man?' We told him, 'If he were not a criminal we would not have handed him over to you.'"

Jeremiah dismissed Pekah with his eyes and resumed his comments, "Pilate said, 'Take him yourselves and judge him by your own law.' That's when we told him, 'We have no right to execute anyone.' Pilate became disturbed and went back inside his palace."

"A couple minutes later after talking to the carpenter from Nazareth, Pilate came back outside," cited Pekah. "He looked at the crowd and said, 'I find no basis for a charge against him. But it is our custom for me to release to you one prisoner at the time of the Passover. Do you want me to release 'the king of the Jews?' Our crowd shouted back, 'No not him! Give us Barabbas.'"

Ruth offered a different point of view, "Your uncle and the synagogue elders persuaded the crowd to shout for Barabbas to be released. Barabbas was in prison. He's an insurrectionist and murderer."

"I bumped into Barabbas in Jerusalem when I was thirteen years old." I recalled then guffawed, "He's was even a rebel as an adolescent."

"Pilate had Jesus taken into the Praetorium and gathered the whole company of soldiers around him. Then we heard Jesus being flogged thirty-nine times," cried Ruth.

Jeremiah continued his account, "I peeked through the Praetorium gate and watched the Roman soldiers strip him, place a purple robe on him, twist together a crown of thorns and set it on his head. They put a staff in his right hand, knelt in front of him and mocked, 'Hail to the King of the Jews!' Then they spat on him, took the staff from his hand and beat him with it again and again."

"Once again Pilate came out to us," Pekah crowed and laughed about the Roman governor. "This time he had Jesus with him. He was wearing the crown of thorns and a purple robe."

"It was dreadful," recalled Ruth, shedding tears. "Blood flowed from his back, chest, and legs. His flesh barely hung on his ribs and his back was raw."

Jeremiah handed his wife a dry napkin and he resumed, "Pilate glared at the crowd and said, 'Look I am bringing him out to you to let you know that I fine no basis for a charge against him. Here is the man!'"

Pekah interrupted him, "As soon as my uncle and the other officials saw him, they shouted, 'Crucify him! Crucify him!' But that pathetic Pilate answered, 'You take him and crucify him. As for me, I have no basis for a charge against him.'"

"But the crowd insisted, 'We have a law and according to that law he must die, because he claims to be the Son of God,'" Ruth sniveled between words.

"Then that gutless Pilate went back inside," laughed Pekah. "When he came back outside we told him, 'If you let this man go, you are no friend of Caesar. Anyone who claims to be a king opposes Caesar.'"

"He sat on his judgment and finally said, 'Here is your king.' But we shouted, 'Take him away and crucify him,'" informed Jeremiah.

"Again the spineless Pilate asked, 'Shall I crucify your king?'" Pekah remarked, stroking his perfectly braided beard. "My uncle shouted, 'We have no king but Caesar'. Finally Pilate handed the misguided teacher over to the Roman soldiers to be crucified."

Jeremiah closed his eyes and summed up, "Pilate asked us, 'What crime has he committed?' But Pilate finally realized he was getting nowhere with the crowd, instead it was turning hostile. So he took a basin of water and washed his hands before the mob. Then he said, 'I'm innocent of this man's blood. It is your responsibility.'"

"The crowd shouted, 'Let his blood be on us and our children.'" Ruth regretfully recalled, wiping tears from her bloodshot eyes.

"The Passover crowd disparaged the impostor from Nazareth as he carried his crossbeam through the Jerusalem streets. He couldn't even carry his wooden cross half way up to Golgotha." Pekah said, shaking his head. "The Roman soldiers picked some weak-minded man out of the crowd and he carried the wooden beam up to the Place of a Skull."

"It was terrible," Ruth spoke between her wailing. "They drove long, iron spikes through his wrists and one through both his feet."

"Sounds brutal. I've never seen a person nailed to a cross. I thought their hands were tied to the crossbeam," I said, feeling sympathy.

"They usually do," replied Jeremiah. "But not this man. He hung on the cross for hours! Then died! After his death, lightning and earthquakes shook the city! The veil between The Holy Place and The Holy of Holies ripped from the top down, the very one your sister stitched together."

"I purchased Jesus' purple robe from one of the soldiers who crucified him. The soldier won the robe casting lots beneath Jesus' crucified body." Ruth clutched the robe with one hand and wiped away tears with the other.

She handed me the robe and I felt a strange power within it. Her following remark caught me off-guard, "He rose from the grave three days later!" There was a vista of joy in her eyes I'd never seen before. "Jesus is the Son of God, the Messiah."

I handed the seeming preternatural robe back to Ruth and looked at her in a perplexed manner. The head elder demanded, "Enough of this talk!"

"I agree," Pekah bellowed. "This mere carpenter isn't our Messiah. He wasn't crowned the king of Jews by the Sanhedrin. He didn't eliminate our oppression. He didn't bring us prosperity."

"Yes!" The congregation members shouted, who had been quietly standing in the foyer.

"The Messiah will be a military leader, political king, eternal provider, and prince of peace. The Messiah would have never been hung on a cross and died in public disgrace. We know that anyone who is hung on a tree is under God's curse. He was just another pious martyr!" the rabbi declared, and then dismissed the informal gathering.

~~

As weeks passed, disturbing news continued to reach Tarsus about numerous Jews becoming believers in this resurrected Jesus. When the rabbi's wife and her brother returned from the Pentecost festival she shared her experiences with the leadership team at the synagogue.

She told us about her social encounters, but the head elder interrupted her and asked, "What of the one they call Jesus of Nazerth?"

She discontentedly changed topics and said, "Hundreds of Jerusalem Jews are following him, even though he was crucified. His followers claim he is the Son of God. His believers are filled with the Holy Spirit. They speak in tongues or languages of all nations. Jewish pilgrims from all over the Roman Empire have heard the story of Jesus Christ in their own language."

"Who is the Holy Spirit?" I asked with a baffled expression.

"The Holy Spirit is the third person of the Holy Trinity; Yahweh, Jesus Christ, and the Holy Spirit," she informed us.

"What does the Holy Spirit do?" I inquired.

"The Holy Spirit convicts us of our sin, leads us to righteousness, and partakes in our eternal judgment," she replied. It seemed like she believed what she told us, "The Holy Spirit dwells in us, fills us with Yahweh's love, guides us, and empowers us."

"You buy this?" I questioned the rabbi's wife.

"It seems real to me," she sheepishly replied.

"Blasphemy," the rabbi shouted.

"So if I can make something appear real, you believe in it," I chortled then left the synagogue.

The Tarsus elders were outraged by the rabbi's wife remarks, Ruth's convictions, and the unceasing reports coming out of Jerusalem during the summer months. The synagogue elders called a special meeting and ruled, "Saul, we would like for you to journey to Jerusalem and investigate these stories. Also, assist in stamping out this new sect and its followers."

They chose me because I was trained in the written law of our fathers and zealous for Judaism. I immediately departed for Jerusalem, the fall of that year.

Chapter Seven
A Time to Question

The partisan, when he is engaged in a dispute, cares
nothing about the rights of the question, but is anxious
only to convince his hearers of his own assertions."
Plato

It took our coast ship eight stormy, turbulent days and nights to reach
Caesarea. We rowed into Caesarea's harbor at daybreak. I immediately
joined a large, but unarmed caravan and began the two day hike up to
Jerusalem. A half day from the Jewish capital, we were robbed by twenty
bandits on a dusty, mountain trail. The robbers intimidated the caravan
travelers by beating several of us up, and then they took everyone's food
and money.

When we finally arrived in the Holy City, I was in a Jerusalem state
of mind. My mouth longed to place itself in the Serpent's Pool, Towers'
Pool, Israel Pool or Bethesda Pool. My stomach dreamed of consuming
food from the food vendors in the Lower City, Business District, Upper
City or Temple Marketplace.

My bruised, starved body walked wearily down the main thoroughfare.
I didn't recognize any familiar faces so I went to my favorite inn, now
called The Way. It was still under the management of Philip, my longtime
friend and fellow schoolmate at Gamaliel School.

"Saul, my dear friend, it's great to see you!" Philip exclaimed as I
entered the inn.

"Same here, Philip!"

"Are you okay?" He inquired with great concern as I collapsed in a
wooden chair.

"Yes. But, I met with some trouble on the road from Caesarea. Ruthless bandits assaulted and robbed our cavern about a day's journey outside of Jerusalem," I responded through swollen lips and a sore jaw.

"I'd hate to see what the bandits look like." Philip ribbed, pushing his black, curly hair behind his bronze ears.

"A lot better than me," I joked as my broken nose began bleeding again. "Can you feed a starving friend without any money?"

"I'd love to fill your belly and satisfy that thirst." Philip replied, handing me a white cloth napkin for my bloody nose. He disappeared for a minute, then returned with a plate full of sweet figs, juicy dates, fresh bread, kosher meat, and a jug of green tea. "Enjoy."

"I will," I affirmed after giving thanks for the food.

Philip watched his starving friend stuff both cheeks and chortled, "A pack of wolves couldn't devour this food any quicker than you."

The two of us started college at the same time, but he graduated a semester behind me. We had the same set of friends during our six years at college. Philip delighted in recalling humorous stories about our fellow classmates at Gamaliel's school.

Philip looked at me, started laughing, and said, "I'll never forget the Arabian stallion incident?"

"Me either," I laughed, wincing in pain.

"I remember it like it was yesterday. Gamaliel took our freshman class to Bethany for a springtime outing," recalled Philip. "He had arranged for an afternoon of horseback riding at the Ben-Judah estate."

"What a day." I replied, shaking my aching skull.

"The stable hand put everyone on thoroughbred mares and fillies. But, he allowed you to pick out a white, Arabian stallion after we were all trotting about in the field. The Arabian stallion and you came flying out of that barn. You chased us all through the woods and fields," Philip added with a chuckle.

"We thought we were Roman cavalry soldiers in a battle." I snickered before dropping three sweet figs on my tongue.

"Until Levi's mare tired in front of the barn. Your stallion mounted the mare and knocked Levi clear off his horse. You were hanging onto the neck of your horse for dear life. Finally, you slid backwards off the Arabian onto the ground." Philip's recollection was punctuated by snorts of laughter.

"We all learned about the birds and bees that day," I hooted, brushing dust from my long tangled earlocks.

"Along with the anatomy of a horse," cackled Philip. "We were all lying on the ground in amazement. The farm workers joined us in front of the barn during our impromptu sex education class. Then Gamaliel came out of the barn and yelled, 'Boys back to school, now!'" Philip tittered before taking a sip of green tea.

~~

I changed topics with a tone of curiosity, "In Tarsus, we hear a large number of Jerusalem Jews have become disciples of the crucified man from Nazareth, Jesus. Is there validity to these stories?"

"Yes!" But, before he could finish his comment, a man about my age, whom Philip treated as a brother, entered the inn.

"Hello, I'm Stephen," he politely introduced himself. Stephen had a clean-shaven face and thick, black hair. I instantly realized he was a Hellenistic Jew who didn't lack spirit. "And you are?"

"Saul, Saul of Tarsus," I proudly said, grabbing the last fig.

"I'm familiar with your scholastic accomplishments under Gamaliel," Stephen responded with admiration. I could tell he was also a man of academic achievements.

"Thank you for your kind remark," I replied, feeling more narcissistic than thankful. My eyes examined him like a hawk searching a field for rodents.

"It's a time of political correctness, humanism, mysticism, secularism, and harassing people with different religious convictions. Which of these bring such an eminent Pharisee and teacher to Jerusalem?" he inquired as we both reached for the same date.

"It seems the Hellenistic Jews in Tarsus much like the Hellenistic Jews in Jerusalem, are receptive to new religious doctrines. I've come to find out about a man named Jesus and to investigate the rumors of his resurrection," I sternly declared before choking on the juicy date plucked from Stephen's fingers.

"Friend, it's true! Jesus of Nazareth arrived in Jerusalem three and a half years ago. His divine teachings turned the city upside down," Stephen exclaimed. "His holy teachings were at odds with Jerusalem's political and religious establishments. Our Jewish leaders formally accused him of blasphemy and treason during this year's Passover. The Sanhedrin's false accusations lead to a Roman flogging, and then they crucified him on a cross during the Passover Festival."

"A couple of my congregants told me of this tale," I responded with resentment.

"It's not a tale, it's the truth," he continued. "Jesus was buried just before sunset on Friday and three days later on Sunday morning, he physically arose from the grave."

Stephen poured us some green tea. I grabbed a clay goblet from the table and said, "Being a Pharisee, I believe in resurrection, but I question your remarks. Did he appear to anyone or say anything after his resurrection?"

"Yes," Stephen affirmed. "When Jesus first reappeared to his disciples, after his resurrection, they thought he was a ghost. Jesus said, 'Why are you troubled, and why do doubts rise in your mind? Look at my hands and my feet. It is I myself! Touch me and see; a ghost does not have flesh and bones, as you see I have.'"

"That's all he said?" Wrath ignited in my words.

"No, after they had eaten he opened their minds. 'Everything must be fulfilled that is written about me in the Law of Moses, the prophets, and the Psalms. This is what is written: The Christ will suffer and rise from the dead on the third day, and repentance and forgiveness of sins will be preached in his name to all nations,'" added Stephen.

"I know the holy scrolls, you don't have to read them to me," I snapped, shooting him a sour grimace. "He didn't rise from the grave. His followers took his corpse!"

"I personally saw him. And the nail holes in his hands and feet," Stephen reassured.

"You saw him in a dream," I growled.

"No, hundreds of people beheld him over a forty day time frame," rejoiced Stephen.

"So what kind of directives did he supposedly give his followers in this resurrected state?" I interrogated.

Stephen took a sip of green tea and said, "He instructed us, 'All authority in heaven and on earth has been given to me. Therefore go and make disciples of all nations, baptizing them in the name of the Father and of the Son and of the Holy Spirit, and teaching them to obey everything I have commanded you. And surely I am with you always to the very end of the age.'"

"Sounds like heresy. Where is he now?" I demanded as hatred slipped into my tone.

"Jesus addressed a sizeable crowd just days before Pentecost in the vicinity of Bethany," said Stephen. "He told us, 'Wait for the gift my Father promised, which you have heard me speak about. John baptized with water, but in a few days you will be baptized with the Holy Spirit. You will receive power when the Holy Spirit comes on you.' Then he ascended before my eyes along with five hundred other sets of eyes into Heaven, where he took a throne seat at God's right hand."

"Blasphemy!" I shouted through quivering lips. I grabbed my walking stick, then stormed into the crowded marketplace, upsetting several fruit and hyssop plant vendor stands.

"See you soon!" Philip shouted over all the commotion.

Chapter Eight
A Time for Conflict

"Passions are generally roused from great conflict."
Titus Livius

I roamed the city streets full of ire as I reflected on Stephen's comments. Throughout the evening I couldn't believe the number of Jesus followers I encountered among Jerusalemites and Jewish pilgrims. It seemed like thousands embraced his teachings and precepts.

Ninety thousand pilgrims were in town for the Feast of Tabernacles. Most had already built their temporary shelters out of willow and palm branches. These shelters were constructed all over the city. They symbolized the housing used by our ancestors when they wandered in the wilderness for forty years.

Just after midnight I roamed into the Akra quarter, the gathering place for Jerusalem's poor, homeless, and downcast sojourners. I approached a family of four, Jewish pilgrims clothed in burlap sacks. They were warming their bodies and souls by a roaring campfire.

"May I sleep by your fire tonight since it's so late?" I inquired, scratching the eyebrows merging above my nose. "I just got into Jerusalem today and lost track of time pondering an acquaintance's remarks. Hate to wake up any friends or family this time of night."

"Friend, please join us," the father offered. "Please, make yourself at home by our campfire and join our conversation."

"Thanks! Where are you from?" I inquired, sitting down next to their blazing fire beneath a black awning filled with bright stars.

"We are from the city where Jesus performed his first miracle," the Galilean grandfather replied while brushing dust from his beard.

"Which is?" I inquired with sarcasm.

"Cana," the patriarch proudly answered before taking a bite of flat cake.

"What was the miracle?" I inquired, displaying a lack of interest.

"Let me give you some background first," a teenage girl said, throwing two small logs on the fire. "One of my friends was getting married in Cana. Coincidentally, Jesus and his disciples were in Cana, so the bride's father invited them to the wedding."

Her twin sister interrupted, "When the wedding party ran out of wine, Jesus' mother approached him and said, 'They have no more wine.' Jesus responded to her, 'Dear woman, why do you involve me? My time has not yet come.'"

"Jesus mother told the servants to do whatever he asked," added her sister. "Jesus noticed six large, stone water jugs and said, 'Fill the jars with water.' The servants filled the jars used for ceremonial washing to the top, then Jesus instructed, 'Now draw some out and take it to the master of the banquet.'"

"When the governor of the feast drank from the cup he called the bridegroom and said unto him, 'Everyone brings out the choice wine first and the cheaper wine after the guests have had too much to drink; but you have saved the best till now,'" their father exclaimed.

"You expect me to believe that story." I remarked, shaking my head in anger.

"It's true. It was the first of his miraculous signs. Jesus revealed to us that evening that he is the Son of Jehovah. He revealed his glory and his disciples put their faith in him. Isn't it great the Messiah chose our hometown for his first miracle?" the grandfather pronounced.

"You Hellhounds! May Jehovah have mercy on your soul," I yelled, walking away from their campfire. My exhausted body laid itself down on a mat of bamboo rushes about twenty fathoms from them. They talked through the night of Jesus' first miracle among themselves and with any pilgrims who would join their campfire.

~~

The next morning I awoke distraught and full of fury. I went to the nearest synagogue, which was the Agape Synagogue. It was a Hellenist's synagogue filled with Jews who still embraced the Greek culture. The elders asked me to take the place of honor as a guest Pharisee.

When I sat down, my periphery vision saw Philip. He approached me just before the morning service and suggested in Greek, "Keep your mind and heart open to Stephen's words. For we have more to share with you."

"I don't want to hear it!" I remarked with disdain. I was shocked by his audacity to bring this subject up in a Jewish synagogue.

"Let me mention one event, you should be aware of. We were worshipping and celebrating the most recent Pentecost festival when a sudden, violent wind from heaven filled my house. Tongues of fire set upon each of us! Then, as Jesus had promised we were all filled with the Holy Spirit." Philip's voice overflowed with enthusiasm far beyond his normal level of elation.

"Not you, too!" I replied.

"Yes, I have found The Way. I'm one of the seven who oversee the widows, orphans, and poor among Jesus' followers," Philip expounded.

"How could you? You were schooled under Gamaliel." I shouted, feeling a friendship being jerked from my life.

"My soul's door swung open when I heard the Rabbi from Nazareth's teachings in the temple courts," Philip said with no trepidations toward his senior classman. "I saw the sincerity of his love and compassion when he healed the lame, fed the poor, and cared for the beggars. The Messiah has come."

"My intellect always saved a seat for you. Are you out of your mind?" I bellowed after noticing a joyful spirit within Philip because he shared his faith with me.

The synagogue rabbi and three elders facing the congregation motioned for silence. They were staring at Philip and me, so we quietly sat down. I gave Philip a look of disgust and moved as fast as possible from him to the seat of honor.

The rabbi conducted the first part of their service, and then said, "We are honored today with the unexpected presence of Tarsus' most eminent Pharisee, an esteemed teacher and a dear friend. Saul, please teach us this morning from any of the holy scrolls and expound upon the verses."

I slowly walked to the front of the synagogue and selected the *Psalms* scroll. I unrolled the long scroll and read aloud in Hebrew from right to left. "Indignation has taken hold of me because of the wicked who forsake your law." I spent the next twenty minutes speaking on the Mosaic Laws and its authority in daily Jewish life.

~~

After the worship service, I refused to speak to or acknowledge Philip and Stephen. However, I did hear Philip tell Stephen, "I'm going home and falling to my knees to give praise to the Lord. For giving me the boldness and courage to share my faith."

Stephen's remarks, Galileans' campfire conversation, and Philip's comments had me in a crotchety frame of mind. So, I decided to visit the home of my astute teacher, Gamaliel, and obtain his insight on this new sect.

"Shalom, dear friend and teacher," I affectionately greeted, bowing to Gamaliel as he opened his door. He greeted me with an amiable hug on his doorstep, invited me in, and we walked to his courtyard. I solicited his thoughts before we even sat down, "Please, share with me what you know about Jesus of Nazareth and his disciples."

"As you know, it has been four hundred years since the voice of God has spoken to us through a prophet. Many believe Jesus was the one to break this silence."

"I think they are out of their minds and have lost their way," I replied.

"Ironically, his followers refer to themselves as 'The Way,' the true way."

"I've seen and heard that term several times within the last twenty-four hours. Now it makes sense."

"I recently sat in on a Sanhedrin hearing and a disciple of The Way, named Peter, shared his faith," Gamaliel remarked as I studied his emotions.

"His aunt and uncle are members of our Tarsus synagogue," I interjected, disgusted. "Their nephew became a follower of the Nazerth carpenter about three and half years ago. I think his aunt is a believer in The Way."

"Many are."

"Unfortunately," I remarked. "What happened in the hearing with the Sanhedrin?"

"The Sanhedrin immediately instructed Peter not to teach in Jesus' name anymore. Peter responded, 'We will continue to teach, for we must obey God rather than men. The God of our fathers raised Jesus from the dead - whom you had killed by hanging him on a tree. God exalted him to his own right hand as Prince and Savior that he might give repentance and forgiveness of sons to Israel. We are witness of these things, and so is the Holy Spirit whom God has given to those who obey him,'" recalled Gamaliel.

"Yes, all his disciples are saying 'He was born to die! He died for our sins so we could have eternal life.' But, what do you say?" I asked in a calculated countermove.

"The Sanhedrin and High Priest wanted to have Peter along with his colleagues put to death. I spoke these words in the council meeting and I still wonder who or what inspired them. 'Leave these men alone! Let them go! For if their purpose or activity is of human origin, it will fail. But if it is from God, you will not be able to stop these men; you will only find yourselves fighting against God.'"

Gamaliel reclined in his bronze chair. I leaned toward him and said, "Forgive me, teacher, for refuting you, but I feel they're a threat to our Jewish customs and oral laws. The Way is tainting Judaism, and we should deal aggressively with these misguided Jerusalemites and pilgrims."

"Saul, remember to pursue the love, not the hate, within you."

"I pursue the ways of our ancestors!"

"Be a builder, not a destroyer. Don't live by your insecurities, because they lead to unhealthy behavior like odium, abuse, and piousness," he instructed.

"I follow our fathers' written and oral laws," I declared with zeal, leaning closer to him. "I detest their claims and beliefs."

"Time will decide if The Way is of human origin or divine inception. We don't want to be guilty of going against Jehovah's will," Gamaliel responded with his usual Hillelite premise. "I met Jesus and spoke with him, he was a godly man."

"Maybe, but he was just a man. He wasn't even a Pharisee or Sadducees. And he had the audacity to speak out against our oral laws!" My voice was full of ferocity.

"The written law is from God, and the oral law is from man. Jesus merely reminded us of this. Don't drown yourself in legalistic righteousness!" responded Gamaliel. I got up from Gamaliel's courtyard table and promptly dismissed myself from his presence.

That afternoon, I decided to stay in Jerusalem and continue investigating this religious sect. I rented a room in the Upper City about five minutes from the Holy Temple. My collegian employer rehired me as a part-time tentmaker. The job had paid my living expenses as a student, and it would do the same as an interrogator.

I was excited to resume my duty in Jerusalem, with abundant pride. A preeminent Pharisee who meticulously followed every Mosaic and oral laws. Over the next couple of months my rage against The Way grew, as did its multitude of believers.

In the winter, this sect totaled over five thousand men. A large percentage of Jerusalem's believers in The Way were poor Hebrew priests. These distraught priests' raiment usually consisted of tattered burlap sackcloth with hemp tied about their waists and no sandals.

Fellow Pharisees and I were extremely baffled by The Way's generosity toward them and others. Followers of The Way would willingly tithe vast portions of their belongings; food, fields, houses, jewelry, and money. They would place all the proceeds and contributions in a general fund then distribute it to those in need.

When I would confront Jesus' followers on this topic, they'd reply, "These worldly things have no value in the Kingdom of Heaven."

Their benevolent acts toward each other as well as non-believers of The Way created animosity with us. By mid-winter water was at a freezing point and my spiritual tolerance was at a boiling point.

Chapter Nine
A Time for Action

"You cannot have a proud and chivalrous spirit if your conduct is mean and paltry; for whatever a man's actions are, such must be his spirit."
Demosthenes

One chilly afternoon in February, I ran into Levi, fellow Pharisee and classmate at Gamaliel School, in the Holy Temple's Court of Women. "Shalom. It's great to see you." My voice revealed its excitement as did my hands, which were holding several sticks of incense.

"Same here," Levi exclaimed in Persian, his parents' native tongue.

"Jehovah has been kind to you over the years," I responded in Persian.

My grandparents spoke Persian as their primary dialect. Their ancestors learned the language when they were held captive under the Medo-Persia Empire about six hundred years ago. My grandfather tried to make it his grandchildren's second language.

"He has blessed you also," replied Levi. His green prayer-shawl rested on his narrow shoulders beneath a crimson beard and curly, red hair parted in the middle above a youthful face.

"I was hoping to run into you. Maybe you can offer some insight into a baffling situation," I said in a puzzled tone.

"Be delighted to help my old horseback riding buddy," Levi teased as we stood by the Eastern Inner Gate.

"You resided in Jerusalem when Jesus of Nazareth supposedly performed his miracles and taught amidst these walls. Tell me what you know about him and The Way," I politely requested of my tall colleague.

"Jesus did perform many amazing miracles among the people," Levi announced in a melodic timbre over the pilgrims' rhythmic chanting. Levi's long, tangled beard hid every movement of his lips.

"Are you serious?" I bellowed in Aramaic, stepping aside as four temple guards carried a young, female leper into the Court of Lepers.

"Yes, I personally saw Jesus heal a leper of his leprosy," Levi replied. My eyes glanced over at the Court of Lepers and he added, "The leper placed his faith in Jesus and as quick as a flash of lightening he was healed.

I studied the female leper's face consumed with the disease and said, "I find that hard to believe."

"Also, I watched him give sight to a blind man!"

"It was probably staged. I've seen that act performed in Tarsus among traveling, false prophets."

"No! That blind man grew up with me in the Lower City. We played together as children. He was born blind! The man always had something like a thick coating of goat's milk over his dilated pupils till the day Jesus healed him of blindness!" Levi spoke with candor while the female leper wiped pus from the stub, once a nose, in the middle of her scarred face.

"Amazing! Did this Nazarene prophet worship in the Holy Temple?" I inquired, giving Levi my full attention.

"Yes. He called it 'My Father's House.' Just days before his brutal crucifixion, he purged the temple of all its greedy moneychangers and parsimonious vendors. He wept over the temple's coming destruction." Levi recalled, charitably tossing a handful of shekels into the Court of Lepers.

"One of our parochialists already told me about his purging the temple. But what is this about the temple's destruction?" I queried as we walked through the Eastern Inner Gate toward the Holy Altar to burn my incense.

"He said, 'One greater than the temple is here. I'm able to destroy the temple of God and rebuild it in three days,'" Levi recalled in the Court of Israel. "The new temple was Jesus' body."

I felt this impious topic shouldn't be discussed next to the Holy of Holies. I suggested, "Let's step outside and into the Court of Gentiles for this conversation."

"No need, but as you wish."

We lifted our prayer shawls and silently headed for the Eastern Outer Gate. After we passed through the Eastern Outer Gate, I asked him with sarcasm, "So this Jesus and his church is the new eschatological temple?"

"Yes. It was validated by Jesus' atrocious crucifixion, tenable burial, and miraculous resurrection," Levi shared on the Eastern Outer Gate's bottom step.

"You're bordering on heresy," I said, shooting him a bemused look. "Tell me about his crucifixion."

"The Sanhedrin thought crucifying Jesus would eliminate their religious problem. They figured such an embarrassing death would disgrace him and discourage his followers. Furthermore, they felt his followers would be filled with fear and denounce him," Levi asserted with raised eyebrows.

"Did you see him crucified?" I shouted in Hebrew, as though conducting an inquisition. My voice was like a gust of wind that could have uprooted a palm tree.

"Yes, I followed the crowd up to Golgotha. It was a dreadful sight to behold! The Roman soldiers drove two iron spikes through his wrists. The spikes severed the tendons that extended into his shoulders. It sent pain throughout his entire body. They drove one long spike through both feet impaling him to the splintered wooden cross. Then they raised the cross upright with a rope," Levi's expressions led me to suspect he might believe in this crucified rabbi.

We passed through an opening in the limestone balustrades and entered the Court of Gentiles. I looked Levi in the eye and said, "I've already heard this account."

Levi ignored my remark and continued, "He had to use his back muscles to support himself and to breathe, since his arms and wrists were impaired. He had to put all his weight on a single nail. He had to alternate between pushing down on his nailed feet and arching his back muscles to breathe. Pain consumed his body! After several hours, he lost his strength and ability to push himself up.

"Before he suffocated on the cross, his bleeding, swollen lips uttered, 'Father, forgive them for they don't know what they're doing.' Then a Roman solider ran a spear into his side and several liters of blood poured from the opening. When all the blood had seeped from his body, water oozed from the wound. Those three barbaric hours still haunt my mind," he concluded.

"So, he's dead!" I announced as my face turned red with rage.

"He died an earthly death, but He has risen," Levi hummed slightly off-key. It sounded like a hymn for The Way.

"I know the stories regarding his resurrection," my voice barked, growing in ire. "Also, I know the tale of the Holy Temple's thick curtain that separates the Holy Place from the Holy of Holies that was supposedly torn in half. My sister helped sew that curtain together, not even a team of oxen could rip it apart!"

"It was torn in two from the top down. His followers believe this graciously opened the way for all to worship God, without having to go through the High Priest. They say, 'We can now worship in spirit anywhere, not just in the Holy Temple, because Jesus is the new Living Temple,'" Levi shared.

"That's blasphemy!"

"It's the precepts of The Way," Levi responded, staring toward Solomon's Colonnade.

"Look at those misguided souls. I can't believe his followers meet every day at Solomon's Colonnade," I retorted with a clenched fist. "Their devotion is like a sundial in the shade, good for nothing."

"The Way has met there since Jesus' crucifixion. The numbers of followers are growing daily at Solomon's Colonnade." Levi responded with animation in his voice. I ignored his tone and focused on the boldness of a dead man's followers. They shared their bane with nearly everyone who walked past them.

"They must be eliminated," I shouted, breaking three incense sticks in half that I forgot to place on the altar. "Crowds are even coming from nearby towns to worship at Solomon's Colonnade."

Levi sat down on a marble bench in the Court of Gentiles and remarked, "The Sanhedrin didn't count on God's son's resurrection and ascension."

"That kind of talk puts a target on the back of a person in Jerusalem," I snarled and sensed a gulf between us.

"Maybe the lowest became the highest," Levi said with a demeanor of hope.

"Do you believe in this heresy?" I asked Levi, circling the marble bench and knocking the dust off my red robe's tassels.

My bloodshot eyes beheld a sparkle in his pupils. I thought for a second, maybe he wasn't bewitched by a magician but touched by a Higher Being. I quickly dismissed that thought, stuck my nose within a finger nail of his face and yelled, "Well?"

"I don't know. Sometimes I think we're more concerned with our external appearances than others' wellbeing. Maybe we are so heavenly good we are of no earthly use. Perhaps we try to please man rather than

God. It seems these days are the darkest, yet brightest of times," Levi mused in earnest reflection.

My hands forcefully lifted Levi off his butt. With the hoarseness of an enraged sea captain I shouted, "How dare you say those things! You are a Pharisee. You have a duty to take drastic actions against this cult."

"I don't know," Levi said, committing to his spirit. "After what I have seen and heard of Jesus, I think he might be our Messiah."

At that moment odium ran through my veins instead of blood. "You besmirch my soul! Here's some incense. Go ask for forgiveness," I screamed at Levi and threw the broken incense in his face. I stomped away past the stonemasons finishing the western corner of the temple, and exited the Huldah Gates for my synagogue.

~~

I daily worshipped and weekly taught at the Synagogue of the Freedman. Our congregation had several Diaspora Jews, ex-slaves and former prisoners who received manumission from their masters. Most of our members were from Cilicia, Northern Africa, and Asia. Some of the Cilician congregants were from my hometown synagogue in Tarsus. The synagogue was extremely zealous in the faith, and some called us "Zionists."

The Synagogue of the Freedman's elders were concluding their monthly meeting when I entered the synagogue's sanctuary. They motioned for me and announced before I even reached them, "We have unanimously decided to eradicate The Way and its disciples from our synagogue and Jerusalem."

"Finally, someone else is willing to take action against this sect that's corrupting our laws and customs," I shouted in delight amidst a dark disposition.

"Our strategy is to have you discredit one of their acclaimed disciples, Stephen, in a religious debate at the Holy Temple. Are you willing to engage him in this manner?" The head elder asked as a light winter breeze blew through an open synagogue window. It caused the few hair strands atop his head to dance about.

"Yes! I briefly encountered his temerity when I first arrived in Jerusalem," I replied without suppressing my ego. "Tell me about him."

"Stephen goes from synagogue to synagogue preaching the crucified carpenter from Nazerth is the Messiah," the head elder informed. "Stephen is an outstanding Greek preacher, and Jerusalemites follow him throughout the city to hear him. He's a Jew, but he thinks, talks, and reasons like a Greek."

An elder with wedlock eyebrows told me, "Those foolish members of The Way say Stephen is full of God's grace and the Holy Spirit. He's supposedly loved by all."

"It may take a week to set up the debate, since Stephen has such a busy schedule," the head elder chuckled, regarding The Way's first deacon.

"What does he do within this sect?" I queried.

"He oversees the caring for numerous Grecian widows, hundreds of Jerusalem orphans, and countless poor Hebrew priests who have joined The Way," a senior elder, who was a blacksmith, stated after greeting me with a brawny handshake that nearly brought me to my knees.

"He seems to be a busy little bee!" I kidded.

"He also helps elderly Jews who moved here from around the Roman Empire to die in Jerusalem, mainly those who have become followers of The Way," the blacksmith added while I shook off his painful salutation.

"These misguided believers hold weekly collections for their poor congregants every Saturday," informed an elder whose sister belonged to The Way. "Then they distribute the food and money based upon individuals' needs each Sunday. Stephen oversees the collection and allocation of those offerings."

A younger elder, jealous of my Pharisee status and education, said with disdain, "You had better be at the top of your game or Stephen will devour you."

"He'll regret the day we debated! Just let me know where and when." I concluded, basking in my arrogance, and then headed off to the tent shop.

Chapter Ten
A Time to Kill

"Thinking to get at once all the gold the goose could give,
he killed it and opened it only to find – nothing."
Aesop

It took a couple weeks for the Synagogue of the Freedman's elders to arrange our Holy Temple debate. The elders finally set up the dialectic for a Sunday afternoon at the ninth hour in the Court of Women.

News of the debate traveled across the city from rooftop to rooftop. Most of the homes in Jerusalem were one-story buildings and residents used their rooftops as extra living space, since they were flat and it rarely rained in the Holy City. Residents shared the news of the debate with great anticipation from their contiguous rooftops.

That Sunday afternoon, the tunnels into the temple were packed with people. The Court of Gentiles was full of bartering merchants, moneychangers, and pilgrims. Jewish musicians played their cymbals, harps, and flutes outside the Holy Temple's entrance. However, minutes before the ninth hour everyone took a break to go hear the debate.

The Levites stopped blowing their bronze trumpets inside the Eastern Outer Gate. Priests quit chanted prayers in Hebrew and Aramaic on the Holy Temple steps. A colorful gathering filled the Court of Women and its galleries. The court was overflowing with excitement and congregants from every synagogue in Jerusalem.

Our Holy Temple debate began with this prideful Pharisee quoting from the holy scroll of Deuteronomy, "If you do not obey the Lord your God and do not carefully follow all his commands and decrees I am giving you today, curses will come upon you and overtake you." Then I recited forty

Jewish decrees and oral laws we were to live by. I dogmatically concluded, "We receive forgiveness by sacrificing animals as atonement for our sins, not through a Nazareth carpenter who was nailed to a wooden cross."

The high priest gave Stephen a paltry introduction, and then Stephen quoted from the holy scroll of Isaiah, "He was pierced for our transgressions; he was crushed for our iniquities: the punishment that brought us peace was upon him and by his wounds we are healed. The Lord has laid on him the iniquity of us all. He bore the sin of many and made intercession for the transgressors.'" Stephen paused and said, "Isaiah's words reveal to us that Jesus is the Messiah."

"Blasphemer!" The Alexandrian Synagogue elders screamed as sunlight toiled to get through the temple's orifices.

My rebuttal attacked his stance. It brought numerous cheers from the crowd. However, three minutes into Stephen's refutation, the audience was temporarily mesmerized by his words, not mine.

Stephen spoke with captivating passion, "We must obey Yahweh rather than men. We are saved by His amazing grace, not by the Mosaic laws or our good deeds. Yahweh's grace enables us to receive what we don't deserve: eternal life. His mercy prevents us from receiving what we deserve: eternal damnation. Our obedience to the law is not the cornerstone for a relationship with Yahweh. Our relationship with Jesus Christ is the cornerstone for a relationship with Yahweh."

Stephen's resolutions and rebuttals were crafted with such wisdom. It seemed like a spirit spoke through him. I was losing my first debate, ever. Every tactic and argument seemed useless against his pensive words.

"Only the Son of Man, who sits at God's right hand, can save you from eternal judgment not the law," Stephen responded to one of my remarks. Some women in the upper gallery and men in The Court of Women began nodding their heads in agreement with him.

Several bewildered elders abruptly concluded the Holy Temple debate, since it was going in the wrong direction. We overheard with great concern numerous congregational members whispering as they left the Court of Women, "Stephen's words seem to ring of truth."

The elders and I were so outraged; we held a meeting after everyone left the Court of Women. Our minds curdled together like spoiled goat's milk. One synagogue elder pounded his fist into his hand and exclaimed, "This man is dangerous. His words may have just converted some of our own congregational members to this damned sect. We must plot his downfall."

"He sickens the soul. We must shut his mouth for good!" An elder from Jerusalem's largest synagogue shouted after throwing his prayer shawl on the Holy Temple floor. Other elders did the same.

Over the next couple of weeks, those elders plotted Stephen's demise. The disgruntled elders convinced most of the Sanhedrin members that Stephen was a blasphemer; therefore, he should be tried, convicted, and executed.

~~

Stephen had three trials during the summer. The first trial was held at the Hall of the Sanhedrin. It got out of hand when Stephen said, "Jesus was crucified on a cross and buried, then arose from his grave after three days." The first trial lasted about thirty minutes and ended in a warning for him not to speak or teach in the name of Jesus Christ.

His second trial was held at the Chamber of the Hewn Stones. It got verbally violent when Stephen stated, "God's blessings aren't limited to Israel, but meant for all nations, including gentiles. May this generation not be like previous generations that opposed Yahweh's will and prophets!" The second trial ended in a flogging because of his remarks and failure to heed the first trial's ruling.

The third trial took place in the Court of Women. Most of the Jerusalem synagogue, elders, and Sanhedrin had run out of patience with Stephen. Once again, Jerusalem's religious leaders lined up false witnesses to accuse the innocent defendant of blasphemy.

I was working diligently in the tent shop during the third trial. The entire shop labored to complete a large rush order of wool tents for the Roman army. Four to eight soldiers usually shared one tent. Two Roman legions had gathered in Jerusalem over the last couple of weeks and were marching in two days for Decapolis to squash a slave revolt. During my time, about fifty-five percent of the people in the Roman Empire were slaves.

A young law student at Gamaliel's School, whom I had been mentoring ran into the tent shop. "Come quick! Stephen is giving his final defense in the Court of Women to the Sanhedrin. He's saying Jesus is the Messiah! Also, God spoke through our great ancestors to reveal this truth." The young law student shouted, breathing heavily.

"Thanks for letting me know!" I bellowed from behind a tall pile of black goat hair. I slipped on a scholarly, black mantle and we sprinted down the narrow backstreets of Jerusalem's Lower City to the temple. We raced up the temple stairs, scurried through the Court of Gentiles, and darted into the Court of Women. We arrived toward the end of Stephen's speech.

"You stiff-necked people, with uncircumcised hearts and ears! You are just like your fathers: You always resist the Holy Spirit. Was there ever a prophet your fathers did not persecute? You stoned Jeremiah to death, sawed Isaiah in half, and sold Joseph into slavery." We were shocked to hear him accusing our forefathers of hypocrisy. "They even killed those who predicted the coming of the Righteous One. And now you have betrayed and murdered him."

Within seconds I became as outraged as everyone in The Court of Women beneath dark, gloomy clouds. A ray of light shined through the dark clouds upon Stephen. He continued his remarks, being full of a spirit, "Look I see heaven open and the Son of Man standing at the right hand of God."

"Blasphemy! Blasphemy!" The Synagogue of the Freedman's congregation, Sanhedrin members, and synagogue elders screamed at the top of their lungs.

"We have a worm in our mist!" yelled a ranking elder with two insignia on his black mantle.

"He's a menace and a liar!" ten Sanhedrin members shouted.

"Stone him! Stone him!" The vehement crowd shouted, pumping clenched fists into the air. My ears rang from the temple crowd's thunderous death-sentence.

All the Sanhedrin members, except for one young member slipped out a side door. They wanted to avoid making Stephen's death verdict a sanctioned event by the ruling Jewish party. That activity could bring the wrath and imposition of Roman officials upon them.

Roman law made it illegal for local leaders to execute an individual, unless the municipality was a "Free City". Jerusalem was not one. However, the temple guards were granted the right of capital punishment, stoning, if needed to keep the temple holy.

~~

Four temple guards grabbed Stephens's limbs. They carried him out of the Court of Women and into the Court of Gentiles. Then the mob threw and kicked him down the temple's marble stairs. They booted him out the Sheep's Gate and pulled him through the dusty Jerusalem streets. The temple guards instructed the crowd to drag Stephen out the secluded

Lion's Gate to Kidron Valley, since two extra Roman legions were stationed by the city's main gates.

When we reached the Rock of Execution several men ripped off Stephen's garments and punched him with their fists. Then they threw him off the Rock of Execution, eight cubits drop-off to the ground below. The ground around us and below us was covered with large stones. Everyone stood at the Rock of Execution's edge and shouted obscenities down upon Stephen.

"Our time as residents here is fleeting. Pain, hardships, and death are constant reminders this is a temporary residence, not our eternal domicile." Stephen proclaimed amidst the pain of two, broken bones protruding through his skin.

"You're about to experience all three reminders." A young Sadducee shouted back.

"May we be God's ambassador, devoting ourselves to serving and helping others. Also, may I boldly stand for my faith because Jesus is waiting for all believers with open arms in Heaven." Stephen said, trying to stand up.

"Death to the Blasphemer! Death to the Blasphemer!" I yelled along with the crowd.

According to ancient Jewish law, those who brought forth the capital charges were required to cast the first stones. Three witnesses, an elder and two congregational members from the Synagogue of the Freedman, eagerly came forward. They removed their mantels of silk, wool, and burlap. "Will you watch over these for us?" they asked me. I nodded, acknowledging my willingness to watch their garments and endorsing Stephen's execution.

The witnesses each picked pick up two jagged rocks the size of softballs. Stephen was surrounded by rocks covered with dried blood. He was getting up when they started hurling their rocks down upon him. The first three rocks missed him as he stood in prayer for his executors.

The fourth rock struck him in the stomach and he sank to his knees in prayer. The fifth rock hit Stephen square in the face. He fell flat upon the ground as blood and pain flowed from his facial features.

Stephen lay lifeless on the ground for several seconds then with great difficulty arose to his knees. He wiped the blood from his suppurating nose and lips with a bruised forearm.

"Stone him! Stone him!" The lone Sanhedrin member, caught up in-the-moment, yelled.

Nearly everyone in the mob laid their garments at my feet and began flinging stones at Stephen. I stood there overseeing the garments and watched Stephen collapse amidst a deluge of rocks. He lay prostrate on the ground as stone after stone began taking away his earthly life.

"Lord Jesus, receive my soul," we heard him say.

Stephen looked up from the ground and uttered these words with his last breath: "Lord, do not hold this sin against them." This remark inspired us all the more with hatred and purpose.

When Stephen finished this prayer, a large stone struck him on the left temple. He instantly collapsed and died in a pool of blood. The crowd continued to bounce rocks and stones off his deceased body for several minutes.

"We will hear no more lies from his blasphemous mouth!" shouted a female proselyte.

"Today, we took our first step to subjugate this sect." The Sanhedrin member declared after throwing the last stone, "Now, let's take this oath…"

"We shall work together to eradicate this sect!" everyone swore the oath on the Rock of Execution.

The Sanhedrin member and five elders surveyed the crowd. They searched for an individual to administrate their oath and religious extermination. Their eyes focused on me because of my reputation as an ambitious Pharisee and lack of tolerance for heresy.

"Saul, we unanimously pick you to be the Chief Persecutor of The Way. Your educational background, devotion to the Mosaic Law, and willingness to participate in this stoning makes you the ideal candidate. May your zealous passion for Judaism guide your actions. Remember, this Jewish sect threatens all we hold dear!" The Sanhedrin member added before I handed him his outer garment.

"I accept the position." I felt the survival of Judaism rested upon my shoulders. Also, I wanted to obtain the esteemed approval of the Sanhedrin. Furthermore, I thought this role might help me gain membership into the seventy-one member Sanhedrin council.

Everyone went back to the city, but I remained behind. I stood alone in silence above Stephen's body nearly buried by bloody rocks. His serene expression vexed me for a few seconds. Then pride overtook my spirit. I turned away from Stephen's carcass and left it to the flies, buzzards, and wild dogs. My ego departed the Rock of Execution to perform its newly assigned duty, eliminating The Way.

Chapter Eleven
A Time for Injustice

"Where you find the laws most numerous, there
you will find also the greatest injustice."
Arcesilaus

The next morning the Sanhedrin summoned me to their monthly council meeting. Midway through their meeting a senior member turned and said, "We have decided to assign twenty temple guards to you. They will assist in your efforts to eradicate this sect plaguing our synagogues."

"Thanks for this opportunity to show my zeal for the law," I declared with a firm voice in the Court of Israel. "I appreciate you offering the temple guards' services, but I don't need them."

"We insist you use the temple guards. We don't want any signs of weakness on this matter," the High Priest ordered.

"Your desire is my command," I replied with obedience.

"Like the Roman army, we shall attack our enemy at its weakest point. We suggest you begin with the Hellenistic Jews. They entertain the claims of these blasphemers, and their religious convictions swim in the shallow end of the pool," a Palestinian member stated.

"Yes, and they're also very lax in upholding our oral laws," I confirmed.

"We have reopened Pompey's Prison for The Way inmates. The old dungeon has been abandoned since Cneius Pompey Magnus captured our Holy City nearly a century ago. Pompey used the jail to torture and murder our insurrectionists." A sage Sanhedrin member informed me.

"The death dungeon is just a couple of blocks southwest of the Hippodrome. The prison is three stories below street level. The place has no sunlight and is infested with rats," another Sanhedrin member added with a grim look.

"I'm familiar with the facility. The temple guards and I will begin our efforts today," I remarked, trying to appear humble.

"Remember your means validate the action which justify our ends." A Sanhedrin council member advised, giving me complete freedom in dealing with the Jewish sect. I bade an honorable farewell to the Sanhedrin council.

Upon walking outside the temple's Huldah Gates, I bumped into Stephen's burial procession. I was amazed at the vast number of mourners and familiar faces for this first martyr. Some called him a saint, and others sang songs of his boldness.

Most of them held tear drop bottles, thin, small vases for catching one's tears, to place by his grave site. The sheer number of Jerusalemites that honored this martyr's death exasperated me but justified my vengefulness.

The Holy Temple guards' barrack was one block from the Holy Temple in the City of David. I barged into the barrack with an air of pomposity and ordered the temple's chief officer, "Give me twenty of your finest guards! They're for a task assigned to me by the Sanhedrin."

"You take what I give you!" The chief officer of the temple answered, laughing in my face. "I'm sick and tried of fledglings like you! You all think you can come down here and tell me what to do," the chief officer growled.

He proceeded to assign the most cold-blooded, bloodthirsty, insubordinate Jewish temple guards to my detail. Their respect for human life must have existed somewhere in the recess of their souls, but I never found it. These men weren't urbane law enforcement officers, they were ruthless brutes disguised as temple guards.

We did, however, have two things in common. First, we hated The Way. Second, our bigotry toward this sect caused us to classify everyone human being into one of two categories; either followers or non-followers of The Way.

~~

Over the next several weeks the temple guards saw themselves above the law. When it came to tracking and imprisoning followers of The Way, abhorrence flowed from their hearts like blood from a severed artery.

All of the temple guards, along with the jailers (ex-temple guards), took pleasure in mistreating our religious prisoners. Their odium toward these inmates usually led to acts of torture. Sometimes they hanged prisoners' upside-down on prison walls for hours. They chained others to dungeon walls and stuffed filthy, oil-drenched rags in their mouths so they didn't have to listen to their babbling. They often used prisoners as punching bags for their daily exercise.

I was ordered to attend the Sanhedrin's monthly council meeting and give them an account of our first month's activities against The Way. When I entered the Sanhedrin Council Chamber, the High Priest stopped the meeting and remarked, "Saul, we have received numerous reports regarding you and your temple guards' actions against the sect." Trepidation filled my soul till the High Priest added, "On behalf of the council, I would like to say, we're pleased with the way you're aggressively pursuing the disciples of Jesus. You are fulfilling our objective, stamping out this religious cult!"

"Thank you. We are merely trying to please the council."

"Over twenty rabbis have informed us of the excellent job you're doing! There is no need for you to give an account today of your activities. Please return to your duties. We appreciate you taking time out of your busy schedule to visit us today," a senior Sanhedrin member said with admiration as he dismissed me.

The High Priest, Sanhedrin members, and synagogue elders frequently praised our zealous suppression of The Way over the following weeks. I was a man on a merciless mission. I sought professional recognition, legalistic righteousness and Sanhedrin membership. The temple guards and I were feared by all throughout the Holy City.

Our acts of persecution were relentless toward believers of The Way. We treated our prisoners like enemies of the state and hardened criminals. The twenty temple guards and six jailers spent the fall and winter months experimenting with ways to torture those followers.

They placed believers in boiling water, threw them into pits full of wild dogs, or flogged them till their bones showed. Others were placed over the fire of judgment, burned with red-hot iron pokers, or had their earlobes pierced and loaned out to slave labor camps.

~~

I bumped into Gamaliel one chilly, winter afternoon at the Pool of Siloam. There was no customary or cordial greeting; instead, he physically ushered me behind a wooden fruit stand. "Saul, you need to stop going from synagogue to synagogue and house to house searching for men, women, and children to imprison," Gamaliel scolded.

"I can't! It's my duty. We have wolfs amidst our flocks."

"Do you not remember what I told you about The Way?"

"Yes, but The Way is growing at a phenomenal pace since the Nazareth carpenter's crucifixion. I'm a Palestinian Pharisaic Jew and their disrespect for our oral laws is what drives my rage." I removed his hand from my forearm.

"I taught you the Golden Rule; do unto others as you would have them do unto you. I didn't teach you hatred at my school. Please, stop devoting yourself to these violent acts of abhorrence."

"I'm only persecuting those who defile our synagogues."

"You have devastated Stephen's old Hellenist Synagogue," Gamaliel remarked, staring into my livid eyes.

"They embraced The Way! Plus, those Greek speaking Jews have always placed less emphasis upon Judaism's rituals and customs."

"Their minds are merely open to a wide variety of Jewish prophets."

"This Nazareth prophet and The Way aren't some harmless faction of Judaism. They threaten all we hold dear!" I glared back into his wrinkled face.

"I thought I planted the seeds of tolerance and love in you. I keep waiting for them to blossom in your soul. Your very breath emits mayhem upon God's ways," said Gamaliel, sighing. His facial skin reminded me of the dry prunes on the fruit stand. "The Sanhedrin should have never assigned you a group to persecute The Way. Your temple guards and jailers are like madmen. How can you place harmless, innocent people in Pompey's Prison?" I noticed the puzzling way his russet eyes looked at me.

"They're not innocent! They have committed the ultimate, crime of heresy and must be punished."

"I taught you, there are two passionate reactions we have toward others, love or hate. Hatred is the opium of human emotions. Furthermore, loathing is the companion of fearful uncertainty which leads to detestation. We abhor people because we make prejudiced assumptions about them and we make prejudiced assumptions about people because we abhor them."

"I'm not full of hate but duty!"

"Hatred is opaque when looking in a mirror but transparent when looking at others. Abhorrence is one of the main reasons we don't receive all of God's blessings. God made us to be beings of love, not hatred."

"It's not about hate it's about religion! These blasphemers are coloring outside our theological boundaries. They are compromising Judaism. You are a Benjamite. You should be sensitive to this!" I snarled with squinted eyes.

"I am, this is why I'm confronting you."

We stepped toward each other. We were so close only silence stood between us. After a minute passed, I said, "It's time to weed Israel's garden for the sake of Judaism. I've taken a stance, and my actions require no defense!"

"I disagree. You have crossed over the boundary of goodness, into the sinister! You drum up false charges, like the Sanhedrin did against Jesus of Nazareth and Stephen, when you arrest people. If they refuse to denounce their faith, you hold hasty trials." The smell of rotten fruit and my fetid soul caused Gamaliel to take a couple steps backward.

"They're guilty of blasphemy! I don't care what you say or think!" I interjected, clenching my fists.

"Their mock trials consist of your temple guards and you casting stones, white for not guilty and black for guilty. Rarely does a defendant receive one white stone against your fabricated charges. After their trials your guards flog them then drag them to that death dungeon. You are doing the Evil One's vocation," moaned Gamaliel.

"Spend your words on someone else."

"My voice is a minority on the Sanhedrin, but as a teacher of God's word I ask you to reflect upon your actions. Please stop! You are fighting against God!" Gamaliel harangued with tears dripping unto his white beard. He turned and left me alone in self-reflection behind the wooden fruit stand.

Gamaliel's words offered a glimpse at the darkness in my soul. The stench from the fruit stand's spoiled melons, figs, and grapes caused me to reflect upon our rancid actions. Then, arrogance overpowered guilt and I saw myself rising above all contemporaries.

Chapter Twelve
A Time to Hate

"Let them hate so long as they fear."
Lucius Accius

Gamaliel's comments spurred my ego. I developed an appetite for combative action against The Way. I decided to feed this hunger in Jerusalem's Greek District, since that neighborhood was usually negligent in following the Torah and Mosaic customs.

I found my temple guards lounging in a Lower City tavern called Brutal Force. "We've got work to do. I got a name this morning from an informer. This religious traitor is one of Stephen the Martyr's associates. Let's go get ourselves a blasphemer!" I commanded, irrespective of Gamaliel's remarks.

"Now you're talking," Amon toasted.

Amon was my temple guards' captain. His muscular legs looked like marble pillars and his brawny arms like oxen legs. Amon's face was severely scarred, not from maintaining peace in the temple, but from fatal sword-fights in local taverns.

His reputation as a sadistic enforcer was frequently displayed within the temple's precincts. Amon patrolled the temple grounds armed with an iron sword in one hand and a leather whip in the other. When Amon wasn't on probation he roamed and searched the temple area for troublemakers.

~~

The temple guards threw their clay goblets against the tavern wall. We departed the tavern and marched to a neighborhood by the Pool of Siloam. I found myself knocking on a familiar door. It was Prochorus' house. Prochorus sold published treatises and manuscripts for a living from his one-room house. He was regarded as Jerusalem's foremost authority on ancient Hebrew scrolls.

Prochorus was a middle-aged widower. His wife and only child had been accidentally run over in the marketplace by a Roman centurion's chariot during a recent rebel uprising. I had been a valued customer and dear friend of his for nearly twenty years. I tutored his adolescent daughter in Latin for treatises during my college years.

The impatient Amon kicked in Prochorus's front door just seconds after I pounded on it. Prochorus's four internal, mud-plastered walls were covered with wooden shelves from floor to ceiling. They were filled with leather and papyrus scrolls.

His floor was filled with cedar boxes full of clay tablets. Prochorus was still seated at the dinner table in prayer when the guards busted in. He quickly read the intentions of the single-minded guards. He jumped to his feet, and his long salt and pepper beard covered his upper torso like a breastplate.

The callous temple guards ransacked his house. They threw his rare scrolls all over the floor as well as outside on the Lower City street. Nearly all the scrolls were in pristine condition and only a few were worn around the edges.

The guards quickly became bored with rummaging through his scrolls. They turned their attention to Prochorus and ripped off his shirt. Prochorus's chest was as bald as his scalp. The temple guards dragged him into the street by his uncombed beard, and then beat him with wooden clubs.

"Are you a believer?" Fat Jesse, a drunken temple guard, slurred. Fat Jesse was really tall and thin; a Roman galley slave's oar had more thickness to it than Fat Jesse. He had a raggedy, red beard and a rusty moral fiber. His oversized nose had been broken five times in fights; it looked like a mountain range.

"Yes, it is as you say!" Prochorus declared, quoting the words Jesus spoke to Pontius Pilate.

"Deny him, and we will set you free!" I impatiently screamed at my old friend while standing over his swollen, bloody body.

"I can't. Jesus is The Way to heaven!" Prochorus claimed without fear.

A young temple guard began savagely whipping him. "Maybe I can expedite your trip to Heaven," the flogging temple guard, Thin Imna sadistically snorted through his eagle nose. Thin Imna was really short and fat. He looked like a tomato. His right eye had been recently poked out in a tavern brawl. His flesh was pale white, while his eyebrows, hair, and beard were as black as octopus ink. Thin Imna's values resided in that gray area between vile and evil.

"If I go to Heaven today, I hope to find a place there for you!" Prochorus audibly prayed for his abusers between lashings as his blood dripped onto the dust from which he had come and would go.

"Quit whipping him! I want him alive not dead," I screamed at Thin Imna.

"He's a blasphemer! Let's end his life right now! Why wait for tomorrow to eliminate this scum from our city streets?" an inebriated Fat Jesse hollered as Thin Imna dropped his whip.

"Do not worry about tomorrow, for tomorrow will worry about itself. Each day has enough trouble of its own." Prochorus spoke, barely managing to quote Jesus while using a palm tree to rise to his knees.

"Today's troubles may do you in before tomorrow even gets here!" Amon remarked then accented that comment with the toe of his boot. Amon stood over him like a vulture deciding how to pick apart its prey.

Prochorus collapsed back on the dusty street and tried to raise his head. "You may eradicate my life, but not the teachings of our divine redeemer. His words will always exist somewhere, someplace, and somehow. You can't eliminate the truth," Prochorus muttered before passing out.

"Amon, take him to the prison. We will deal with him when he awakes!" I commanded. Fat Jesse tied Prochorus to his horse, and then dragged him off to the death dungeon.

~~

We were greeted at the prison's gates by another informer. "You know the Galilean teacher had twelve disciples. I know where one of his twelve disciples is working in Jerusalem." He said, raising his eyebrows.

"Yeah, now you're talking!" Amon said between belches.

"Let's go get that one!" Several temple guards roared in harmony.

"What a prize catch that would be! The Sanhedrin would honor you for his arrest, maybe even make you a member of their special group," mocked Amon.

"Cut that prisoner lose. Let's go get a blasphemer, who was in the inner circle." I ordered. Fat Jesse cut Prochorus's nearly lifeless body from his horse.

We left Prochorus bleeding and broken body outside the prison gates. Our black stallions followed the informant into the Hippodrome Marketplace. We barged into a tanner's shop where Bartholomew was busy working his craft. Six temple guards seized and threw him out on the marketplace street. A crowd of water carriers, hairdressers, magic potion vendors, cheese cutters, camel drivers, and artisans gathered around us.

My stallion snorted above Bartholomew's prostrate body, and I shouted down. "Renounce this false prophet as Lord!"

"Abolish his sect! Abolish his sect!" A Zionist mob chanted, encouraging the temple guards to take harsh actions against Bartholomew. The rabble grabbed pebbles from the street and threw them at Jesus' disciple.

"I refuse to deny my faith in the Righteous Redeemer. His resurrected body appeared before me at the Sea of Tiberias." Bartholomew moaned in agony as several temple guard plucked handfuls of long, curly hair from his scalp and face.

"Deny or die!" Amon shouted after smiting him on the lips.

"As long as these lips can breathe and speak, I will share the Gospel of Jesus Christ!" Bartholomew declared, trying to stop the steady flow of blood dripping from his mouth with one hand. The other hand was raised toward Heaven.

Amon picked up Bartholomew by the scruff of his neck and slammed his left elbow into Bartholomew's face. "Put him in chains!" Amon ordered.

"My faith is my link to Jesus Christ. You can chain my body, but not my spirit," Bartholomew boldly spat out those words, blood, and teeth, before the temple guards lugged him off to prison.

The temple guards threw Bartholomew inside the prison gates. Amon announced to the jailers. "We've got a gem for you guys, one of the carpenter's twelve disciples."

Then Amon turned to his men and said, "It looks like our other rat crawled back into his hole! Let's see if we can find him."

"Fat Jesse and I will check his house of scrolls. The rest of you follow the trail of blood," Amon directed his temple guards.

The temple guards and I successfully followed Prochorus's trail of blood into a back alley. Prochorus had somehow crawled into the alley where we assumed some followers of The Way stumbled upon him and took him to their home.

When we got back to prison gates, I told the guards. "Take the rest of the day off. We had a good haul, today."

"What are you going to do boss?" asked Thin Imna.

"I'm going to the dungeon and taking care of some long, overdue paperwork."

Upon entering the prison, I noticed the guards had already dragged Bartholomew down the dungeon's stone steps. When I reached the bottom stair, I saw them taking turns spitting and urinating all over him. Ahab, head prison guard at the Pompey Prison, had just defecated on him. Ahab was fittingly named after the most corrupt king of Israel, King Ahab.

"Take him to the dungeon's torture chamber and tie him to a chair," I heard Ahab shout as I pushed aside thirteen empty wineskins on my desk adjoining the torture chamber room.

Ahab drank from the second he awoke to the moment he passed out. He spent his off duty hours drinking in taverns with harlots. He had been convicted several times for physically abusing prostitutes in back alleys and brothels. Ahab was continuously in and out of the city prison for his crimes. That is how he got this job.

"Let's give our special guest the Melt!" I overheard one of the deranged prison guards hollered, tying Bartholomew to the chair. These dungeon guards delighted in their brutality toward prisoners.

"Great idea," Smart Samuel, who was really stupid, bellowed while grabbing a torture chamber candle.

Within seconds, Smart Samuel and two other sordid prison guards held Bartholomew's hand over a burning candle while his skin melted. Bartholomew screamed in agony. We were always amazed at the torture and pain these people endured for their faith.

"Your faith is built of wax, not rock!" Smart Samuel yelled after a gut-wrenching belch.

"Jesus said, 'Everyone who hears these words of mine and puts them into practice is like a wise man that builds his house on the rock." Bartholomew divulged with his voice full of excruciating pain, as the malodorous smell of his burnt flesh filled the torture chamber room.

"I can take your life right now!" Bright Bilhan, who was really obtuse, chortled while placing his burnished bronze sword against Bartholomew's throat.

"Only God can give and take life. Only fools try to keep what they can't keep," Bartholomew rebuked the prison guards.

"Let's show him what we can give!" Ahab guffawed, thumping a large club in his palm.

Bright Bilhan threw his sword on the dungeon floor and grabbed a wooden club. Then Bright Bilhan and Ahab began beating Bartholomew's torso.

"Enough! Stop it," I ordered from behind the pile of old, brittle wineskins. Ahab shot me a dirty look then dragged Bartholomew's unconscious body into a three by three by three cubits prison cell.

For weeks Bartholomew battled rats unceasingly chewing at his body. The pesky rodents kept his eyelids from resting for nearly a month. The prison guards insulted, whipped, and starved him for thirty days.

Smart Samuel and Bright Bilhan mistakenly released Bartholomew from the death dungeon one Sunday afternoon. In due course, Bartholomew left Jerusalem. He took a long mission trip to Armenia and India where he joined another disciple of Jesus, Thomas. Bartholomew's lips continued to share the Gospel for three more decades till he was flayed alive, and then crucified upside down.

Chapter Thirteen
A Time to Persecute

"Help me, for men persecute me without cause."
Psalmist

Our harassment didn't ease up over the winter months. Instead, the temple guards and I took our maltreatment to another level. We continually sought out and brutally tormented followers of The Way. The dark clouds of persecution intensified over Jerusalem.

It was still winter, and we were riding our black stallions through the Hippodrome Marketplace, on the prowl for followers of The Way. My stallion rounded a corner in full gallop and knocked down an elderly man. I looked down and it was Gamaliel.

Gamaliel struggled to get up but exclaimed, "Saul, phobia is the appetizer to the entree of animus. People who fear the most are the ones who generally persecute the most."

"I don't want to hear it, Gamaliel." I shouted, pulling back on my horse's reins.

"Friend, for some it's easier to flex the muscles of religious maltreatment than religious tolerance. Hatred leads to persecution and persecution leads to lasting scars and lasting scars lead to revulsion."

"Save it for your students!" I barked, looking about the marketplace.

"There's Nicodemus!" yelled Amon. Nicodemus, a Pharisee and former Sanhedrin member, was teaching thirteen Hebrew priests beside the marketplace fountain. Jesus had called Nicodemus the "Teacher of Israel."

We had heard that Nicodemus converted to The Way and taught it. Furthermore, he'd been recently baptized by two of Jesus' disciples, Peter and John. We galloped straight into their circle. Somehow, Nicodemus and the thirteen Hebrew priests avoided our cavalry charge. The temple guards jumped off their stallions and began beating the men with their fists.

"Confess your sin, or death will come to you heretics!" Amon screamed as several guards kicked, whipped, and clubbed the priests.

"We have nothing to confess! We have received salvation through the sacrificial love of God's son. We are not afraid to die for our faith in Christ!" a Hebrew priest boldly declared.

"Blasphemy! Don't you realize these guards can take your life?" I informed them of their dire status from my saddle.

"It's God's grace that allows us to take another breath, not your temple guards." Another Hebrew priest screeched between beatings.

"You priests are fools! You were trained to teach the holy edict, and it is called the Mosaic Law," Amon yelled at them after he took a brief break from thrashing three priests.

"We receive eternal salvation through God's grace, not the Mosaic Law. God's grace has a name, and it is called Jesus Christ." Nicodemus responded as blood flowed from his right ear after being kicked there several times by Fat Jesse.

All thirteen Hebrew priests and Nicodemus were lying prostrate on the wintry, stone street from their beatings. "Chain them!" I ordered the temple guards standing over their quarry like a lioness over her prey. The temple guards placed cold chains around their bloody wrists and ankles; meanwhile, Nicodemus and the priests sang praises unto their Lord.

"Stop singing, or you'll regret the day you were born!" Thin Imna yelled at them.

"Fortunately, we were born twice! Flesh gives birth to flesh, but the Spirit gives birth to spirit. You must be born again to see the kingdom of God," Nicodemus said, glancing up at me with blood, not fear in his eyes.

"Then, I'll kill you twice." Thin Imna yelled.

"Our Lord said, 'Do not be afraid of those who kill the body but can't kill the soul. Rather be afraid of the One who can destroy both soul and body in hell.'" Nicodemus encouraged the Hebrew priests before Thin Imna's foot rubbed his face into the rough stone pavement.

"Take their condemned souls to the Pompey Prison." I shouted with fury burning in my soul like a ceramic bowl inside a red, hot kiln.

It took all twenty guards to haul the fourteen prisoners to jail. The temple guards dragged them behind their horses. The detainees' bleeding legs looked like shredded paper when we arrived at the dungeon's gates. "People discover what they truly believe at death's door!" Nicodemus asserted to me before being untied from Thin Imna's horse.

"Well, you are at death's door," I claimed as my horse's hoofs threatened his life.

"Only if the One who gives and takes life wishes it to be that way," Nicodemus mused amidst his pain.

"Amon, throw all fourteen of them into just two prison cells!" I commanded. Each cell was designed to hold two criminals.

The temple guards kicked Nicodemus and the thirteen Hebrew priests down the dungeon steps, and then dragged them by their facial hair to their cells. The cell's stench from human waste and vomit was already unbearable when Ahab opened the cell doors.

Neither cell had been cleaned for months. Amon threw eight priests in one filthy hole and five priests along with Nicodemus in another soiled stall. The priests gathered up inside their cells like a covey of wild quail in a sorghum field.

"These boys are all yours. The one named Nicodemus is nearly as valuable as one of the carpenter's twelve disciples. He's the one who prepared their Lord's body for the tomb." Amon snarled to the prison guards after Ahab locked the cell doors.

~~

The temple guards bade farewell to the prison guards, Amon, and me. I stayed behind to retrieve a scroll for the Sanhedrin. I was searching my desk beneath empty wineskins, when I overheard Ahab and the prison guards laughing at the prisoners. They garnered immense pleasure and amusement in the way these prisoners had to lean against each other just to fit their battered bodies inside both cells.

"Which one of you is named Nicodemus? We want you to hang out with us." Ahab said with a strident snicker.

"I am!" an elderly Hebrew priest bellowed.

"No, I am!" shouted four other priests.

The prison guards grew in their wrath. They unlocked both cell doors to beat the dung out of every prisoner. After the first cell door swung open Nicodemus crawled over several priests and said, "Gentlemen, I'm Nicodemus. My friends were just being honorable." The prison guards dragged Nicodemus into the torture chamber room after locking both cell doors.

Ahab, Smart Samuel, and Bright Bilhan held a three minute mock trail. After their miscarriage of justice Ahab chortled, "You're a blasphemer and have been judged - guilty! You're sentenced to a life of harsh punishment!" They chained all four of Nicodemus's twisted limbs to the dungeon wall.

"Do not judge, or you too will be judged. For in the same way you judge others, you will be judged, and with the measure you use, it will be used to measure you." Nicodemus preached even while hanging on the dungeon wall like a broken picture frame.

"Measure this, old man!" Smart Samuel yelled, before swinging a wooden club into Nicodemus' midsection.

"May your soul beat to the drums of God's grace." Nicodemus moaned over the agony of a broken rib. He wore this new pain like a cheap tunic.

Nicodemus spent several months on and off the dungeon wall, being abused by prison guards. A Sanhedrin friend eventually got Nicodemus released from prison. Not long after his release, he was exiled from Jerusalem.

~~

The Way started meeting in believers' homes after Nicodemus was captured. These congregational gatherings were known as house churches. A house church consisted of ten to thirty believers. House churches began replacing synagogues and the Holy Temple as safe places for The Way's worship services during those late winter months.

We discovered our first house church one frigid winter morning by the Amphitheater. Ten temple guards surrounded the house and the other ten guards stormed into the house church. They were outraged by what they saw. The congregational members were reenacting their Galilean Messiah's crucifixion. The guards immediately started clubbing the worshippers and taking their jewelry as bounty.

Meanwhile, the ten temple guards surrounding the house became chilled. So, they set all four corners of the house church on fire to warm themselves.

"How dare you profane our religion!" coughed Thin Imna from the black smoke.

"Deny the crucified Nazarene! Admit your transgressions!" I demanded of the flock inside the house church as flames began to surround this congregation.

"We will not deny Jesus the Nazarene in this house of worship or anywhere!" One courageous teenage girl shouted back at me. I stared into the flames dancing around her silhouette and realized it was Uncle Elisha's daughter, Rachel.

"How could you? You are from the tribe of Benjamin! Forsake this cross!" I screamed at my young cousin, while backing out the door.

"Anyone who does not take this cross and follow me is not worthy of me. Whoever finds his life will lose it, and whoever loses his life for my sake will find it." She paraphrased Jesus before two temple guards threw her into the street. During our family dispute, two other temple guards threw their wooden cross into the flames.

The temple guards continued to club the congregational members inside the house church. The heat and smoke eventually forced all ten temple guards outside. Before exiting the burning house church, they threw congregational members into either the fire or street. All who survived the inferno and the beatings were chained and hauled off to our death dungeon.

~~

When we reached the dungeon, I ordered the temple guards, "Toss the severely burned prisoners into cells. The others, leave on the torture chamber floor." Amon and the temple guards threw ten crisp bodies into filthy, crowded cells and seven onto the torture chamber room's stone floor.

"Amon, you and the others may have the rest of the day off after this haul." I informed Amon and the temple guards inside the dim dungeon. "Ahab, I want to interrogate our new prisoners one at a time. First, bring me a male follower of the Nazarene rabbi!" I commanded.

"We should call them 'Nazarenes' since they follow the carpenter from Nazareth." Amon joked with Fat Jesse and Thin Imna before leaving the dungeon.

"Yeah!" all the other temple and prison guards yelled.

"Can anything good come from Nazareth?" Ahab sarcastically bellowed to Amon, who was walking up the dungeon steps.

The first prisoner Ahab threw at my feet for questioning was Levi, my old classmate. His pallid mantle was covered with blood, soot, and footprints of Amon's sandals. "How could you? You're a Pharisee," I shouted in disappointment.

"Saul, there's one thing I didn't get to mention to you in the Holy Temple. I saw Jesus' glorious ascension into Heaven. I can't erase that scene from my mind. Like Jesus, one day I'll leave behind this broken earthly body for a new one in Heaven," Levi declared through a broken jaw.

Ahab became so outraged by Levi's response that he clubbed him on the side of the head with a long wooden bludgeon. "Looks like today is the day," he roared.

Levi's body crumpled to the dungeon floor. Ahab and two of his prison guards picked up Levi. They threw his nearly lifeless body into a dark, rat-infested pit.

"Here's your heaven!" Ahab laughed as Levi lay unconscious and bleeding from the ear in a pit of human waste.

Ahab grabbed another adult male and kicked him like a mud ball till he reached my feet. The man's face was covered with bloody hair and black soot. "Throw a bucket of water on his face, so I can see who I'm talking to!" I ordered. "Not you, too!" I screamed as water revealed the kneeling man's identity.

"Yes, I have found the truth. I no longer dwell in the ignorance of darkness!" Uncle Elisha boldly declared, spitting muddy water and blood from his mouth.

"As a Nazarene, you could spend your life in this dungeon! Disown him!" I cried at Uncle Elisha as rats nibbled at his bare feet and my sandals.

"Whoever acknowledges me before men, I will also acknowledge him before my Father in heaven. But whoever disowns me before men, I will disown him before my father in heaven." My uncle quoted Jesus as two prison guards picked him up. Both of his legs were fractured.

"Look at what you have done to your family and yourself by following that Galilean rabbi," I said, kicking the rats away from our feet.

"I've found the most precious jewel of all, Jesus! He's a flawless rock who willingly suffered and died for all of our sins!" Uncle Elisha evangelized to everyone in the torture chamber room.

"Maybe this will help you catch up to your rock's suffering!" The bloodthirsty Bright Bilhan snorted, flogging Uncle Elisha.

"Stop it! Stop it!" I ordered. My spirit all the sudden felt itself caught in a dichotomy. The thrashing my uncle just received pained me as much as it did him.

"Animals die for our sins, not Galileans! The High Priest determines what animal is pure and without flaws for a sacrifice. Only then will Jehovah accept a blood offering as atonement for human sins. Not some carpenter's blood from Nazareth who was shamefully crucified on a wooden cross!" I shouted at Uncle Elisha before noticing the house church flames had disfigured the left side of his face.

"God looked down from Heaven. He saw Jesus' holy and sinless body hanging upon that wooden cross. Jehovah accepted His Son's blood offering as atonement for our sins. This one sacrifice enabled all of humanity's sins to be forgiven. Forever," Uncle Elisha added in pang of pain.

"I remember that day! I worked that man's crucifixion! The whole city was in an uproar," Ahab snarled.

"Yeah, and we had a major earthquake!" Bright Bilhan guffawed after licking green snot from his index finger.

"Later that evening some crazy Roman centurion came into the Brutal Force and claimed, 'Surely he was the Son of God.'" Ahab recollected before his anger caused him to start clubbing Uncle Elisha in the stomach.

"Drop that club! I'm talking to this man," I commanded Ahab.

"O Lord, I yield my soul into your hands." Uncle Elisha murmured before passing out from the burns, pain, and beatings. His remark echoed in my soul.

"Take a break!" I ordered the prison guards. They dropped my uncle like he was leftover food scraps. Ahab pulled out a bottle of cheap wine from beneath the Rack. He took several gulps while all the other prison guards fought for the next swig.

I picked up Uncle Elisha and carried him out of the torture chamber room. Meanwhile, Ahab handed Smart Samuel the wine bottle. Ahab went about the torture chamber room, ripping off male prisoners' garments. One detainee resisted his actions with minor success.

The guards who were waiting for a swig shouted. "Kill him! Kill him!"

So Ahab grabbed the skinny, adult prisoner and savagely slammed him against the wall. Then Ahab ran a bronze sword through the detainee's boney ribcage and into his heart. The man instantly dropped dead amidst the tears of fellow prisoners and cheers of the guards.

Chapter Fourteen
A Time to be Perplex

"To have little is to possess, to have plenty is to be perplexed."
Lao-tzu

My troubled soul searched for direction. Loathing and love no longer co-existed within my heart; they fought for dominance. I had just overseen the persecution of my favorite relative. My Jewish heritage and family ties were at odds with each other.

I had been shaped by familial relationships, but I received professional worth from the Pharisees and Sanhedrin. Ima always told us that blood was thicker than water. But, blasphemy was a sacrilegious act that couldn't be overlooked in Judaism. Therefore, my kith and kin were in conflict.

Amidst personal turmoil, these quivering arms carried my unconscious uncle to a secluded prison cell. I paused outside the cell and pulled a ruby ring off my finger, then placed it inside Uncle Elisha's tunic pocket. It was the one he'd given me on my bar mitzvah. I prayed he'd use it as a bribe with Ahab to get his family out of this death dungeon.

When we entered the cell, a Hebrew priest looked up at us. He had his hands tied behind his back on the assumption it would keep him from praying to the Nazarene carpenter. He was lying on his stomach on the cell floor that was covered in human waste. He was trying to eat his paltry daily rations. He ignored us and went back to head-butting the rats who were trying to devour his food.

I cleaned a spot on the cell floor with my sandals and set Uncle Elisha down. He briefly regained consciousness, so I whispered into his burnt ear, "I put my ruby ring in your pocket. The one you gave me for my bar mitzvah. Use it to get your family out of this hellhole. Then, go back to your estate and stay silent like the stone carvings in the Holy Temple."

"There is no estate. We sold our villa and gave all the proceeds to Jesus' disciples. They shared the money with our needy brothers and sisters. Furthermore, we gave our most valuable possession to Lord, our souls. May you do the same!" Uncle Elisha uttered between painful breaths.

"What is wrong with you!" I moaned. Then my eyes noticed a wide gash on his left arm from a temple guard's sword. The deep wound was still bleeding, so I ripped off part of my mantel and dressed the wound.

"Saul, may this crossroad open your mind. There is no hatred in my heart for you, only love. The redeemer of Israel has come, and his name is Jesus." He passed out again. His piercing words became like termites eating at the foundation of my Pharisaic soul. We had just beaten him into unconsciousness, and still he had love for me.

~~

Upon returning to the torture chamber I found Ahab, Smart Samuel, and Bright Bilhan attempting to rape a female congregational member. "Stop it!" I yelled. The guards dropped her broken, partially dressed body on the grimy stone floor. The woman's mangled torso and legs swam in a puddle of her own blood.

"Pick her up and bring her to me!" I shouted above the other congregational members' songs of praises and prayers. We were successfully crushing their bones, but not their faith.

"Man, you're no fun!" Bright Bilhan growled before putting his loincloth back on.

"Ahab, move the hair from her face," I ordered.

I nearly fainted. It was the woman who was present at my birth, Aunt Helah. "We've imprisoned your whole family today. Is this where you want them to spend their lives? Deny this doomed prophet," I demanded.

"I can't! Peter the Apostle told us of the anguish he experienced after denying Jesus. He prayed none of us would ever encounter that ." Aunt Helah remarked through the throbbing pain of broken nasal bones.

"Peter the Sham!" Ahab screamed in anger.

"Yeah, he's that burly fisherman who nearly caused us to be beheaded when we were working in the public jail." Smart Samuel recalled before wiping Aunt Helah's blood from his muscular body.

"He escaped on us! I had the jail securely locked, with guards standing at the doors: but when we opened them, we found no one inside." Ahab, the ex-captain of the temple guard, growled.

"The fisherman cost us our jobs!" Smart Samuel shouted after spitting on Aunt Helah.

"Why do you voluntarily go through this suffering? Are you still sane?" I questioned my aunt while growing irritable.

"Yes, we're still sane, but sometimes we'll suffer in life like the Lord did for us. We accept all events and give thanks for all circumstances." Aunt Helah labored to catch her breath.

"Free yourself from this false Messiah's spell. You will never know peace as one of his followers!" I pleaded with her.

"The kingdom of God expands one soul at a time. I hope your temple guards, prison guards, and you find the point to life - eternal peace in the Lord." Aunt Helah prayed with her last breath before blacking out.

"Let me help you find the point. The point of this sword!" An intoxicated Bright Bilhan maliciously screamed, drawing his sword from its cracked leather scabbard.

"No! She's already full of a poison that will kill her. Put her in a cell with that teenage girl!" I ordered Ahab in a forceful voice while pointing at Rachel. If Ahab or other prison guards knew Uncle Elisha, Aunt Helah, and Rachel were my relatives, they'd kill them out of spite after I left the dungeon.

Ahab and Bright Bilhan grabbed them by their long, bloody hair, then dragged them to the cell area. They threw Aunt Helah and Rachel into a prison stall. I heard the haunting sound of their skulls bouncing off the mucky stone floor.

"Put a couple of those fanatics on The Rack! That will help straighten out their priorities!" Ahab bellowed when he returned to the torture chamber room.

They placed several congregational members on The Rack. The Nazarenes were stretched to their limits but didn't break. Every one of them uttered that it was an honor to endure persecution for the name of Jesus, since he suffered and died for their sins. Their faith, to our amazement, provided them strength in spite of our oppression. Also, we were all astonished by their valor and perseverance while being tortured on The Rack.

Over the next two days our house church prisoners were given jail sentences from three to eight years. The severely burned prisoners, with blistering burns over three-fourths of their bodies, were thrown outside the prison gates to die.

When I arrived at the prison three days later for additional interrogations, my ears heard agonizing screams coming from Uncle Elijah's dungeon chamber. I immediately went to his cell to investigate the shrieking. My eyes and nose were overwhelmed upon entering the cell.

"Your left arm is completely infected with gangrene!" I exclaimed, holding my nose.

"I know, he replied through clenched teeth.

"If your arm isn't amputated now, you will die. We have to amputate it!" I shouted, watching an ocean of pain swell up in his body.

"Please help, please!" His thoughts were barely coherent because of the terrible pain.

"How? No doctor or medical professional is going to step foot in this dungeon."

"You can do it. You once saved your abba's life. Now save mine."

I called three guards to Uncle Elisha's cell. They wouldn't enter the cell because of the stench. So I tricked them by saying, "We're going to torment this old man, who kept you up all night with his screams."

"Yeah, now you're talking boss!" cackled Smart Samuel.

They held down Uncle Elisha as I cut away his dead flesh with Ahab's knife. I had Smart Samuel get a saw. Ahab cut off his arm just below the left shoulder. Without much enticing, Bright Bilhan fetched a hot rod from the fire pit that they had been using to burn out prisoners' eyes. I successfully cauterized my uncle's severed veins and arteries with the red-hot rod. Finally, we all took some grease from the Rack and took turns throwing it on his mid-arm stump. The guards returned to their torture chamber room, thinking they had just performed a splendid act of torture.

Uncle Elisha gained consciousness for a minute after the crude surgery and uttered, "Thank you, Saul! You saved my life. Now, let the Lord save your life." I shook my head, still not believing he had sacrificed an arm and nearly his life for a carpenter.

~~

Most prisoners' family members and friends disowned them, once they were incarcerated as Nazarenes. Even with the reality of harassment and imprisonment, Jerusalem citizens still sought out this sect. The

Way remained contagious among the populace. It was spreading like a smoldering fire in the refuse behind the temple's western wall.

We stepped up our efforts over the next couple of weeks, but mysterious events began to occur. Several times we tried to enter house churches; however, some unexplainable force prevented us from entering their services. Twice, we busted into house churches and suddenly found ourselves lacking the energy to beat up or arrest anyone.

Also, during this time Ahab informed me, "Nazarenes' prison cell doors are bizarrely unlocking and swing open! One day, seven inmates walked right out of their cells, up the steps, and out the prison gates without any of us even seeing them."

These extraordinary occurrences inspired my desire to track down Nazarenes. I was convinced, along with my Sanhedrin friends: every possible avenue should be pursued to exterminate The Way.

We daily searched Solomon's Porch and the Jewish neighbors for followers and teachers of The Way. By winter's end only a few underground house churches, believers, and apostles remained in the Holy City.

God knew, but I was clueless; this was my first act of evangelism. My spirit wasn't even conscious of this heavenly antithesis - every negative has a positive just like every dark cloud has a silver lining. In other words, God was using my bad for His good – later in life I'd grasp this godly insight.

Our ruthless persecution forced thousands of believing Jews out of Jerusalem. They fled to their previous provinces or sought refuge in Samaria (like Philip), Asia Minor, Syria, and areas beyond. Upon entering these lands, they shared the Gospel of Christ with its inhabitants. All these exiled believers helped lay the cornerstone for the world's churches.

Chapter Fifteen
A Time to be Prejudiced

"Dogs bark at a person who they do not know."
Heraclitus

The stories of our persecution spread throughout the region as our oppressed brethren fled Jerusalem. The spring brought numerous rabbis along with synagogue elders from Samaria, Galilee, Decapolis, and Syria to Jerusalem. They were all seeking my tactical advice on how to eliminate this new sect from their congregations.

They all had similar comments: "The Way is taking up residency and being embraced in our synagogues! Also, gentiles are converting to this sect and trying to worship in our synagogues!" My blood would boil with fury every time rabbis and elders shared these accounts.

These reports from distant synagogues became a daily occurrence. By mid-spring these continual communiqués exhausted our tolerance. My volcanic wrath erupted in late spring when a group of elders from Damascus and their rabbi approached me.

They were in town for meetings with the Sanhedrin on judicial issues. The Damascan delegation tracked me down in the Hippodrome Marketplace during a late morning recess. I had just finished an inflammatory speech to a vast crowd, condemning religious fanatics.

"Saul, can we speak with you about these radicals?" the Damascan rabbi inquired.

"Rabbi, my ears are all yours," I responded, jumping off a couple bundles of grain sacks.

"These heretics, who call themselves The Way, have the audacity to worship some man from Nazareth as their Messiah. They worship together on the first day of the Roman week, Sunday, in our synagogue! They invite our congregational members to join them," the rabbi declared to a sizeable gathering.

"Sometimes they meet on the Sabbath in rooms adjoining our sanctuary. Their worship service frequently interrupts our liturgies because of their hymns unto this Nazareth carpenter." A senior elder with broken, yellow teeth added in frustration.

"We have a lot of Hellenistic proselytes and God-fearers in our synagogues. Their minds are breeding grounds for The Way! Our city has become the gateway to the Orient for this sect," a young, Syrian businessman remarked. He wasn't a synagogue elder but had joined the religious delegation, since he had commercial trading interests in Jerusalem and Damascus.

There were two gentile groups in most Jewish synagogues. The *proselytes* were circumcised and lived by the Mosaic as well as the oral laws. Because of the first requirement, there were more female than male proselytes. The *God-fearers* were less committed to the ways of Judaism. They were usually uncircumcised men who didn't want to endure the surgical procedure.

"You have found the right person to help you!" a drunken Fat Jesse yelled from a nearby flea infested inn's outdoor café.

"Enough of this damned sect! Saul, tell them about the importance of spiritually staying in line!" Thin Imna roared amidst the captivated throng. Then he toasted the crowd, spilling spirits all over him and others.

"Our earthly life is a finite line. God draws the length of that line. We usually cast out our line in adolescence, then walk that line through adulthood. However, some now claim they can read between the lines." I preached while passing the vendors' stands that lined the Temple Marketplace's main thoroughfare.

"Yes!" Several zealot sandal-makers shouted from their wooden booths. Zealots strongly opposed Rome's secular rule, heavy taxation, and religious blasphemers. Furthermore, they were the most vocal and rebellious of all Jewish people.

"The Way continues to cross the line with stories of a new lifeline. Now is the time to sever their line and hold tight to ours!" I shared the party line, cursing those with a different line of thought.

"They have crossed the boundary lines in our synagogues!" A Damascus elder bawled with the type of anger that causes neck veins to become visible.

"Followers of The Way are tainting our synagogues' worship services throughout our regions. These itinerant lunatics must be dealt with, now!" I bellowed to the marketplace throng.

"Yes!" The fuming horde screamed back at me.

~~

I bade farewell to the marketplace multitude and Damascan delegation, then headed to Caiaphas's abode in the Upper City. My feet gaited with purpose up a nearby hillside, leaving the city below. Rage was boiling inside me. When I arrived at Caiaphas's palace, surrounded by lush palm trees, my face and spirit were fire-red.

Caiaphas answered his door in a plain purple mantle and said, "Saul! Shalom!" It was the first time my eyes had ever seen Caiaphas not wearing his High Priest's garments.

"Shalom!" I replied as he escorted me into his spacious courtyard.

"Your zealous persecution against the Nazarene sect in Jerusalem has far exceeded our expectations! You are doing a great job eradicating these rabble-rousers." He praised.

We had barely stepped into his courtyard when I declared, "I'm the most committed Pharisee in Jerusalem and Palestine for our traditions."

"Yes, you are, my son."

"So, I'm asking you as our High Priest and head of the Sanhedrin to issue me an official document, granting me unlimited power to go throughout the land, to arrest any Jew who claims that Nazarene carpenter is the Messiah. Give me the authority to bring these fugitives back to Jerusalem for their trial and imprisonment," I exclaimed.

Rome granted religious governance and extradition rights to the Jewish High Priest. Caiaphas had permission to pursue Jewish criminals who fled Jerusalem and bring them back to Jerusalem for trial. Also, under Roman law, the High Priest had authority to sentence Jews guilty of blasphemy to incarceration or death. However, the High Priest could only issue the death penalty in extreme cases and with Roman approval.

"Saul, you can embark upon that crusade this afternoon! Please rid Palestine and our neighbors' lands of these blasphemers! Where will you begin?" Caiaphas gleefully inquired after broadening my scope of religious persecution.

"Damascus! It's the hub of caravan activity, crossroads for the Babylon, Egyptian, and Red Sea trade routes." I declared. "Numerous travelers pass through that city's thoroughfares, and The Way uses those trade routes as an avenue for sharing their foolish faith. Also, we receive more dispatches about The Way from Damascus than any other city!" My wrath continued to erupt.

"Wise choice!"

"We will haul them in by the hundreds." Damascus had thousands of Jewish residences. I knew capturing Hellenistic, Jewish followers of The Way in Damascus would be like throwing out fishing nets during spawning season.

"Take plenty of supplies, because Damascus is a six to eight-day journey. The Sanhedrin and I will draft the official Letters of Plenipotentiary tomorrow morning. They will grant you extradition rights, so you can bring those blasphemers back to Jerusalem for disciplinary actions."

"Sir, I had hoped to leave today?"

"No problem, I'll send the letters by courier to Judas of Damascus's house. He will share it with the Damascan synagogues. By the time you get to Damascus everything will be in place. I suggest you stay with him. Also, don't drink the water in Damascus. It comes from the Abana River and it will disrupt your bowels," Caiaphas meted.

"Thanks for the insight," My sour voice and face replied.

"Give my regards to the residents of the Nabatean Kingdom. And Aretas IV, the Arabian prince, whom Rome has appointed as Damascus's overseer." Arabia reached from the Sinai Peninsula to east of Damascus. Aretas IV ruled the Nabatea kingdom and desert thoroughfares from his capital city in Petra.

"Will Aretas IV cooperate with our wishes?"

"Yes, he's always seeking Jewish favor. Aretas will endorse this mandate from Jerusalem. Make us proud of your actions!" Caiaphas concluded, giving me a confirming pat on the back. He picked up a papyrus map of Palestine from his courtyard table and gave it to me.

"I will, High Priest!" I promised. Then my callous fingertips rolled up the map, and I took immediate leave of his sacrosanct presence to prepare for the journey.

Upon descending from Caiaphas's hillside villa, I met Amon and eleven temple guards, who were waiting for me in the Lower City. "We found some stinking Essenes in the marketplace getting supplies. They are preaching that John the Baptist, who baptized the carpenter from Nazareth, lived among them before he was beheaded by Herod the Tetrarch," Amon shouted.

"You can deal with them. I've got other fish to catch!" I informed

Amon. "Get nine temple guards to escort me to Syria! Have them meet me at the Temple Marketplace in half an hour!"

~~

Nine temple guards and I joined a small caravan near the Temple Marketplace at noon. Just as we were exiting the Damascus gate for Syria the Roman cavalry came galloping back into Jerusalem.

The cavalry was in full gallop and nearly stampeded three pilgrim families in our caravan. The Roman soldiers were returning from Jericho with several political prisoners, people who couldn't or refused to pay their taxes.

The Roman soldiers were dragging several of our brethren from Jericho behind their horses and libidinously riding with their ransomed daughters. Along with them ran a sizeable herd of goats, cattle, and sheep. They had taken these animals as payment for taxes, in addition to deeds of the men's olive groves.

We were barely five hundred paces outside the city gate when we beheld six young, Jewish men who had just been crucified alongside the Damascus Road. Their families were gathered at the foot of their crosses, cursing the Romans and weeping for their love ones.

"They were convicted yesterday of treason and sedition by the Roman court. Too many Jews have died at the hands of Roman soldiers!" Thin Imna's lips curled in disgust.

"I'm weary of Roman oppression, taxation, and suppression," replied a Jerusalem traveler. But we tolerated it, because we knew a Messiah is coming to free us from Rome's tyranny. We anxiously waited for the Messiah as the yoke of Roman despotism became heavier and heavier. My temple guards' brutal acts toward the Nazarenes paled in comparison to the way Jews were treated by Roman soldiers and governmental officials.

Just a short distance outside the Damascus gate, we passed one of the most important shrines for The Way. Thin Imna remarked, "Up there on Golgotha is where the carpenter was crucified."

"The place looks like a skull from down here," a young temple guard observed as we all shook our heads in agreement.

"It has looked like that, since the stonemasons started excavating boulders for the Holy Temple," Thin Imna stated.

I embarked upon this journey to Syria's capital with one objective; persecute the heretics of The Way. My hatred grew with each passing step for those blasphemers who had fled Jerusalem and were defiling our religion in other regions. Some felt we were Jewish terrorists, but we merely sought to keep Judaism pure! Regardless, my band had unlimited authority in dealing with betrayers.

Not far from Jerusalem our caravan took a left turn to Bethel instead of a right turn to Jericho and Perea. The caravan commander's wife had acquired an illness, so we spent the night in Bethel not far from his sister-in-law's house. Then in the morning our caravan commander decided to take the longer, safer route through Samaria to Damascus.

When we reached the boundary of Samaria, I barked, "Samaritans are immoral and spiritually bankrupt people. We have no desire to travel through their land!"

"I'm sorry sir, but I have no choice." He remarked, then turned and motioned the caravan into Samaria.

"There is no kinship between these heathen Samarians and us righteous Jews. You are defiling our bodies!" I barked again regarding their secular detestation.

We hiked through the upland's extremely fertile soil full of grape orchards, olive trees, and Samaritan villages. Our caravan continued through the mountains of Ephraim toward Mount Gerizim. When Mount Gerizim came into sight, I pointed to it and told the temple guards, "See that mountain?"

"How can I not see it!" Smart Samuel replied, sarcastically.

"It's one of the main reasons we look down upon the Samaritans. Over five hundred years ago King Cyrus of the Persian Empire conquered the Babylonian Empire. After his conquest he allowed some Judean Jews to return to Jerusalem. Those ancestors rebuilt the Holy temple in Jerusalem. The Samaritans were not permitted to go back and help with the reconstruction." I informed them.

"And that was a good decision," declared Menahem, the one in charge of the guards.

"Eventually, King Cyrus released the Samaritans and they built a temple on Mount Gerizim. They believe that is the dwelling place of God, not Mount Moriah in Jerusalem where our Holy Temple stands. That fallacious temple on Mount Gerizim is about four hundred years old." I imparted my knowledge to them.

"But, my great, great grandfather helped to destroy most of that temple over hundred and fifty years ago!" Menahem proudly bellowed. We were all shocked by his historic knowledge of the event.

PALESTINE

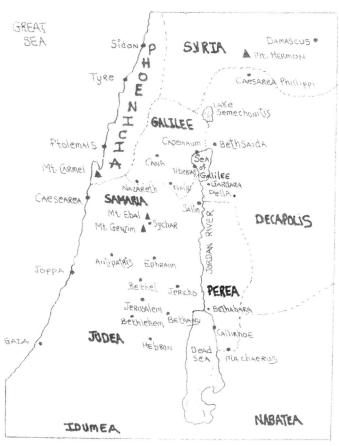

Chapter Sixteen
A Time for Anger

"Anger is a short madness"
Horace

About three thousand paces from the base of Mount Gerizim, our caravan took an afternoon break. The sun's full glare was baking us like clay pots inside a kiln. We were feeding our horses along side the road when five Samaritan men passed by.

Menahem looked over his horse and shouted at the travelers, "You Samaritans are apostates and idolaters! You will marry anyone, even gentiles. You're a land of a mixed race!"

"We should have crossed the Jordan River around Jericho to avoid this pagan region," Fat Jesse barked to the other temple guards.

"Sorry our race offends you. You gentlemen must be from Judea." A young man said.

"At least they know a thoroughbred when they see one!" Menahem boasted.

"Do you know a Jerusalemite Jew named Philip? He was here not long ago. He showed us The Way! Do you know The Way?" Another young Samaritan man graciously inquired. Samaritans warmly embraced The Way, especially when compared to Judeans.

"A Samaritan and Nazarene all wrapped up in one!" Menahem yelled, grabbing his thrusting sword from its leather scabbard and pushing aside his black stallion. Menahem punctuated his response by running the length of his blade through the young man's chest. The Samaritan fell dead in a pool of his blood.

"Is it his unlucky day because he's dead, or is he dead because he's unlucky?" Fat Jesse laughed after spitting on the Samaritan's bleeding fatal wound.

"Any other questions?" Menahem barked to the remaining four Samaritan believers before loosening his mail corselet.

"Let us show you our way," hollered Fat Jesse. Within seconds, all nine guards were punching and kicking the Samaritan believers. After five minutes of savagely beating them, the temple guards mounted their horses and galloped toward Mount Gerizim.

I followed after them. They stopped in the valley that lies between Mount Gerizim and Mount Ebal to fill their goatskin canteens at Jacob's Well. Menahem was the first to reach Jacob's Well. He threw aside a Samaritan woman drawing water, so he could wash the heathen's blood fragment from his sword and pommel.

"Welcome to Sychar!" The Samaritan woman greeted us after getting up from the soiled ground and brushing the dust from her garments. "Are you a Jew from Jerusalem?" She asked me. The temple guards were fighting each other to fill their goatskin water bags.

"Yes. I live there now." I answered piously and immediately attempted to remove myself from her presence, because she was a Samaritan.

"Do you know of the one named Jesus? He taught in Sychar for a couple days."

"Yes, but how dare you even speak to me! You're a Samaritan! I'm a Pharisee!" I angrily responded before turning my back to her.

"Forgive me! However, I feel led to tell you Jesus had a conversation with me at this very well." I turned back around. "He told me, 'Everyone who drinks this water will be thirsty again, but whoever drinks the water I give him will never thirst. Indeed, the water I give him will become in him a spring of water welling up to eternal life.'" The middle-aged woman remarked.

"Blasphemy!" I rancorously screamed and knocked the water jug from her hand.

"He wasn't speaking of drinking water but the water of spiritual life. Now, my soul never grows thirsty. I faithfully worship your Messiah, as do many Samaritans in this city." She looked like others who had drunk from The Way's intoxicating well.

"The Messiah will come to the Jews, not to the lowly Samaritans and heathen gentiles. Let's get out of here, men!" I yelled. The guards grumbled aloud then jumped back atop their horses, digging their boots into the stallions' flanks.

We galloped out to meet the caravan commander. My anger was boiling over in the late-day's full glaring sun as I told him, "You have thirty minutes to refill your goatskins. Meet us on the edge of town. We're heading due east to get out of this region! We'll cross the Jordan River at Salim!"

"Why?" The baffled caravan commander asked me.

"I'm sick and tried of hearing stories about the Galilean carpenter on this side of the Jordan River! I have no desire to pass through or near his hometown of Nazareth."

"Fine! We'll cross the Jordan River at Salim, and then continue to Damascus through Decapolis and Trachonitis." The caravan commander conceded with ire before heading the caravan to Jacob's Well.

~~

There was no peace within my soul as we journeyed eastward. We continued for a couple thousand paces then camped for the night. The next morning we headed toward the forests and chards overlooking the Jordan River valley. We crossed the Jordan River at Salim, but my conscience was still tormented by those Nazarenes' sacrilege.

For days we hiked up the Jordan River's eastern riverbanks then along the Sea of Galilee's eastern shoreline. We continued hearing stories from Jews as well as gentiles about Jesus' teachings. My pace quickened along with my desire to persecute Jewish followers of The Way as we passed the Sea of Galilee.

We were just north of the Sea of Galilee when our caravan stopped in Bethsaida for food supplies and a night's rest. Bethsaida was a regional center for selling and buying freshwater fish. It was late, and only one fish vendor was still selling fresh fish in the Bethsaida Marketplace.

"These fish are fresh. I just caught them this afternoon." The fish vendor informed as my taste buds were deciding between musht and barbels for dinner.

"They look fresh." I mumbled.

"Where are you from, friend?" He inquired.

"Tarsus, but I live in Jerusalem!" I answered briefly.

"Do you know a man named Simon Bar-Jonah in Jerusalem? Maybe you know him by his Aramaic name, Cephas, or his Greek name, Peter? Our Lord gave him that name. This is his hometown!" The fish vendor informed me with an amiable tone.

"Yes, I've heard of the blasphemer! As well as the carpenter from Nazareth you call Lord!" I declared with obvious anger in my voice.

"Sir, I was asked not to tell others of this event, but for some reason I feel compelled to share it with you. Nearly all in Bethsaida know of it, but not from my lips." He spoke quietly after selling a fellow caravan traveler a basket full of fresh sardines.

"Jesus and his disciples came to Bethsaida about four years ago to minister and visit Peter's mother. I didn't see Jesus enter our village, because I was born blind! However, my friends did, and they took me to Jesus, since he had preformed many miracles in Galilee." The fish vendor spoke with excitement. "Jesus took me by the hand and led me outside the village. I spent the morning with him and his disciples. We became friends that day!"

"Good for you," I responded with acrimony.

"Around noon, Jesus and I sat down on a hillside. He spat saliva on my eyes then placed his hands upon my eye sockets. He asked, 'Do you see anything?'"

"Spare me the story." I yawned.

"I looked up and I said, 'I see people they look like trees walking around.' I was only partially healed of blindness. Jesus did this for a purpose! It showed that we don't always see what God is doing in our lives." The fish vendor finished with exhilaration.

"I had to listen to the same dung before he sold me some musht," Menahem declared as he passed by the fish stand.

"Jesus placed his hands on me again! My eyes were opened and my sight was restored, and I saw everything clearly. I was able to see things for the first time in my life!"

"Do you expect me to believe this story?" I shouted with unbridled rage.

"Friend, it's true!" A local woman interjected after buying two barbels. "I grew up with him. He came out of his mother's womb blind as a bat! He was blind until he spent that day with Jesus of Nazareth."

"Then Jesus bade me farewell and said, "Don't go into the village of Bethsaida.'" So, I went home to my village a short walk from Bethsaida." The elated fish vendor concluded.

"Try that tale on someone else!" I shouted.

"Faith opened up my eyes to his love." the vendor said.

"You are distorting Judaism, with your story of this man. He's just a carpenter from Nazareth!" I shouted, sticking my nose in his face.

"He's more than a carpenter. He is the Son of God. You can have a personal relationship with God's son by simply embracing him in faith." He ministered as I shot him a disgusted look.

"Keep your stinking fish! You think by putting your faith in some Jewish carpenter you now have religious insight and eternal life? You people are crazy!" I yelled while backing away from his stand and nearly falling into a perfume vendor's booth.

"I pray you will soon be healed of your blindness." Those were the last words I heard him say before I turned away.

~~

The following day my mind was outraged by the fish vendor's remarks. I couldn't even speak to fellow caravan travelers or to the temple guards. Finally, by mid-afternoon I was able to calm down because Caesarea Philippi came into sight.

Caesarea Philippi was named after Augustus Caesar and Philip the Tetrarch of the Herod family. The city was situated by a spring on the southwestern edge of snow capped Mount Hermon. It's one of the most beautiful places on earth.

This spring was one of three springs which marked the source of the Jordan River. Caesarea Philippi was a religious center for pagans' fertility gods, dating all the way back to the Canaanites and their god, Baal.

A stone temple stood just outside Caesarea Philippi honoring fertility gods. We stopped about two hundred paces from the temple to spend the night. Two locals approached us and pointed to Mount Hermon. One of them said in Aramaic, "Seriously? That's the place of your Messiah's transfiguration. People say two of your old prophets, Moses and Elijah, spoke with Jesus while he was up there."

"A goat farmer tending his herd saw Jesus' face. He said it shone like the sun, and his clothes were brighter than lightning. Also, the goat herder heard your God say, 'This is my son, whom I love; with whom I am well pleased. Listen to him.'" The other local resident said.

"He's not our Messiah!" Thin Imna barked before chasing them away with his whip.

"I need something stronger than water to drink. I'm going into town for some spirits." Menahem growled after drinking a handful of cold water from the glacier stream.

"I'll join you. I didn't have dinner last night, and I want to get away from this Garden of Evil," I remarked. The two of us departed for Caesarea Philippi, one of the wickedest places in the world.

The city was full of idolaters and sleazy taverns. Menahem chose a seedy Jewish inn with cheap wine and bad food. The proprietor approached our table and asked, "You Judeans looking for food or trouble?"

"We are looking for people who follow the carpenter from Nazareth," I firmly responded.

"We don't cater to that kind here!" The burly inn keeper responded while picking some dry snot from his left nostril and flicking it on the table beside us._

"My kind of place." Menahem's mangled teeth rattled, then he added, "Give him your kosher special, and I'll have a bottle of your cheapest wine." The innkeeper nodded and left to fill our order.

"This is about as far north as the carpenter's Galilean ministry went," the man sitting at the table beside us offered up after brushing the gratis appetizer from his table.

"Leave us alone!" snarled Menahem.

"Please, let me tell you a story. My younger brother, the perfume mixer, was a follower of the carpenter from Nazareth. A couple weeks before the Nazarene was crucified in Jerusalem, he came to Caesarea Philippi with his gang of twelve. They stayed at my brother's house, out by the temple." He added the last sentence as the wine bottle arrived.

"Congratulations. You want me to give you another free appetizer!" Menahem growled.

"No, thanks," he amicably replied, watching Menahem's thumb rub the wine bottle's rim.

"My brother awoke early one morning and followed them. He hid behind some rocks, but he thought the prophet knew he was there. He overheard the prophet's conversation with his disciples. Apparently, the prophet taught with questions. He asked his disciples, 'Who do people say the Son of Man is?'" He moved closer to us.

"I don't want to hear it!" Menahem screamed.

"Go ahead. I'm curious how you spin this tale." I encouraged.

"His disciples answered him in the shadows of the stone temple, 'Some say, John the Baptist; others say the Elijah; and still others, Jeremiah or one of the prophets.'"

"Even his own disciples didn't know who he was." Menahem laughed with derision.

The man joined our table at the same time as my cold dinner and cited, "'But what about you?' Jesus inquired of them. 'Who do you say I am?'"

"The big fisherman from Bethsaida answered him, 'You are the Christ, the Son of the living God.'" Our uninvited table guest eyed Menahem's wine bottle.

"Another Peter story!" I moaned to Menahem while wrestling with my stale food.

"Ever since my brother heard that Bethsaidian's confession, he thought the prophet from Galilee was more than a human being. He believed Jesus was the Messiah." Our sober visitor, having reached the climax of his story, now reached for Menahem's bottle.

"We were just in Bethsaida and already heard too many tales about this burly fisherman called Peter." My tongue shrieked, since I was drunk on hatred.

The man whispered over our table: "Then the Nazarene said while standing on the rock foundation of our fertility gods' temple, 'Blessed are you Simon son of Jonah, for this was not revealed to you by man, but by my Father in heaven. And I tell you that you are Peter, and on this rock I will build my church, and the gates of Hades will not overcome it. I will give you the keys of the kingdom of heaven; whatever you bind on earth will be bound in heaven, and whatever, you loose on earth will be loosed in heaven.'"_

"Cheap wine is what binds me to this earth!" Menahem snickered, grabbing back his wine bottle and guzzling its contents.

"My brother said Jesus approved the fisherman for comprehending the messianic mission that Jehovah had bestowed upon him." Our visitor shared while coveting my leftovers.

"Then he warned his disciples not to tell anyone he was the Christ, since the masses were still trying to grasp the truth." He added before I pushed my nearly empty plate toward him.

"Later that day my brother heard Jesus tell his disciples he would go to Jerusalem. While he was in the Holy City the chief priest, elders, Sadducees, and Pharisees would have him killed, but he would be raised to life on the third day." He concluded before licking the plate clean.

"Blasphemy!" I bellowed.

"Where's your brother? We have something for him." Menahem shouted, jumping up from the table and knocking it as well as our visitor over.

"His heart stopped about six months ago." Our frightened table visitor replied from the floor. I grabbed Menahem by the forearm, and we left the tavern.

~~

My wrath had reached new depths when we rejoined the caravan. We left Caesarea Philippi early the next morning. Nearly two days later Mount Hermon stood to the west and behind us; when my inner turmoil, rage, hatred, and thirst for bloodshed reached its summit.

May's noontide heat was baking us. It was as hot as a mid-summer day and it was getting hotter with every step. Everyone in the caravan spoke of stopping for the day beneath the steamy, cloudless sky. The heat was so overpowering everyone wanted to seek cover.

"We'll set up camp to escape the afternoon sun since the temperature is rising. We'll spend the night here beneath these trees." The caravan commander suggested with sweat dripping from his forehead.

"No way! We're only several thousand paces from Damascus! It's Friday afternoon, and I want to be in Damascus before sunset! I don't journey long distances on the Sabbath. Plus, we have a plague to eliminate!" I barked.

My inner demons longed to reach their destination. The closer we got to Damascus, the further I seemed to get from God. Legalism's billows had knocked the winds out of my spiritual sails. I was adrift in the Sea of Hatred.

"I insist we continue our sojourn!" I demanded pridefully, wiping sand chunks from the corners of both bloodshot eyes.

"Fine, but any hardships we encounter are on your hands!" The caravan commander angrily conceded.

Chapter Seventeen
A Time of Awakening

"In so far as the mind is stronger than the body, so are the ills contracted
by the mind more severe that those contracted by the body."
Cicero

The caravan travelers and temple guards reluctantly resumed the journey.
It was so blistering hot everyone but I dismounted their parched horses,
donkeys, and camels. They led them by their reins across the sweltry Syrian
landscape and sandy road.

The scorching road baked their sandals like bread in a clay oven. We
loosened our cloth turbans to catch some of the gentle breeze. Our teeth
chewed sand kicked up by the wind and our feet. Everybody's lungs felt
like they were filled with sand rather than air.

We were just four thousand paces from the Damascan gates when the
most pivotal incident of my life occurred beneath the sultry noonday sun.
I was ambushed once again in life.

~~

A bright light from Heaven shone down upon us. It was far more
luminous than the sun but lasted for only a short period. The light's power
knocked all of us, including our animals, off our feet. We were ambushed
by an omnipotent source.

Everyone slowly got back up on their feet, while I lay prostrate on my
leather breastplate. I rolled over onto my red robe and looked up. My eyes
beheld an epiphany, a heavenly being in a purple robe. He had nail holes in
his hands and feet. I was seized by his omniscient presence. He completely
eradicated my hatred and murderous desires.

"Saul, Saul, why do you persecute me?" He asked in Aramaic. Those in the caravan were speechless.

"It is hard for you to kick against the goads." Goads were wooden poles with pointed ends. Farmers used goads to keep plowing oxen moving forward. If the oxen resisted or kicked against the goads, it caused them painful consequences.

"Who are you, Lord?" My dust-covered lips inquired. The brilliant light and voice came from Heaven, but I didn't know if it was an angelic being like a seraphim, cherubim, or archangel. I only knew it was a heavenly being of grand authority and awesome power.

"I am Jesus of Nazareth, whom you are persecuting." He replied before my eyes were overwhelmed by his radiance. I quickly realized the goads this zealous persecutor had been kicking against were Jesus' divine teachings and ministry. He had risen and He was alive.

"I will rescue you from your own people and from the Gentiles. I am sending you to them to open their eyes and turn them from darkness to light, and from the power of Satan to God, so that they may receive forgiveness of sins and a place among those who are sanctified by faith in me." As he spoke, benevolence filled my heart.

"Now get up and stand on your feet. I have appeared to you to appoint you as a servant and as a witness of what you have seen of me and what I will show you." He commissioned me and I surrendered my will unto him.

I stood up, but my eyes couldn't see anything. I cried out from a parched mouth, "I can't see! I'm blind!" "What shall I do, Lord?" I desperately inquired amidst a broken will and sightlessness.

This arrogant Jewish Pharisee found himself, helpless for the first time in his life on a dusty road outside Damascus. I humbly realized Jesus was the Lord, after placing me in an odium-filled corner. The more one selfishly elevates self above others the further and harder one falls.

"Go into Damascus. There you will be told all that you have been assigned to do." The Lord said, and then departed as quickly as he had appeared.

I desperately shouted to temple guards, "Help me! I'm blind! Please, take me to Damascus! Please, take me to Damascus!"

Everyone was spooked by the supernatural event and the gray film or scales that now covered my eyes. I was totally blind, like the Bethsaida fish vendor once was, the person who insightfully prayed I'd be healed of blindness.

An elderly, gentile couple who lived north of Damascus approached me. "We couldn't see who or what was making those noises," the man's voice kindly offered.

"It was Jesus of Nazareth, the son of God. My eyes just beheld the resurrected Lord." I exclaimed, searching the air for his hand.

"We heard sounds but couldn't make them out," added his wife after taking my hand.

" I need to get to Damascus!" I shouted, releasing her hand to find my temple guards.

~~

I followed the laughter of my nine temple guards, who were huddled about twenty paces away finding humor in my calamity.

"He must have looked into the brightness of the light. He has lost his eyesight!" I heard Menahem whisper to the other guards.

"He's now useless to us as a leader. Look how lost he is!" Thin Imna chucked.

"Let's just leave him here in the desert!" Fat Jesse suggested between sniggers.

"Yeah, he'll just be an anchor around our necks!" Thin Imna agreed.

"You boys are on something. If we ditch Saul, we can pillage Damascus and keep all the bounty for ourselves. All in favor of leaving the blind Pharisee say – 'aye,'" suggested Menahem.

"Please help me. I need your help to get to Damascus!" I shouted, tripping over a caravan traveler's burlap sack.

Every temple guard laughed then bellowed, "Aye."

"Take his horse! We can use it for our bounty," ordered Menahem. I heard them jump on their horses and dig their boot heels into the black stallions' breasts. Dust filled my nostrils as they galloped off for Damascus to plunder The Way.

The elderly, benevolent couple once again had pity on me. "We'll take you to Damascus," they offered. They took turns escorting me by the hand to the Syrian capital.

I willingly and blindly accepted the change along with my initial commission on that torrid road to Damascus. My heart instantly discarded Satan's rage and embraced God's grace. The Lord directed me and my faith flexed its first missionary muscle of obedience. This is something I would do until my earthly death.

Meanwhile, my remaining four senses were expanding into unfamiliar realms. My sense of touch felt tiny sand particles landing on exposed flesh. For the first time I tasted the sweetness of a tear drop. My nose sniffed fragrances it never smelled before in arid breezes. I heard sand forming around footprints and wind whistling around bodies.

My female friend broke our silence just outside the Damascus gate, ""Will you be all right? This is major change in your life?"

"Yes, and thanks for caring. Some feel if we're not changing we become part of the past instead of the future. Others deem our merit is reflected in our ability to change those around us. But God put us on this globe to be His constructive agents of change. We must remember things perpetually change. Our life course is determined by our response to an inevitable reality – change." I replied over the activities outside the city gates.

~~

We arrived in Damascus an hour before sunset. The smell of the oasis' vegetations filled my nostrils. Once inside the city I could hear teenagers finishing their daily chores. I felt small children on their way home for dinner bouncing off my frame like rain drops off a clay roof. Now I knew why the blind man Jesus healed at the Pool of Siloam, whom we persecuted and threw into a death dungeon, refused to deny him.

"Where should we take you?" the Syrian couple asked, helping me avoid the street's droppings of donkey, camel, and horse dung.

I wasn't quite sure where to go or what to do, since I'd just become a disciple of Jesus. The High Priest's prearranged plan of residing with Judas seemed to be my only option.

"Please, take me to Straight Street, to Judas of Damascus' house." Straight Street was a long, linear street that stretched from the west city wall to the east city wall.

The three of us bumped our way down that lengthy, crowded street asking tanners, potters, and other residents for directions to Judas's house. Meanwhile, I was overwhelmed by my acute sense of hearing. My ears even heard a commotion two blocks away. The nine temple guards were being arrested by Roman soldiers for stealing a Jewish citizen's belongings.

We located Judas' house just after sunset. Judas reluctantly opened his door, and the Syrian couple explained, "This is Saul of Tarsus. A bright, blinding light from the sky struck us all down on the road outside of Damascus. The light blinded Saul and only Saul!"

"Thank you for bringing him here. I have been waiting for him. I will now take care of him," Judas gracefully declared to the gentile couple, then tried to slip them several silver coins.

"No, thank you! We brought him here out of friendship and duty." My Syrian eyes hugged me goodbye and departed for an inn.

"Saul, glad to meet you! Sorry it's under these circumstances," Judas said.

"Same here!"

"I received a correspondence yesterday from Caiaphas and the Sanhedrin about your duty in Damascus. I have your sealed Letters of Plenipotentiary for the Damascan synagogue and Aretas IV in my study. What can I do for you?" Judas loudly shouted after he closed his front door.

"First, I'm blind, not deaf." I humorously responded. "Second, do you have a room where I can lie down and not be disturbed?" I inquired hoping not to impose upon him.

"I already have a room prepared for you," Judas confirmed, gently guiding me to a second-story bedroom.

"Thanks for your kindness and hospitality!"

"Delighted to help. Can I call a doctor or rabbi?"

"No! I just want to be left alone to pray and fast."

"The cistern is full of fresh rain water. How about a drink?" He asked with a concerned heart while directing me to the bed.

"No, thanks. I'll call you if I need anything." I remarked after sitting down on the bed's edge, embracing my new mooring.

"Okay." Judas replied before closing the bedroom door.

Within minutes, my sweaty hands searched the walls for a window. My body temperature rose as this new believer's soul incinerated old convictions. My left shin painfully banged into a night stand and bitterness tried to slip into this soul. But the joy residing within my heart crushed that attempt. Upon opening the window, I heard the sound of children's voices transformed into angelic praises.

That evening all four senses battled to dominate my mind with their expanded capabilities. However, the first sightless night was spent on bended knees confessing numerous sins and endless acts of persecution. I exhaustively searched my memory for godly insight spoken by persecuted disciples we had dragged off to Pompey's prison. The stench of my religious oppression kept me from sleep.

Over the next thirty hours Christ was my constant companion while praying and pacing upon that bedroom's wooden floor. I had lost physical sight but gained spiritual vision. My soul's eyes now followed a different spiritual compass.

By noon on the third day, my senses firmly grasped why God sent Christ to earth as a man; *to teach His absolute truths and plan of eternal salvation.* Wrapped in God's grace, I comprehended why Jesus was crucified upon a wooden cross – *to atone for everyone's sins.* Also, amidst God's omniscience, I realized why Jesus Christ arose from the grave after three days and ascended into heaven – *to give us hope and the path for eternal life.*

Chapter Eighteen
A Time for Guidance

"Things that are holy are revealed only to men who are holy."
Hippocrates

On the third day of my blindness, I had a vision about a person in the Damascan Jewish community named Ananias. I supernaturally saw him returning to his flat during the mid-day break to find a letter beneath his door. The correspondence was from a female friend in Jerusalem, who had shown him The Way.

The letter read, "Greetings, Ananias, my dear friend. Saul of Tarsus, The Persecutor, is in or soon will be in Damascus! The High Priest has granted Saul permission to arrest Jews in Damascus who call on the name of Jesus. Also, Saul has been given authorization by the Sanhedrin to carry these believers back to the Holy City for their trials and imprisonment. Be careful!"

In the vision as in reality, I was a living nightmare to Ananias and every other Damascan follower of The Way, because of my brutal treatment toward Jerusalem's believers. My mental image beheld Ananias falling to his knees and praying for the city's Jewish believers.

"God, please protect us from Saul of Tarsus. Jesus, please keep him from beating down the doors of our house churches and dragging us off to Jerusalem's death dungeon. Holy Spirit, if persecution comes our way, please grant us the courage to endure it and not deny our faith." I heard Ananias pray at his bedside.

Suddenly, I heard a powerful voice fill Ananias' bedroom and my vision. "Go to the house of Judas on Straight Street and ask for a man from Tarsus named Saul."

Ananias was startled by the omnipotent voice. He frightfully stuttered, "Lord, I have heard many reports about this man and all the harm he has done to your saints in Jerusalem. And he has come here with authority from the chief priests to arrest all who call on your name"

"Go! In a vision he has seen a man named Ananias come and place his hands on him to restore his sight," commanded the Lord. My mind's eyes watched Ananias faithfully arise from his knees and depart for the opposite end of town.

~~

That afternoon I heard a knock on Judas' front door. "What do you want?" I overheard Judas bitterly greet someone upon opening the door.

"I come as a friend, Judas."

"You are no friend of mine! You have forsaken the Mosaic Law and become a believer in The Way." Judas shouted for his neighbors' sake.

"I wish to speak with Saul of Tarsus." Ananias responded in a humble voice, while standing outside Judas' threshold.

"Saul is ill and doesn't want to be disturbed! He hasn't eaten or drunk anything in three days. He's delirious and wishes no visitors, especially a blasphemer like you!"

"He's expecting me."

"Saul has no desire to see a pig!" Judas harshly barked. Judas didn't want any of his nosey, pious neighbors thinking he was embracing The Way.

"Please, let him know I'm here."

"I think not! Now, be gone!" Judas snarled, trying to slam his door shut.

I heard Ananias scream in pain like he stuck his foot in the door frame. Ananias politely remarked in severe pain, "The Lord has sent me to speak with Saul."

"Five minutes! And never come back to my house again!" Judas shouted, loud enough for all those watching to hear.

Judas pushed Ananias up the narrow staircase toward my guest room. They knocked and entered the bedroom at the same time. I was kneeling in prayer at the bedside. Ananias didn't behold a malicious tyrant, but a trodden soul ready to be used by the Lord.

"This man says the Lord has sent him to you!" Judas declared, shoving Ananias backward toward the bedroom door. Judas nearly pushed Ananias into the burning wall torch he lit upon entering the room.

"Yes, I was instructed in my prayers to expect him." I thankfully affirmed from my knees. It sounded like Judas' jaw dropped to his collar bone.

"I must inform you; this man has recently become a follower of The Way." Judas grunted before leaving and slamming the door.

Ananias approached me and laid his hands upon my head. He said, "Brother Saul, the Lord Jesus who appeared to you on the road as you were coming here has sent me so that you may see again and be filled with the Holy Spirit. Brother Saul, receive your sight!" I instantly felt the mercy of the Lord upon me.

Then something like fish scales fell from my eyes and my vision was restored. I gazed upon God's human instrument and gratefully shouted in Hebrew, "Hallelujah!"

"Alleluia!" Ananias exclaimed in Greek.

"I had a vision you would come, place your hands upon me, and restore my sight! It took courage and faith to come to this house with your foreknowledge of my tyrannical acts." I acknowledged.

Ananias shared with me his vision while still standing over me. "The Lord also said in my vision, 'This man is my chosen instrument to carry my name before the Gentiles and their kings and before the people of Israel. I shall show him how much he must suffer for my name.'"

"The Lord did divulge some of those turbulent storms I'll encounter ministering to Jews and Gentiles in his name. Now I know, no spiritual victory can be won without a battle. No emblematic cross is too heavy to bear. No religious fire to hot too confront," I revealed from my knees.

"Also, the Lord said, 'The God of our fathers has chosen you to know his will and to see the Righteous One and to hear words from his mouth. You will be his witness to all men." Ananias stated and reinforced the Lord's apostolic duty for my life.

"During my three days of blindness, I viewed life with the eyes of Jesus. I saw God's will for me and it is as you say." I humbly acknowledged before falling prostrate on the wooden floor in submission to the Lord.

"Now what are you waiting for? Get up, be baptized and wash your sins away. Nobody is too far from God to be saved!" Ananias said, helping me up.

"Yes, I've kept God waiting long enough! He chose me when I was still in my mother's womb! Please baptize me, now!" I remarked with the excitement of a Jewish child at Hanukkah.   ~~

Joy flowed from our hearts as we left the guest bedroom and walked downstairs. Our host was whitewashing Ananias's footprint from his door frame.

"Judas, the Lord has restored my vision through this man! Thank you for your hospitality during my blindness. May the Lord bless your kindness!" I said with sincere gratitude as Ananias and I exited his house.

"Saul, what happen? Where are you going?" Judas asked in amazement.

"I've been healed and this soul longs to wash sin's footprints from its past." I announced, descending Judas' steps.

"Your previous transgressions will not impede your role in God's divine plan. Your past has been forgiven! Today, you have been blessed with a new life and purpose!" Ananias avowed as we headed toward Straight Street.

"Alleluia!" My vocal cords and soul cried out. It was praise unmatched by any sound of worship or gratitude ever uttered by my lips. "One can be brilliant and still not understand or see. I was one of the most educated men in Jewish theology but was spiritually blind."

"Knowledge puffs up, but love builds up," Ananias quoted.

"Yes, my relationship and love for the Lord have gone from secondhand knowledge to firsthand reverence."

"Let love and faithfulness never leave you; bind them around your neck, write them on the tablet of your heart," Ananias remarked as we turned onto Straight Street.

My childlike eyes beheld the triple row of marble colonnades on both sides of Straight Street. The multihued petals of garden flowers I could only smell yesterday, my eyes now beheld. When we walked through the marketplace, my eyes had a new appreciation for the colorful wool woven into merchants' tapestries and the vibrant colors painted on the artists' canvases.

"Where are we headed?" I asked as we trekked toward the city gates.

"Brother, heaven captured a rebel this week. I'm taking you to the Abana River to symbolically celebrate this transformation within your soul. We are going to baptize you in river water. It will be your public announcement of a new life in Christ."

"Thanks for referring to me as a brother," I declared, walking out the city gate.

"In the Lord's family, we refer to each other as brothers and sisters. We live as kindred spirits, embracing all personalities, nationalities, races, colors, sexes, and social classes." Ananias proclaimed as the sounds of river life emerged in front of us.

"An earthly attempt at God's heavenly bliss: I like it!" I replied before we passed twelve women returning from the Abana River with their washed garments. Several were women I had chased out of Jerusalem. They tactfully hid their faces with clean laundry when we passed by them.

"Sometimes faith grows better in the winter than spring of life. Even though a warm, reviving breeze refreshes the spirit – often - it's the cold, harsh winds of fear and persecution that sprout human convictions." Ananias said, trying to offer insight into my past actions.

"I have learned, where there is a need there is hope – where there is hope there is God."

"There is always hope. And today, like yesterday, marks another day in your spiritual growth. It's a continuous journey till the day of our earthly death," Ananias informed.

"What are the different levels of spiritual growth?" I asked.

"It seems like there are at least three phases of spiritual growth. The first phase is the new believer or child stage. It's when you are spiritually born again by placing your faith in Christ. All your past, present, and future transgressions are washed away through the death and sacrificial blood of Jesus. This parturition gives us a new life, a life of forgiveness through grace."

"I remember a man named Nicodemus, whom we arrested one afternoon in the Jerusalem Marketplace. He told me, before we dragged him off to the death dungeon, 'You must be born again to see the kingdom of God.'" I recalled his words.

"Yes. The second phase of spiritual growth is the growing believer or adolescent stage. It's when you begin to grow in your daily walk with the Lord. You build upon the cornerstone of your spiritual conversion through studying His word, praying, and fellowshipping with other believers. Also, it's when you comprehend there are spiritual battles going on around us, so you spiritually prepare yourself to combat the forces of darkness," Ananias declared.

"I'm still in the initial phase. But, the Lord has opened the eyes of my heart and the ears of my mind."

"That would make for a good hymn" said Ananias.

"What's the third phase?"

"The third phase is the mature believer or adult stage. It's when you seek to become more Christlike in your actions, thoughts, and character. You put others first. You daily praise God for everything he does in your life; moreover, you allow God to work through you for his glory. You focus on the things of heaven, not earth." Ananias spoke over the commotion of camel drivers herding their animals from the river.

"May we both be quick to reach this phase in our spiritual lives!" I exclaimed as we stopped at the river's bank.

Chapter Nineteen
A Time to be Reborn

"I would rather be adorned by beauty of character than jewels. Jewels
are the gifts of fortune, while character comes from within."
Plautus

We stepped into the Abana River with a purpose that warm, Sunday
afternoon. "Brother, is there anything you would like to say, before I baptize
you?" Ananias asked, before we waded into the springtime current.

"Over the last three days, I've learned to be dependent amidst
independence, to behold life through divine eyes instead of temporal
blindness, and to praise God not oneself. I submit my life to you, Lord!"
I claimed with unwavering commitment as our bodies created waves in
the river current.

Ananias squeezed my nose with his left hand's thumb and forefinger.
His other hand pressed into my stiffened spine. "I baptize you in the name
of the Father, Son, and Holy Ghost." His left hand pushed my head and
upper torso into the chilly river water.

During those few seconds beneath the river's surface, I felt my sins
being washed away. My heart and mind were awash in spiritual bliss. My
soul bathed in the awesome veracity that the Holy Spirit is the Sanctifier,
Jesus is our Savior, and God is the Creator.

"We are buried with Christ through baptism into death. We are raised
from the dead like Jesus to glorify God in our new lives." I vaguely heard
Ananias through waterlogged ears after he lifted me out of the swift
current by his right hand. I was drenched in the Holy Spirit.

"That was refreshing," I said, spitting words and water from my
mouth.

"You have just been baptized. It's an external act to proclaim your internal transformation and rebirth," Ananias added, while I tilted my head and shook the river water out of both ears.

"Now I know it was love, not nails that held Jesus on the cross. May the time I have left on this earth be spent bringing glory our Lord," I enthusiastically asserted before climbing the riverbank.

"Since you are going to be God's instrument unto the Gentiles, maybe we should call you by your Latin name, Paul?" Ananias jokingly but sincerely suggested after ascending the river bank.

"I haven't been called Paul since taking philosophy classes in Tarsus over twenty years ago," I announced in Greek, stepping atop the riverbank.

"Still can't believe a Jewish tyrant was transformed into a Gentile apostle." Ananias exclaimed.

"Yeah, from rebel to saint in three days," I quipped as we walked back to Damascus.

"Paul, I'm taking you to our sunset church service. For the first time, you will be a participant rather than a persecutor of The Way's worship service." Ananias remarked as we entered the city gates at dusk.

~~

When we reached the house church, I noticed ten people nervously milling about. Before we entered the house church, Solomon Ben-Hadad, the owner of the home and a Jew, approached me. As our eyes met, I remorsefully recalled his anguish when the prison guards cut off the tongue of his son and father-in-law for blasphemy.

"Sir, I'm so sorry for what we did to your family. Please forgive me for what I've done!" I pleaded as tears welled up in my bloodshot eyes.

"The Lord has forgiven you for what you have done to my family and others! How could I not forgive you?" Solomon Ben-Hadad replied with a compassionate spirit. Then we entered his spacious courtyard full of fellow believers dressed in mantles ranging from burlap sackcloth to hand-woven Oriental silk.

Ananias and I sat down by the marble fountain in the middle of the courtyard. Sitting to our left were the Ben-Hurs, Jewish believers from Jerusalem, who fled the Holy City two months ago to escape my wrath. To our right was the Ben-Judah family, whose grandparents I had thrown into the Pompey Prison. The City of David's Ben-Geber and Ben-Deker families were behind them, staring at me in utter horror. Meanwhile, two other Jewish families got up and slipped out the courtyard's side gate.

"Allow me to get started with tonight's service." Ananias tried to calm the nervous congregation. Those families from Jerusalem gazed upon me in a state of shock. Fear flamed through the house church like an out of control forest fire.

"Saul has come to kill us!" Several teenage congregants screamed.

"It is fine!" Ananias declared, trying to settle them down. He wasn't having much success. It didn't help that the river water had my receding and facial hair jetting in all directions; I looked like a possessed man.

"How dare you bring the Angel of Death here!" Someone shouted from behind the fountain.

"Where there's thunder, there's lightening! Where there's Saul, there's persecution!" The patriarch of the Ben-Dekers said with trembling lips. They assumed that at any moment temple guards would come bursting into the worship service.

"Saul is now a believer. He publicly confessed his faith in Christ! I just baptized him in the Abana River," informed Ananias. It was amazing how the Lord used my selfish ambitions and ungodly behavior to spread his Gospel all the way to Damascus.

"Ananias did right. Saul's presence here this evening is not a trap. We spoke before the service. The Author of Salvation has spoken to his heart!" assured Solomon Ben-Hadad.

Everyone's nerves were still on end when Ananias unrolled the papyrus scroll of *Psalms*. He stopped near the scroll's end and read, "But with you there is forgiveness."

"Yes," mumbled a few congregational members.

Ananias went on to teach the congregation about forgiveness. "Not to forgive is one of the biggest mistakes we can make. Forgiveness overcomes all things. Our inability to forgive leads to bitterness, and bitterness is a poison that reaches into the marrow of our bones."

The Holy Spirit was at work in the congregation through Ananias' message. Those Damascan brothers' and sisters' hearts softened during that sermon. After the church service, they showered my starving soul with forgiveness and fellowship.

Before Ananias and I left the house church, Esther Ben-Hadad filled our empty stomachs with leftover lamb porridge. Then she filled our spirits with these words: "Before my conversion, I put my faith in possessions! We purchased an estate with numerous rooms, but I found less room in my heart for others. The more clothes I bought, the harder it was to bare my soul. The more servants I had to care for me, the less I cared for others."

When Ananias and I finally departed the house church, the acclaimed charioteer, Judah Ben-Hur, who was visiting his Damascan family, accompanied us outside. He offered a word of encouragement. "God never gives up on us, even when we are racing amiss. He's always rooting for us!"

"You're right! I was racing on an iniquitous track and focusing on the wrong finishing line. My pharisaical lifestyle was being pulled by the four horses of vanity, pride, odium, and selfishness."

"Those four beasts will slam you into the wall every time," Ben-Hur acknowledged.

"From now on, my chariot will be drawn by the four stallions of faith, humility, love, and altruism," I confirmed.

"Sounds like a winning team!" Judah Ben-Hur agreed with a smile.

"By the way, I'm a big fan of yours. You are The Man!" I said with admiration.

"Thank you. I have been blessed by God on this journey through life. He has been with me as a wealthy land owner, galley slave, charioteer, and now a Nazarene." Ben-Hur humbly declared.

"Please forgive me for all the trials and tribulations I put your family through before finding the truth," I expressed, looking up at the towering Judah Ben-Hur.

"Saul, forgiveness surpasses revenge. We grow in character when we forgive our friends and enemies. Love and forgiveness are gifts from God that we can share with others."

"Thank you, but guilt still resides in my soul."

"It took me a while to replace guilt with truth," Judah Ben-Hur said pausing at a fork in the street.

"I agree," Ananias interjected.

"My life was hastening on an ignominious track till I saw Jesus' earthly body nailed to a wooden cross. I discovered the truth at his bloody, nail-pierced feet." Judah Ben-Hur celestially remarked with a voice commanding one's attention.

"Same here, when I saw his nail-scarred hands and feet. He appeared to me in his heavenly body on a road outside of Damascus. It rendered my heart helpless!" I marveled beneath a starry sky.

"Praise is to those who never see Jesus' nailed-scarred hands and feet, but still race toward him," Ananias said.

"Yes, for we are like the children of Rome, watching a chariot race outside the Circus Maximus through narrow gaps in the arena's wooden gates. We only see a small portion of track, not the whole race. But, God sees life's entire track and knows the outcome of the race before it's even run." Judah patted us on the back with his powerful, charioteer hands.

"What's taking place on the track that we can't see?" I asked.

"A spiritual battle."

"Please expound," Ananias requested.

"The forces of darkness had two desires for Jesus. First, for him not to die on the cross for our sins. Second, was for people to misunderstand the purpose of his crucifixion so his generation and other generations would not believe in him as God's son. Plus, the dark side has two desires for us. First, is for us not to believe in the deity of Jesus Christ. Second, is for us not to give praises unto God." Ben-Hur stated before departing to care for his Arabian horses.

~~

The next six days were spent with Ananias' family and the Damascan saints growing in The Way. On Friday night at dusk, Ananias lit the fish oil in his Sabbath lamp. It acknowledged the beginning of our Jewish day of rest and worship. After lighting the lamp, we ate a delicious meal prepared earlier in the day by Ananias' wife, Miriam.

The next morning, as was custom, Ananias, Miriam, and their two sons departed for the local Diaspora synagogue's worship services. I accompanied them beneath a beautiful rainbow from an early morning storm.

We arrived at the synagogue just before the start of their Sabbath service. The head elder, an ardent oppressor of The Way, recognized me upon entering the synagogue. He was unaware of my conversion and asked, "Saul of Tarshish, student of Gamaliel, and a leading Pharisee of Jerusalem, would you read from one of the Holy Scrolls, then teach us?"

"Sure!" I approached the table holding the Holy Scrolls.

"This man was sent here by the Sanhedrin to place followers of The Way in chains. He has been commissioned to drag those religious blasphemers back to Jerusalem and put them in the Death Dungeon! Saul has come to eliminate these imprecators in our city!" The head elder announced in a piqued manner as I unrolled the Holy Scroll of *Isaiah*.

I stopped unrolling the scroll. My brown eyes raised themselves toward the congregation. I quoted these verses in Hebrew and from memory. "'The people walking in darkness have been sent a great light...to us a child is born...he will be called the Prince of Peace...He will reign on David's throne...with justice...forever.

"Yes," murmured several elders.

"The Prince of Peace Isaiah wrote about appeared to me on the way here. I experienced a spiritual transformation this season. Moreover, my spirit is like a springtime garden, growing in spiritual truths, blooming in endless faith, sprouting unconditional love, and budding in Jehovah's grace." I proclaimed.

"I'm at the end of a novena. I was physically blind for three of those nine days. You can verify this blindness with Judas," I added. Judas shook his head yes with reluctance. He barely shook it long enough for half the congregation to be reassured of my claim. "These eyes have been spiritually blind for thirty-four years, not just three days. This divine event has given my soul insight into God's eternal plan. I now know the law is bankrupt!" My lips reported to a shocked congregation.

"What did he say?" I heard an elderly man ask his son, who motioned, "Wait a Minute."

"I was once a blasphemer and a persecutor and a violent man. I was shown mercy because I acted in ignorance and unbelief. The grace of our Lord was poured out on me abundantly, along with the faith and love that are in Christ Jesus. Here is a trustworthy saying that deserves full acceptance, Christ Jesus came into the world to save sinners, of whom I'm the worst," I pronounced. You can image their stunned glares, open jaws, and enraged emotions.

"Have you come to our worship service drunk on wine? Or, wine that has been poisoned with The Way's folly!" a senior elder shouted. The congregation began to link the chain of spiritual events together and realize my bond had changed.

"I'm only intoxicated on the power of the Holy Spirit! I'm no longer a persecutor, but a proclaimer of The Way!"

Then this novice preacher expounded on Jesus being the Messiah prophesied in *Isaiah*. My teachings exposed the congregation to insights on messiahship they never fathomed. I spoke with zeal unmatched throughout the history of those synagogue walls.

After sharing this new revelation, a heated debate took place inside the synagogue. The elders were speechless, since my words were adorned with the Lord's knowledge and wisdom. It was during this worship service that I realized the Holy Spirit gave and would continue to give me the words to speak throughout my life.

The rabbi began to frantically wave his arms covered with a white silk and red tassels mantle. He irefully shouted, "You were sent here by the Sanhedrin. You are a Pharisee! How dare you speak these words of blasphemy in our synagogue!"

"You came to Damascus to rid our synagogues of Jesus' followers, not to teach he is the Messiah!" the head elder finally screamed.

"I was spiritually ambushed on my way here."

"You mean you were mentally ambushed," the rabbi barked.

"No, I haven't. The earthly tomb is empty, and the heavenly throne is occupied. He has risen!" As I informed the synagogue leaders, several Gentile proselytes and God-fearers felt the scales of spiritual blindness falling from their soul's eyes.

"Your words are like clanging cymbals to our ears!" The head elder screamed before the congregation erupted into total chaos.

"This service is over! Saul, leave our synagogue!" The rabbi shouted above the commotion. Some ears heard, some eyes perceived, and some hearts understood the truth. Most eschewed my christophanic remarks.

Chapter Twenty
A Time to Loath

"You have endured worse things; God will grant an end even to these."
Virgil

Ananias' family and I respectfully left the synagogue. Nearly all within the synagogue followed us outside and made derogatory remarks.

"I don't think they're going to honor you with a dinner tonight." Ananias joked as we descended the synagogue steps.

Several Jewish teenagers followed us down the synagogue steps. They began throwing pebbles at us when we reached the street. "Go back to Jerusalem, you stinking apostate!" They yelled at us till we rounded the street corner.

Even amidst verbal abuse, my soul exploded with unparalleled bliss. Upon arriving at Ananias' apartment in a Jewish housing project, everyone realized we had not stopped praising God since leaving the synagogue.

Ananias changed topics outside their flat. "Saul, will you please accompany me into the community courtyard to see if that early morning rainfall filled our water jugs?"

My host picked up one of three full clay jugs, then jumped right back on the spiritual track. "Jesus took on and conquered humanity's curse, sin! May humanity take on and fulfill its duty, faith."

"So the cornerstone of faith is acknowledging God, the one who gives us the inimitable liberty through grace to embrace or reject Him?" I inquired, picking up a rainwater jug.

"Yes, God's grace and our faith is the foundation for an eternal relationship. May you exercise your muscles of faith, today." Ananias replied, several steps ahead of me.

From out of nowhere, a ripe melon hit the back of my skull. Somehow, I managed to keep the full jug and myself upright. I turned around and observed seven pre-adolescent boys from the synagogue smirking.

My upper torso shook off the pain, melon seeds, and childish prank. I joined Ananias inside the housing project and heard him saying, "Followers of The Way will experience pain on earth exercising their faith, but may these hardships guide and shape us as believers."

"Over the last couple of days, the Lord has given me foresight into my future hardships: beatings, shipwrecks, robberies, insomnia, dehydration, starvation, spiritual rejections, stonings, and imprisonments. Also, he revealed our rewards in Heaven will far exceed our earthly sufferings." I acknowledged this between breaths while carrying the jug up three flights of stairs.

"After my conversion, I have come to comprehend that hardships are provisions from God for our spiritual growth," Ananias articulated after we entered his home and set down the two water jugs along with our exhausted bodies beside his dinner table.

"The best example is Jesus' earthly hardship on Good Friday," Miriam remarked, setting a plate of sweet dates and dried figs on the table. "Look at what grew out of Christ's brutal crucifixion and death; his resurrection, ascension to Heaven, forgiveness of our sins, and path to eternal life." She removed the coiffure and white veil from her youthful, oval shaped face. "We make it through our hardships by praying to the Lord. Prayer is our lifeline to God!" Miriam added with the social freedom only woman in The Way had. They could freely join males' spiritual conversations within their churches and households.

"Yes, through prayer we bring our praises and petitions unto the Lord. He hears our entreaties and intercedes on our behalf," Ananias insightfully asserted after instructing his twin seven year old sons to bring up the remaining clay jar from the courtyard.

"Ananias, you are living proof to me that God hears our prayers," I affirmed with joy as the twins left the apartment.

~ ~

Sometimes people find the hatred within them is easier to express than the love within them. Loathing is a toxic waste that few if any can successfully handle. It is hard to be religious and full of abhorrence at the same time, but Ananias' neighbors were determined to find that common ground.

"Prayer doesn't inform God. It enlightens us." Ananias spoke loudly over the profanities yelled by his disgruntled neighbors returning from the synagogue.

"God loves to give us more than we pray for," Miriam said with jubilance before we heard a clay jar break in the courtyard. Miriam nearly tripped over her pink stola running to the window.

"What was that?" Ananias said, turning his head toward the window.

"Like now, when I pray for the safety of my children. He blesses me with his virtues of comfort, peace, and self-control," Miriam remarked as she dashed to the window.

Ananias joined her at the window amidst a heavy storm of profane remarks. Their eyes searched the common courtyard for their sons. They couldn't see them, but they saw five grown men uprooting their vegetable garden.

Ananias and I immediately ran toward the apartment door to go find his sons. The last thing Miriam saw before closing their shutters was four men throwing mud at her clean laundry. The moment we opened the apartment door, both boys came running in, with bloody lips and noses.

"They beat us up! They beat us up because of your friend!" The twins cried.

"Who beat you up?" Ananias inquired with mounting rage. Ananias was a usually large and strong man. He was a blacksmith and annually won the anvil-throwing contest at the Damascus Merchants' Carnival.

"Five older boys beat us up in the stairwell. They said we are children of blasphemers, and scorpions crawl from the mouth of your friend." One of the twins sobbed.

"Love your enemies, do good to those who hate you, bless those who curse you, pray for those you mistreat you. If someone strikes you on one cheek, turn to him the other," quoted Miriam. She used the Lord's words to comfort her weeping sons, irate husband, and woebegone visitor.

Her words taught a valuable precept to all the males in that apartment. We grasped the merit of turning the other cheek. However, Ananias struggled with this principle because he wanted to go outside and whip those teenage boys' fathers.

Miriam took their two sons into the bedroom, the only other room in the place. The two rooms were separated by a thick, black, wool curtain. Ananias and I stayed where we were.

"Ananias, I'm sorry to have caused your family and you so much grief.

I'm the reason you're being physically and socially maligned by your peers."
I raised my voice over the sound of squalling children.

"Saul, it's not your fault. This has been brewing in the synagogue for weeks." Ananias paced the floor to calm himself down. Trying to change his heart, he switched topics. "The conversion of Saul is a miracle. God gave us an apostle for the Gentiles. This could be the most important event in church history since Jesus' crucifixion, resurrection and ascension."

"Now, that's an overstatement," I remarked while Ananias tried to relax by pouring us some fresh rainwater.

"May you not express prejudice to others in your life. But sometimes it's a struggle - because we run toward intolerance faster than we sprint towards forbearance. The key is to daily pray for patience and tolerance."

"Brother, may we all emulate your patience, steadfastness, tolerance, self-control, and faith. Hopefully, I can display a disposition like yours when confronted by others!" I added with admiration as the boys began to calm on the other side of the black curtain.

"Remember, when you go through life in Damascus, Jerusalem, Tarsus, or wherever, your actions and reactions are like pebbles thrown into a large pond. Each ripple spreads into the uncharted emotional and spiritual water of others. Those ripples enlarge your circle of faith and influence." Ananias spoke this piece of edification as pebbles began bouncing off his wooden shutters.

"Also, may we never forget that God is a rock, not clay to be molded by our earthly desires," I exclaimed over what now sounded like large rocks pounding against the wooden shutters.

The twins got upset again when a large rock broke two shutter boards. Miriam cuddled with them on the bed and sang a psalm. "I will fear no evil, for you are with me; your rod and staff, they comfort me." Meanwhile, Ananias and I reinforced the window's shutter with some boards from a wooden stool.

"Reveal, don't conceal! Never be ashamed of your faith!" Ananias said with discernment before investigating the noise at his front door. Opening it, he chased away three teenage boys who were painting profanity on the door. "Saul, the faith you had been persecuting didn't come from man but from God – a God who is timeless and unchanging!"

"You're right!" I agreed then added, "The creator of this universe does not change to meet the whims of a certain decade, century, or millennium. Jehovah enlightened us for years through prophets. Now he has blessed us with His one and only son to intercede on humanity's behalf."

Both boys finally calmed down after several choruses of *Psalms,* but the exterior commotions didn't let up until after dusk. Ananias and I prayed his neighbor would see the light, then fellowshipped for hours beside the flicking flame of a lamp lit by vegetable oil.

Just after midnight, Ananias went to bed, and I slumbered on their kitchen floor till sunrise. When I awoke, there was an intense spiritual yearning in the caverns of my soul to spend time alone with the Lord.

~~

Ananias and his family invited me to their sunrise service at the Ben-Hadads' house. I agreed, hoping our absence in the housing project might calm things down. On the way to the house church I informed them, "I will be leaving Damascus after the worship service."

"Please, stay! Your conversion and presence in Damascus have been a blessing to all of us," Miriam sincerely entreated.

"Thank you, but I have caused your family too many hardships. Plus, I need time to myself to grow in the Lord," I humbly responded.

"It pains my heart to hear you are leaving, but you must do what the Lord is leading you to do." Ananias spoke with remorse as we reached the Ben-Hadads' house.

Miriam and Ananias went on to become saints in the early church by embracing people of all races from every social background amidst any personal circumstance. They endured numerous hardships fighting against society's racial and spiritual bigotry.

Chapter Twenty One
A Time of Solitude

"A mind without instructions can no more bear fruit than
can a field, however fertile, without cultivation."
Cicero

Prior to walking inside the Ben-Hadads' residence, I noticed several of
Ananias's malicious neighbors following us. Once inside the Ben-Hadads'
house church, the Damascan congregation showered us with love. I
regretfully announced my travel plans before the sunrise worship service.
Nearly every family pleaded with me to spend a couple more days in
Damascus.

Ananias began the worship service by teaching on The Family of
God, the church. He concluded by saying, "The Lord didn't give me the
church I wanted! The Lord didn't give me the fellowship I longed for! The
Lord didn't even give me the congregation I hoped for!" Nearly everyone
in the church was shocked, and they mumbled to themselves in Greek,
but Ananias wasn't finished. "Instead, He gave me something better than
I asked for. You!" Ananias shouted, drowning out the sound of rocks
bouncing off the Ben-Hadad's house.

"Halleluiah!" The congregation roared. The similarities between that
morning's and previous night's events were becoming a concern to me.

"This church is not about a building. It is about fellowship. It's a place
for the body of Christ to grow together in faith." Ananias concluded over
malicious remarks coming from outside.

"Fellowship isn't just sharing food – it's about worshipping together,"
Miriam added. Then we prayed for the situation outside as Solomon Ben-
Hadad went to his front door to reason with those zealots.

Suddenly, out of a clear sky came thunder, lightning, and rain. It caused the riotous gang to dash home. Solomon came back inside and said, "You never know which direction fellowship is going to pull you. When we focus only on our selfish interests, we lose sight of others and God." The sound of pouring rain nearly drowned out his comment.

"Thanks to you, Damascan saints, I've learned God is the source of love and fellowship. Also, trust is born out of intimate companionship and community." I spoke as the rain let up.

"Yes! There's nothing like the trust between those who worship, pray, and cry together." Miriam declared before she and the congregation departed for work amidst a light sprinkle.

~~

The Ben-Judahs invited those who could to their home for a farewell breakfast and about twelve others joined us. When the sun popped above the horizon, everyone left the Ben-Judah's house for work. Meanwhile, I stayed and helped the Ben-Judah family put on a new tile roof.

I enjoined the Ben-Judah's company so much I agreed to spend the night with them and leave in the morning. Just before dark Joseph Ben-Judah, the family patriarch, and I went to the marketplace and purchased lamb chops for a house church supper. We were about four blocks from his house when six male synagogue members surrounded us on a side street.

"Look what we bumped into. Two blasphemers!" a synagogue elder of large stature barked while poking his index fingers into our chests.

"I think we need to show this scum what we think of them!" Another burly man, the leader of the pack, chimed in.

They formed a circle around us then began pushing us back and forth. They knocked the lamb chops from our hands. The sphere grew tighter till Joseph and I stood back to back.

One of the instigators pulled a butcher's knife from his tunic and remarked with threatening glee, "Maybe we should cut the religious fat from their chops." Joseph and I were pushed to our knees as the circle engulfed us. We both prayed for the Lord to deliver us from this predicament.

A thundering blow struck the back of my skull. I lay prostate and barely conscious beside Joseph on the stone street. For the next couple of minutes we felt like ripe grapes being squashed by feet.

Looking up from the ground with blurred vision, my eyes beheld the six men backing away from us in silence. I vaguely saw ten Roman soldiers' plumes turning onto the side street. Joseph helped me to my feet as I grabbed the lamb chops. We used the distraction as an opportunity to escape and sprint back to Joseph's house.

"It seems every neighborhood I stay in becomes filled with hatred and mayhem," I told Joseph after dinner. Damascus' Jewish community was truly divided over my presence. I prayed this would not be a prelude of future events. We spent the evening in fellowship, nursing our wounds, and thanking the Lord for saving our lives.

The desire to be alone with God was growing in my soul like water levels during the Great Flood's forty days of rain. This yearning to deepen my relationship with Christ rose with each passing hour. I had drunk the entire first–second-and third-hand knowledge that Damascan believers had to share. I desired to drink directly from the fountain of knowledge, to drown my thirst in a quenching relationship with the Lord.

~ ~

The people I had come intending to imprison over ten days ago now tearfully bade me farewell. The Damascan disciples filled my burlap sacks with flat cakes, dates, and figs. I departed this beautiful Syrian oasis and headed east, toward Arabia. The Pharisaic, oral laws had been my life's temple, and it had just been imploded to the ground. I needed time to lay a new cornerstone, build a foundation of faith, and frame my apostolic commission. I needed time to meditate and be alone with the Lord, as I had in those three days on Straight Street.

Thoughts filled my mind of saints told of in the Torah, who intensified their relationship with God through times of solitude. Moses spent forty years as a lonely shepherd in barren Midian. Joseph served two years in a filthy, Egyptian prison cell. Jonah endured three days in a whale's smelly belly. God took these prophets' times of solitude to expand their individual knowledge, insight, and relationship with Him. God knew before He could use them, He had to instruct and redirect them in His will. During their seclusion, it was God's voice they heard, not human babble.

It didn't take long to reach Arabia. Arabia and its desert land stretched from just east of Syria to the Dead Sea's eastern shore to the Gulf of Aqaba into the Sinai Peninsula and the northern part of the Arabian Peninsula.

Arabia was part of the Nabatean Kingdom. The capital of this Bedouin kingdom was the invincible city of Petra. It was where the powerful King Aretas IV resided. The Nabateans traced their ancestry back to Nebajoth, son of Ishmael, son of Abraham.

In northern Arabia, I slept beneath the stars or by social outcasts' campfires. During daylight hours, I infrequently joined caravans. Most of the caravan travelers told stories about being attack by Arabian sheiks. There were several sheiks in the Arabian Desert who robbed and pillaged caravans for a living. Only one or two sheiks delighted in killing and mutilating their caravan prey. The worst of these sheiks was Sheik Abdul bin Qaboos Al-Thani, know to most as Sheik Abdul.

Occasionally, I stumbled across desert dwellers' worship serivces at sandstone obelisks. I spent time in fellowship with these residents of Arabia, and then shared the Gospel with them. The Arabs were receptive to my teachings; however, King Aretas VI of the Nabatean Kingdom wasn't euphoric about it. He eventually placed a bounty on my head, because a Jew was preaching a novel religion to his people.

Arabia was the setting for my spiritual reflection. The purpose of life was being revealed through an intimate relationship with the universe's center character. Everywhere I went, the Lord's voice and hand instructed me. My days were filled with listening, praying, and praising.

Meanwhile, the desert's fields of endless dunes took their toll on me. Only hope and faith saw me through this barren land. Billions of grains of sand wore my body down day after day. The unremitting desert sun's heat nearly took my life several times. It felt like my entire body and soul had been sandpapered by a carpenter.

Chapter Twenty-Two
A Time to be Brave

"We become just by performing just action, temperate by performing temperate actions, brave by performing brave action."
Aristotle

I was somewhere in the western Arabian Desert surrounded by sand mountains. There was not a stream or well to be found among the reddish sand dunes. Three days passed without water. My thirst grew by the minute beneath the torrid sun.

Around high noon an oasis miraculously appeared in the distance. When I staggered onto the oasis's perimeter, four heavily armed Arab warriors assaulted me. They threw me on the scorching sand just shy of a palm tree's shade.

"Are you a spy for Sheik Abdul?" one warrior asked in Arabic, placing his sword to my throat. Sweat rained down from my forehead.

"He's a damn Jew, not a spy, you idiot!" Another soldier shouted before I could answer.

"Then let's kill him!" a sword-swinging warrior suggested. When someone desires to take away your breath, it's a frightening experience. It was comforting to be able to take up the shield of faith.

"Or, we could tie the stinking Jew down in the sand, then watch him die of thirst." A muscular warrior spit his insult and saliva on me.

"Too long! Let's throw lots to see who passes his sword through him."

"No. We will take him to Sheik Fahad. He may want to question this wandering Jew. Let the Sheik decide what to do with him," stated an elderly warrior who seemed to be in charge.

"Good idea!" I tittered in Arabic, much to the surprise and laughter of the warriors.

Being dragged through the oasis, I noticed other soldiers as well as the entire nomadic clan diligently preparing for battle. I counted at least eighty Arabian horses and forty camels in their camp.

Outside the sheik's tent I noticed several fresh graves. There was a rock at the head and foot of every grave. "In the desert we have no wood for coffins. The clothing atop the graves are for those who need garments." A warrior barked in Arabic, noticing my curiosity.

Just before being pushed into Sheik Fahad bin Mohammad Al-Nahyan's tent, I noticed a grave in the shape of a dromedary. Sheiks' tents were usually long, rectangular structures with two sections: the mag'ad for men, guests, and a fireplace, and the maharama - for women. The two sections were divided by a ma'nad, a thick woven wool curtain.

"We captured this Jew on the edge of the oasis. The men would like your permission to kill him after you interrogate him!" the elderly warrior announced.

"What are you doing out here in the middle of this desert by yourself, Jew?" Sheik Fahad inquired in Aramaic while studying a papyrus map.

"Searching for spiritual insight!"

"My men want to run their swords through you. Why should I stop them?" the sheik asked, still studying his map.

"I mean no harm. I'm merely a tentmaker from Tarsus," I answered in Aramaic.

"Are you, The Jewish Tentmaker of Tarsus?" The sheik curiously asked raising his eyes for the first time from his battle plans.

"Yes, I'm his son. My abba and I made this tent." I pointed to our initials stitched into the tent's ma'nad.

"This is the man who makes the quality tents we buy in the Egyptian marketplaces and steal from the Roman caravans." The sheik merrily shouted to his soldiers and wives in Arabic. He motioned for a lieutenant to give me some fresh cardamom spiced coffee.

"I may let you live so you can make more tents for us to steal!" Sheik Fahad chortled.

"Thank you, Sheik Fahad!" I said in Arabic after taking a swig of coffee.

"You speak our tongue, Jew. You must be a wise man!" he remarked, while rolling up the map. "I have heard many intriguing stories about you Jews. Some say your great ancestors separated the Red Sea to escape Pharaoh's army."

"Yes, what you say is true!"

"My favorite Jew story took place in Jericho, the old city just north of where the Jordan River empties into the sun-baked Dead Sea. They say seven of their religious men blew ram horns as they marched around the city. They did this seven times around the mighty walls of Jericho. Then all the Jews shouted, and Jericho's fortress walls collapsed. The Jewish warriors easily captured Jericho." Sheik Fahad spoke in Arabic for his wives' sakes.

"Our people attribute these two miracles and many others to the one true God, Jehovah, the God of Abraham," I declared, standing beside one of the poles supporting his wool tent.

"Abraham is the father of my people. It seems all Arabs and Jews come from his two sons, Ishmael and Isaac. Do you think we are distant relatives?" The sheik laughed.

"We have the same heavenly father!" I replied.

"He thinks he's kin to us!" The sheik said, chuckling to his staff and wives, then added in a more serious tone, "You don't even know where our ancestors are from, Jew."

"I'd guess, after my experience with your warriors' swordsmanship and their lack of fear, you're Ishmael's descents from Yaman, part of the ancient Sabaean Kingdom." I complimented the sheik in Arabic so all could understand.

"We are, my friend!" He swelled up with pride. "Since we left the Fertile Crescent, we have lived in this trackless terrain. We make our livelihood raiding Roman trade routes. The Roman soldiers chase us into this dry desert, but they have no appetite for its daytime heat and nighttime cold. They use the desert as an excuse to stop pursuing us, but really, they fear us!"

"In God I have put my trust; I will not fear what flesh can do unto me," I boldly quoted from Psalms.

"I admire your lack of fear."

"My heart and mind are full of faith; therefore, there's little room for fear. During challenging times, we must reach inside our souls to find the vigor to overcome trepidations. Heavenly faith always conquers earthly consternations! I only fear the God of Abraham!"

"I think I like this Jew!" Sheik Fahad remarked to his military staff.

"We spit in the face of fear!" the sheik's first lieutenant shouted in my ear.

"This is true, but sometimes it causes us to fight too much among our own race. We often find ourselves at war, not at peace, with our Bedouin brethren," the sheik remarked with some regret in his voice.

"It looks like you're getting ready for a battle," I remarked, not knowing what else to say.

"Yes. Yesterday, we traveled here and set up camp. My favorite camel was grazing on the oasis's outer grass when Sheik Abdul bin Qaboos Al-Thani's tribesmen killed her. They maliciously shot twenty arrows from behind a sand dune into my camel! She smelled them in the distant dunes and was about to give away their position," the sheik added, putting on his armor.

"They say a dromedary can smell a man over three thousand paces away," I acknowledged as a lizard crawled across my foot.

"That camel carried my belongings for many moons."

"A camel can be a man's best friend in the desert."

"She was." He polished the cutting edge of his ivory-handled sword.

"We are about to go into battle with Sheik Abdul. I have one favor to ask of my new Jewish friend," the sheik revealed as the horses and camels became restless outside.

"What is it?"

"Watch over my family. Their lives, and yours, depend upon it." He buried the Arabian sword between my feet, then walked out of the tent.

Sheik Fahad jumped on his white Arabian horse. I walked outside the tent with a couple of his wives. Within seconds, arrows began landing in the oasis. "Release the arrows! Send out the infantry!" yelled Sheik Fahad.

One of Fahad's second lieutenants, about five paces away from us, was hit in the neck with an arrow. The sheik reached down from his horse and grabbed the dead warrior's spear. "Either you're with us or against us!" he demanded.

"It seems God moves about in your camp to protect you and to deliver your enemies to you." I quoted from Deuteronomy. Sheik Fahad saluted me with his index finger, then turned toward the battle.

"I hope Fahad kills that evil Abdul! He murders innocent women and children from caravans as well as those from our tribes for pleasure," Harissah, one of Sheik Fahad's seven wives, commented. We watched

Sheik Fahad's infantry leave the oasis' palm trees beneath a sky full of arrows flying in both directions.

The infantry headed straight for Sheik Abdul's stronghold, a nearby sand dune. Sheik Fahad's brave warriors marched across the hot desert floor with wooden shields partially protecting them from the enemy's thunderstorm of arrows.

"Camels, attack!" Sheik Fahad commanded from the edge of the oasis. The camels galloped toward the middle of the sand dune. Then we heard Sheik Abdul's trumpets ordering his men to attack Sheik Fahad's infantry and camel riders.

~~

The sound of battle cries filled the desert air. Halfway between the oasis and sand dune, a great, bloody skirmish broke out. Men were cutting off each others' hands, limbs, and heads. We could see sparks and blood flying from soldiers' swords.

"Horses to the left! Horse to the right!" Sheik Fahad ordered from the oasis' fringes. He galloped off leading the left frontal charge, and his third lieutenant the right attack. The sheik planned to out flank his enemy by going two hundred paces off the center attack point.

Sheik's Fahad's oldest wife, Jabbarah, was standing beside me, and all of a sudden she blew a ram horn with all her might. Then she turned to me and said, "Last night, my husband sent some of his foot soldiers out into the desert. Those soldiers buried themselves in the sand behind Sheik's Abdul's camp. They rose out of the sand to attacked Sheik Abdul when I blew the horn. He will be surrounded and destroyed!"

Jabbarah blew the horn again with all her might because Sheik Fahad's infantry and dromedary attack were meeting strong resistance. Then, the tide turned; the rear attack completely caught Sheik Abdul off-guard and threw his forces into temporary chaos. This allowed Sheik Fahad and his horsemen to cut through the enemy's flanks like a school of tilapia through minnows.

"Look at how well Sheik Fahad's men fight. That's because his warriors respect him! Even though we are outnumbered three to one, we are the superior force! Watch Sheik Fahad. Nobody can handle a sword like him," Bahieh, his only blonde wife, gleefully announced.

My eyes beheld Sheik Fahad decapitating eight men in sixty seconds. We lost sight of him when an arrow dropped his horse. The archers on both sides had killed most of each others' horses and camels. We could see tribesmen stabbing each other with daggers, swords, and spears as dead corpses piled up atop each other.

"I love the sight of bloodshed in the afternoon sun!" Jabbarah shouted.

Our ears were filled with the screams of pain and death. We continued to hear the sound of metal swords clanging for awhile. Blood from fatal wounds streamed into the air like geysers. Blood covered the desert surface, but like footprints in the sand it was quickly covered over by arid breezes.

Finally, metal sparks no longer appeared on the desert battlefield. The hand-to-hand combat had lasted for twenty minutes. The arid landscape was filled with triumphant screams. The echoing sound of victory came from Sheik Fahad and his warriors.

I retrieved Sheik Fahad's Arabian sword, because Sheik Abdul and his warriors were fleeing in all directions. My lips silently prayed, "Lord, may I not have to mêlée with any of Sheik's Abdul's men. I have no quarrel with them."

Some defeated warriors ran toward and through the oasis. One of them was Sheik Abdul himself. He paused in front of the sheik's tent and laughed. "Fahad now recruits Jews to baby-sit his women!"

He reached for his sword but realized he had lost it in the battle. He quickly turned, looked behind himself, and decided to put distance between Sheik Fahad's men and himself. Before departing, he screamed, "Jew, you will pay for meddling in our affairs!"

Sheik Fahad's troops returned to the oasis after vainly chasing Sheik Abdul and his men. The women and children of Fahad's clan ecstatically ran out to greet their victorious warriors. Only Fahad's wives, mistresses, and I remained by a tent. Sheik Fahad graciously accepted the praises of his people, then walked over to his tent where his female family members and I stood.

"Tentmaker, thank you for guarding my family! I will spare your life, since mine has been spared this day." Sheik Fahad laughed after grabbing his ivory-handled sword back from my hand.

"He had an easy task. The real action was out there in the desert," Harrissah remarked while helping Fahad take off his armor.

"After you have helped us bury our dead, you are free to go," Sheik Fahad said after thrusting his sword into his scabbard.

"Thanks!" I gratefully answered as he turned and walked inside his tent.

I noticed blood dripping from three deep battle wounds on his arm, leg, and upper torso. "Sheik Fahad, may I join you inside your tent to sew up your wounds? I've had experience sewing up lesions since childhood."

"If you can sew human skin like goat hair, come on in." He guffawed. Within seconds, Bahieh handed me a needle and thread.

"Sheik would your wives, staff, and you like to hear some good news?" I asked while stitching up the sheik's wounds.

"Yes." They all shouted. So, I told them, "His chariot was a donkey, his crown made of thorns, and his throne was a cross." They listened and asked many questions as I sewed them up.

"You have given us a fresh perspective on Jews. We always thought your race was lazy since you didn't work on Saturday, barbaric because your religious badge is circumcising eight-day-old males, and overly pious since you worship only one God." Sheik Fahad stated before putting on his casual mantle.

"Unfortunately, some of my brethren feel the world is divided into two types of people, Jews and non-Jew."

"There are only two types of people, Arabs and non-Arabs," laughed one of the sheik's lieutenants.

"Go, help my people with our dead," the sheik said, dismissing me. We buried Sheik Fahad's warriors in sand, and then sparingly outlined their bodies in stones. It took us well past sunset to inhume all of Sheik Fahad's warriors in the crimson sand. Fahad left the enemy's bodies to the lizards, scorpions, dung beetles, and Egyptian vultures.

Late that evening I shared the Gospel with Sheik Fahad's entire tribe. The next morning, they packed their belongings and a burlap sack full of food for me. We bade a friendly farewell at noon. I headed southeast to Mount Sinai. They headed northeast to raid Roman trade routes for food, horses, and dromedaries.

~~

My cracked lips spit and hooked nose blew out great amounts of sand over the next couple of days. It felt like my teeth were sandblasted white. Meanwhile, the sun's actinic rays turned my skin black with blisters.

I aimlessly walked for weeks in that arid land. My feet stumbled through shifting sand, but my soul stood firm upon solid rock. My leather sandals wore thin but my heavenly relationship grew thick while roaming Arabia amidst heavy, buffeting winds.

There's only one river and one lake on the whole Sinai peninsula, so

I would fill up my goatskin water bag at every deep well and oasis. Still, numerous days would pass without water. Several times, friendly Bedouins shared their water, and their generosity spared this Jewish nomad's life.

Late one afternoon I ran into a peaceful, Bedouin family. They were camped about a two day walk north of Mt Sinai. My lips had gone three days without water. The Bedouins were kind enough to share their water. I repaid them by repairing their tents beneath the afternoon sun and sharing the truth beneath a starry sky.

The next afternoon my eyes beheld a mountain towering above all others. Upon approaching the lower mountains, I was baffled how nomadic herdsmen could support their herds with so little grass. After months of walking the sandy Sahara surface, my crooked legs began climbing granite ridges.

The following morning during a walking quiet time, my feet found themselves at the base of Mount Sinai. My whole body collapsed onto the rocky ground. I thanked God for letting me reach this mountain in the bottom of the Sinai Peninsula. Also, I was grateful to meander for only a couple months through the same wilderness Moses and the Israelites had wandered through for forty years.

Chapter Twenty-Three
A Time of Spiritual Growth

"A journey of a thousand paces must begin with a single step."
Loa-Tzu

Mount Sinai holds tremendous, religious sufficiency within Jewish history. The mount was also known as Mount Horeb, the Mountain of God. The Nabateans called it Mount Moses or Jebel Musa in Arabic. The prophet Moses had climbed the mountain for divine insight fifteen centuries before me. Atop Mount Horeb he received God's laws, the Ten Commandments, for daily living.

The prophet Elijah fled to this mountain during his period of depression and discouragement. The Lord also spoke to him on this mountain. Then God sent Elijah from Mount Horeb to the Desert of Damascus.

I sang a couple psalms at the base of the mountain then began climbing it. With each passing step the ascent became more rugged, barren, and steeper. The climb consumed any remaining energy left in my already fatigued 36-year-old body.

Upon reaching the summit, I collapsed and took a brief nap. Upon awakening, I found a sharp jagged stone, and two massive boulders. I began scratching the Ten Commandments given to Moses by the voice of God on the holy mountain's rocky boulders.

On one boulder I inscribed the four commandments regarding our relationship with God:

1. YOU SHALL HAVE NO OTHER GODS BEFORE ME
2. YOU SHALL NOT MAKE FOR YOURSELF AN IDOL

3. YOU SHALL NOT MISUSE THE NAME OF THE LORD
    YOUR GOD
4. OBSERVE THE SABBATH DAY BY KEEPING IT HOLY

On the other boulder I etched the six commandments regarding our relationship with people of all races, color, religions, sexes, and creeds:

5. HONOR YOUR FATHER AND YOUR MOTHER
6. YOU SHALL NOT MURDER
7   YOU SHALL NOT COMMIT ADULTERY
8. YOU SHALL NOT STEAL
9   YOU SHALL NOT GIVE FALSE TESTIMONY AGAINST
    YOUR NEIGHBOR
10. YOU SHALL NOT COVET YOUR NEIGHBOR'S HOUSE,
    WIFE, AND BELONGINGS

The Ten Commandments were God's moral and civil laws for humanity. Moses received them while leading the Jewish race from Egypt to the Promised Land. A few Gentile societies lived by the Ten Commandments, but most merely marveled at their intention.

Sitting atop Mount Sinai, I remembered a Judean believer we had imprisoned in the Jerusalem dungeon. We were dragging him from the torture chamber to a prison cell when he shared, "Jesus taught us during his Sermon on the Mount that 'anyone who breaks one of the least of these commandments and teaches others to do the same will be called least in the kingdom of heaven, but whoever practices and teaches these commands will be called great in the kingdom of heaven.'"

Then I recalled something a Damascan believer told me just before leaving Syria: "Jesus summarized all Ten Commandments when he said, 'Love the Lord your God with all your heart and with all your soul and with all your mind. This is the first and greatest commandment. And the second is like it. Love your neighbor as yourself. All the Laws and the Prophets hang on these two commandments.'"

Several seconds later, thoughts of Solomon filled my mind while I paced the summit. Solomon was the wisest man to have ever lived on earth outside of Jesus. Solomon knew God directed the stars in the sky and paths of people. Therefore, he sought God's wisdom because it's the companion of the wise and absent friend of the folly. Still, throughout his book, *Ecclesiastes,* he thought life was meaningless and made no sense.

However, he found the purpose of life and wisdom by the time he wrote the last sentences of *Ecclesiastes*. "Here is the conclusion of what matters:

1. FEAR GOD AND KEEP HIS COMMANDMENTS, FOR THIS IS THE WHOLE DUTY OF MAN.
2. GOD WILL BRING EVERY DEED TO JUDGMENT, INCLUDING EVERY HIDDEN THING WHETHER IT IS GOOD OR EVIL."

After contemplating Solomon's words, I realized the Holy Spirit had led me to this mountaintop where God gave Moses the Ten Commandments. I prayed God would reveal unto me his Gospel of grace and my direction.

Accepting a new foundational stone was a major step for this man of religion. I had been using the pharisaical and oral law as the guide to eternal life. My earthly traveling companions throughout adulthood had been religious fervor and legalism.

For several days, waves of dark clouds surrounded Mount Sinai's summit. Cold rain and divine insight fell from the clouds. My body was drenched in rainwater while my soul was soaked in the knowledge that God is not the author of sin.

One rainy afternoon the Holy Spirit saturated my mind with the thoughts, "Truth doesn't evolve, it's created."

When the rain finally lightened up, my emotions wrestled with the reality of being an apostle to the Gentiles. Once the rain stopped my fingers wrote in the mud, "I am the least of the apostles and do not even deserve to be called Apostle, because I persecuted the church of God. But by the grace of God I'm what I am, and his grace to me was not in vain."

It seemed my role as an apostle would be different from the twelve apostles who walked and talked with Jesus. They had lived with him for three years, versus my three days of blindness plus a couple weeks. Those disciples had first-hand knowledge of Jesus. They beheld his miracles, teachings, death, resurrection, great commission, and ascension. Surely, they had more knowledge and insight than this nomad dweller.

For weeks I prayed atop Mount Sinai to find, follow, and fulfill God's will as an apostle. I had been on that mountain for twenty-five days when, on the twenty-sixth night, I roamed back down toward the base of Mount Horeb. I fell asleep in a cave not far above the desert floor, possibly the one Elijah was in when God spoke to him.

I was awakened by a painful, stinging sensation. Upon opening my eyes I noticed a scorpion crawling off my right arm. It was the Arabian scorpion, the most deadly scorpion in the world. The scorpion's erectile tail had just deposited its poisonous venom in my forearm vein. The venom would kill me in six to seven hours.

My upper body and arm became filled with intense pain as well as stiffness. I started drooling, having muscle spasms, abdominal pains, and struggling to breathe. Without a Nabatean antivenin, I'd be dead before sunrise. From the mouth of the cave, I searched the dark desert landscape for a Bedouin campfire. Thankfully, my eyes beheld one not far from the base of Mount Sinai.

I headed toward the campfire but went into a violent, raucous convulsion. Fortunately, the nocturnal Bedouins heard me. They ambled over to investigate the noise and saw a trembling Jew. The desert dwellers immediately recognized the symptoms and gave me a scorpion antivenin, a cocktail of herbs, spices, roots, and blood from an infected horse. Most Nabateans carried antivenin with them for these kinds of emergencies.

The next afternoon, upon gaining consciousness, I thanked the Bedouins for their medical assistance and kindness. They shared their camel milk yogurt, dates, unleavened bread, and ghee with me.

I shared my most precious gift with them: "Eternal life is not based on our race but our relationship with Jesus." They thanked me for the insight then moved on with their small herd of sheep. I crawled back up Mount Sinai and successfully battled death for a couple days. My body experienced a week of severe pain, double vision, and swelling. It took about eight days to totally recover from the sting.

On the fortieth day atop Mount Sinai I was praying for insight into my apostleship, when suddenly, it was like the Holy Spirit raised me above the mountain and desert landscape. I was looking down upon earth and saw the ten principles of my apostleship. The Holy Spirit engraved these upon my heart.

The first six are regarding our relationship with the Holy Trinity:

1. ILLUMINATION LEADS TO TRANSFORMATION
2. A CULMINATION IS THE BEGINNING, NOT THE END
3. SACRIFICE LEADS TO VICTORY
4. SOMETIMES THERE'S ONLY ONE WAY TO A DESTINATION
5. BE EXHAUSTED IN YOUR WORK AND INVINCIBLE IN CONVICTION

6. THERE'S A SPIRITUAL VOICE WITHIN ALL OF US

The last four have to do with our relationship with other believers and people:

7. A SOUL FLOUNDERS WITHOUT VERITY
8. CHOICE, THEN GRACE, ALTERS ONE'S DESTINY
9. THERE'S A U IN UNITY
10. LOVE ENABLES DEEDS AND OVERCOMES ADVERSITY

These ten principles along with the Holy Spirit inspired me to write thirteen epistles. Also, these initial ten principles framed the bridge to my apostleship.

My life like Moses' life, I had been transformed after forty days on Mount Sinai. I fell to my knees on Mount Sinai and praised God for revealing my apostleship. I prayed for obedience and patience in the life ahead.

Chapter Twenty-Four
A Time to Return

"If a scholar has not faith in his principles how
shall he take a firm hold of things."
Mencius

I got up from the rocky surface then climbed down Mount Sinai's gorges
and cliffside trails. After reaching the lower plain, I headed northeast on
the desert floor. My feet took a slight detour in the desert terrain to avoid
some black scarabs, Egyptians' symbol for resurrection, eating a camel's
carcass.

My eyes beheld a spice caravan journeying northeast about two
thousand paces away in the afternoon horizon. I decided to head toward
the caravan and see if I could join it. The months of solitude had sparked
a desire for human companionship.

The caravan commander was on his way out to investigate and question
me, when the sound of camels and horses came roaring out of the lower
mountains. Sheik Abdul and his band of bandits were headed straight
toward us.

"Run for your life!" The commander shouted as he turned around and
galloped back toward his caravan.

I stood between Sheik Abdul and the caravan's bounty. The sheik's
warriors were waving their swords and screaming death threats. Their
voices got louder and louder. I dropped my few belongings and took off
across the sandy desert.

After a few minutes, I stumbled to my knees in exhaustion and prayer,
then quoted from Psalms, "Rescue me, O Lord, from evil men; protect me
from men of violence, who devise evil plans in their hearts."

The bandits stopped and ransacked my few belongings. I could hear Sheik Abdul shouting in Arabic, "That's the stinking Jew who was with Fahad! He's the one telling the Bedouins about this new religion. Kill him then chop him into pieces!" He shouted to his warriors as the sound of hoofs nearly drowned out his words. It was then I realized we don't need to tell God about our enemies but we need to tell our enemies about God.

"Sheik Abdul, God will forgive and deal with each man according to all he does!" I screamed in Arabic over my shoulders.

"Form a circle! A tight circle! " I vaguely heard the caravan commander screaming to his people in the other direction.

"Kill him! Kill him!" Sheik Abdul and his men yelled. They were about a hundred cubits away. Spears were landing close to me.

Within a few minutes, this new apostle was either going to being sharing the Gospel with Sheik Abdul or enjoying a feast with Jesus in heaven. I feared the Lord, not Sheik Abdul. My nerves were calm even though an army of Arab warriors was about to overtake me. Fear couldn't find a foothold, because I stood firm in the Prince of Peace.

Suddenly, from nowhere a grand simoom came out of the northeast. A great sand wave engulfed the desert around us. The simoom instantly turned sunlight into darkness. Nobody could see the hand in front of his face and our eyes were full of sand. Even the camels, with their extra-long eyelashes, couldn't keep the grains of sand out of their eyes.

Sand pounded against our bodies. The warriors were knocked off their camels and horses. The powerful, sand-laden winds tore all the loose clothes from our bodies except for undergarments. The simoom's sandy force was like having one's skin combed with a metal brush, blood dripped from our skin.

I decided to outsmart Sheik Abdul by crawling northeast, right into the simoom. The caravan commander did the same with his people since they were all in a tight ball. We marched right into the teeth of the sandstorm.

The caravan moved at a slower pace, but we both made some progress. It sounded like we were only a hundred paces from each other. Meanwhile, Sheik Abdul screamed and screamed to his men, "Kept the simoom to your backs, like the weaklings will do." The warriors allowed themselves to be blown southwest by simoom.

The sandstorm lasted for thirty minutes. The impossible became the possible through prayer. Death's door stayed closed even though the bloodthirsty Sheik Abdul and a lethal sandstorm were pounding on it.

The simoom's overpowering winds erased everyone's footprints. Sheik

Abdul and his men couldn't see us or begin to track us. They assumed we also headed southwest with the overwhelming winds. So they galloped off in that direction.

~~

For weeks I struggled to find shelter in the desert after escaping Sheik Abdul and the simoom. The scorching sand was like walking across burning coals. The bottoms of my feet looked like camel hoofs. The sun parched the flesh on my bones. The winds blew sand into every dimple of my body.

Like the desert plants I stored up sunshine all day long to stay warm at night when the temperature fell. It was hard to sleep at night since most animals in the desert are nocturnal. I had toads, snakes, scorpions, or spiders crawling on or near me every night.

I continued trekking northward on a sea of sand and occasionally surfed down the brown ocean's waves. The sandy currents pounded against my body every day. Once I got motion sickness from just watching the wind reshape the waves of sand. The barren desert played tricks on my mind several times, I found myself with a mouthful of sand instead of water.

My tongue was daily sandblasted. Fortunately, the Bedouins taught me how to gather the morning dew from plants and rocks for drinking water. This skill kept me alive in the desert. When Bedouins crossed my path they would graciously tend to my personal needs. They shared their clothes, food, and water with me. I would in return, repair their tents and share the Gospel with them. Their souls were hungry and their hearts were thirsty.

~~

I wandered the desert like Moses and the Israelites fortnight after fortnight. Those months of spiritual solitude passed like days, but physically they seemed to last for decades. The solar calendar revealed this reclusive sabbatical had lasted nearly three years.

Amidst solitariness the Lord revealed - It takes time for us to mature spiritually and for God to develop our character. We have to unlearn secular falsehoods to relearn His truths. Wisdom and understanding occur as our minds embrace His verity. When the truth of God's word flows through our hearts, we have inner peace. Truth and wisdom are the passports for divine awakening.

I roamed over to Khirbet Qumran on the northwestern shore of the Dead Sea. Moreover, I stayed there for a week and was physically rejuvenated by the Essenes, a small Jewish sect. They were a monastic group who religiously practiced communal possessions, ceremonial purity, and celibacy. They all walked around in white garments even while farming. Their culture had strong Hellenistic and Oriental influences.

Two weeks after I left the Essenes, a severe rainstorm brought a flash flood and life to the desert. It also brought the desert locusts from their nymphal stage beneath the sand to the surface. It took a while for the nymph hatches to turn from crawlers to hoppers to flyers. For a couple weeks, they were my daily source of protein like manna from heaven.

The first day a locust took flight I cherished its novel, buzzing sound. The next day the sky was blacked out by a swarm of locusts for two hours. Their sound almost drove me crazy. Three days later, it took seven hours for the locusts to pass. Within eight days, a plague filled the land, as locusts consumed nearly all the vegetation in sight.

Walking in the direction of the Oasis of Ghouta, I realized God had given me several insights for humanity. First, if we take time every day to be alone with God, He will show us His will for our lives. He speaks to us through providential circumstances, nature, people, variety, love, prayers, His Son, and the Holy Spirit. Our earthly direction becomes clearer after time in solitude with the Lord.

Second, God created us to worship Him through our daily activities. We should live our earthly lives like His Son and emulate His righteousness. Also, let His truths and those He places in our lives change our direction.

Third, be thankful God has chosen us as His instruments. Then patiently wait for God's hand to pick us off His earthly workbench for our assigned tasks. Realize being His human tool may chip our pride, nick our torso, or go against the temporal grain.

I was more than ready to be used as God's tool. I had been transformed as well as reshaped and was ready for my mission! And why would He not use me right now? I had placed my faith in His grace, not in legalism, humanity, or secular ways.

In the spring of my thirty-seventh year, I found myself within eyesight of Damascus. I was elated to see and return to this metropolis. A nomad vendor sold me the enclosed leather map outside the city gate. My mind wanted a visional remainder of the thirty-six months spent in the wilderness. It's where I learned to listen to God, walk with Jesus, and be guided by the Holy Spirit.

NAHOR
TYRE
DAMASCUS
MEDITERRANEAN SEA
SEA OF GALILEE
NABATEA EMPIRE
JORDAN RIVER
JERUSALEM
DEAD SEA
ARABIAN DESERT
SINAI PENINSULA
EGYPT
MT. SINAI
RIVER NILE
RED SEA

Chapter Twenty-Five
A Time to be the Enemy

"He is a man of courage who does not run away, but
remains at his post and fights against the enemy."
Socrates

My dusty body plunged into the Abana River, then staggered through the main city gate. Meanwhile, my fervent soul hoped God was ready to pick up this neoteric tool from his earthly workbench to lead Jews and Gentiles unto the Lord.

I stumbled down Straight Street to Ananias' apartment on a cool spring evening. My last ounce of earthly energy was used climbing his three flights of stairs. None of the neighbors recognized me on the stairwell. My face was covered with blisters. I looked like a leper with festering lesions.

It spiritually felt like I was dressed in a silk bridegroom's robe and garnished with priceless jewels. However, I was wearing a worn out Bedouin thawb. There was barely enough burlap sackcloth left to cover my tattered, linen loincloth. The kufiyya headgear was merely wool threads tangled in my unctuous hair.

One of Ananias' neighbors handed me alms on the third floor stairwell, thinking I was a beggar. Nearly every bone was visible beneath my skin.

Ananias instantly recognized me upon opening the door. He joyfully greeted me with a hug and exclaimed, "It's great to see you!" Then he helped my exhausted frame into his flat.

"Forgive me for imposing upon you again, especially after what happened the last time I was here. But, I have nowhere to go."

"It is long forgotten!" Miriam said. "You are one of God's chosen instruments. You are always welcome to stay with us, regardless of the length of time and consequences."

"Thank you."

"How was your time in Arabia?" Ananias anxiously asked.

"Challenging! The sand and sun wore me out," I replied between gulps.

"How did you survive the desert?" one of the twins asked as Miriam took care of the burns and blisters covering my head.

"Like an elephant. My oversized feet helped me trek across the sandy desert surface, and my large, floppy ears kept my head cool," I joked.

"You seem different," the other twin insightfully remarked as Ananias handed me a small loaf of bread.

"I am. The Lord baked his virtues of patience and wisdom into me. Also, the desert and Holy Spirit sandblasted my soul clean." I chuckled before taking a huge bite of bread.

"We can see your body was sandblasted." Miriam laughed before handing me one of Ananias' old robes.

"How is the Damascan church?" I inquired through a mouthful.

"It's alive and well! We haven't experienced any religious persecution for two and half years," Ananias replied while fixing me a mat in the far corner.

"Praise the Lord."

I tottered over to the mat and collapsed on it. I slept for twenty-two hours and awoke the next evening when the Sabbath began. Miriam had already prepared a dinner for us. Over dinner and throughout the evening, we discussed those insights the Lord revealed to me in the desert.

The next morning I awoke to the noise of Ananias' family leaving for the Sabbath's sunrise service. Miriam greeted me as I gained consciousness. "Paul join us for the Sabbath worship service."

"I don't have anything to wear." I yawned. Ananias handed me one of his clean mantels and tunics. Minutes later, I looked like a child in adult clothes, walking down Straight Street to the synagogue.

"The orthodox Jews have been reluctantly coexisting with The Way," Ananias said as we approached the synagogue. Upon entering the building, we directly went to an empty pew, and the service started when we sat down.

"Visitor, would you like to read from the scrolls this morning?" the new rabbi asked me. It was a common Hebrew custom to invite visitors to read from the Holy Scroll.

A couple of elders behind us thought they recognized me but dismissed the thought. All the facial blisters and oversized garments made it difficult to identify me. Once again, the congregation was in store for divine insight and a surprise.

I approached the dais, nervously cleared my throat, straightened my posture, then read from the Holy Scroll of Isaiah, "He was despised and rejected by men… he was pierced for our transgressions… he was crushed for our iniquities… by his wounds we are healed… The Lord makes his life a guilt offering… He bore the sin of many and made intercession for the transgressors."

"Teach it," mumbled an elderly lady from Jerusalem.

"Jesus of Nazareth is the Messiah that Isaiah spoke of in his writings over seven hundred and forty years ago. Jesus Christ was despised, rejected, pierced, and crushed for our sins. His wounds, life, and intercession eliminated the need for blood sacrifices. Jesus is God, and God is Christ!" The orthodox members grew restless as I spoke.

"Isn't this the man who raised havoc in Jerusalem among those who call on Jesus' name three years ago?" An elder asked.

"Yes, it's Saul! But remember, he turned into one of them!" Another elder shouted.

"Leave our synagogue! Never speak those words again in this building, or to any members of our congregation." The head elder motioned for three muscular congregants to escort me out the door.

I was carried out of the synagogue; however, I repeated this message throughout other synagogues in Damascus over the next several days. I boldly instructed the Jewish population about God's new revelations. With God's blessings, I grew more persuasive and powerful in teaching that Jesus is the Son of God.

Numerous Jews committed their lives to The Way. The Jewish elders throughout the city were full of rage and jealousy. The Gospel stirred up a fuss in the Jewish community. Within ten days, the synagogues' elders banned me from all their buildings in Damascus.

So, I took the Gospel to the Gentiles. I taught them the truth in their marketplaces, on street corners, and by the Abana riverbanks. Damascus is where I implemented the missionary strategy of first going to the Jews then to the Gentiles with the Gospel.

The Damascan Gentiles I ministered to were mostly Nabateans or Bedouins. Damascus had an extremely large Nabatean population since the Nabataean Empire was not far from the city. Also, Damascus was frequently visited by transient Nabateans trading for goods, attending chariot races, and participating in the city's lascivious lifestyle. These nomadic Nabateans usually stayed in tents outside the city gates. Some of them were tents I had made.

I spent several hours every day evangelizing to Nabateans. I befriended these residents and visitors by sharing humorous stories about my time in the Arabian Desert. They especially loved hearing of Jesus' parables. The Way was rejuvenated in Damascus as a flock of new Jewish and Nabatean believers sought a relationship with Christ.

King Aretas IV of the Nabatean Kingdom heard quite a few of his tribesmen had become Nazarenes. He disapproved of them committing their alliance to another king, even if it was a heavenly king. He became furious; furthermore, King Aretas IV placed a bounty on my head: "Wanted died or alive. No questions asked."

Aretas instructed his Damascus Ethnarch to deal with this situation as quickly as possible. The Ethnarch had partial authority over the Nabatean community within the city walls, since Damascus was a free Roman city. The Romans had absolute jurisdiction over all races inside Damascus.

The Nabatean Ethnarch obtained permission from the Roman Prefect of Syria to search inside as well as outside the city walls for me. Then, he was granted permission to arrest and sentence me.

The Nabatean soldiers combed the synagogues, house churches, friends' homes, Ananias' flat, and the marketplaces. I always managed to stay a step ahead of them. On the street, they even stopped people, whose height resembled mine, thinking it was me in disguise.

~~

Unfortunately, the thunderous power of the Gospel caused jealousy among most synagogues' elders. They took righteousness and tried to twist it into something appalling. Division, anger, and homicidal thoughts were raining down all over the Jewish section of Damascus.

One blustery afternoon, after Ananias and I finished teaching some Nabateans in the marketplace, we were joined by two of Ananias' cousins. They ushered us into a back alley and his youngest cousin said, "We just finished some woodwork in King Aretas' place. We overheard several zealous Jewish elders speaking with the Nabatean Ethnarch. They have agreed to undertake a mutual alliance against Paul."

"What kind of an alliance," Ananias remarked as they remained silent for several seconds.

"Deadly." The older cousins said, while looking over his shoulder, "One of our elders said, 'We know King Aretas IV is trying to catch Saul, the religious troublemaker. It's said that Saul sides with King Aretas' political enemies. Also, he is an agent for those you war against.'"

"Lies. What else did they say?" Ananias inquired.

"They said, "We have figured out a way to catch Saul. We will invite him to speak at one of our synagogues, tomorrow afternoon. Before Saul enters the synagogue, you can overtake him and arrest him. We'll convict him of treason and blasphemy. Then you can take him outside the city wall and stone him to death,'" the older cousin said.

"The Nabatean Ethnarch shouted, 'Great idea!'" whispered Ananias youngest cousin.

Meanwhile, Judah Ben-Hur had just arrived in Damascus to visit some relatives and to race in the Annual Oasis Chariot Race. The local odd makers at the Hippodrome had him favored to win by two to one. He had already won the Rome Championship, Ephesus Open, Tarsus Classic, and the Alexandria Series.

Judah was at the marketplace purchasing grain for his Arabian horses. A wealthy, Grecian Jew, who was an admirer, recognized him and yelled, "Ben-Hur, your white Arabians are the quickest horses in the Empire."

"Thank you."

"I have followed you since your early days in Rome's Circus Maximus. You've won six hundred and ninety-nine races out of eight hundred and forty-nine races! If you win the Oasis, you'll become only one of five charioteers to win seven hundred races!"

"Thank you, I was unaware of that statistic."

"My favorite race of yours was ten years ago in the Caesarean Hippodrome. Your chariot accidentally ran over a fallen horse on the home stretch, and your right chariot wheel came off. And you somehow jumped from your chariot onto the back of your left inside horse to win the race."

"That was a blessing not to have missed the Arabian and been trampled to death. Youth delights in flirting with death."

"So do religious zealots."

"What do you mean?" inquired Judah Ben-Hur.

"Well." Judah's fan whispered, "Allow me to share a secret with you, I just heard the Nabatean and zealot Jews are plotting to kill your Nazarene friend, Paul, tomorrow."

"How do you know this?"

"My brother-in-law is the head elder at the Hellenistic Synagogue. I overheard him talking with an elder from another synagogue on this matter." He said with hesitation.

"What else do you know of the plan?" pleaded Judah.

"To make sure he doesn't escape, the Nabatean Ethnarch has posted soldiers at every city gates. They say, 'Paul will be forgotten by tomorrow's sunset.'" The fan reluctantly added, then shouted, "Hope you win tomorrow!"

"Thanks on both accounts," Judah acknowledged while bidding his fan farewell.

Judah dashed over to Ananias' abode. Several Damascan believers and I were in the apartment having a concert of prayer. We were asking for God's guidance and His blessings upon the Damascan church. Judah apologized for interrupting, then told us about the murderous plan.

"This confirms my cousin's information," Ananias said.

"We need a unique escape route to get Saul out of this city, tonight! They have guards positioned at every gate." Judah exclaimed with building fury.

"My wife has a friend, who lives in a fourth-story apartment on the southern wall. Its over three hundred paces from any city gate, tower, or guard stand. Her apartment has a large window that overlooks the Damascan countryside," suggested Ananias.

"I like it! The moon is black tonight. The walls will be full of darkness," Judah Ben-Hur added.

"We could put Paul in my masonry basket, the one I use to lift and lower large stone for repairing the city wall," a member from Ananias' congregation offered.

"I have a rope that is over thirty cubits long, we could use," a hemp craftsman added while getting up from his knees.

Just before midnight my small frame curled up inside a builder's basket. Two black wool blankets and several small builders' rocks were gently placed atop me. Four strong, young men carefully lowered this human cornerstone of the Damascan church to the ground.

The wooden basket bounced off the city wall as it descended the four story wall. The rocks in the basket painfully bounced off my head and shoulders. When the dusty basket landed on the ground, I tossed off the rocks and blankets, jumped out of the basket, grabbed the wool blankets, and hid for awhile in a city wall niche.

Nobody saw us. I waved farewell to the Damascan saints. My feet quickly raced through the olive groves, past several oil-presses, and finally into the dark, barren land.

Three years before I had approached Damascus full of pride, but I now departed the city fasting in humility. God taught me the importance of spiritual fellowship, love, and reliance upon others. The glittering stars and Holy Spirit guided me toward Judea.

Chapter Twenty-Six
A Time to Proclaim

"They should proclaim this word and spread it throughout their towns."
Nehemiah

I headed southwest, battling the desert's sweltry days and chilly nights. My soul cherished the insights gained from the last three years in Arabia. Now, I longed to meet Jesus' apostles who lived with him during his earthly ministry. My mind longed for their knowledge, the wisdom they obtained from hearing his teachings for three years in Palestine.

I periodically stopped in Syrian villages to share the Gospel and buy food. Upon reaching the Sea of Galilee's northeastern shore, I sauntered into a small Decapolis village. After I shared The Way in the marketplace, a believing man and his daughter invited me to their home for dinner.

His wife already had supper set out on the roof's dinner table when we entered the small one room house. The husband blessed the fresh sardines, bread, and beets. Then he asked, "Did you know Jesus ministered on both sides of the Sea of Galilee?"

"Yes, I heard he had a ministry on the western and eastern shores."

"Mother, tell Paul your two favorite stories about Jesus," their only child exclaimed.

"He has probably heard them already."

"I would love to hear them," I requested as the sun winked good night on the horizon.

"Well, the first story took place on the western side or Jewish side of the Sea. It was just before your Passover feast. Jews in the seaside towns heard Jesus was coming to their area so a large crowd gathered to hear him. When Jesus' small boat reached the shoreline he had compassion on them, even though he was grieving the death of his cousin, John the Baptist who was beheaded by King Herod. Jesus healed those who needed healing and taught the crowd of twenty thousand many wonderful things." She stopped, waiting for my expressions or words to reveal themselves.

"Please continue," My voice and face communicated.

"Late in the afternoon the twelve disciples came to Jesus and said, 'Send the crowd away so they can go to the surrounding villages and countryside and find food and lodging, because we are in a remote place here.'" She paused to give me another plate of sardines. "'They do not need to go away. You give them something to eat. How many loaves do you have? Go and see.' Jesus said.

"He already knew how much food they had to eat." My male host added with a mouth full of bread.

"When the other disciples left, Jesus asked Philip, 'Where shall we buy bread for these people to eat?' Jesus knew what he was going to do but was testing his disciple's faith. 'Eight months' wages would not buy enough bread for each one to have a bite,' responded Philip. Then the disciple Andrew returned and he said, 'Here is a boy with five small barley loaves and two small fish, but how far will they go among so many?'" she resumed.

"Only five loaves and two fish?" I sought confirmation.

"Little is much when placed in the hands of the Lord," she replied after cutting me another piece of bread. "Jesus instructed his disciples, 'Bring the five loaves and two fish here to me. Have the people sit down in groups of about fifty each.' Looking up to heaven, he gave thanks and broke the bread and musht. Then he gave them to the disciples to set before the people."

"When everyone ate till they were full and Jesus said, 'Gather the pieces that are left over. Let nothing be wasted.' The disciples collected twelve basketfuls of broken pieces of bread and musht!" The young daughter exclaimed.

"The twelve baskets of leftovers represent the twelve tribes of Israel. Jesus preformed that miracle for his fellow Jews, to illustrate to them that God is the one who spiritually and physically feeds the twelve Jewish tribes." I belted out upon grasping the symbolism.

"I never thought of it that way," my male host responded.

"The second story deals with another great crowd and miracle. This time Jesus was on the eastern side or Gentile side of the Sea of Galilee. About sixteen thousand people came to him in a remote area of Decapolis." She began after serving us more beets.

"I'll never forget that day," said her husband.

"People brought their lame, the blind, the crippled, the mute, and many others and laid them at his feet: and he healed them," she resumed.

"You would never know it, but my mother was mute till that day," The young girl interjected with a smile, "Jesus placed his hands on her throat, and she spoke for the first time in her life. She hasn't stopped talking or praising since then."

"The people were amazed by this miracle and all the other ones he performed. But, the greatest miracle was our spiritual transformation!" her father reminded.

"Yes, praise the Lord," the mother agreed then continued her story. "Jesus met with his disciples and said, 'I have compassion for these people; they have already been with me for three days and have nothing to eat. I do not want to send them away hungry, or they may collapse on the way, because some of them have come a long distance.

"He cares so much for us." I mumbled, caught up in the story.

"'But where in this remote place can anyone get enough bread to feed them,' his disciples pondered. 'How many loaves do you have?' Jesus knowingly inquired of his disciples. 'We only have seven loaves of bread and a few small fish. How will you feed them?' a disciple asked."

"Oh, we of little faith," her husband tossed in.

"Jesus instructed all of us to sit down on the ground. Then he took the seven loaves and the fish, and when he had given thanks, he broke them and gave them to the disciples, and they in turn to the people. All ate till their bellies were full. When we were all finished the disciples picked up seven baskets of leftovers. Then he got in a boat, and we all went home," she concluded.

"The seven baskets of leftovers represent the seven tribes of the Canaanites. Jesus performed that miracle for the Gentiles, to let us know God is the one who also spiritually and physically feeds us," the Gentile man surmised, helping his wife with the dirty dishes.

"Thanks for sharing your story," I said, trying to hide a yawn.

"It's gotten dark on us. It's past our bedtime. Paul, you can sleep here on our roof. There's a comfortable straw mat over there in the corner." My head bobbed several times in agreement with the host's remarks.

"I'll be gone before sunrise. Thanks for your hospitality!" I said as they went downstairs to go to bed.

~~

The following day I was about a half day's hike south of the Sea of Galilee, on the eastern side of the Jordan River. It sounded like the sky was pounding its chest. Then hail started shooting down from the clouds like pebbles from slingshots.

I hurried into a small, nearby Gerasenes village. The ten faded white plaster houses and I were getting pulverized with pellets of ice as my eyes desperately searched for a protective place. An old man with pure white hair stood at his humble abode's threshold. He motioned for me to seek shelter in his home.

"Hello," he greeted me as I ran inside his house.

"Thank you for the shelter!"

"No problem. My name is Legion."

"Legion, that's a unique name. How did you get the name Legion?"

"I was once possessed by a legion of demons," he stated. The skin between his eyebrows was wrinkled like a wad of paper from years of crazed, glaring stares.

"My name is Paul. I was once possessed by pious demons."

"Welcome, Paul. Please, sit anywhere. Sorry, I have no furniture. It's an old habit from a previous lifestyle, living in caves."

"I once lived the same way. I appreciate your hospitality on such a nasty day."

"Where are you headed, my friend?" Legion inquired while scratching a bug bite on his flabby earlobe.

"To Jerusalem."

"What's a Jewish man doing on this side of the Jordan River? I thought you considered this pagan country?" His chapped lips and penetrating brown eyes inquired.

"Not me. I'm going to the Holy City to learn about a Jewish man who changed my life and the world. I'm sharing this wonderful news with Jews and Gentiles!"

"My world was also changed by a Jewish man."

"Was his name Jesus?"

"Yes!" Legion exhilarated as he handed me a bowl of figs.

"How did he change your life?" I inquired before grabbing a handful of figs.

"Well no human is completely full of evil spirits, but I was once close to it! Numerous chains hung from my feet and hands where people had unsuccessfully tried to chain me. No chain was strong enough to hold me." He said, pulling his wrists in separate directions.

"Wow," slipped out of my mouth.

"I was living then in a solitary cave on the Sea of Galilee's eastern shoreline, just north of here. One evening during a furious squall I was inside the cave, cutting myself with sharp stones. Then this fishing boat sailed to the shoreline just outside my cave. The squall mysteriously disappeared, and this captivating Jewish man got out of the boat. My nude, bleeding body ran out the cave toward him and fell at his feet." He resumed.

"Then what happened?"

"The evil spirits within me yelled as loud as they could, 'What do you want with me, Jesus, Son of the Most High God? Swear to God that you won't torture me!' I had no idea who he was, but the evil spirits certainly knew! They knew he could eradicate them!"

"For sure!"

"Then Jesus said, 'Come out of this man, you evil spirit!' Meanwhile, there was a large herd of pigs feeding on the nearby hillside. Pigs on this side of the Sea of Galilee are considered sacred animals, unlike Jerusalem where pigs are regarded as unclean animals. They are a ceremonial part of our local fertility ritual. The evil spirits within me begged Jesus, 'Send us among the pigs; allow us to go into them.'" Legion gestured excitedly as he spoke.

"What an amazing story," I remarked with growing curiosity.

"Jesus gave them permission, and the evil spirits came out and went into the pigs. The herd, about two thousand in number, rushed down the steep bank into the lake and were drowned."

"Awesome metaphor, the lake represented Hades and the pigs the demons. You saw the evil spirits return to their Abyss, their home," I said.

"Yes, those spirits didn't want to go back into the air but home to hell! Meanwhile, those tending the pigs reported this in the town. The townsfolk came out to see what had happened and saw the change in me. The people began to plead with Jesus to leave their region because they were overcome with fear."

"What did Jesus do?"

"He got back in his boat. I begged Jesus to let me join him, but he said, 'Go home to your family and tell them how much the Lord has done for you, and how he has had mercy on you.'" Legions' lips and heart were acting in unison not separate.

"We serve a God who delights in showing mercy! That is why God sent His Son instead of just a book. What an awesome testimony Jesus gave you!" I said.

"I have spent every day since then telling others how much Jesus has done for me. Every time I tell the story in marketplaces or house churches, people are amazed on both sides of the Sea of Galilee and Jordan River." He concluded as the frozen raindrops stopped falling.

"I can image."

"It goes to show you don't need special training to share the truth. All you have to do is tell what God has done in your life. God's actions and one's testimony speak volumes in the empty, spiritual chambers of peoples' hearts," he concluded.

We spent that afternoon together. I told Legion about my unique encounter with Jesus and the things He taught me in Arabian Desert through the Holy Spirit. I encouraged him to keep up the good work, then bade my new friend farewell before the sun went to sleep. I continued my journey southwest to Jerusalem.

~~

I hiked the Jordan River's eastern riverbanks for approximately four days sharing the Gospel with Decapolis' residents. The river's elevation drops more than the height of a large adult every thousand paces as it twists from the Sea of Galilee to the Dead Sea. This causes a quick current in the spring, making for a treacherous crossing.

Early one morning I decided to traverse the Jordan River over to Samaria. My foot slipped on a mossy rock in mid-stream. The chilly springtime current carried me downriver. I was suddenly fighting the cold, swift current; furthermore, I found myself at the mercy of the river of judgment and God.

I banged my head off a rock, went under the swift current, and nearly filled my lungs with river water. It seemed drowning was inevitable! In the distance I noticed a large tree that had partially fallen from the western riverbank.

With split-second timing I desperately leaped for the limb. I missed it with my right hand but caught it with my left hand and pulled myself to shore. Upon reaching the western side of the Jordan River, I yelled, "Alleluia! Alleluia!"

A few minutes later my soaked body resumed its journey. I trekked the thick-wooded, western riverbank by day for coolness and slept on the river's edge at night for safety. This novice apostle continued southwest into Judea and eventually to the outskirts of Jerusalem.

Chapter Twenty-Seven
A Time to Mend

"Forgiveness is the fragrance the violet sheds on the heel that crushed it."
Unknown

My weary body finally beheld Jerusalem's Damascan gate on a cloudy, spring morning. It was the day of my 37th birthday. I was not as pious or pompous as when I had departed thirty-seven months ago.

A weathered, sackcloth mantel covered my torso as I approached the gate. Somewhere in southwestern Decapolis a simoom had blown off my headgear. Dusty pus from broken sun blisters covered my face. The bottoms of this desert dweller's feet were woven calluses; they felt and looked like leather.

Huge crowds of residents and pilgrims were pouring out of the Holy City. I had to swim upstream amidst frenzied masses to get through the Damascan gate. They were escaping the violence and smoke that engulfed the entire city.

Rome's Jerusalem garrison was squashing a major revolt; furthermore, Roman soldiers had set ablaze most of the Lower City. The houses in that part of Jerusalem were made of wood and built side by side. Hundreds of one room homes were on fire or smoldering.

It was great to be back in Jerusalem, even though the city was in complete chaos. I immediately went to the Lower City to help put out fires and salvage belongings. Several of us worked for awhile assisting those poor and working-class homeowners.

"Did your face catch on fire?" one small child asked after I helped her father lower furniture off their roof.

"No, too much sunshine!" I laughed before jumping onto her neighbor's roof. The flames from those wooden homes were like giant candles lighting up the cloudy sky. After helping the last family rescue their household items I headed to the Holy Temple.

The thoroughfare was littered with dead Jewish insurgents. Some of their hearts were still spurting out blood. Others had fluids seeping from spears thrust deep into their rib cages, and a few had membranes oozing from their shattered skulls. I took the back alleys to avoid the sight of warfare and Roman soldiers.

The Holy Temple was under Roman guard but they were allowing groups of three or less through the Huldah Double Gates. I entered then climbed the steps to the Court of Gentiles. This court's namesake now held a totally different meaning. My soul humbly proceeded through that court to the Court of Israel to worship God and His Son, the blessed redeemer.

Two hours later I exited through the Sheep Gate and spent that night in prayer at the Pool of Bethesda. I arose from my stiff knees at sunrise to seek out Jesus' disciples. Upon entering the Hippodrome's Marketplace I confronted numerous followers of The Way. Some of them I had persecuted over three years ago.

"I am the one you once called Saul of Tarsus. Please forgive me for my past behavior and what I've done to your families and friends! I've seen the light! Could you please introduce me to Peter and the other pillars of the Jerusalem church?"

"Please, leave us alone!" A few would reply in fright.

"Your actions have pierced our families like arrows from an archer's bow," another said.

"I was converted to The Way on the road to Damascus! I am one of you, now!" I'd exclaimed.

Most timorously shrugged their shoulders then politely walked away, except for one bold woman in the marketplace. She declared, "This is just another move by the Sanhedrin to infiltrate our church and imprison our leaders."

"Please, introduce me to the apostles," I pleaded to nearly two hundred Nazarenes in the marketplaces that morning and afternoon. They were all suspicious of my motives. The haunting, painful memories of our maltreatment kept them at bay. Our horrid acts had left no believing family untouched in Jerusalem.

Around the ninth hour (3:00 p.m.), I sought out Pompey's Prison. The closed building brought back numerous memories of our oppressive, brutal acts. I fell to my knees in prayer outside the locked prison gate.

"Saul, are you okay? What's wrong?" One of my old Pharisee compatriots asked, hurrying to the Holy Temple for the ninth hour of prayer.

"Nothing, but I've been spiritually transformed. I have found The Way."

"Oh, no! You have turned into one of them, a religious blasphemer!" he screeched before storming away.

After the ninth hour of prayer, most of my former Pharisee friends and fellow scribes turned their backs on me. For years, I had been admired by the religious elite in Jerusalem, but within minutes I was being rejected by them.

I spent the rest of the afternoon hoping and praying someone would introduce me to the apostles, but the Nazarenes avoided me. My Pharisees peers now mocked and spat upon me. At sunset I wondered over to Dung Gate (where the sick, suffering, and slaves dwelled) and they even questioned my motives.

~~

Later that evening, after I preached outside of Herod's Palace, an old Gentile camel driver from Damascus informed me, "Your Uncle Elisha, Aunt Helah, and cousin Rachel are living in the Lower City. Elisha is selling precious stones from his house and joyfully sharing the Gospel with your Jewish brethren."

That night I went back to the Lower City. My uncle's one room home was built into the City of David wall. It was one of the few abodes that survived the Roman soldiers' torches. Because of our last meeting my knuckles reluctantly knocked on their door. Aunt Helah and Uncle Elisha both answered the door. Their eyes were filled with love, fear, and tears.

"Helah, it's our nephew Saul!" Uncle Elisha shouted in excitement and gave me a hug with his one arm.

"I don't deserve to be considered your nephew after the way I treated your family," I declared before falling into their arms.

"Saul, we never stopped loving and praying for you! Even when you were persecuting us," Aunt Helah avowed as they escorted me into their home.

"Thank you for your prayers over the years. They were heard and answered!"

"We are blessed for the role you played in our lives!" My aunt remarked before getting some aloe for my burns.

"How can you say that, after what the temple guards and I did to you?"

"You were our saving grace! Three years ago, you got us out of the death dungeon with your ruby ring." Rachel piped up as my mind agonizingly recalled the incident.

"The word on the street is you had a spiritual apocalypse," stated Uncle Elisha with a grin.

"Yes, the Lord with His five wounds appeared unto me. I'm devoting my life to Him!"

"Hallelujah!" Aunt Helah shouted.

"Tell us of your conversion!" Rachel insisted. I told them of the events on the Damascus road and insights obtained during those three years in Arabia. Around midnight, Uncle Elisha retrieved a small wooden box from beneath his bed. With his right hand, his only hand, he opened the wooden box and approached me.

"Happy Birthday!" hummed Aunt Helah and Rachel

"It took us nearly three years to earn the money to buy this back," said Uncle Elisha. He handed me my bar mitzvah ruby ring.

I now saw a ruby not resembling the blood of religious lunatics but redemption. My head clasped into both hands and I said, "Thank you Lord, for forgiveness and family."

"Through the sacrificial blood of Christ, you have been forgiven! Now, it's late and time for rest. Nephew, no debating, you're spending the evening with us," my aunt demanded.

I conceded then went upstairs to sleep on their stone roof, relying on faith for guidance and prayer for solace.

"God, please put another Ananias in my life like you did in Damascus," I prayed beneath the starry sky before falling asleep.

The next morning at breakfast, Uncle Elisha asked. "Why the long face?"

"I came up to Jerusalem to get to know Peter and the other apostles. However, followers of The Way think I'm plotting to capture them then imprison them. I've been rebuked by everyone except for you. Can you help me gain access to Jesus' disciples?"

"Nearly all still vividly recall your reign of terror," Aunt Helah explained. "It was like yesterday for most. That's why many question the sincerity of your conversion. But, I know the Lord has spoken to your heart! He has great plans for you."

"Yes, but the doors of believer's hearts are being slammed in the face of my faith. I don't know what to do?"

"Go to the Pool of Siloam at noon," Uncle Elisha suggested. "There's a man there who aids the weak and gives them words of encouragement. He may be able to help you meet the disciples."

"Who is he?"

"His name is Barnabas. He's from a wealthy, Jewish aristocrat family in Cyprus," remarked my uncle.

"Cyprus, the winter playground for the Roman Empire's rich and famous. I've never been there but they say it has the best winter climate in the Eastern Mediterranean," added Rachel.

"People say Barnabas is an extremely successful Jewish businessman with real estate holdings in Cyprus and Jerusalem. He is highly regarded by the Jewish community and The Way." Aunt Helah said, ushering her family and herself out the door for their daily activities.

~~

At noon I went to the Pool of Siloam bathing in prayer and hoping to find an advocate. I instantly recognized the gentleman of whom Uncle Elisha spoke, a striking man my age, who was assisting handicapped people around the Pool and offering words of confirmation to all.

"You are so kind to these people with your time and energy," I remarked admiringly after approaching him.

"I'm merely substituting one of my wants for one of their needs."

"Is your name Barnabas?"

"My given name is Joseph, but I am also called Barnabas, it means son of encouragement. What is your name?"

"I was once called Saul, but now I'm known as Paul."

"What can I do for you, Paul?"

"I need your help?"

"What kind of help do you need from me?" he asked while filling an elderly lady's water jug.

"First, do you know who I am and what I've done?"

"Yes, a friend recently told me of your past and conversion. He said you are going to be a blessing unto the Gentiles?"

"I hope so. Will you introduce me to the disciples?" I eagerly asked over the screams of magic potion vendors.

"Many have heard of your incredible conversion, but most question its validity. I believe in your transformation, because God changes people. Plus, the Holy Spirit spoke to me this morning about being your advocate to the apostles," Barnabas revealed with a smile.

"Alleluia!" I shouted. The Lord blessed me with Barnabas to intervene on my behalf. "Could you share your story with me?" I added.

"I was raised as a Levite in Cyprus, where I helped the chief priest with animal sacrifices and led our music worship services. About five years ago, I traveled to Jerusalem for the Passover festival to fulfill my Levite duties."

"Sounds like you're faithful in your duties."

"I am. When I arrived in Jerusalem, I heard Jesus teaching in the Holy Temple. Suddenly, my heart started pounding like it was a hundred paces from finishing a marathon. My mind began absorbing his omniscient treasures of wisdom like a sea sponge. It was the kind of riches you share with others and don't horde. Meanwhile, every sinful impulse swam for my soul's shoreline but a tidal wave of righteousness drowned them."

"It's like being changed from the inside out," I proclaimed.

"Yes, it is. Initially, I had a difficult time separating my old way of thinking from his insightful teaching. My mind was a mess. Religion had been throwing soiled thoughts in the same mental pile for years. The simplicity but depth of his teachings rearranged my spiritual frame of mind." Barnabas said while leaning down toward a lame man by the Pool of Siloam's gate.

"There is a difference between religion and The Way. Religion is an effort, works, and awareness of a higher being, whereas The Way is a gift, faith, and relationship with the Lord." I remarked.

Barnabas nodded his head in agreement as he lifted the paralyzed man. "My spiritual journey in The Way began with the Lord at one end and me on the other end. He traveled the entire distance I just had to embrace him."

"Three days after my spiritual awakening Jesus was crucified. I decided to stay in Jerusalem another fifty days till Pentecost. During that time I beheld Jesus' resurrection, befriended the disciples, and saw His ascension into heaven." Barnabas added.

"You're a blessed man!"

"Also, during the Pentecost we were all together in one place. A sound like the blowing of a violent wind came from Heaven and all of us were filled with the Holy Spirit. It was the day the church came into existence.

Now, we are all blessed because the Holy Spirit knocks on every heart's door."

"It took a dramatic event for me to answer that knock!" I said.

"The Lord knows when and how long to sift our hearts."

"For the last three years God has been preparing my heart to teach his word unto Jews and Gentiles."

"That's a unique ministry! Just remember, it's not us working for Him, but Him working through us. May we remain obedient so we'll not be haunted at death by what we could have done for his kingdom." Barnabas placed the paraplegic man's legs in the pool.

"I'm no longer confident in myself, but in Christ."

"Good, because that is what changes us," he said, helping an elderly woman out of the pool.

"When do you think the apostles' hearts will be open to meet with us?" I impatiently asked.

"Tomorrow! Meet me here at noon." The Lord blessed me twice that afternoon – I found a man to introduce me to the disciples as well as a new friend.

Chapter Twenty-Eight
A Time for Insight

"Grasp the subject, the words will follow."
Cato the Elder

All the apostles and church leaders who were present in Jerusalem that evening met with Barnabas. Every one of them respected his judgment of character, but Barnabas had to put his reputation on the line as they listened to and debated him. He enlightened them on my conversion, epiphany, and fearless teaching of the Gospel in Damascus. Barnabas relentlessly pleaded my faith was sincere. Finally, around midnight, the Holy Spirit moved in them to forgive and trust me.

The following day, Barnabas arrived at the Pool of Siloam. It was a few minutes before noon when he greeted me, "Good day, my friend. Are you ready to meet the apostles?"

"They will meet with me, today?"

"Yes!" he exclaimed as we departed the Pool and headed over to a neighborhood by the Fortress of Antonia. On an alley way behind the Pool we passed an insurgents' hospital disguised as a butcher shop. Some insurgents were making recoveries from Roman sword wounds but most were now fighting an even more imposing enemy, death.

The streets outside the Holy Temple were busy as numerous brethren hurried into the temple for prayer. Three times a day followers of Judaism paused for prayer; third hour of the day (9:00 a.m.) and sixth hour of the day (noon) and ninth hour of the day (3:00 p.m.).

"The apostles are waiting for us at the home of James, the half brother of Jesus. James and Jesus had the same mother, Mary of Nazareth. James' father was Joseph of Bethlehem, the carpenter, and Jesus' father was God, the Creator of heaven and earth." Barnabas informed over the noisy crowd.

"Could you give some more insight into James?"

"James was not one of Jesus' twelve disciples, but possesses tremendous wisdom from living with Him for thirty years. James came to Jerusalem not long after Jesus' crucifixion to investigate His ministry. Within days he embraced The Way, devoting himself to Christ and the Jerusalem congregation."

"What is his ministry?"

"He teaches the Gospel with unmatched clarity, performs numerous miracles among the needy and baptizes new believers. His sermons attract followers from all walks of life: brethren from depressed neighbors, poor priests, inquisitive Pharisees, and orthodox Jews. James helps the physically challenged, financially oppressed, widows and orphans. His selfless acts and wisdom along with his leadership skills have catapulted him into a prominent position within the Lord's first church."

"Thanks for your remarks about James and praise the Lord for your perseverance!" I said as we approached the door. "You must have been a one man play last night?"

"I was, but the Holy Spirit wrote the script. May none of us ever be filled with pride because we perform on an earthly stage full of actors. There are no main characters in this terrestrial theater. All the roles that God gives are equally important. He directs our earthly actions while Satan is backstage trying to create chaos and destruction." Barnabas knocked on James' door.

A young lady named Martha greeted and invited us into the house. Barnabas politely introduced me to everyone. James and Thomas were the only apostles in town. All the others apostles were on missionary journeys outside Jerusalem. Also present were a small handful of Judean saints.

"Good afternoon!" James welcomed us while getting up. He was lengthy in stature with a slender frame.

"Many feel it would be easier to believe an ant lifted an elephant than to believe you are an apostle of Christ." James offered as I lowered my head and noticed his large, bony feet.

"I am. Plus, this meeting is not a plot to capture you and the leaders of the Jerusalem church!"

"We're not worried about that outcome. Please sit down in this chair. My brother made it."

"Thanks." I replied, relaxing in the most comfortable wooden chair I had ever sat in.

"Our brother Barnabas feels we should embrace you. He believes you have seen the light and found the truth," James remarked.

"It's true! I literally saw the light and heard the voice of Jesus."

"Please, don't perceive me as someone with unique illumination. Jesus enlightened many during His earthly ministry. His resurrected body appeared unto me as well as over 500 other people. I didn't become a follower of The Way till after His death."

"Still, you have been blessed, James. The Holy Spirit chose you to be the head elder for the Jerusalem church, His first church."

"Thank you. But I'm still extremely stern in my observance of the oral and Mosaic Law, like you were when you were known as Saul. I eat no impure meat and only break bread with Jews."

"I have shared table of fellowship with both Jews and Gentiles," I informed James.

"That is your choice. I still go to the temple three times a day for prayers. The Pharisees know of my god-fearing piety and devotion to our ancestral traditions, so they leave us alone," declared James.

"Thanks for abbreviating your sixth hour of prayer to meet with me."

"It is rare that I miss this hour of prayer in the Holy Temple, but it was a good time to meet you. What can I do for you?" James brushed back the uncombed, black locks from his face.

"I've come from Damascus seeking the wisdom the disciples and you attained from Jesus. I hope to share it in my ministry with believers and non-believers."

"Your visit is timely. I'm currently writing a short but practical letter for the church. The words have been inspired by the Holy Spirit and our Lord," replied James.

"Could you please share some of its content with me?"

"Sure! 'Every good and perfect gift is from above... Our Lord doesn't show favoritism... God cannot be tempted by evil, nor does he tempt anyone, but each one is tempted by his own desire... Come near to God and he will come near to you.'"

"What practical insight."

"Faith by itself, if it is not accompanied by action, is dead... Believe that there is one God, even the demons believe that and shudder... Anyone who chooses to be a friend of the world becomes an enemy of God."

"Please tell me more!"

"Everyone should be quick to listen, slow to speak, and slow to become angry, for man's anger does not bring about the righteous life that God desires... The tongue is a restless evil, full of deadly poison may we learn to control it... Anyone who knows the good he ought to do and doesn't do it, sins."

~~

I was blessed to be surrounded by individuals who were personally taught by Christ. They began to introduce themselves to me individually by asking questions or sharing insightful stories of Jesus.

"Tell us about your life since leaving Jerusalem over three years ago," said the one they called Thomas, one of Jesus' original twelve disciples. He still seemed to doubt my transformation.

I told them about my spiritual conversion, those years in Arabia, and the plot against my life in Damascus. Within a short period of time, everyone realized the sincerity of my faith and warmly accepted me as a fellow believer, even Thomas.

"My heart, mind and soul are like bottomless pits seeking to be filled with the words of Jesus! Could you share some of His teachings with me?" I eagerly asked the saints.

"He said 'I am the way and the truth and the life. No one comes to the Father except through me. If you really knew me, you would know my father as well. From now on, you do know him and have seen him,'" said Thomas.

"Please, tell me more," I pleaded with him to continue.

"I was alone in my sorrow and missed Jesus' initial resurrection appearance unto the disciples. My stubbornness and desire for evidence prevented me from believing my colleagues. I had seen the Roman soldiers drive bronze spikes through His hands and feet then pierce His side with a spear. Still I needed to put my fingers in His wounds to believe." He recalled.

"Tell him the rest!" encouraged Barnabas.

"Eight days later he reappeared to us again. He told me, 'Put your finger here; see my hands. Reach out your hand and put it into my side. Stop doubting and believe.'"

"Wow, what did you do?"

"'My Lord and my God!' I shouted without even needing to touch

Him. He responded, 'Because you have seen me, you have believed; blessed are those who have not seen and yet have believed.'"

"Thomas, we all want proof he has conquered death. I'd be lying if I didn't say the same thing about my faith. We all have your doubts. It's human nature," Barnabas consoled.

"Thankfully, Jesus comforted me with His presence and transformed my pessimism into evangelism," testified Thomas.

Then a man who looked like he had been given a second chance in life spoke up. "I'm Lazarus. I loved his Sermon on the Mount. He taught us, 'Blessed are the poor in spirit, for theirs is the kingdom of heaven. Blessed are those who mourn, for they will be comforted. Blessed are the meek, for they will inherit the earth. Blessed are those who hunger and thirst for righteous, for they will be filled.'"

"What judicious beatitudes," I interrupted then added, "Are there more?"

"Yes. 'Blessed are the merciful for they will be shown mercy. Blessed are the pure in heart, for they will see God. Blessed are the peacemakers, for they will be called sons of God. Blessed are those who are persecuted because of righteousness, for theirs is the kingdom of heaven.'"

Two ladies who looked like sisters were sitting beside Lazarus. The older sister was the lady who had greeted us at the door, and she articulated, "The day Jesus raised my brother, Lazarus, from the grave He said, 'I'm the resurrection and the life. He who believes in me will live, even though he dies; and whoever lives and believes in me will never die.'"

"He raised Lazarus from the grave?" I remarked, leaving my mouth and eyes wide open.

"Yes, from the dead! Another time He told me, 'You are worried and upset about many things, but only one thing is needed. Chose what is better, and it will not be taken away,'" Martha proclaimed then left the room to finish fixing lunch.

The other elegant lady remarked, "I'm Mary, Martha's and Lazarus' sister. I cherish His comment, 'Who of you by worrying can add a single hour to your life? Since you cannot do this very little thing, why do you worry about the rest?'"

Barnabas turned to his left and said, "This is Joseph of Arimathea. He gave his stone tomb to Mother Mary for Jesus' burial place."

"But, now it's empty," Thomas interjected with joy.

"I treasure the words he taught us on how to pray. 'Father, hallowed be Your name, Your kingdom come. May Your will be done on earth as it is in heaven. Give us each day our daily bread. Forgive us our sins, for we also forgive everyone who sins against us. And lead us not into temptation but deliver us from the evil, for yours is the kingdom and the power and the glory forever. Amen.'" Joseph shared with me.

Right after Joseph finished his remarks, Martha reentered the room. She announced, "It's time for lunch!" James blessed the food, and we all filled our plates.

At lunch I sat down next to an elderly gentleman and asked him, "Excuse me, but aren't you a Pharisee and former-Sanhedrin member?"

"Yes, I was once part of the highest ruling body among our race."

"Are you not Nicodemus, the one Jesus called the 'Teacher of Israel?'"

"You have a good memory."

"I imprisoned you, didn't I?"

"Yes, you did my friend."

"I apologize for all the abuse inflicted upon you at my hands. Please forgive me for what the guards and I did to you."

"God has forgiven you. How could I not forgive you?"

"Praise the Lord for his blessing of forgiveness," I replied humbly and asked, "You never lost your convictions, while in prison! How did you do it?"

"Faith and Hope! May they be your companions if you should ever find yourself in prison. Because followers of Jesus will face tough times, but they will make us stronger! We are like tea, when the heat is turned up we perk a strong, uplifting aroma for others."

"Were you in Jerusalem during Jesus' crucifixion?" I asked Nicodemus.

"Yes, I saw His crucified body. These hands helped prepare His body for the tomb with myrrh and aloes. Then we wrapped it in linen just before the Roman soldiers sealed the tomb."

"You touched his corpse." I replied before choking on a mouthful of olives.

"Before His death, He told me. 'No one can see the kingdom of God unless he is born again.' Till his death I couldn't comprehend how an adult could be born again. Now I know how easy it is – it's a rebirth of our soul and an innocent, childhood like faith in Him!" Nicodemus concluded.

"Paul, tell us what the Lord told you?" inquired James.

"I'm sending you to your own people and the Gentiles to open their eyes and turn them from darkness to light, and from the power of Satan to

God, so that they may receive forgiveness of sins and a place among those who are sanctified by faith in Me."

"Those words regarding a ministry unto the Gentiles are new to us," Thomas sharply responded.

"The kingdom of God is for everyone, Jews and Gentiles. The way to God is not through the Holy Temple or a synagogue, but through Jesus. Now, everyone has access to God." I asserted.

"Your words ring of truth, if they come from the Lord. But, our Jewish brethren who uphold the oral laws will struggle to accept this teaching," offered James.

"The oral law has caused too many to stumble. It's the reason I fell," I replied.

"These words would cause much distress in our synagogues," James said uneasily, fidgeting in his chair.

"True! I saw it firsthand in the Damascan synagogues. My heart aches for the pain and rejection this will cause among our brethren. But, it is part of God's plan for eternal salvation."

"Do you seek a commission from us?" Thomas asked.

"I've already received my apostolic commission from the risen Lord. Like you, I've been commissioned by him. I came for your blessings and companionship, not your permission."

"You have our blessings and comradeship!" James remarked. We shared the Lord's Supper and spent the afternoon in fellowship. Everyone left James' house just before the ninth hour. They all departed for the Holy Temple, but I went to Herod's Marketplace to share the Gospel with the Gentiles.

That evening while walking back to Uncle Elisha's house, I thanked the Lord for Barnabas' trust, his friendship, and letting the Nazarene community embrace me. I realized two valuable lessons that day. First, we all have a Barnabas, a peer, in our life. We just have to let them into our sphere, so God can spiritually use them in our life.

Second, when God calls us to do his work, He will occasionally leave obstacles in our path. Moreover, when we overcome these impediments, the glory for God is greater than if He would have removed the obstacles and made our course easy.

Chapter Twenty-Nine
A Time to be Acknowledge

"I will send them prophets and apostles, some of whom
they will kill and others they will persecute."
GOD

Two nights after my meeting with the Jerusalem saints, Barnabas and
James escorted me to Simon Bar-Jonah's residence. James knocked on his
front door in the House of Records neighborhood. Simon answered the
door and exclaimed, "Good evening!"

"Welcome home!" James responded. Simon had just returned from a
mission trip in Galilee. "This is Paul, whom we once knew and feared as
Saul of Tarsus."

"This is a surprise! Please come in," He remarked as I noticed the heavy
bags beneath his eyes.

"Thank you!" I replied, excited, and stepped inside his one room home.
Barnabas and James excused themselves to help believers in the Lower City
reframe their burnt homes. James, like Jesus, was a carpenter.

"Simon is my birth name, but the Lord called me Cephas, Peter to our
Greek friends. When the Lord needed to reprove me, He called me Simon.
When there was a need to be strong or a leader, He called me, Peter, the
Rock. He saw the fleshly and spiritual sides of me. You can call me what
you wish." He closed the door.

"I'll like the Lord's name for you, Peter."

"And I shall call you by your conversion name, Paul."

"That works. They say you were a fisherman on the Sea of Galilee."

"Yes, but when I met Jesus, I left behind my cloth nest and became a fisherman for human souls." The strong, burly disciple replied then asked, "And you?"

"I was trained as a Pharisee in Jerusalem." We were close in age and conviction but came from different, social backgrounds.

"What brings a renowned Pharisee to my home?" My response was delayed as I stared at his large, calloused hands. They were offering me a clay goblet filled with water.

"I came to hear about Christ," I replied after accepting the clay goblet.

"I've heard you've found The Way," Peter remarked as I sat down on one of the twelve wooden benches that filled the single-room house.

"Yes, and I've traveled a long distance to inquire many things of you, since, you were present at the epoch of Jesus' earthly ministry, all the way through to his ascension. You knew the earthly, crucified, and resurrected Lord. I only know the heavenly, highly exalted Lord. Would you share stories of His earthly ministry with me?"

"It would be a blessing and an honor to share them."

"They say you were the first disciple to recognize Jesus as the Messiah. Also, you personally witnessed his numerous miracles, intellectually grasped the depth of his teachings, and faithfully traveled with him during his Palestinian ministry," I remarked before taking a drink.

"True, except for the grasping the depth part," Peter joked. "I heard there are still many in Jerusalem who question your spiritual conversion. Unfortunately, many have scars on their backs and hearts. It causes them to question your apostleship." He sat down on a bench beside me.

"Yes, I've found this out firsthand over the last couple of days."

"We must soften their hearts," Peter declared. "Where are you staying in Jerusalem?"

"Not far from here, with my aunt and uncle."

"Please stay with us while you're in the city. It's the least we can do for you. Also, it might help others accept the truth of your conversion and apostleship."

"Thank you. I accept your kind offer."

"Our friend James stayed and slept here right after he became a believer. Let's go upstairs to enjoy the night air, check out your sleeping quarters, and meet my wife," he suggested. We got up from the wooden benches and went upstairs to the roof. Peter's wife and his young friend, John Mark, were sitting in wicker chairs, identifying Greek constellations.

"Erev tov!" They responded in harmony.

"This is Paul. He will be staying with us for a while." I could tell by Peter's tone he was the kind of individual who could make things happen.

"I will fix you some flat cakes and get some bed linens," Peter's wife kindly offered.

"Thank you!" I said as she and John Mark went downstairs.

"I hear you have a unique ministry. You preach the Gospel to both Jews and Gentiles!"

"Yes, for there is no difference between Jew and Gentile in the Lord's eyes. He is Lord of all and richly blesses all who call on him, for everyone who calls on the name of the Lord will be saved."

"I'm a Jew! I'm proud of my Hebrew heritage! I have never eaten anything impure or unclean food. Your words sound like they may cause dissension in the Jerusalem synagogues and churches. But, I've been known to deny another's ministry." Peter's dominant personality echoed throughout his remarks.

"The Gospel is for Jews and Gentiles!"

"Five years ago during the Pentecost, after Christ ascended to Heaven, God sent down another gift from Heaven, the Holy Spirit. The Holy Spirit descended upon a large group of Jews. But now, you think this gift is for Gentiles, too?" Peter asked. He sought information through questions like a good leader does when seeking clarity.

"Yes! Both Jews and Gentiles can be filled with the power of the indwelling Holy Spirit."

Peter took a deep breath and shrugged his shoulders. We were two peas in a pod, but different pods. Peter was still extremely orthodox in his Jewish thoughts. I was more accepting of non-Jewish behavior because of my childhood years in Hellenistic Tarsus and the events over the last three years.

"Jesus eliminated all racial barriers. Jews and Gentiles are equal in God's eyes. Gentiles can come to the Lord without converting to Judaism or becoming proselytes. They are saved by faith in Christ, just like us! As James said, 'Our Lord doesn't show favoritism.'"

"We are both tools of the Lord, but we have a slightly different point of view on Gentiles. Allow me to pray about this topic," he stated.

"Tell me about the earthly Jesus." I changed topics to a more comfortable subject.

"His ministry was filled with unconditional love, compassion, forgiveness, sharing, humility, humor, and wisdom," Peter stated, taking this opportunity to teach me. He expounded upon these virtues of Jesus throughout the evening. Peter shared the Gospel with an unmatched passion. One could easily see his sinful life had been altered by Christ's sinless life.

Over the next forty eight hours, I was a fixture at Peter's side. The daylight hours were spent helping people rebuild their homes in the Lower City and evangelizing in the Jewish marketplaces. The evening hours were devoted to listening to Peter expound on Jesus' Palestinian ministry.

During those two days I couldn't help notice Peter's selfless, management skills he learned from an incredible leader. Jesus taught him to embrace individuals, counsel them in their issues, bring out the best in others, and not belittle them. Peter focused on the potential of people and inspired a godly maturity in their character. His integrity created an atmosphere of unity and caring. He was a supportive, truthful, and humble decision-maker, with a firm focus on the goal at hand.

～～

People were knocking on Peter's front door at all hours of the day and night. Zealots would stand at his threshold, cursing him. Roman soldiers would periodically harass him. Orthodox Pharisees would express their distain for his teachings. Believers would seek his apostolic insights. The sick and lame prayerfully asked for his healing touch. He reverently answered every knock.

On my third night at Peter's home, John Mark and I kept him from sleep. It was already late when I asked Peter, "Could you tell us of Jesus' miracles?"

John Mark got out his stylus and papyrus scroll. He was always taking notes when Peter spoke.

"Yes. The disciples and I were blessed to behold countless miracles. I vividly remember watching Jesus heal my mother-in-law. She was suffering from an extremely high fever. He took her hand, and the fever left her body! Another time, there was a lady who had been experiencing twelve years of an endless menstrual cycle. She simply touched His cloak and she stopped bleeding!"

"Amazing!"

"Jesus healed a deaf mute man when He placed his fingers upon the man's ear and tongue! A paralytic man was miraculously restored to health by his friends' faith in Christ! A man's son, suffering from epileptic seizes since childhood, was cured by his father's belief in the Lord."

"The power of faith," I acknowledged.

Peter paused for a second, then continued, "We also saw Jesus take the hand of a synagogue ruler's recently deceased daughter. The young girl immediately stood up and walked around the room! That miracle left me speechless for days."

"Awesome!" John Mark exclaimed, scratching his scalp with his strong, lean, scribe's fingers.

"Even nature responded to His commands! One day, a violent storm beset our boat on the Sea of Galilee. We were about to sink and perhaps drown. We awoke Jesus from His sleep. He arose and said, "Quiet! Be Still!" The mere sound of His voice calmed the sea. Another time, He walked on water from the shoreline out to our boat in the middle of the Sea of Galilee!"

"Wow, he had power over his father's creation." I acknowledged.

"What behavioral characteristics did you observe in Jesus?" the young writer inquired. John Mark was a very loquacious person. He had a zest for the Gospel and recording accurate events.

"Jesus spent the hours of every morning, every afternoon, and every evening in prayer to God. He prayed without ceasing. He loved little children and always made time for them. Jesus taught all ages with heavenly authority and love. Also, He treasured ministry work. On one occasion, Jesus sent us out two-by-two to share the Gospel, and gave us authority over evil spirits."

"How did Jesus view people's response to the Gospel?" I asked.

"That can be summarized by his *Parable of the Sower.* Jesus said, 'A farmer went out to sow his seed. As he was scattering the seeds, some fell along the path and the birds came and ate it up. Some fell on rocky places where it did not have much soil. It sprang up quickly, because the soil was shallow. But when the sun came up, the plants were scorched, and they withered because they had no root. Other seed fell among thorns, which grew up and choked the plants, so that they did not bear grain. Still other seed fell on good soil. It came up, grew and produced a crop, multiplying thirty, sixty, or even a hundred times,'" Peter responded.

"Did he interpret the parable for you?" I asked.

"Yes. Jesus explained, 'The farmer sows the word of God. Some people are like seed along the path, where the word is sown. As soon as they hear it, Satan comes and takes away the word that was sown in them. Others, like seed sown on rocky places, hear the word and at once receive it with joy. But since they have no root, they last only a short time. When trouble or persecution comes because of the word, they quickly fall away.'" Peter's voice revealed his overwhelming passion for the Gospel.

"The others?" John Marked inquired impatiently.

"Still others, like seed sown among thorns, hear the word, but the worries of this life, the deceitfulness of wealth and the desires for other things come in and choke the word, making it unfruitful. Others, like seed sown on good soil, hear the word, accept it, and produce crops thirty, sixty or even a hundred times what was sown.'"

John Mark and I sat there hugging our knees for a while, comprehending the parable. Both of us were amazed how Jesus' parables revealed the truth to those who sought it, but veiled the truth from those who didn't seek it. We stored this parable in our memories, realizing the impact one believer has on humanity. Both of us wanted to make a difference, not be indifferent.

"The last group is the one who leads others to heaven," Peter announced.. His caring tone and sincere mannerism revealed how the Lord shaped his apostleship.

"How about the events that occurred during His last week on earth?" I asked.

"It's nearly a new day. Let's get some sleep. Tomorrow night, I'll share with you those events surrounding Jesus' last week." John Mark and I both shook our heads yes. We all went to bed mats or wooden benches for a few hours of sleep.

Chapter Thirty
A Time of Passion

"Take heart. Suffering, when it climbs the highest, last but a little time."
Aeschylus

The next day John Mark, Peter, and I helped people in the Lower City frame their walls. Several hours after sunset, we returned to Peter's house. "I know it's late, but my mind can't rest. It's filled with questions regarding Jesus' last week on earth."

"Same here. Please, share your insights," John Mark chimed in.

Peter sat down on a wooden bench. "Several days before the Passion Week, we were walking south in Palestine. Jesus took us aside and said, 'We are going to Jerusalem, and the Son of Man will be betrayed to the chief priest and teachers of the law. They will condemn him to death and will hand him over to the Gentiles, who will mock him and spit on him, flog him and kill him. Three days later, he will rise.' We didn't understand what he meant at the time."

"But, now we do!" John Mark exclaimed while recording Peter's words.

"We arrived outside Jerusalem late Sunday afternoon before the Passover. Jesus sent two disciples into the city to retrieve a donkey. It was a colt no one had ever ridden. When they returned, Jesus mounted the donkey atop the Mount of Olives. He looked down upon the city and He wept. Large crowds of Jerusalem's residents and Passover pilgrims gathered outside the city gate. Several people spread their cloaks on the road, while others laid palm branches before Him as He rode the donkey from the Mount of Olives into the city. The huge crowds were joyfully shouting, 'Hosanna! Blessed is He who comes in the name of the Lord! Blessed is the coming kingdom of our father, David! Hosanna in the highest!'" said Peter.

"This was the fulfillment of Zechariah's ancient prophecy. Our Messianic King would enter Jerusalem on a donkey," I responded.

"Yes. The city was abuzz about Jesus. We went to the temple and stayed there for a while, then left since it was already late. There were no vacant rooms in Jerusalem's inns because they were filled with Passover pilgrims. So we went to Bethany for the night."

"A suburb of Jerusalem," John Mark interjected, then sheepishly realized everyone in the room was aware of Bethany's location.

"Monday morning when we left Bethany, Jesus was hungry. He saw a fig tree with leaves but no figs and said, 'May no one ever eat fruit from you again.' On reaching Jerusalem, Jesus entered the temple area and drove out those who were buying and selling there. He overturned the tables of the money changers and the benches of those selling doves, and would not allow anyone to carry merchandise through the temple courts. He said, 'Is it not written: My house will be called a house of prayer for all nations? But you have made it a den of robbers.' The chief priests and teachers of the law heard what he did in the temple and began looking for a way to kill him, for they feared him."

"I agree! The Court of Gentiles is a den of robbers. I've felt that way, since my first visit at age thirteen," I said.

"Tuesday morning, we returned to Jerusalem after spending the night in Bethany. Jesus used the now withered fig tree to teach us to have faith in God. He healed the lame and blind, while teaching the growing crowds in parables. Once we were inside the Holy Temple the chief priest, teachers of the law, and elders questioned Jesus' authority, several times. They were all trying to trap him."

"Could you share an encounter?" I asked, opening a new jar of octopus ink for John Mark.

"One of your Pharisee colleagues asked Jesus if they should pay taxes to Caesar. He knew of their hypocrisy and said, 'Why are you trying to trap me? Bring me a denarius and let me look at it.' A Herodian gave Him a coin, and Jesus asked, 'Whose portrait is this? And whose inscription?' They all responded 'Caesar.' Jesus said, 'Give to Caesar what is Caesar's, and to God what is God's.'"

"His humanity didn't take away from his deity," John Mark uttered.

"They immediately comprehended His wisdom and quit trying to entrap him. His eminent words overwhelmed them. He did many wonderful things that day. The Jewish leaders grew extremely jealous of His parable teaching and vast following, so they plotted among themselves to kill Jesus. Unknown to us, before we headed back to Bethany for the night, Judas, a disciple and our treasurer, met with the High Priest and Jewish leaders to betray Jesus."

"Was Caiaphas the High Priest during those days?" John Mark inquired.

"Yes, he was. Wednesday, the Lord concluded His public ministry and went into seclusion. Thursday afternoon, Jesus instructed John and me to go into the city and prepare for the Passover dinner. A few hours later, just before sunset, all the apostles gathered in an upper room not far from here. We were all arguing our case for the seats of honor, next to Jesus, when He arrived for the Passover meal.

"Upon entering the room, Jesus washed everyone's feet. He did this to show us how we should humble ourselves unto others. He wanted us to know we're all servants in God's work. Then He revealed, 'I tell you the truth, one of you will betray me – one who is eating with me. Woe to that man who betrays the Son of Man! It would be better for him if he had never been born.' Judas got up from the table and ran downstairs into the street.

"Jesus took the bread and said, 'Take, eat this is my body.' Then he took the cup of wine and passed it among us, saying, 'This is my blood of the new covenant, which is shed for many. I tell you the truth, I will not drink again of the fruit of the vine until that day when I drink it anew in the kingdom of God.'"

"Hence, the Last Supper!" John Mark interrupted.

"I guess you could call it that. Again, we debated among ourselves who was the greatest of the disciples. Jesus said, 'You will all fall away.' I declared, 'I will not!' He looked at me and said, 'I tell you the truth, today yes, tonight before the cock crows twice, you yourself will disown me three times.'" Peter recalled painfully.

"That would have been when the Roman guard changes the Cock Crow Watch, before sunrise. With all the people in Jerusalem for Passover, the Roman sentry would have blown his trumpet twice, once to the east and once to the west, to inform the additional Roman soldiers throughout Jerusalem it was time to change watch," John Mark enunciated.

Peter nodded then continued, "After the Passover meal, we went to the Garden of Gethsemane and Jesus said to us, 'Sit here while I pray.' Jesus took James, John, and me into a remote section of the garden. He became deeply distressed and troubled then said, 'My soul is overwhelmed with sorrow to the point of death. Stay here and keep watch.'

"Jesus went on a little ways and fell to His knees in prayer. To my amazement, I noticed Him sweating drops of blood. I heard Him praying aloud about the hour at hand. 'Abba, Father, everything is possible for You. Take this cup from me. Yet not what I will, but what You will.' Then I fell asleep while an angel from Heaven appeared to Him and strengthened Him.

"Then Jesus returned he awoke me from my slumber, 'Simon, are you asleep? Could you not keep watch for one hour? Watch and pray so that you will not fall into temptation. The spirit is willing, but the body is weak.' Jesus came back later, and we were all asleep again. We did not know what to say to him. Jesus came back a third time and said, 'Are you still sleeping and resting? Enough! The hour has come. Look, the Son of Man is betrayed into the hands of sinners. Rise! Let us go! Here comes my betrayer!'

"It was then I saw Judas and the armed crowd, sent by the chief priest, teachers of the law, and synagogue elders. Judas had arranged a signal with them: "The one I kiss is the man.' Judas walked over to Jesus and kissed Him on both cheeks. Within seconds, the men seized and arrested Jesus." Peter paused and took a drink of water.

"The betrayal happened just as Jesus predicted!" I marveled as Peter shook his head.

"I violently reacted by grabbing a sword from a temple guard's scabbard. I cut off the ear of the High Priest's servant. The Lord grabbed his ear, pressed it against the side of his head, and it was miraculously healed."

"He loved even those who came to kill Him," mused John Mark while recording Peter's remarks.

"Jesus said, 'Am I leading a rebellion, that you have come out with swords and clubs to capture me? Every day I was with you, teaching in the temple courts, and you did not arrest me. But the Scriptures must be fulfilled.' Jesus insisted His arrest be a peaceful event. Then Jesus persuaded the crowd's leaders to let His disciples go free. They reluctantly freed us while binding His hands. We deserted him and fled in the Garden of Gethsemane, amidst the olive groves and oil presses. We watched Him from a distance."

"Caring, grace, and truth were exhibited in his life," I proclaimed.

"It was just after midnight when Jesus voluntarily left the Garden of Gethsemane with the blood-thirsty mob. They took Him to Annas' and

Caiaphas' house. The Sanhedrin were there and searching for evidence to execute Jesus. They listened to numerous, false testimonies, but the stories conflicted with each other."

"Lies have no foundation to stand upon," interjected John Mark.

"The High Priest asked Him, 'Are you the Christ, the Son of the Blessed One?' Jesus responded, 'I am. And you will see the Son of Man sitting at the right hand of the Mighty One and coming on the clouds of heaven.' The Jewish leaders shouted, 'He has just condemned himself worthy of death. This is blasphemy!' They spat on Him and struck Him with their fists."

"Where were you during Jesus' trials?" I inquired.

"During Jesus' mock trial I was in Caiaphas' courtyard warming myself by a fire. Caiaphas' servant girl asked me, 'Were you with Him?' I said, 'I don't know or understand what you're talking about.' I went into Caiaphas' entryway, and she told those there, 'He's one of them,' but I denied it a second time. Not long after that, others claimed, 'Surely, you are one of them, for you are a Galilean,' but I swore, 'I don't know this man you're talking about.' Then, the Roman trumpet sounded twice for the changing of the Cock Crow Watch. I had disgracefully disowned Jesus three times before the cock crowed twice." Peter sniffed.

"Thrice!" We both were shocked by what was said by this apostle and saint.

"Yes. Just like He predicted," Peter contritely replied.

"A female, congregational member from the Tarsus synagogue and a male, classmate from the School of Gamaliel told me about Jesus' last day. Would you please share your insights on what happened that day?"

"Jesus was unjustly tried six times Friday morning: once by the former High priest Annas, his son-in-law, the High Priest Caiaphas, the Sanhedrin, Herod Antipas, and twice by Pontius Pilate.

"The smell of moral decay filled the city. It was such a pungent smell it made me ill," John Mark remarked.

"Pilate found no fault in Jesus either time! So he decided to offer the crowd Rome's customary gesture of releasing a Jewish prisoner during the Pentecost Festival. Pilate offered to free Barabbas, the insurrectionist, or Jesus, the Messiah. The Jewish leaders planted conspirators throughout the crowd and encouraged the multitude to call for Barabbas' release. After those shouts, Barabbas was set free. Pilate asked the crowd, 'What shall I do then with the one you call the king of the Jews?' They shouted, 'Crucify him! Crucify him!'"

"I remember that day. Pilate handed Jesus over to be crucified then literally washed his hands of the crowd's demands," chimed in John Mark.

"The Roman soldiers manhandled Jesus into the Praetorium. This was after they had dragged Him across Jerusalem for eight hours without letting him sleep. The entire company of soldiers assigned to Pilate watched Jesus be flogged thirty-nine times.

"After His flogging, a company of Roman soldiers spat on Him and pulled hair from His beard. Then they put a cloth bag over His head and ruthlessly beat Him in the face, with their fists and a staff. They scoffed, 'Prophesy who's hitting you!' The soldiers placed a woven chaplet on Jesus' head. The crown was made from palm pine branches with finger length thorns. Also, they dressed Him in a faded, red military cloak since it looked like a royal, purple robe. Then the soldiers mocked Him as a king."

"He endured all this without calling down an army of angels," I thought out loud.

"Just after the second hour (8:00 in the morning) the centurion on duty ordered the Roman soldiers, 'Have the prisoner carry his crossbeam up to Golgotha for crucifixion. Tie the beam to his shoulders.' Jesus struggled carrying His heavy, wooden beam up the steep road after all the beatings. He collapsed, and the centurion ordered a man in the throng, Simon of Cyrene, to carry the crossbeam. It was the third hour when they reached the top of Golgotha. The Roman soldiers drove iron spikes, half cubit long, through each of His wrists into the wooden crossbeam. They placed his feet atop each other on the upright beam and drove another enormous spike through both feet. Then they raised the wooden cross into a vertical position." Peter excruciatingly recalled the events.

"It pains me just to think about it!" John Mark flinched in agony.

"The Roman soldiers removed Jesus' garments. They cast lots for His clothes beneath the wooden cross. The chief priests and the teachers of the law mocked him among themselves, 'He saved others, but he can't save himself.'"

"These events fulfilled numerous passages from the *Torah, Prophets,* and *Psalms,*" I said.

"Yes. Jesus struggled for about three hours to breathe. With a loud cry, Jesus breathed his last, yielding His life as an atonement for our transgressions. The Roman centurion on duty saw Jesus give up the ghost and told his soldiers, 'Truly, this man was the Son Of God.' One of the centurion's soldiers shrugged his shoulders, then stuck a long spear into

Jesus' side to make sure He was dead. It was around the sixth hour or noon."

"There was a severe earthquake and total darkness filled the city from the sixth hour till the ninth hour," John Mark recalled.

"What did they do with his body?" I inquired.

"Joseph of Arimathea, a prominent member of the Council, boldly asked Pilate for Jesus' body. Pilate approved thinking no harm would come from the gesture. Several of us carried Jesus' deceased body on a bier to Joseph's tomb. His sepulcher was cut out of solid rock. It had two rooms, typical of a rich person's grave, one room for the corpse and another room for grieving visitors.

"Several women washed the Lord's body and wrapped it in linens. Unfortunately, they didn't have time to buy spices to line the linens because it was nearly dark. And as you know by Mosaic Law, his body had to be buried by sunset."

"Yes, before the start of our Sabbath." I interjected.

Peter took a drink of rain water then said, "The Roman officials, at the urging of the Sanhedrin, had a huge circular stone rolled against the entrance of the tomb, so nobody could steal his body. Then they sealed the tomb."

John Mark added, "The Roman officials refused to post their soldiers there, so the Chief Priest hand picked four highly respected temple guards. They were posted outside His tomb with their weaponry. Meanwhile, we went to Peter's house to honor the Sabbath and mourn the Lord's death." He couldn't resist helping Peter tell the story.

"Saturday, the temple guards stood watch at Jesus' tomb." Peter continued, "Early on Sunday; the third day after his crucifixion, Mary Magdalene; His mother, Mary; and Salome, the mother of James and John, took spices to anoint Jesus' body to express their devotion to the Lord. Upon approaching the tomb, they noticed the very large stone was rolled away from the entrance."

"To their amazement, they found the tomb, empty!" John Mark interjected.

"Yes, and an angel standing at the tomb told them, 'He has risen! He is not here.' The angel sent the women back to us. They returned to the house breathless, and then blissfully told us of the wonderful news. In disbelief, John and I ran as fast as we could to the tomb. Our eyes couldn't believe what they saw: an empty tomb! John and I quietly stood there in bemusement till we recalled Jesus' words: 'After three days, I will rise again.' Then John shouted, '*He has risen!*'"

"How do you deal with accusations or clouds of suspicion that someone took His body?" John Mark inquired.

"When we reached the empty tomb, all that was in it were his funeral linens. The flat linens were still wrapped up in the shape of His body. Anyone stealing a body would have taken the body and linens, not rewrap the linens in the shape of a body with guards outside," answered Peter.

"You found an empty tomb, the foundation of faith in Christ." I remarked, reading the story's impact written all over Peter's face.

"Sunday evening, we bolted the doors to my house, because we feared the Jewish leaders would come for us. Instead, Jesus miraculously appeared unto us in this house without entering through a door or window. He breathed upon us and said, 'Receive the Holy Spirit. If you forgive anyone his sins, they are forgiven. If you do not forgive them, they are not forgiven.'"

"Our Lord appeared unto hundreds of others over the next forty days," John Mark added.

"The last time we saw Jesus was on the forthieth day after His resurrection. He instructed us, 'Go into the entire world and preach the Good News to all creations. Whoever believes and is baptized will be saved, but whoever does not believe will be condemned.' Then Jesus ascended into heaven to sit at the right hand of God and prepare an eternal place for all who believe in Him." Peter concluded.

"That is where Christ was when he spoke to me!" I exclaimed.

I was amazed at how Jesus took a cadre of fishermen, common laborers and tax collector, and placed the Good News of the Gospel in their hands. He entrusted them with the foundation for His Gospel here on Earth. I was in awe of how God designed a plan of eternal salvation that can save anyone, at anytime, in any place, simply through faith in the Lord.

"Once again, it's late. We'd better get some rest. Tomorrow is the Sabbath. Paul may have a busy morning," suggested our host. A few minutes later, Peter's house was filled with the sounds of deep sleep.

Chapter Thirty-One
A Time of Trouble

"Man is born unto trouble, as the sparks fly upward."
Job

Just before sunrise, there was a loud knock on Peter's front door. John Mark groggily got up from a wooden bench and answered the door. It was James, barely recognizable in the pre-dawn's gray sky. "If we're going to make the synagogue's morning worship service, we need to leave in five minutes." James' voice echoed throughout the house and all the way up to the rooftop. Four minutes later, we were all dressed in our Sabbath attire and headed out the door.

"Glad you have a positive, working relationship with the Pharisees and Sadducees," John Mark announced as he followed the pillar of the Jerusalem church down a narrow alley.

Peaceful times existed between Judaism and The Way, because James strictly followed the Mosaic and oral laws, and he strongly encouraged all believers to adhere to those edicts. James took great effort in making sure the church didn't violate any Jewish laws and traditions. All this kept the High Priest, the synagogue elders, and the zealots at bay. Church violence had drastically abated over the last three years.

"Thankfully, those religious leaders don't keep that close an eye on us these days!" James whispered over his shoulder. One could easily see Jesus' fingerprints all over his half-brother's life.

"That may change today, since the whole city is in an upheaval over Saul," exclaimed John Mark.

"Yes, let's hope we're not placing the pot on the fire!" Peter's wife expressed.

"This city was at a boiling point long before Jesus' and Paul's ministry!" Peter seethed.

"It doesn't take much to heat things up in this city." Barnabas chuckled after joining us just two blocks from the synagogue.

The late night session with Peter and his numerous stories of Jesus' ministry had my evangelical boldness boiling. I was mentally and spiritually prepared to speak on behalf of the Lord even though the hair on the back of my neck was standing at attention.

~~

When we entered the City of David Synagogue, Jerusalem's largest congregation, it was busting at the seams. A large assemblage from Stephen's Greek-speaking synagogue was among the congregation. His murderers had come to get a glimpse of their former accomplice.

The congregation's elders reluctantly welcomed me. The High Priest was present that morning but refused to acknowledge me. His presence was meant to be more daunting than threatening. Once we were seated, the High Priest signaled for the worship service to begin. This synagogue's Sabbath service consisted of six parts including a set cycle of 154 homilies.

The Sabbath service began as normal. First, everyone stood and quoted the Shema. Then Salomon Ben-Ammi, a synagogue elder and Sadducee, directed the second part of the worship services. He leaded us in prayer and recited several blessings from *Psalms*.

Next, a layperson was chosen from the congregation to read from the *Torah*. A baker from Herod's Marketplace stood up and read, "Man does not live on bread alone, but every word that comes from the mouth of the Lord."

A visiting elder from a Caesarean synagogue fulfilled the fourth stage of the worship service, reading from the *Prophets*: "A shoot will come up from the stump of Jesse; from his roots a Branch will bear fruit. The Spirit of the Lord will rest on him – the Spirit of wisdom and of understanding, the Spirit of counsel and of power, the Spirit of knowledge and of the fear of the Lord – and he will delight in the fear of the Lord."

The visiting Caesarean elder, who only knew of my past, turned to me and asked, "Saul of Tarsus, would you deliver the 121st homily?" Jerusalem Jews who believed in Christ were no longer given an opportunity to proclaim the fifth part of any Sabbath service.

"Yes! It would be an honor," I replied, thrilled. This was my first time to speak publicly in a Jerusalem synagogue since the conversion.

I prayerfully walked to the front of the synagogue amidst total silence. "Jehovah revealed his sovereign plan of eternal salvation and the shoot from the stump of Jesse to me, over the last three years," I said. The congregation moved toward the edge of their wooden benches, intensely listening to my every breath and word.

"Jehovah first instructed me on a road outside of Damascus, when a brilliant light shone down from Heaven." I paused and said with boldness, "The shoot, Jesus, the Son of God spoke to me and changed the direction of my heart. Your temple guards are witnesses to this event. Then the Lord said, 'This man is my chosen instrument to carry my name before the Gentiles and their kings, and before the people of Israel.'"

The High Priest stood up and made an unfriendly gesture before storming out of the crowded synagogue. He lived only a stone's throw from the religious center of the Jewish universe, the Holy of Holies, but was no where near its spiritual source.

"Those words the Caesarean elder just read, reveals Jesus as the Messiah. Isaiah also said, 'He bore the sins of many and made intercession for the transgressors.'" Several visiting elders stood up, took off their outer garments, and ripped them into pieces while walking out of the synagogue. This symbolized their disapproval of my message.

"Heresy!" two resident elders yelled. Three other elders from that synagogue motioned for four well-built servants to escort me outside.

I quickly continued, "Death doesn't discriminate. It doesn't see sex, race, color, creed, Jew or Gentile. It embraces everyone with open arms! May you spiritually do the same! May your hearts not differentiate among races! Don't miss the meaning of the Lord's words: love thy neighbor."

"Remove that Hellhound from our Synagogue!" the head elder shouted.

"Suppressing the truth is an act of unrighteousness." I declared while being grabbed by four brawny men.

"Blasphemer!" The majority of the congregation screamed as those men physically escorted me from the pulpit. I prayed my words would echo throughout their souls as they dragged me down the aisle.

Several zealots covered me with saliva while others opened the bronze doors. Inside, the head elder quickly performed the sixth and final part of the worship service. He angrily read the blessing from the Torah and gave the departing prayer. Meanwhile, I was being tossed down the synagogue front steps.

When the congregation left the building I was still lying on the dusty street, slowly recovering from the pain of being thrown down twenty marble steps. There were a few, emphatic looks of praise and pity, but most were stares of hatred with murderous thoughts woven into them. Solomon Ben-Ammi, along with a majority of the congregation, turned their shoulders away.

Peter, James, Barnabas, and John Mark helped me up. Then we silently walked back to Peter's house. When we turned onto Peter's alley, Barnabas broke the silence.

"How does our race possess so little wisdom with so much knowledge? The true sign of wisdom is acknowledging what you don't understand."

We went to Peter's house for breakfast, but I was restless as a caged lion. So I excused myself and headed to the Hippodrome Marketplace where the Gentiles did their morning food shopping.

When I passed by the Holy Temple's towering southern wall, another confrontation occurred between Solomon Ben-Ammi and me. He grabbed me by the left arm and bellowed, "Have you lost your senses?"

"No," I responded amiably.

"Yes, you have! Your new faith is futile! Jesus of Nazareth is dead! You are to be pitied above all men." He shouted for everyone to hear who passed by.

"Christ was raised from the dead! You have been to his empty tomb. Your own wife and children saw his resurrected body. Your mother beheld his ascension to heaven!" I replied.

Solomon stood speechless and growing in anger. "You will never find that which you seek. The door upon which you knock is closed. You can't receive the blessing for which you ask!" He screeched in frustration while squeezing my forearm.

"Thankfully, one can obtain those blessings! I've sought and have found the Messiah. I've knocked and heaven's door has been opened. I've asked and received eternal life."

"Why can't you be like James? And try to maintain harmony within our community." Ben-Ammi shouted in disappointment then released my flexed forearm.

"Each person has his own godly gift. James is blessed with the gifts of unity. Sorry my gift of evangelism offends you."

"Your words scratched at the core of my soul."

"My words ring of truth. You walk the line, but don't embrace the

Living vine. You know the plan, but not the Man. You focus on who you are, not whose you are." I replied with kindness.

Solomon shot a dirty look at me then walked away. He hollered over his shoulder, "You'd better watch out for your safety while in Jerusalem! Hope you're dying to depart the Holy City, because you're flirting with death, and death is flirting with you."

"Thanks for the warning. Even if death knocks on my door, I'll remain faithful to the Lord," I stated boldly.

The next seven days remained relatively peaceful. During the morning hours I taught Gentiles in the Hippodrome Marketplace. I spent the afternoon preaching in the Holy Temple and evening hours were devoted to speaking outside the Amphitheatre.

~~

During my second week as Peter's house guest, things got a little unstable in Jerusalem. People reacted in either a positive or negative way to my teaching. Unfortunately, the Jewish community became split again as hatred and strife filled the city. Jerusalem's quarters were spiritually divided for the first time in several years.

People began throwing fruits, vegetables, and verbal insults at me when I evangelized in public places. The marketplaces turned into debating grounds. Orthodox Jews constantly disputed the Gospel; however, my God-given dialectic skills overwhelmed them. The Holy Spirit used these disputations to show several synagogue elders The Way. This really angered the Sadducees and Sanhedrin.

Harsh words dominated conversation between Jewish believers and non-believers in residential neighborhoods. Religious fights broke out in city streets and on synagogue steps. Zealots started beating up church leaders on their way home from work. House churches were being set ablaze. Religious fever accounted for the hostility among the populace.

Hundreds of Nazarenes were excommunicated from their synagogues. Some were fired from their jobs; this religious discrimination caused serious financial dilemmas for those unemployed families.

The Pharisees wanted me gone; the Sadducees detested me; and the High Priest plotted against me. Those who partook in Stephen's stoning and Jesus' crucifixion suggested aggressive actions against this troublemaker from Tarsus. It seems only bloodshed satisfies some. Several zealots recommended they kidnap Peter's wife and only release her once I left the city.

There were even enemies within Jerusalem's church. Some still questioned the validity of my conversion. Others disapproved of my mission to the Gentiles. Several of those who spoke out against me were believers who had quit their jobs and were merely waiting for Jesus' return. They were a financial yoke on the church. Now, they were also a verbal burden to my efforts. It seemed my ministry eased the troubled and troubled those at ease.

Everywhere I went, people shouted abrasive remarks. There were only a few in Jerusalem who firmly stood beside me: Barnabas, James, Peter, and John Mark. Humility became a close friend, it eliminated the I in pride. Peter's wife was right; I had ignited a spiritual fire and placed the pot over the flames of religious odium.

The dark side was attacking The Way. Even James was being threatened by the zealots. The apostles were extremely concerned about the unrest. Plus, relationships were stressed and patience was thin within the church in Jerusalem.

Chapter Thirty-Two
A Time to Egress

"A man's homeland is wherever he prospers."
Aristophanes

Jerusalem became increasingly split over my ministry as the hours passed. The city was in complete turmoil. The zealots seemed capable of unleashing brutal actions upon any believer.

The atmosphere outside Peter's house was getting precarious. Zealots surrounded the holy saint's habitat every night around sunset yelling profane remarks at me. On my fourteenth night in Jerusalem, we had to stay downstairs with his shutters closed. Stones bounced off his external walls, shutters, door, and rooftop throughout the evening.

I excused myself three hours after sunset, against Peter's wishes, to visit the Holy Temple. My soul sought guidance upon Jerusalem's holy ground. Half of the zealots outside the disciple's dwelling followed, harassed, and shoved me through the city streets. Others joined them along the way, tossing pebbles and insults at me.

Upon reaching the Huldah Gates, the zealots blocked my entrance to the Holy Temple. They spat, shouted obscene words, made rude gestures, and threw wild punches at me. One zealot yelled, "We are not going to let you desecrate our Holy Temple!"

Fortunately, Gamaliel strolled by and demanded, "Let this man worship in peace within the Holy Temple. I told you once before, if their purpose or activity is of human origin, it will fail. But if it is from God, you will not be able to stop them; you will only find yourselves fighting against God." They reluctantly stepped aside.

Forty minutes later John Mark found me praying in the Court of

Women. He informed me, "The zealots are still waiting for you outside the Huldah Gates. However, the zealots at Peter's place have gone home."

"Thanks for the update, but what caused the zealots to leave Peter's house?" I asked looking up from my knees.

"After your departure, a large group of saints arrived at Peter's house. They decided to have a prayer meeting. They knew in times of crisis the Lord's saints fall to their knees."

"Those prayer warriors know, things happened when God's people pray!" I remarked, standing up.

"Peter began the prayer meeting with some insightful words from the Holy Spirit. His inspirations were part of two short letters he has been working on."

"What did Peter say?" I asked, brushing dust from my knees.

"He said, 'We have an inheritance that can never perish, spoil, or fade, kept in heaven for you... Like newborn babies, crave pure spiritual milk, so that by it you may grow up in your salvation.

"Always be prepared to give an answer to everyone who asks you to give the reason for the hope that you have... Be self-controlled and alert. Your enemy the devil prowls around like a roaring lion looking for someone to devour... If you are insulted because of the name of Christ, you are blessed." John Mark recalled.

"Those words will bring hope and comfort to people being persecuted for their faith."

"After those words, Peter prayed for the situation at hand because he knew prayer releases God's power. Then everyone prayed and the apostle's abode was physically quaked by the presence of the Holy Spirit! Clay dishes fell from the kitchen cabinet, five large jars full of rainwater toppled over, and wooden benches filled with praying bodies tumbled to the floor."

"What did the zealots outside do?"

"They became frightened and ran home. Inside the saints continued to pray. Their prayers focused on God and only glimpsed upon the problems at hand." John Mark concluded.

"Thanks for letting me know about Peter's prayer meeting. If you don't mind, I have some praying of my own to do. I will meet you at Peter's house in a little while; I wish to continue worshipping, praising, and petitioning the Lord." I needed to step back from horizontal conversations and focus on a vertical orison. My mind sought earthly silence to hear a heavenly voice.

In quietude I prayerfully recalled my commission to preach the Gospel to Jews and Gentiles. Then I fell into a trance. The Lord appeared and said, "Quick! Leave Jerusalem immediately, because they will not accept your testimony about me."

I arose from my knees and exited the Court of Women. My short legs briskly walked through the Court of Gentiles, down the marble steps and out the Golden Gate. I jogged back to Peter's house to bid a regretful farewell to the apostles and saints.

Upon entering the house, James remarked, "Saul, Jewish antagonism against your ministry is mounting. We have just heard of a plot against your life. Please depart this city now, for your safety!" Before anyone else could speak, James added, "You've put confidence and boldness in the hearts of believers. You have shared your spiritual insights with this city. We are grateful for the way God has used you to enlighten us on Gentiles."

"Faith has trustworthy belief. Hope has confident expectations. Wellbeing has you leaving Jerusalem." Barnabas counseled, putting his arm around me.

"May the sound judgment that dwells in your soul's well be brought to the surface by wisdom's pail." John Mark mused.

"Yes, because it wasn't prudence Samson called upon when he revealed the secret of his strength unto Delilah. It wasn't discretion David yielded to when he lustfully stared upon Bathsheba from his palace roof. It wasn't forbearance Abraham drew on when he twice referred to Sarah as his sister. It wasn't courage this apostle displayed when I denied Jesus three times. Don't let foolishness dribble from your mouth regarding your stay in Jerusalem," Peter advised.

"Thanks you for all your concerns and remarks. The Lord just spoke to me in a vision at the Holy Temple. He instructed me to leave Jerusalem. I'm headed back to the region of Syria and Cilicia tomorrow morning."

"Halleluiah!" the saints cheered in harmony.

"Unfortunately, my teaching has caused too much strife here," I said.

"We have prayed and prayed the Jerusalem populace would hear God's words in your teaching, but they didn't have a teachable spirit. We hoped they'd receive God's new covenant with an open hearts, but they have had hardened hearts. Maybe they will change from the inside out and be dwelling in God's grace when you return to Jerusalem," James remarked.

"I hope they are. I have learned the church isn't built on one saint, one apostle, one preacher or one teacher, but on Jesus Christ. Plus, those who teach His word are not called to fame but to obedience," I acknowledged.

"Paul, you have been blessed to be a blessing to others. God will use you in His time and place. Be patient my brother. Throughout life the Lord changes our settings, conflicts, actions, and resolutions to shape us," encouraged Barnabas.

We all prayed together, late into the night. We asked for a servant's heart, the Lord's boldness, the Holy Spirit's guidance, and God's mercy upon the Jerusalem church. Everyone went home around midnight. Peter's house was dark within minutes, since tomorrow held a long journey for this homeless apostle.

~~

I awoke early and packed my belongings. As I was about to depart, my host informed me, "Barnabas, James, John Mark, and I are accompanying you to Caesarea."

"I appreciate your gesture, but there is no need for you to journey all the way to Caesarea."

"We insist!" said Peter and we all departed the Holy City before sunset.

Upon leaving the city limits, I didn't kick the dust from my feet as a sign of having nothing to do with a metropolis. Instead, I prayed the Lord would bring me back to Jerusalem to preach the Gospel to all races.

It took us two days to walk from Zion's hilly countryside down to Caesarea's seaport. We arrived in Caesarea just before dusk on the second day of our journey. The ship captains' vendors were still hawking transits in the marketplace. I booked passage on an Egyptian grain ship leaving the next morning.

"There's a Jewish family in Caesarea who gracefully opens its doors to traveling believers," Peter informed us in the marketplace. We found the spacious house not far from the harbor. They warmly welcomed us, fed us, and allowed us to bed down early, since they knew we were exhausted from our journey.

The next morning, we arose before sunrise and headed to the dock. While walking past Herod's Mediterranean Palace, John Mark quoted from *Proverbs*, "Do not set foot on the path of the wicked or walk in the way of evil men. Avoid it, do not travel on it; turn from it and go on your way. God be with you."

"John Mark thanks for sharing Solomon's advice."

"Encouragement brings joy. So upon your journeys lend a hand to the needy, embrace all in love, strengthen troubled hearts, be patient with perplexed souls, and reassure the oppressed." Barnabas offered as we approached the dock.

As we stepped onto the Caesarean dock Peter said, "Make every effort to add to your faith, goodness; and to goodness, knowledge; and to knowledge, self control; and to self control, perseverance; and to perseverance, godliness; and to godliness, brotherly kindness; and to brotherly kindness, love."

"Your words of wisdom have been a blessing!" I emotionally declared to everyone in the shadow of the Egyptian ship.

"May they keep you from being ineffective and unproductive in your knowledge of our Lord Jesus Christ," Peter bellowed over the poorly trained crew's final preparations for departure.

"Remember, we who teach will be judged more strictly and remain humble. Also, anyone who chooses to be a friend of the world becomes an enemy of God," James reminded me. Before I stepped onto the gangplank, he added, "Ships are steered by a very small rudder. Likewise the tongue is a small part of the body, but it makes great boasts. The tongue corrupts the whole person, sets the whole course."

"Thanks you for your fellowship." Melancholy and gratefulness accompanied my remarks. Our friendships were woven together like threads in a colorful tapestry.

I boarded the Egyptian boat just before several deck hands raised the fore and aft anchors. My hand and heart bade farewell to those saints as the crew rowed from the dock. I prayerfully gave thanks to the Father of Grace and Son of Salvation for their companionship.

My new friends waved goodbye and returned to Jerusalem as our ship sailed out of the Caesarean harbor. Shortly after they returned to Jerusalem, the church experienced a time of peace. The Holy Spirit temporarily abated the turmoil between Judaism and The Way.

Chapter Thirty-Three
A Time to Speak

"Then words came like a fall of winter snow."
Homer

Our Egyptian grain ship yawed along the Mediterranean crescent because of strong westerly winds. We were caught in a spring storm, but it seemed like a winter gale. Violent, white-capped waves crashed against the port side of our vessel.

Those endless waves pounding against our hull reminded me of sin's incessant assaults against humanity's morality. If one wave didn't overwhelm the boat, the next one took its turn, just like Satan's relentless attacks.

I climbed aloft from the damp, smelly hull to the cold, drenched deck. From the stern I beheld Mount Carmel jutting toward the sea. The fierce storm prevented me from seeing much of the mountain. I imagined my torso leaning against the twisted trunk of an olive tree or resting on the roots of a towering oak tree on Mount Carmel's sloping mountain side.

This mountain was the sight of a famous showdown between God's prophet, Elijah, and four hundred and fifty prophets of Baal. Both religions' prophets made animal sacrifices then prayed to their divine being, "Ignite our altar's fire." Only Jehovah performed a fiery miracle that day. The people fell prostrate and cried, "The Lord – He is God." I prayed beneath flapping canvas sails that one day Jerusalemites would cry out, "The Lord – He is Jesus."

Suddenly, a strong wave nearly capsized the ship. It knocked everyone on the deck off their feet. My hands barely grabbed hold of a starboard lifeline to stay aboard.

Upon pulling myself up, I noticed a Jewish pilgrim emerging from the cuddy. His face was white with seasickness, but still he bawled over the thundering squall. "You're a heretic! You turned Jerusalem upside-down and ruined my pilgrimage from Cilicia to the Holy City!"

I grabbed one of the ship's starboard halyards for additional support. Then, recalled audibly something Peter shared with me, an insight Jesus taught him, "Men will hate you because of me, but he who stands firm to the end will be saved. When you are persecuted in one place, flee to another.'"

"Keep this up, and you will also have to flee Tarsus!" The pilgrim declared, and then spat into the air. A sheet of salt water and his saliva simultaneously splashed against my face.

"The Lord said, 'No prophet is accepted in his hometown," I stated as salt water soaked into my lips.

"I won't listen to your words!" he yelled, storming off toward the stern to vomit.

An Egyptian crewmember working on the bowline overheard our conversation. "Do you speak on behalf of the Jewish God?" He inquired like a soul searching for a spiritual lifeline amidst the deadly sea.

"Yes, I believe in Jehovah and preach the words of His Son."

"What is His Son's name?" the sailor asked as a large, splintered piece of the wooden bowsprit flew over our heads.

"He is called Jesus Christ, Prince of Peace, Morning Star, Blessed Redeemer, Wonderful Counselor, Son of God, Holy One of Israel, The Truth, Light of the World, Lamb of God, King of Kings, Messiah, Son of Man, Lord, Emmanuel, and Savior. Those are just a few of His glorious names!" I wiped away the raindrops flowing down my face with the back of both hands to see this inquisitive sailor's face.

"Please stay on deck! Join me on my watch and share more of His sayings. There are too many waves on this ocean, too many philosophies in this mind, and too many deities upon this earth. I can't figure out which one will guide my vessel home. I seek the truth but I'm dwelling in spiritual darkness!" His brown eyes pleaded beneath one long, heavy black eyebrow.

"Jesus said, 'I'm the light of the world. Whoever follows me will never walk in darkness, but will have the light of life.' Also, 'My kingdom is not of this world. I came into this world to testify to the truth. Everyone on this side of truth listens to me.'" I quoted Jesus as hail the size of large pebbles started to pound against our bodies.

There are dangers in the sea of teaching, like drowning your pupil in information. But the turbulent waves washed those concerns overboard. We spent the next three hours navigating through an uncharted course in The Way. Together on that rocking vessel's deck we swayed from guilt to grace. We were awash in rain and saltwater as well as fellowship and truth.

Before I went below deck to sleep in the hold, my sailor friend said, "Thanks for opening the eyes of my soul and igniting my faith."

"The Lord said, 'Everything is possible for him who believes.'" I exclaimed, climbing down the teak steps.

Wading through ankle high seawater in the hull, I grasped how God places his people in others' lives, especially when others need His help and guidance. God conducts a multitude of events amidst what seems like random circumstances to spark one's faith. We just have to be receptive to His leading regardless of the setting. It's amazing the difference one person can make in another's life.

The next several days, the sea was calm and the skies were clear. Nearly all the crew and passengers stayed aloft to dry out themselves along with their belongings. I spent one of those afternoons helping my sailor friend, tie together the splinter mast with heavy hemp. The vessel's wooden cross enabled him to envision Jesus' selfless act of being crucified for our sins.

～～

Our Egyptian vessel sailed into Tarsus' hectic harbor at high noon. The crew dropped sails, then rowed up a wide, manmade channel into a huge, naturally protected lake fed by the Cydnus River. The lake was filled with Persian costal boats, Greek merchant ships, Egyptian grain vessels, and private Roman crafts.

The crew rowed to the northern edge of the lake. The captain laid anchor next to a colorful private craft belonging to a Roman senator. Rome's privileged usually summered in Tarsus to escape Italy's heat. This Italian bureaucrat was getting an early start on the summer.

Our vessel was immediately surrounded by small water taxis. Barefoot, unshaven taxi rowers climbed Jacob's ladder soliciting business. They wanted to paddle passengers the remaining ten thousand paces up the Cydnus River to Tarsus. Nearly all the passengers boarded dinghies.

I stayed aboard for another hour, encouraging my nautical friend and fellow believer. Then disembarked the vessel, walking north past blooming crape myrtles, budding birch trees, flowering oleanders, and sprouting river communities. Wild red poppies embroidered the Roman road's edges into Tarsus. The aroma of fresh-plowed, brown soil filled the springtime air. I arrived in Tarsus just before sunset.

Tarsus was preparing to feast upon the season of pagan festivals. The city's appetite for Greek culture and knowledge showed up on every street corner. However, I was now ready to feed Tarsus' didactic hunger a new entree, the Gospel of Jesus Christ.

Upon my arrival at my parent's house, Abba embraced me and exclaimed, "Saul, what a blessing to see you! We haven't seen or heard from you for nearly five years, ever since our elders sent you to Jerusalem to investigate reports on that misguided Nazarene carpenter."

"A lot has changed since then!" I said as Ima and Abba hugged their beloved son for nearly three minutes.

"We're going to throw you a huge homecoming feast, tonight! I'm inviting all our family members, friends, and the synagogue elders!" Abba declared.

"Please, don't!" I begged Abba, but he would have it no other way. Ima and all my aunts began cooking numerous kosher dishes. Abba and all the other male relatives went about town inviting people to our feast.

Dinner was spent catching up on Tarsus news and synagogue events. During the meal Abba repeatedly hugged, boasted, and toasted his eminent Pharisee son. Every other minute someone would ask, "Where have you been? What have you been up to?" or "Will you give us an update after dinner?"

When the kashrut feast was over, Abba stood up at the end of our dinner table and demanded, "Saul, tell us of your journey over the last five years."

"Are you sure you want to hear what happened?" I inquired.

"Yes!" my abba ordered.

"Please!" All the dining guests shouted.

"Leave no details untold!" Abba encouraged.

I stood up at the other end of our long, wooden table. Full of lentils, the Lord's boldness, and the Holy Spirit, I told them about being a Pharisee in Jerusalem and all my atrocious acts in Pompey's Prison. Then, I spoke of my conversion and apostleship in Christ.

"How could you? You were a prominent Jerusalem Pharisee! You were my pride and joy! You left an Arabian thoroughbred and return a useless mule!" My father screamed as I silently swallowed my self-worth to abate his disappointment. "You now have nothing and are in the last half of your life!"

"I have my faith in Jesus. He was deity wrapped in humanity."

"This is a nightmare! Your soul has erected a shrine to a sect!" He screamed at me like I was an adolescent.

"The only temple in my soul is an altar to God and His Son, Jesus Christ."

"You've become a pagan like our Gentile neighbors. You selfish...!" He caught himself but continued, "How could you? Since childhood, you were taught to obey the Mosaic and oral laws! You were raised by a Pharisee and you are a Pharisee!"

"The Lord spoke to me!" I responded as an earthen lamp filled with animal fat shined on me. The house became silent, except for the noise our kitchen helpers made slipping out the back door.

"You swapped Judaism for a cult! Those Nazarenes don't even obey our sacrificial laws. They no longer sacrifice animals on the Holy Altar!" He barked, pacing behind our dinner table.

"There is no longer a need for blood sacrifices. The Lamb of God shed his cleansing blood to save humanity. All our sins have been forgiven through his sacrificial death on the cross. We now have direct access to God. I now possess the one true treasure, eternal life in Jesus Christ. So can you!"

"No! No, you don't! You've given up your true treasures - your family, status as a Pharisee, and your convictions to Judaism!" Abba yelled, his volume increasing with each word.

"Jesus said, 'For where your treasure is, there your heart will be also.' My treasure now lies beyond the earthly grave, in Heaven with Christ."

"Your words are like a tooth being pulled from my jaw! You speak like a man who has lost his senses!"

"I'm sorry, Abba. You said leave no details untold. I've been transformed! You gave me earthly life, but the Lord gives me eternal life."

"You are like a finger with leprosy! It must be cut from the body before it inflicts the rest of us!" Abba hollered with flaring nostrils. "Leave this house! Don't come back till you gain your sanity! May God have mercy on your soul!" Abba shouted before throwing several clay dishes and bronze goblets at me.

"Yes, sir." I ducked out the front door, then dejectedly wandered down a busy city street. The party broke up within seconds of Abba's final outburst.

Chapter Thirty-Four
A Time to Heal

"Illness strikes men when they are exposed to change."
Herodotus

I spent the night on the Tarsus Plains praying for family members, friends and Jewish leaders. Before I knew it, the sun was peeking over the horizon at these weary, bloodshot eyes. I got up from my knees and jogged to the Tarsus Marketplace for breakfast.

The sun's rays were still yawning and stretching on the distant horizon when I arrived at the city gates. However, the marketplace was wide awake and preparing for another heathen festival. Street vendors were hawking pagan trinkets; dancing girls lasciviously shook their extremities; and greedy merchants shouted vulgarities at pilgrims.

Within an hour, festival music filled the streets. Cheers poured out over the Coliseum walls, and drunken bodies stumbled from taverns. Gentile pilgrims worshiped pagan idols on street corners while others sought priestly prostitutes in back alleys and on temple steps. I marveled at the difference between Jerusalem and Tarsus. These activities didn't publicly take place in the Holy City.

Aeolus, an elderly Greek gentleman and casual acquaintance, approached me in the marketplace. He was wearing a white toga and had gold rings on every finger and toe. "Paul, I hear you're having problems with your abba and Jewish brethren."

"News travels quickly in Tarsus."

"In some circles, it does."

"It's true. Neither approves of my faith in Jesus Christ, the Son of Jehovah."

"Some Jews are saying you have lost your wisdom and way."

"No, I have found The Way and it has blessed me with heavenly wisdom. Unfortunately, this revelation has turned my abba's pride into bitterness."

"It seems his Hebrew convictions has abducted his love for you. Let me help you through these difficult times." Aeolus offered part of his morning flatbread to an undernourished slave.

"How?" I inquired after side stepping a drunken pilgrim.

"Well, I have always admired your tent-making skills," Aeolus said while purchasing three cilicium bundles from a wool vendor.

"Thank you, but I'm done as a tentmaker. Abba has disowned me! He won't let me in his shop," I declared handing the rest of my breakfast to a starving beggar covered with flies.

"You may or may not know: I'm also a tentmaker, but my old fingers can barely work the needle and wool. Will you work for me? You can teach me about this Jesus while we weave!" Aeolus suggested as several dirt washed nomads walked between us.

"It would be an honor to work for you. Isn't your abba the one who befriended Julius Caesar with a black cilicium saddle? When Caesar visited Tarsus about eighty years ago?" I grunted while picking up two bundles of cilicium for the old craftsman.

"Yes, but let me tell you the rest of the story, since we're talking about our abbas. Not long after Julius Caesar's assassination, Cassius occupied Tarsus during the Roman Civil war. Cassius heard of my abba's kind gesture to Julius Caesar and had him sold into slavery. Abba wore a wooden manumission tablet around his neck for years bearing the name of Aeolus Eneas, his owner and my namesake." He wheezed, carrying the other cilicium bundle to his workshop.

"I never knew that part of the story!"

"Not long after Abba was sold into slavery, Mark Antony and Octavian defeated Brutus and Cassius in Philippi." Aeolus panted, pausing to catch his breath. "Many moons later, Mark Antony journeyed to Tarsus for a romantic rendezvous with Cleopatra. Both were fond of our hometown, since they met here. Mark Antony heard what Cassius had done to my abba. He found abba then set him free! Abba thanked Antony with a black cilicium tent as well as one for Cleopatra." Aeolus concluded as we reached his modest shop.

That morning, I began working for Aeolus as a tentmaker. He was a kind and generous man. He granted me flexibility during the workday, because of the quantity and quality of my craftsmanship, to teach the Gospel in Tarsus.

~~

One summer afternoon when we were about to take a break for lunch, Aeolus asked. "Paul, would you like to join me and watch the Olympic trials at the Coliseum?"

"I guess so. I've never attended a Greek sporting event."

"You've lived an isolated life! Don't you know our hair color reflects how hard we make our guardian angels work? Mine works around the sundial, that's why it's snow white!" Aeolus snickered.

"It looks like my angel is able to take some time off," I joked, rubbing my nearly bald head. "Jewish families don't support the games, since athletes perform their events in the nude."

When we walked out his shop door, five naked athletes jogged past us on their way to compete in the coliseum. "Look at those young men's pectoral muscles and sculpted bodies. Physical perfection is wasted on the young." Aeolus remarked as we headed to the coliseum.

The multitude's cheers inside the coliseum that afternoon motivated me to get back into shape. I started spending lunch breaks at the gymnasium lifting, boxing, and running. These exercises proved useful in tuning up my body and providing illustrations for teaching Gentiles. My exhausted frame shared the Gospel at the gym after nearly every workout.

Several Greek athletes approached me one afternoon outside the gymnasium. A javelin thrower shared, "Some of us might follow The Way, but the circumcision surgery is painful and dangerous. Plus, it diminishes our crowd appeal during the games."

"Circumcision is not necessary or required to be a believer in The Way, just faith in the Lord." I informed them. After that remark my fellow athletes and Gentiles' interest in the Gospel increased twofold.

~~

I started spending Monday and Tuesday evenings at Tarsus' universities. I'd devote the early evening hours to reading the works of Greek writers, like Aristotle's *Discourse on Conduct*, Plato's *Republic*, and Homer's *The Odyssey*. I studied Greek poets like Callinus and Solon, humorous writers of Greek comedy such as Menander, transcribed works of orators like Lyses and Isocrates, and historic writers like Herodotus.

Greek literature was the foundation for Rome's intellectual thought. Greek writers had an economy of words that stimulated one's thoughts. Their works influenced some of my writings.

Wednesday and Thursday nights were spent in cavernous caves by our city dump aiding as well as teaching lepers. Like the Lord, I tried to look at peoples' hearts, not their external appearances, and embrace all in love.

Friday through Sunday nights were devoted to preaching at Tarsus' synagogues. There were probably over a hundred Jewish synagogues in Tarsus. Jewish law stated a congregation only needed ten families to be recognized as a synagogue. The Hellenistic synagogues were the most receptive to my teachings. They frequently called upon me to deliver the Sabbath homily. The parishioners marveled, debated and tolerated my sermons, but their elders did not.

The Diaspora congregations and elders publicly disowned and barred me from their synagogues. They detested my teaching of The Way and visiting Gentile households. Also, family and friends who strictly obeyed the Mosaic and oral laws were at extreme odds with me. I was continuously confronted with verbal harassment in the Jewish community.

"You're a blasphemer and religious heretic!" Local Pharisees shouted at me inside and outside synagogue walls as well as in the marketplaces. Those months of denunciation were difficult, but the bells of heavenly joy daily rang in my soul.

The Jewish elders throughout Tarsus eventually ran out of patience. They believed my religious teachings and actions required a legal proceeding. So several elders accused me of impious acts. The Jewish leaders held an undisclosed trial and within minutes reached a unanimous verdict: "Guilty of Blasphemy!"

Because of Abba's pharisaic status, they decided my behavior wasn't worthy of death. Their punishment instead was a flogging before my entire family and congregation. Jewish law permitted scourging up to forty lashes minus one, in case the lictor miscounted.

Immediately following the Jewish leaders' verdict, four former classmates dragged me from Aeolus' shop. They tied me to a whipping post outside our family synagogue. My feet barely touched the ground because of the wrist straps' height.

A professional flagellant was chosen for the flogging. He chose a whip with metal fragments, broken glass, bone chips, and sharp rocks woven into its leather thongs. It was designed to cut deep into the flesh.

He brutally lashed me thirteen times from the chin down to the navel.

It seemed like a hundred lashes. Then he rested and walked to the other side. He flogged me twenty-six times from the collarbone to my tailbone. Each lashing painfully ripped into me, tearing away chunks of flesh and exposing nerves that shot excruciating pain throughout the body.

Blood flowed from my tattered flesh forming large puddles on the ground. It dripped from my forehead where one of the thong tips ripped open the scalp. When I was within in a lash of death, someone cut loose my hands. I collapsed to the bloody ground, not far from our synagogue's back steps, where I had played as a child.

My father along with several male family members shamefully retrieved and dragged my hemorrhaging body home. Ima lovingly nursed the thirty-nine wounds on my marred body.

The scourging was the most severe, physical pain I had ever experience in my life. Each lashing brought back painful memories of the agony the temple guards and I inflicted upon Jerusalem believers. Also, each thrashing reminded me of the spiritual pain Christ endured for our sins when the Roman soldiers flogged and crucified him.

~~

Over the next five days, I only recall the aroma of prayers filling our stressed household. On the tenth evening of my recovery Ima and Abba pleaded with me, like every other night: "Please denounce The Way! Otherwise, your death is just beyond the sundown's shadow!"

"I can't. I've seen the Lord and felt the scars He endured for our sins."

Not long after that remark Ima's five brothers stopped by our house. Since childhood I referred to them as fingers on a hand, as their personalities and body structures resembled phalanges. All five siblings were Sadducees. The Sadducees didn't believe in resurrection or immortality, because Moses never discussed these topics in the Mosaic Laws. For the same reason, they didn't give much merit to the oral law.

Within minutes Uncle Thumb, who was the closest to me, implored, "Saul, you nearly died because of your convictions to The Way. Death is knocking at your door! Please denounce this religion!"

"Jehovah is more concerned about my holiness than my health. Death is a threshold everyone passes through. Funerals, serious diseases, incapacitating accidents, and physical abuse prompt our minds to wonder what is behind death's door. I now know eternal bliss with Jehovah and His Son, Jesus Christ lies beyond the grave."

"There is no life after death! Our death is a crumb on the floor of life's banquet feast!" Uncle Pinkie barked, perched on the balls of his feet to be seen over his taller brothers.

"Jesus died for our sins. When we place our faith in him, we receive forgiveness for our sins and are blessed with life after death, eternal life." I responded.

"Boy, death is the last course your body will taste. There is no dessert called eternal life!" Uncle Index irately yelled poking his second digit into my blistering chest.

"You have allowed your emotions to override your theology!" Uncle Ringo tetchily shouted. He was the weakest of the brothers but loved jewelry, especially precious stones.

"Jesus' death created a fault line for humanity. We are either on one side or the other side when it comes to Jesus Christ." I responded after turning my head to see where everyone stood, which caused excruciating pain to shoot through my entire body.

"He can only speak words of blasphemy!" Uncle Index angrily screamed, leaning away from my bed.

"Death is the end! Plus, you know we oppose the Nazareth carpenter's teachings! We sent you to Jerusalem to silence his ministry, not spread it!" Uncle Goliath yelled. He was the tallest and leader of the brotherhood.

"Please, don't be like those who have eyes but do not see, who have ears but do not hear," I pleaded. "They're causing you to forsake your First Love, God and His Son, Jesus."

"Revoke those remarks, or you will be expelled from our synagogue. Even worse, it may cost you your life!" Uncle Thumb barked.

"Every moment we spend in these earthly bodies is time spent away from our eternal home in heaven with Jesus." I replied.

"Son, why do you speak these words to your uncles? You know their beliefs on the Nazarene carpenter and death!" Abba snapped, realizing the Gospel can put people at odds.

"Jesus said. 'Do you think I came to bring peace on earth? No, I tell you, but division. From now on there will be… family divided against each other. They will be divided, father against son and son against father.' He is the fork in the road that changes one's direction."

"He is a polarizing figure. He has turned my love into hatred!" Abba shouted.

'He is the stumbling block Isaiah spoke of, 'A stone that causes men to stumble... many will fall and be broken.' There will be division on this earth till Jesus comes again." I responded.

"God didn't punch a hole in the universe and send down His Son! Also, Death isn't the beginning, it's the end!" Uncle Goliath retorted, drawing the battle line in the sand.

"We'll all drink from the fountain of eternal judgment. Death is Satan's conquest over our physical bodies, but the cross is Christ's redemption for our spiritual bodies. May your hearts embrace God's Son before you die, so we can spend eternity together in Heaven."

"That's it! We are going to hold a funeral for you. You are dead to us!" Uncle Goliath barked. Then all five uncles spat on the tile floor beside the bed. This symbolized their denouncement of my family heritage and existence.

"You're out of here tomorrow morning!" Abba screamed as twelve clenched fists stormed out of the house.

The next day I left my childhood home, permanently excommunicated from our synagogue and Tarsus's Jewish community. I was publicly denounced by all family members and abandoned by all Hebrew friends.

It took several more weeks to recover from the flogging. Aeolus was kind enough to let me recover and spend those weeks in his tent shop. Meanwhile, I experienced tremendous growth in my faith, faith that seemed irrational within the Jewish neighborhoods and beyond rationale in the Gentile communities.

So I turned to other cities. I spent my days off traveling throughout Cilicia and along the Mediterranean coastline, visiting first the synagogues, then the Gentiles. Many hardships were experienced during those months, but adversities have a way of clarifying priorities. They can created a change in direction and offered spiritual insights which otherwise may not have been grasped.

Chapter Thirty-Five
A Time to visit Heaven

"Heaven is my throne and the earth is my footstool."
GOD

Four months after the brutal flogging, I returned to our family's orthodox synagogue, hoping time had abated its disdain for the Gospel and me. Once again I was seized by synagogue elders and zealots. They viciously flogged me for blasphemy and heresy.

I was a religious liability as well as a personal embarrassment to my family, synagogue, and Tarsus' Jewish community. Jesus' words echoed in my mind: "I tell you the truth, no prophet is accepted in his hometown.'"

My residence became a Tarsus foothill cave. I moved there after my second flogging and eviction from Abba's house. My Pharisee education meant nothing among fellow cave dwellers. I spent days in solitude and weeks with nearly nothing to eat.

The seven years that followed have been referred to as my Silent Years. They were full of challenging times and wonderful evangelical memories. I guess you could say they were the bleakest of times and the merriest of times.

Several times I was ambushed by bandits in the Tarsus foothills, beaten by zealots in Phoenician villages, and enslaved by barbarian sheiks in Syrian border towns. I was buried alive beneath a Tarsus Mountain avalanche and nearly lost several extremities during the winter months in my Cilician cave. I was shipwrecked three times and spent several sleepless nights adrift fighting hypothermia in the sea. However, most nights were spent entertaining insomnia on a damp cave floor, rocky mountain trails, cold sand dunes, prickly pine needles, or damp ship decks.

Through these taxing times, God taught me the importance of trust, patience, and perseverance. Also, the Lord taught me how to deal with adversities and challenges that might arise in the future.

A lot of time was spent in prayer and seeking direction for my Gentile commission, during those seven years. My ego anxiously sought a course, while the spirit patiently waited for guidance. It took time to break my prideful human nature, but eventually I lost all faith in the flesh and placed it in the Lord.

~~

One Friday evening during those later, Silent Years, I knelt in prayer on my cold, rocky cave floor, praying for direction. That night I was taken or caught up to the third heaven. My ears heard and eyes beheld eternal rewards awaiting those who placed their faith in the Lord, not in the flesh.

The next morning Akilah, Bedouin neighbor who dwelled in the cave beside me, curiously wandered into my glistening cave. Her Arabic name meant one who reasons. Her native tongue was Aramaic, but she could speak ten languages. She was slender, dark-skinned, and of head-turning beauty. Furthermore, she was dry-witted, inquisitive, thoughtfully articulate, and handy with a sword. She had a pleasant disposition, but was aloof and always had an empty look in her eyes.

Akilah was raised in the Negev Desert, but hastily left there during a deadly skirmish with Sheik Abdul. The sheik massacred her entire clan at a Negev oasis; furthermore, Akilah killed one of Abdul's favorite sons while gallantly trying to defend her youngest sisters. Akilah somehow escaped the genocide and Negev Desert, but Sheik Abdul had a bounty on her head.

Akilah looked at me and frightfully shouted in Aramaic, "Are you all right? Your skin is glowing! Your eyes are blazing. And your hair is sparkling."

"I've just been to the third Heaven!" I ecstatically responded from my knees.

"What is the third Heaven?" Akilah inquired with interest.

"There are three heavens. The first heaven is our atmosphere and clouds. The second heaven is the stars and planets. The third heaven is Paradise, the dwelling place of heavenly hosts. I was caught up to Paradise!"

I exclaimed, using the word Paradise since it was of Persian origin and Akilah knew its meaning.

"Is that why you are glowing?" she queried, covering her eyes.

"Yes, I've just left the presence of God. It is His glory that's radiating from my body," I exclaimed with joy as my voice echoed off the cave walls.

Akilah looked about the cave noticing rock indentations she'd never seen before and remarked, "We don't need this fire for light with you glowing like the sun."

"There's no sun or darkness in Heaven," I mumbled, recalling Heaven's brilliance. "God is the light and Jesus is the lamp that illuminates Paradise. Darkness has been defeated."

"Okay," she replied with skepticism. "How did you get to Paradise?"

"Whether in the body or apart from the body, I do not know, but God knows," I said, getting up from my knees.

Akilah brushed aside her hijab. She partially looked upon me as Heaven's gleam abated and implored, "Let's start from the beginning."

"I was praying, right here!" I elucidated, walking about the cave. "Then suddenly, I found myself in Heaven. A brilliant, radiant light filled the space around me. I was surrounded by God's glory."

"Could you see anyone or anything?"

"The illumination temporarily blinded me, but I could hear others around me dancing and singing praises to God."

Fully able to gaze upon me, my friend asked, "What did you do?"

"In awe, I fell prostate and speechless," I replied as my soul leaped with joy. "After awhile my eyes adjusted to the brilliant light and I beheld God, the Creator."

"Where were you in Paradise?"

"I was in the Father's house, and it had many rooms!"

Akilah looked at the cave's rocky floor then back at me and inquired, "What room were you in?"

"The Throne Room," I said, seeing it again in my memory. "I saw God seated on a throne made of gold, emeralds, sapphires and other gems. A rainbow of magnificent colors encircled His throne."

"Tell me about Allah."

"Our God is so big! He can measure the waters of the world in the hollow of his hand. He held the dust of the earth in a basket and weighed the mountains of earth on a scale."

"Wow."

My throat exploded with excitement, "Grace and mercy flow from His throne."

"Who else was in the Throne Room?"

"At God's right hand sat Jesus, His son. A masculine deity with greenish blue eyes, thick dark eyebrows, brown hair above his shoulders, and short groomed beard. Jesus' clothes were dazzling white, whiter than anyone in the world could bleach them. He had a pure purple sash across his chest, the color purple kings wear.

"He wore a gold crown with diamonds, topaz, onyx and other gems embedded into it. His wrists had healed wounds the size of a large spike. Jesus' mother, Mary, stood and kneeled before his throne. The gifts of forgiveness, salvation, sanctification, joy, and eternal life lay at his nail pierced feet."

Akilah cleared her throat and matter-of-factly asked, "Who was on Allah's left side?"

"At God's left hand sat Gabriel, an archangel, the messenger of God. Gabriel foretold of Jesus' first coming. He will announce his second coming when it occurs and he will be the trumpeter of the Last Judgment. He had huge wings. Beside him stood another archangel, Michael, and a lot of other celestial beings."

"Was anyone else in the Throne Room?"

"Yes, surrounding those thrones were twenty-four other thrones, and seated on theme were twenty-four elders. They were dressed in white and had crowns of gold on their heads. From their thrones came flashes of lightening, rumblings and peals of thunder."

"Sounds frightful," she imagined. "What did God say to you in the Throne Room?"

I marveled at the thought of having heard God's voice and uttered, "Much."

"So tell me about your mystical conversation," Akilah requested, standing with her hands on her hips.

My lips suddenly felt like they were glued together. I recalled God's instructions and said, "I heard inexpressible things, things that man is not permitted to tell."

"Tell me something!"

"Since I can't tell you what these ears heard in the Throne Room, I'll tell you what these eyes saw in Throne Room and Paradise," I offered after sitting by the fire's orange sparks.

"Okay," Akilah responded with disappointment. "What kind of objects did you see in the Throne Room?"

"I saw seven golden lamp stands and an altar. Upon the altar lay a scroll with seven seals as well as the Book of Life. Also, I observed a sea of crystal-clear glass that enabled me to see you, others, and myself here on earth."

"I know what earth looks like, what did Paradise look like?"

"Heaven's splendor is beyond explanation. It has idyllic scenery and outstanding panoramas that exceed anything we've ever seen on earth. A rainbow of colors filled the space above us in Heaven. The Water of Life, a river clear as crystal, flowed from the throne of God throughout Paradise. On each side of the river stood the tree of life, bearing twelve crops of fruit, yeilding its fruit every month."

I continued, lifting the veil to give her a peek at Paradise. "Heaven's entrance gates were made of one giant pearl. The city walls were like jasper, clear as crystal. The streets were made of pure gold like transparent glass. The city's foundation and buildings were made of stones not marble or granite; precious stones like amethyst, carnelian, chalcedony, chrysoprase, diamonds, emeralds, jacinth, pearls, rubies, sapphires, and sardonyx."

~~

Akilah roamed about the small cave contemplating what she had heard. She put a pot of rain water on the flicking flames and said, "Tell me about these other celestial beings."

"Angels?"

"Yes."

"They must have numbered ten thousand times ten thousand. They surrounded God's throne and stood in His presence, it was unbelievable. There were cherubim, four-winged angelic beings that covered their eyes with two wings, and seraphim, six-winged angelic beings."

"Were they carrying anything?"

"Some carried an object that looked like a sword," I shared. "It was to keep Satan, ruler of the fallen angels, out of Heaven. Satan hasn't descended into the pit of fire, hell, yet."

My remark nearly caused Akilah to burn her fingers on the hot coals. She quizzed, "You saw the Evil One?"

"Yes," I replied, feeling a chill run up my spine.

"What did he look like?" She quizzed, brushing a spider from her brown jilbab.

"Like a dragon, but I don't want to go there," I stated still trying to wipe his image from my mind.

"Okay, who else did you see in Paradise?" she asked, untying a bag of cardamom.

"I saw people I knew. Most looked similar to the last time I'd seen them."

"Did they recognize you?"

"It seemed they did."

"Then our memories are not erased at death?"

"I would assume our recollections are not erased. Everyone in Heaven knew me. The saints I had brutally persecuted all remembered my impious behavior, but every one of them embraced me in forgiveness and love. Even Stephen, whose stoning and death I personally oversaw comforted me."

Akilah reached for two coffee mugs then queried, "We are ignorant of activities in Paradise, but Paradise is aware of our actions?"

"Yes."

"So it's like the Olympian Games, where we watch from the stands to see how poorly or effectively athletes perform their physical challenges. Paradise dwellers watch from the Third Heaven to see how poorly or effectively we responded to spiritual challenges."

"Perhaps," I cautiously replied, knowing my limitations.

"Can you comment on these Paradise dwellers' frame of mind?"

"They have no pessimism or fear. Optimism, compassion, love, encouragement, and peace abounded in them. Heaven is a place full of joy and fellowship."

I tossed another log on the fire as Akilah threw me a curve, "What didn't you observe in Paradise?"

"There was no sorrow, pain, death, suffering, sickness, loneliness, poverty, horrid acts, ignominy, deceit, impurity, or abuse. The pleasures of earth paled in comparison to the joys of Heaven. It made me realize our earthly frame of minds' need to be more positive and less negative as well as more vertical and less horizontal."

"Did Paradise have different types of ethnic groups, foliages, animals, rivers, and cities?" Akilah asked, pouring the cardamom coffee.

"Yes. Jehovah is a God of variety, endless variety. There are people from all races, tribes, tongue, and nations in Heaven. Everyone speaks a universal language. Also, Paradise is full of endless types of blooming flowers, leaved trees, gleaming evergreens, mountain ranges, bodies of water, colorful birds, affable animals, and a booming metropolis."

Between sips Akilah asked, "What were the heavenly dwellers doing?"

"Some were embarking upon adventurous activities, participating in sporting events, and preparing elaborate banquets. Others were singing, serving, exploring, sculpting, talking, dancing, merrymaking, laughing, baking, feasting, listening, watching, building, learning, and worshipping. All were full of joy and singing praises unto God. For grace is the currency in Heaven."

"Were there physical infirmities among Paradise dwellers?"

"Everyone had healthy, infinite, unblemished, and beautiful resurrected bodies."

"Nobody in Paradise experiences illnesses or pains?"

"Nobody. People on earth who were mute, sang songs of worship. The deaf heard the voices of heavenly choirs. The lame knelt in praise. The blind beheld God's awesome majesty in Paradise. We were all created to praise God, and nothing hindered a soul from doing this in Heaven."

"What were the ages of Paradise's residents?"

"All ages were represented. But nobody had a preference for a particular age. Everyone was healthy, beautiful, and full of energy. Everyone was in the youthful, prime of their lives."

Akilah's mouth fell open and she solicited, "So nobody is old?"

"There is no such thing as chronicle age in Heaven. Some choose to have gray hair and winkles because they like the look, but they are as healthy as others in Paradise."

"Is there anything else that makes Paradise dwellers look different compared to their time here on earth?"

"Yes, our new heavenly bodies will have wings, but they are slightly different than the angels' wings. It looked like a great way to travel. Everyone wore snow white clothing, but had different color sashes across their chests. I saw Daniel the Prophet and his sash was red."

Akilah poured more coffee and inquired, "How much time did you spend in Paradise?"

"Time as we know it doesn't exist in Heaven. Time isn't linear in Heaven."

"What do you mean?"

"The way we move our hands through space is the way God moves through time. It's like the apostle Peter said, 'With the Lord a day is like a thousand years, and a thousand years are like a day.'"

"Interesting," Akilah remarked, trying to imagine a place not dictated by time.

"Heaven encircled me and displayed its eternal splendors," I declared as the fire's blue flames danced within its pit. "I'm forever changed."

"This place must seem like a hollow shadow of Paradise."

"It does, Heaven is the place to eternally seek," I confirmed. "Jesus said, 'Enter through the narrow gate. For wide is the gate and broad is the road that lead to destruction, and many enter through it. But small is the gate and narrow the road that leads to life, and only a few who find it.'"

"I'll never be able to stop thinking about this place called the Third Heaven," Akilah confided. "My mind is captivated by your descriptions of Allah, Throne Room, Paradise dwellers and its settings. My soul seeks the peace of Heaven."

"Me too."

We both sat there in silence for what seemed like an hour. Akilah and I reflected on our earthly hardships and the awesome bliss of Heaven.

Chapter Thirty-Six
A Time to Endure

"We survive on adversity and perish in ease and comfort."

Titus Livy

Our souls danced to glorious thoughts and vivid images of Heaven. Akilah reached for her flute to express the emotions running around within her soul. She always carried a bamboo flute with her. But it was her voice that broke the long silence, "What kind of music is there in Heaven?"

"All kinds. There were endless songs with creative beats and rhythmical crescendos. My eardrums couldn't vibrate enough," I shared. "It was like my soul sang the songs not my voice."

Akilah's eyes lit up with heavenly inspirations as she blew into her flute. She paused and declared, "A paradise of sound."

"Yes, the music in Heaven had an awe-inspiring melody. I joined the choruses of praises that filled the air. All around God's throne thousands of cherubim chanted psalms. Seraphims' wings and voices composed a descant worshipping God's majesty."

"I can only imagine what celestial songs would sound like."

"Songs were performed in all types of genres. Every creature's voice sang praises unto God. The lyrics were filled with words of exaltation. It was a polyphonic sound that completely lacked any hint of dissonance. Endless hymns were sung with tonality and a joyful rhythm. There were hundreds of string and wind instruments, some I have never seen or heard before."

"Incredible!"

"It truly was." I replied, still hearing several songs in my mind.

"Excuse me for going back to a previous topic, but tell me what happened when the Lord came unto you."

"When the Lord approached me, I was instantly engulfed in His glorious illumination. My soul cried out, 'My Lord, My God!' I fell to his feet temporarily blinded."

The skin between my eyebrows wrinkled as I recalled, "Before losing my sight, I noticed He wore a purple robe reaching down to His feet and with a gold sash around His chest. His head and hair were white like wool, as white as snow, and His eyes were like a blazing fire. His feet were like bronze glowing in a furnace, and His voice was like the sound of rushing water. His face was like the sun shining in all its brilliance."

Akilah laid down her flute and begged, "Please tell me what you heard."

"I can't, but some of the things I heard will be shared with the Lord's people through another," I assured. "I can tell you that I lost my fear of death."

"That's insightful, but if Paradise is so wonderful why did you return to earth?"

"I didn't want to return! But the Lord still has a purpose for me down here. The Lord taught me, there are two types of people in life, those who take more than they give, and those who give more than they take out of life. I've been given an opportunity to be a giver rather than a taker."

Akilah stared into the amber coals, reflecting upon her life and mumbled, "Am I a giver or taker? I've been given a lot of hardships and had taken them fairly well." Her thoughts were followed with another round of silence.

~~

Akilah took a few minutes to assimilate her thoughts, and then inquired, "Has anything else besides temporarily glowing like a star happened to you since returning from Paradise?"

"Yes, to keep me from becoming conceited because of these heavenly revelations, there was given me a thorn in my flesh, a messenger of Satan to torment me. I pleaded with the Lord to take it away from me. But he said to me, 'My grace is sufficient for you, for my power is made perfect in weakness.'"

"If this thorn weakens you, what will you do?"

"I will boast all the more gladly about my weakness, so that Jesus' power may rest on me. For when I am weak, then I am strong."

"Sorry to hear you have a thorn in your flesh," my friend sympathized. "Thorns really hurt! I recently had a thorn in my palm from weaving baskets. Fortunately, they're not fatal, just painful."

Akilah stood up to stretch her stiff back as I explained, "The thorn in my flesh is figurative not literal."

"Okay, then what is your thorn?"

"I prefer to leave it anonymous."

"Come on, is it a wife, child, vision, gout, epilepsy, stammering, guilt from persecuting early believers, or organ damage from floggings? With your past I could go on and on," she teased.

"The purpose of my thorn is to cultivate humility and dependence upon God," I informed. "Everyone has a thorn within them; they vary from person to person. Thorns can be physical, spiritual, emotional, sexual, psychological or relational."

Akilah paced about the cave like a lioness in captivity. She paused by the cave's threshold then turned toward me and said, "So, you have this thorn because great secrets were laid before you in Paradise?"

"Correct. God lifted me up, but I pray I won't lift myself up, because when we lift ourselves up it's a long, hard fall. So as a reminder I have this thorn. It's to keep me from getting intoxicated on pride."

"It sounds like this thorn has clearly pricked you!"

"It has. For thorns try to keep us focused on our hardships instead of our eternal rewards."

"Satan's uses our thorns and hardships to diminish our faith?" She asked, pacing once again about the cave.

"Yes."

"Also, you're saying Allah uses our thorns and hardships for our spiritual growth?"

"He can."

"Even someone like me?" she cried out. "Who watched her family be murdered, killed a sheik's son, and sold her body to Bedouin warriors to escape the Negev Desert?"

"Yes, God reaches out his loving hands to everyone, even you. He is always there for us," I assured. Akilah's pacing accelerated as she mused on my remarks.

~ ~

Upon spending time with Akilah, one could easily sense her spirits were low. She dwelled in a frame of mind where skies were gray and dreams never came to fruition, a place where hardships rained down like hail. Hers was a hopeless soul crawling beneath tenebrous clouds.

"Where does one find Allah and His son, since we can't all be caught up to Paradise?" she inquired with curiosity.

"God is omnipresent. He's patiently waiting everywhere; to reveal Himself to everyone, somewhere."

"Everywhere, Somewhere?" Akilah looked at me quizzically after putting another log on the smoldering fire.

"God is everywhere! But, I don't know where your somewhere is for spiritual awakening. It's a different place for all of us. Your somewhere might be giving birth in a bed, an emotional meltdown on a city street, battling a life-threatening disease in your home, genocide in the Negev Desert, or being blessed with good news at a friend's house. My somewhere was on a dirt road outside Damascus."

"But, I feel like I'm nowhere."

"The Lord is patiently waiting everywhere for you with open arms. You can embrace Him anywhere at anytime, I just pray you will do it somewhere."

"You're making me feel like my somewhere is this Tarsus cave."

"I pray it is."

Akilah continued to wear her grief like her father's sapphire ring, she never took off. Her sorrowful expression glazed upon me and she said, "My thorn is the haunting memory of seeing my entire family murdered by Sheik Abdul. It prickles my heart and soul every day."

"May God's grace and peace be with." I sympathized, and then heartened, "The good news is Jesus removed the eternal sting of thorns and death through his crucifixion, resurrection, and accession to Heaven."

"But if Allah's son is in Paradise, who's here on earth to help me?"

"The Holy Spirit."

Bewilderment engulfed her facial features as she implored, "Who?"

"There are three divine person of the Godhead or the Holy Trinity; God, Jesus, and Holy Spirit," I stated. "God gave us the Holy Spirit, to change us from the inside out."

"Please, tell me more?"

"The Holy Spirit resided within Jesus during his earthly ministry. When Jesus returned to Heaven he sent the Holy Spirit to reside within our souls and energize us with heavenly power."

"You mean when I grasp words of wisdom, feel inspired, exercise my spiritual gifts, filled with joy, and sense the presence of Allah that comes from the Holy Spirit?"

"You got it. The Holy Spirit encourages, teaches, guides, and comforts us amidst our hardships. Just let your mind, heart, and soul bath in the power of the Holy Spirit," I reassured.

"How do I know when the Holy Spirit resides within me?"

"When the Holy Spirit resides with you, you'll receive the Spirit's fruits; faithfulness, goodness, gentleness, kindness, joy, love, peace, patience, and self-control."

Akilah sat back down and poked the dying fire with a long cypress branch and thought aloud, "Allah may be using my thorn, so the Holy Spirit can get my attention?"

"Yes, we can rejoice in our sufferings, because we know that suffering produces perseverance; perseverance produces character; and character produces hope. Hope does not disappoint us, because God has poured out his love into our hearts by the Holy Spirit."

She continued to stare at the smoldering ashes and asked, "But why does Allah let bad things happen to good people?"

"Because we live in a fallen world."

"A fallen world?" her perplexed voice inquired.

"We all have sinned and fallen short of God's righteousness. When Adam and Eve allowed themselves to be tempted by Satan in the Garden of Eden, they violated God's command. Their faithless rebellion corrupted the nature of humanity. In Adam all die, but in Christ all live."

"Who is Christ? I've not heard you mention that name."

I inhaled for words of wisdom and exhaled this lexis, "Christ is Jesus, and Jesus is God's son. Jesus is the first person you will see in Heaven. He will be your tour guide in Paradise."

"Awesome."

"God's son came to earth to die for our sins, since we're all destined for Hell. Jesus' crucifixion on the cross bore the sins for all of humanity. Christ's resurrection from the grave overcame the powers of evil and death. Jesus Christ's accession to heaven marked the beginning of his reign and intercession for all believers in the Throne Room."

"But wickedness still exists here on earth."

"Wickedness is not God's will, but humanity's response to Satan's prompting. A lot of our hardships and thorns are self inflected because we choose to follow Satan. The Holy Spirit shows us the way, but sometimes we refuse to follow that path. Way to often our free will, given to us by God, chooses the thoroughfare of Satan's sinful, wicked ways."

"Did Jesus experience thorns, here on earth?" echoed Akilah's voice throughout the cave.

"Yes, Jesus endured numerous thorns, especially on the cross. The diadem the Roman soldiers placed on his head was made of palm pine branches with thorns the length of your thumb and they dug into his scalp. His hands and feet were pierced with three barbed iron spikes. He bore humanity's thorns of adultery, slander, murder, and moral depravity. All of our sinful acts pricked his body on that splintery wooden cross."

Her body flinched with pain as she acknowledged, "Oh, the agony he suffered."

"Jesus was God's Sacrificial Lamb. His death took away the sins of the world. Jesus' shed blood atones for the sins of everyone who believes in him."

"What a divine being. I hope to meet him in Paradise."

"To get to Heaven you have to have Jesus in your soul."

Akilah closed her eyes and examined her soul. I saw a smile appear on her face for the first time since we'd know each other. She said, "The soul is the source of life and I feel his presence in my spirit. I believe and trust in the one who died for me."

"Alleluia," I exclaimed jumping up from my rock.

Akilah continued to grab the reins of her soul and added, "I no longer fear death having seen the glory of Paradise through your eyes. I will live my life to reside in Heaven."

~~

We embraced in celebration, and then I felt her body go limp. "What's the matter?" I asked.

"I just remembered something," she cried. "I was recently in an Asia Minor city where followers of Jesus were being persecuted by Roman officials and pagan priests because of their faith. I chanted and encouraged the city officials along with the mob to torture them."

"How were they being persecuted?" I inquired as we went outside for a stroll.

"The soldiers tied their wrists to a tall, wooden cylinder, then chained their ankles to metal rings driven into the stone pavement," Akilah recalled, realizing her new faith might cause her some suffering.

"Unfortunately, our faith is going to be challenged. Sometimes, there is a cost. Jesus said, 'If the world hates you, keep in mind that it hated me first. If you belonged to the world, it would love you as its own. As it is, you do not belong to the world, but I have chosen you out of the world. That is why the world hates you.'"

"I saw hate that day in the eyes of those Roman magistrates and pagan priests," she recalled. "Every time a follower refused to deny the Jesus, their soldiers turned the wooden cylinder. Each turn stretched their limbs and muscles beyond their limitations. Some held firm even though their limbs were torn from their bodies!"

"That's terrible," I agonized. "But don't worry for the Lord will comfort us, for he knows firsthand the pain and challenges of standing firm."

"I don't know if I could endure that kind of persecution."

"If those days ever arrive; keep the faith, let adversity fuel growth, reach deep for courage, pray, and focus on Paradise."

"Thanks for lifting Paradise's curtain so I know what to focus on and how to stand firm."

I spent that afternoon with Akilah sharing Jesus' parables. Our hours together passed like seconds. It was awesome to witness the transformation in her soul and to watch the fruits of the spirit come alive in her.

~~

On the last day of winter, Akilah was shopping in the Tarsus Marketplace. One of Sheik Abdul's bounty hunters recognized her as she tried on hijabs. Without hesitation, the bounty hunter ruthlessly ran his sword through Akilah seven times. I grieved for weeks over the loss of my dear friend, but rejoiced knowing she was waiting for me in Heaven.

Throughout the following spring this lonely apostle sought out other friendships in Tarsus, but people preferred to shower me with malice. I was perceived and treated as a religious lunatic. Jewish leaders constantly placed a yoke of oppression upon me. Local magistrates tolerated all injustices directed toward me.

My soul clung to the Lord like a newborn infant to its mother. Meanwhile, I longed to open my heart like a book to an earthly friend, so we could multiply each other's joy and diminish one another's grief. I sought someone to share thoughts with and to hold me accountable.

Chapter Thirty-Seven
Time of Friendship

"We secure our friends not by accepting favors, but by doing them."
Thucydides

On the day of my forty-fourth birthday this weary soul wandered into Tarsus. I was still recovering from a mutinous voyage on an Egyptian coastal ship when a familiar image appeared before my eyes.

"Hallelujah!" the voice shouted from the other end of the Cydnus River dock.

My spirit exploded with ecstasy. It was Barnabas! We hadn't seen one another for seven years. Barnabas looked exhausted; the white mantle he wore was nearly brown, his black beard was dusty, and his hair was oily. But, those hazel eyes were shining with endless joy.

"Paul, my dear friend, it's great to see you!" Barnabas exclaimed.

"Same here! You don't know how my ears have longed to hear those words!"

"Happy birthday, young man!"

I laughed. "It's been years since I've received a birthday salutation," I shouted upon receiving the best birthday gift since I turned thirteen.

"I've been looking all over Cilicia and Syria for you!" he remarked as we embraced.

"Why?"

"I need your help."

"Mine?" I responded with a puzzled look as if he were a madman.

"Yes! I have needed it for months!"

"What for? I'm merely a dim candle flickering in the relentless breezes of life."

"No, you're a spiritual lighthouse that radiates the Lord's wisdom upon all races! We need your illumination in Antioch!"

"Antioch?" I queried.

"Antioch of Syria!"

"Why Antioch?"

"Jerusalem's church elders sent me to Antioch a year ago to investigate the numerous stories about Jews and Gentiles converting to The Way."

"You were the right choice, with all your connections in Syria. Were the stories you heard in Jerusalem true?" I inquired as we walked down the dock.

"Yes! The church of Antioch is experiencing the biggest revival we've ever seen. Their congregations have as many Gentiles as Jews! The grace of God is upon Antioch."

"Alleluia!"

"Hundreds of Jews and Gentiles make up this church!" Barnabas announced.

"So, it's not a church of Jews that has Gentiles seeking unity, but Jews and Gentiles dwelling in a church of unity."

"Exactly! I need you help to minister unto them."

Barnabas understood asking for help is like playing chess. One needs to know which chess piece will accomplish one's objective. He needed a piece that could jump over racial lines.

～～

When we reached the dock's end our stomachs led us left toward the marketplace. Several zealots recognized me just outside the Harbor's Marketplace. A brawny man shouted, "It looks like the blasphemer finally found a sucker to listen to him." His remarks were followed by a chorus of obscene remarks and gestures.

"Please, pay no attention to them," I whispered to Barnabas.

"What did you just say about us, blasphemer?" yelled another burly man.

I ignored him but painfully felt his two fists land upon my cheeks. The blows nearly lifted my sandals off the street. The man was amazed his punching bag remained standing. We stood there exchanging dirty looks until I noticed Barnabas was about to retaliate in some manner. I grabbed Barnabas' flexed forearm and pulled him into the marketplace. The lazy zealots stayed on their neighborhood street corner, merely shouting crude comments.

"Awesome! You just displayed Jesus' teaching, 'If someone strikes you on one cheek, turn to him the other also,'" Barnabas complimented.

"Yes, but that was painful tutoring," I joked rubbing my jaw. "But, please, tell me more about Antioch."

"Jewish and Gentile believers are worshipping together in Antioch. God has glorious things in store for you there!" Barnabas resumed his beseeching.

"Those Jewish brethren are probably Nazarenes I chased out of the Holy City, Jerusalemite fugitives who successfully escaped my brutal persecution," I muttered after wiggling a sore jaw. "Some days, guilt blows through my mind like a strong wind. And the ghosts of time past flaunt their tenure in my soul."

"Don't let your past capsize your future! God has forgiven you. Forgiveness moves in concert with God's mercy and human absolution."

"You're right. We diminish our testimonies if we don't accept others' forgiveness."

"Jubilant times lie ahead. Focus on your dreams. We have Jewish along with Gentile souls to save and nourish." Barnabas stated, taking a mountain top view of the situation.

"I've really missed your encouraging words." I reflected then added, "We can make an eternal difference when we invest time in others."

"Paul, we're in desperate need of qualified teachers. We need someone who can instruct Jewish and Gentile believers! The Holy Spirit continuously brought you to mind. You're the one we need!"

"Why me?"

"I couldn't forget your convictions to teach the Jews and Gentiles in Jerusalem. You speak several languages, grew up in a multi-cultural city, and have a firm understanding of Jewish as well as Gentile literature. I come on behalf of the Lord! Will you help us?"

"I don't know if you have the right person," I pondered aloud as Barnabas bought us some flatbread.

"You're the perfect person to teach the Gospel in Antioch. You won't compromise the veracity of God's word. Your cross-cultural insights and enthusiasm for teaching the Gospel to Gentiles far exceed mine."

"Thank you for your kind comments."

"In addition, you know how to find the common thread in people from different cultures. You possess the unique ability to take that which separates us and use it to unite us. You were blessed to be a blessing," said Barnabas.

"I like spending time with you." I joked. This marked the second time the Lord used Barnabas, Son of Encouragement, to intervene on my behalf.

"Opportunity knocks when swords are clashing at the city gates, not when harps are playing in the king's chambers." Barnabas roared with encouragement like a trainer inspiring his gladiators for combat. "Paul, it's time to get into the arena!"

"It is time!" I screamed like a fan at the coliseum.

"So you will help us advance the Gospel in all strata of Antioch's society?" he solicited. Barnabas knew in mission work it is grace and passion that keep people devoted to their duties.

"Yes! Thank you for answering my endless prayers and providing a change in direction!" I blurted out. The feeling of being a rusty old tool on God's workbench quickly disappeared.

"Great, because you are the missing piece of the puzzle I've been searching for. You can teach the truth like a simplistic math problem or a complex mathematical formula."

"Let's leave now for Antioch! I've been in God's waiting room for seven long years. Every day, Satan has been trying to remove my last ounce of patience! Fortunately, I've clung to James' remark: 'Patience must finish its work so that you may be mature and complete, not lacking in anything.'"

Barnabas shook his head in agreement as we stopped at a food stand and bought provisions for our journey.

"You have shown great patience waiting for God's guidance," Barnabas lauded while I stuffed our food supplies into an old burlap sack.

"At times I felt like Moses and the Israelites wandering in the wilderness." My lips declared behind long graying bread.

"Sometimes, we just have to keep on moving till we find the right direction."

"Since we've found my divine direction, I need to go out to my cave and gather a few belongings." I suggested as another group of Jewish zealots began mocking us.

"Good idea, since the future doesn't always emulate the past but it does harmonize with it. In other words, let's get out of here before trouble returns," Barnabas readily agreed.

~~

One can find friendship in the likeliest and unlikeliest of places.

Furthermore, there is nothing like a good friend to nourish the soul. The impact we have on one another is eternal.

"It seems you've been ostracized and beset by the people of Tarsus," Barnabas remarked as we left the marketplace.

"The fruit of fellowship has soured on me in this city."

"So, who have you been spending your time with?" Barnabas asked, swatting flies from his sweaty brow.

"I've been spending my time in prayer with Jesus. He's become my best friend!"

"Awesome. One of the problems we're experiencing in the Antioch church is a lack of spiritual intimacy. There's a need to deepen the congregation's fellowship with the Holy Trinity," Barnabas informed after searching the sky in vain for a cloud.

"Nobody knows us like the Lord! His intimate hand of fellowship is offered to all! God seeks spiritual companionship and an eternal relationship with everyone," I stated, walking out the city gate.

"Yes! The Lord has blessed us with endless access to Him; because of prayer we are never destitute of fellowship." Barnabas announced as five Jewish adolescents started throwing stones at us from the city gate's wall.

"We need to teach people daily to share their thoughts and activities with the Lord. We must encourage them to engage in conversation with the Holy Trinity as they commute, converse, eat, exercise, meditate, relax, teach, and work. God is waiting for us to call out His name in fellowship!" I remarked after ducking a large stone.

"His friendship patiently endures our insults and defiance. The earnestness of our commitment may wane, but His love never diminishes. The Lord showers us in love so we'll shower others in love," Barnabas remarked, wincing, after a stone bounced off his collar bone.

"Now, that's sticking your neck out for a good friend," I consoled him and we both laughed. While, ducking more rocks I admitted, "I'm not always a good friend to Jesus. Sometimes my pride pushes aside His glory, my anger rejects His love, my self-centeredness snubs His presence, and my wickedness ignores His righteousness."

"Jesus is a friend of sinners. He loves us more than we could ever imagine. In Him, we have a friendship that changes our inner being and alters our outer acts." Barnabas acknowledged after we were out of firing range from the adolescents' catapulting arms.

"My desire is the fellowship I have with Him, will narrow the space that exists between us!"

"Same here and may our egos never forget, we're the ray, and Jesus is the light. We're the murmur, and He is the thunder. We're the tingle, and Christ is love. We're the drop and He is the fountain of life," Barnabas remarked as we stopped at a watering hole to fill our camel-skin canteens.

After filling our canteens, I switched topics and inquired, "How are the apostles?"

"Most have left or been chased out of the Holy City."

"I was afraid that would happen."

"A vast majority of the synagogue elders, Sadducees, and Herodians are waging war against the church in Jerusalem Church. James, John's older brother, was executed last year. He was the first of Jesus' eleven faithful apostles to be called home."

"What happened to him?"

"A zealot falsely accused James of blasphemy. James was unjustly condemned and sentenced to death. The accuser was so overwhelmed by James' convictions, faith, and forgiveness during the hasty trail that he also became a believer. Furthermore, the accuser requested and was put to death with the sword along with James."

"James boldly stood on the front line of martyrdom. I always admired him."

"Me, too! He fully grasped the Lord's teachings of godly grace over personal glory, heavenly love over human anger and enduring patience over reactionary aggression." Barnabas responded.

"Are the other apostles safe?" I asked, slowing our pace beneath the sweltering sun.

"Yes, and doing their best to spread the Gospel throughout Palestine!" Barnabas answered, wiping away drops of sweat.

Hiking across the Tarsus Plains, I realized friendships are like muscles, we must work at them, or they'll experience atrophy. It's as Solomon said, 'A friend loves at all times. Do not forsake your friend.'

Chapter Thirty-Eight
A Time to Embrace

"Manifest plainness, Embrace simplicity,
Reduce selfishness, Have few desires."
Lao-tzu

We continued across the Tarsus Plains and into the foothills still we reached my cave near the Tarsus Mountains. The view from my cave was breathtaking, a panoramic view of the snow capped Tarsus Mountains. The mountains were shedding their white, winter coat as brown rocks began to appear like blemishes on an adolescent's face.

Barnabas was reluctant to enter the cave. He peeked inside and teased, "Paul, the belongings in there reflect the residence of a nomad."

"That's what I've been for the last seven years." I chuckled before ducking into the cave. Barnabas looked inside once again before entering the cave.

He looked around and examining the debris in the far corner, he surmised, "I would say this cave was used by; wild breasts to give birth, nomadic herdsmen seeking shelter from winter storms, and lepers after being evicted from their community."

"Barnabas, you have a writer's imagination, but this cave is concluding its final chapter on my residency."

I'm going to make us some coffee while you pack," said Barnabas. He knew the best way to converse with an old friend was over some caffeine.

"Sounds like a good idea," my words echoed throughout the cave. "Since leaving the marketplace, I've been meaning to ask you a question. How is our friend Peter doing?"

"He's fine now! However, King Herod Agrippa saw how James' death delighted the zealots, so he began targeting other apostles. Just before I left Jerusalem last spring, Agrippa put Peter in prison!"

I continued, gathering my sparse belongings. My life was not about possessions but who had possession over my soul. Packing my canteen, I asked, "Was he imprisoned during the Feast of Unleavened Bread?"

"Yes! Herod had Peter guarded by four squads of four soldiers each. Herod intended to bring him out for public trial after the Passover. Meanwhile, the church was earnestly praying to God for him. The night before Herod was to bring him to trial, Peter was sleeping between two soldiers, bound with two chains, and sentries stood guard at the entrance. Suddenly, an angel of the Lord appeared, and a light shone in the cell. He struck Peter on the side and woke him up. 'Quick, get up!' he said, and the chains fell off Peter's wrists.

"The angel said to him, 'Put on your clothes and sandals.' And Peter did so. 'Wrap your cloak around you and follow me.' Peter followed him out of the prison, but he had no idea that what the angel was doing was really happening; he thought he was seeing a vision."

"I would too."

"They passed the first and second guards and came to the Iron Gate leading to the city. It opened for them by itself and they went through it. When they had walked the length of one street, suddenly the angel left him."

"Then what happened?"

"Then Peter came to himself and said, 'Now I know without a doubt that the Lord sent his angel and rescued me from Herod's clutches.'"

"Where did Peter go?"

"He went to the house of Mary, the mother of John Mark, where many people had gathered and were praying. Peter knocked at the outer entrance, and a servant girl named Rhoda came to answer the door. When she recognized Peter's voice, she was so overjoyed she ran back without opening it and exclaimed, "Peter is at the door.'"

"Everyone probably thought she was out of her mind."

"At first we did, and then we thought it was an angel. But Peter kept on knocking, and when we opened the door and saw him, we were astonished. Peter motioned with his hand for us to be quiet and he described how the Lord had brought him out of the prison. Then Peter said, 'Tell James and the brothers about this,' and he left for another place."

"I'm sure the church gave numerous praises that night for Peter's miraculous escape."

"We did and in the morning, there was no small commotion among the soldiers as to what had become of Peter. After Herod had a thorough search made for him and did not find him, he cross-examined the guards and ordered that they be executed." Barnabas concluded.

~~

I packed the last of my meager belongings. It felt as though we were about to undertake the most amazing journeys one could imagine. We were traveling to a city in the Roman Empire, where thousands of Jews and Gentiles were making similar spiritual decisions and crossing racial boundaries.

Those thoughts inspired me to ask, "Has Peter changed his view on Gentiles?"

"Yes! A couple weeks before Peter's imprisonment, he was in Joppa staying with a tanner. Peter was on the roof praying and became hungry around noon, when the Lord used a heavenly vision to show him, that he should not call any man impure or unclean. Also, in this vision the Lord revealed the gift of the Holy Spirit had been poured out even on the Gentiles."

"What was the vision?"

"Peter saw heaven open and something like a large sheet being let down to earth by its four corners. It contained all kinds of four-footed animals, as well as reptiles of the earth and birds of the air. Then a voice told him, 'Peter, kill and eat.' Peter replied, 'Surely not, Lord! I have never eaten anything impure and unclean.' Three times the voice said, 'Do not call anything impure or unclean that God has made clean.'"

"That's the third time I've heard Peter rebuff God's will."

"While he was wondering about the meaning of the vision, three Gentile men from Caesarea stopped outside the tanner's house. The three men where sent to Joppa by Cornelius, a God-fearing man and centurion in the Italian Regiment. The Spirit told Peter, 'Simon, three men are looking for you. So get up and go downstairs. Do not hesitate to go with them, for I have sent them.'"

"Events seem to happen in threes to Peter."

"Peter had lunch with Cornelius' emissaries, much to the surprise of his hosts. Their lunch lasted till late afternoon, so the next day some of the brothers from Joppa, the three Gentile men, and Peter went down to Caesarea. The following day they arrived at Cornelius' house. That is where the last piece of the puzzle fell into place for Peter, where he finally realized Gentiles are part of God's family."

"How?" I inquired before guzzling the tepid coffee.

"Peter went inside the house and found a large gathering of Cornelius' relatives and close friends. He was confident that Peter would come. Peter said, 'You are well aware that it is against our law for a Jew to associate with a Gentile or visit him. But God has shown me that I should not call any man impure or unclean. I now realize how true it is that God does not show favoritism, but accepts men from every nation who fear Him and do what is right.

"Awesome! Did Peter fellowship with the Gentiles?"

"Yes, he preached the Gospel to them, while he was still speaking; the Holy Spirit came on all who heard the message. Peter said, to the circumcised Joppa believers, 'Can anyone keep these people from being baptized with water? They have received the Holy Spirit just as we have.' So he ordered that they be baptized in the name of Jesus Christ."

"Hallelujah! He has grasped the equality that exists in all believers."

"Peter stayed with them for a few days to instruct them in their faith, and then he went up to Jerusalem. The circumcised believers in Jerusalem criticized him and said, "You went into the house of uncircumcised men and ate with them.' Peter insisted, 'God gave them the same gift as He gave us, who believed in the Lord Jesus Christ. Who was I to think that I could oppose God?'"

"What did the circumcised believers say?" I asked after tossing a small burlap sack, containing all my earthly belongings by the cave's entrance.

"They had no further objections and praised God saying, 'So then, God has granted even the Gentiles repentance unto life.'"

"The Jerusalem church now embraces Jewish and Gentile believers!" I joyfully shouted.

"Somewhat. That is why the Jerusalem elders sent me to Syria. They wanted see how Gentiles were impacting the Antioch church. The church leaders wanted to see if these new Gentile converts were obeying the Torah, Mosaic Laws, oral laws, and Jewish traditions."

"And?" I prodded.

"I found the Gentile believers full of faith, positively impacting the church, and following God's commandments."

"That's great news! Faith and the Ten Commandments are foundational stones for building a God-centered life." I claimed.

"Yes, but they're not following all our Jewish traditions and oral laws."

"Don't be so legalistic. Let's be thankful for a godly, bi-racial church," I chided then asked. "What has become of King Herod Agrippa since he imprisoned Peter?"

"Not long after Peter's escape, Agrippa pridefully sat on his throne accepting praises meant for God. He was struck with a serious illness. Herod painfully lingered for several days then died. Recent news from Jerusalem says the church is experiencing a time of peace since his passing."

"God is amazing! He can use any of His creations to do His work: a donkey, fish, locust, raven, serpent, farmer, fisherman, mother, soldier, tent-maker, or wicked king," I proclaimed

"Yes, the Lord can use any of His creations to do His will!" Barnabas agreed, kicking out the fire. Then he asked, "What did the Lord teach you while biding time in this stone waiting room?"

"Humility and patience! Over the last seven years, this lump of human clay has placed itself on the Creator's pottery wheel, and now I know, I've been kneaded and sculpted to do the Lord's work in Antioch," I said, visually bidding farewell to that cold, damp dwelling.

Barnabas and I knelt in prayer outside the cave, asking for a safe, fruitful journey. We vowed to approach the world from a godly point of view and to influence positively those we encountered. Both of us promised to do God's will and to seek to be Christlike

Barnabas and I got up from our knees and hiked back to Tarsus' harbor. On this trip along with other sojourns, we would be accompanied by three lifelong friends: faith, hope and love. Just after nightfall, we boarded a coastal vessel to sail southeast to Antioch. This marked the public commencement of my missionary life, the most rewarding activity I would ever encounter.

Chapter Thirty-Nine
A Time to Commence

"I have made known the end from the beginning."
God

Barnabas and I blistered our tongues during the voyage to Antioch sharing stories about Jerusalem, Tarsus, and The Way. Our vessel sailed the coastline for four days; it seemed like four hours. Before sunset on the fourth day, we saw Seleucia, a seaport town near Antioch, on the horizon. Its countryside had green, rolling hills and lush woodlands.

The port's reputation for turbulent currents and strong winds had the crew on edge. All hands breathed a sigh of relief when mild breezes blew us safely into Seleucia's harbor. Sails were lowered as our rowers maneuvered past merchant vessels into the city's manmade basin.

"Lay anchor!" The captain screamed in Greek. He decided to spend the night in Seleucia's basin since the sky was pitch black.

"We can spend the night on this ship and be rowed upstream in the morning to Antioch. Or, we can catch a water taxi to shore and walk up the banks of the Orontes River to Antioch, tonight." Barnabas restlessly suggested beneath a new moon.

"Let's take a stroll!" I exclaimed, hailing a water taxi from the aft.

During the brief water taxi ride, I noticed boats from all over the Mediterranean navigating up and down the Orontes River. Vessels traveling in both directions were full of goods. Antioch sat on the North-South and East-West trade routes. It was the largest trade center between the Orient and Mediterranean. The city was also a major agricultural hub, regional headquarters for every craftsman's guild, and military post for Rome.

"I always feel like putting on blinders when I trek the Orontes River.

Its riverbanks are full of idolatry and lustful acts," Barnabas remarked stepping ashore.

Fleshly activities quickly supported his comments. I beheld Apollo's priests on the shoreline, pouring oxen blood over their disciples' heads. The riverbanks were full of pilgrims pursuing sexual relationships with priestesses and priests of Apollo. Several pilgrims wandered into nearby groves to engage in bestiality.

Accompanying us on the half day journey were hundreds of Greek, Persian, Roman, and Syrian merchants. They were carrying their goods to Antioch for the annual Apollo Festival. Pilgrims' fires lit up Mount Silpius in the distance and Antioch beneath it. Antioch was the Roman Empire's third largest city; only Rome and Alexandria were larger.

Well after midnight, we befriended an Antioch professor at a riverside café. The Chaldaean history professor as well as Barnabas and I had stopped for some green tea. When we finished our teas the academician offered, "We're only two-thirds of the way to Antioch and you both look exhausted. Why don't you both join us on my boat?"

"Thank you, we'd be delighted to!" Barnabas responded. So we boarded his small skiff and squeezed in among three male students. His craft was pulled up the Orontes River by two weary mules.

"You Jews have been dwelling in Antioch since it was founded," the senior history lecturer volleyed.

"We have a tendency to get around," I bantered. Everyone laughed then I shared the Gospel with four curious minds as we glided past the moonlit riverbanks adorned with cypress trees, laurels, black berries brushes, blooming lilies, and colorful oleanders.

~~

Barnabas and I awoke from our slumber when the boat docked in Antioch. We departed the vessel beneath a rising sun. Barnabas exclaimed, "Behold, Antioch, a city established over three hundred years ago by Seleucus Nicator, one of Alexander the Great's four Macedonian generals."

"And Seleucus named the city after his father, Antiochus, another famous Macedonian general. If my historical knowledge serves me correctly; Seleucus reigned as King of Babylonia, Syria, and Asia Minor for thirty-two years. Antioch remained the Seleucid Empire's capital city till Rome took possession of it in about one hundred years ago."

"Very good, you did listen to your synagogue teachers," teased Barnabas.

"Sometimes," I replied with a chuckle then asked, "Is Antioch, still the capital city for the Roman Province of Syria?"

"Yes, but be prepared for this metropolis is unrivaled in the Orient for carnal activities, drunkenness, gambling, and pagan festivals. Locals from the surrounding villages as well as foreign travelers called it Sin City."

"It appears to be more Hellenistic and depraved than Tarsus!" I shouted in a loud voice as we passed through the festive city gates.

"It is!" Barnabas agreed, watching my head oscillate from side to side.

"Syrian Antioch, like Tarsus, is a Free City. Its residents are able to govern themselves within Rome's edicts. Also, Antiochenes are exempt from certain Roman taxes and are permitted additional freedoms. One of these liberties is religious freedom, which has enabled The Way to expand in Antioch without restraints," explained Barnabas.

"Hallelujah!" I roared and asked, "What is the population of Antioch these days?"

"Approximately, six hundred thousand people; its residents are from all four corners of the eastern world. Antioch has a large Jewish population of about fifty thousand and a small percentage of those are Nazarenes. The Jewish residents are actively involved in the city's governmental affairs, political issues, and commerce. Our brethren predominately resided in the southern part of Antioch, a neighborhood the Gentiles call, Jew Town," informed Barnabas.

The city was a symphony of sounds as it prepared for the Apollo Festival. Caravans of pilgrims poured into the city singing merry tunes. Slaves were setting up wooden grandstands and moaning from the whip. Blacksmiths were stridently pounding out metal souvenirs of Apollo.

I noticed the streets were laid out in a grid. Antioch had two lengthy main streets. Both were lined with rows of marble colonnades, palm trees, and statues. Behind the marble colonnades were architectural marvels: Roman Administrative buildings, the massive stone Forum, the Imperial Palace, the Hippodrome, and numerous bathhouses. Behind all those buildings arose another concerto of marble structures: Greek temples and lavish amphitheaters.

"Your friend Judah Ben-Hur occasionally races there, Barnabas remarked, pointing to the Hippodrome. "He holds Antioch's all-time record for most charioteer victories. He's a hero among the local residents. He frequently speaks of his faith. His belief in Christ has helped spark awareness and growth in The Way."

We turned off Singon Street, one of the two main thoroughfares, and walked through the back alleys. "I'm amazed at the level of poverty and broken dreams behind these architectural wonders.

My eyes were also astounded by the obsession with sexuality and false deities we saw in the alleys. Barnabas observed my line of sight and said, "Antioch has a larger number of pagan beliefs. Most residents worship Apollo and the Greek goddess Daphne. Unfortunately, during the annual Apollo Festival, morality is thrown to the wind."

"It looks like it! My eyes are beholding sights they've never seen before."

Pilgrims were having tattoos of the Olympian goddesses and gods engraved upon every part of their anatomies. Apollo's priests were bloodletting themselves beneath Greek gods' statues. Lustful harlots of Daphne were successfully enticing pilgrims with their naked flesh. Apollo's prostitutes were performing sexual acts on street corners for one copper coin.

"This city is filled with seekers of pleasure, not seekers of God. Tarsus is known for moral mayhem, but Antioch looks like it's known for physical pandemonium." I added.

"Now you know another reason why I brought you here!" Barnabas announced, turning onto the other main street as twenty naked priestesses of Apollo danced past us. Within seconds, idol vendors were pushing statues of Daphne and Apollo into our hands to purchase.

"My old employer, Aeolus, once lived in Antioch. He felt it was the most immoral city in the Roman Empire. He said, 'Even Rome, over a million and a half paces away, is acquainted with Antioch's sewage of eroticism and profligacy.'"

"It's hard to argue with his assessment."

"It's amazing how decadence has such a mellow, negative, pervasive influence on cultures. People don't even collectively notice moral decay till their society has collapsed." My observations appended.

"That is why Antioch needs to hear the truth. However, we all have sinned, not just the decadent ones! Everyone needs God's mercy and grace. Salvation is for all!" Barnabas declared as we passed a huge Roman military fortress. It was the headquarters for the Eastern Roman army. These legions were assigned the task of keeping peace in the Orient and Asia.

"I hope someday to witness to Roman soldiers and officers. With their mobility, Roman soldiers could spread the Gospel across the Western and Eastern Empire," I remarked as we approached a ten cubits high, stone wall.

Chapter Forty
A Time to be Re-named

"Nomen est omen (In a name is destiny)."
Roman Saying

There were numerous immured communities within Antioch. City officials had built balustrade barriers or stone walls throughout the city to separate its racial districts. The city's different nationalities, races, and creeds lived within these segregated neighborhoods.

"This stone wall is the border for Jew Town," informed Barnabas. "People crawl over these neighborhood walls every morning and night to worship together in someone's home."

"It's great to know, Jesus' love goes beyond balustrade barriers and stone walls. He's not just for one group, bloodline, or ethnic group; but for all."

"You're right," Barnabas agreed the way some men do, and then said, "Just so you know, the Jewish section is made up of Diaspora, Hellenistic, Judean, Palestinian and Nazarene brethren." We headed through an opening in the stone wall twice as tall as me.

"This looks like one of the city's larger districts."

"It is and it's an isolated basin of righteousness amidst a terrain of immorality during the Apollo Festival." Barnabas remarked as we approached a large mansion. It looked like the biggest house in the Jewish section.

An aristocratic-looking gentleman answered the door and greeted us. "Shalom!"

"Shalom," I replied.

"Manaen, this is Paul, of whom I spoke, the one I've been looking for to teach the Gentiles."

"Welcome to Antioch!" Manaen, a large Hebrew man, politely remarked. He was a wealthy architect, who was highly regarded among Antioch's secular elite, Jewish community, and Nazarenes.

"Thank you!" I said, and then asked, "Weren't you the schoolmate of Herod the Great's son?"

"Yes. I was raised and tutored alongside Herod the Tetrarch within the Herodian Palace.

"You must have had an interesting childhood."

"I did. The good news is that I was blessed with a quality education in Rome and Jerusalem. I got to tour the Orient and Roman Empire as Herod's traveling mate, and became fluent in six languages. The bad news is, I was his playmate and whipping boy. Whenever Herod misbehaved, which he frequently did, I received his lashes."

"Maybe we should compare backs someday," I joked.

"Gentlemen, stay here during the Apollo Festival, since all the inns are full," Manaen offered, then quickly added, "No, stay here as long as you would like!"

Manaen was one of the founders of the Antioch church. So there was a steady flow of believers as well as non-believers from all nationalities in and out of his spacious house throughout that day and night.

~~

The following morning was the Sabbath. Manaen's spacious mansion was one of several locations throughout Antioch for The Way's Sabbath services.

"Our church is organized like Jewish synagogues, with elders and teachers. However, our congregation is made up of Jews and Gentiles. The Gospel of Jesus Christ has struck a chord with all races and economic classes in Antioch," Manaen informed me as we arranged wooden benches for the first of six worship services that day.

Parishioners began arriving at Manaen's house before sunrise. Some worshippers were Hellenistic Jews I had personally persecuted and chased out of Jerusalem fourteen years ago. They had escaped to Antioch for religious asylum.

These Nazarenes immediately recognized me and became gripped with trepidations; however, within minutes faith overcame fear. They showered me with love and hospitality before the first hymn. The Holy Spirit can change anyone!

After the third service, Barnabas suggested, "Paul, let's hike out to the Grove of Daphne."

"Okay, but why?"

"The Grove is where Seleucus built a temple honoring Daphne, the goddess of love. You need to see what goes on out there. It will deepen your conviction for the work to be done here."

So we ate a quick lunch, then walked four thousand paces south over freshwater aqueducts, through fruit orchards, and on worn-out stones to Daphne's temple.

Upon reaching the Grove my lips uttered in amazement, "I'm staggered by people's preoccupation with sexuality. There must be thousands of pilgrims engaging in lustful activities with Daphne and Apollo priests and priestesses."

"I wanted you to behold, there's a spiritual longing in everyone's heart. Unfortunately, some are misdirected. Death sparks the spiritual flames in all of us. Everyone knows that one day our mortal bodies will step on death's trap door. We don't know how, when, or where, but the reality of it haunts our souls." Barnabas said, walking back toward the city's southern gate.

"It does, because we can't escape death; a few ignore death before death, some neglect life before death, while others find life after death. Also, some ponder if death is Satan's or God's tool." I remarked.

"Satan tries to focus our minds on fear, the opposite of faith, along with the noise of the world. He seeks to steer humanity away from God's truth before death, because he knows God's word is the guide to a heavenly life after death."

"You're right. When God's truth is rejected, evil is called good and good is called evil! So, let's teach God's truth at Antioch's southern gate!" I claimed.

"What?"

"Let's set up a tent shop by the southern gate. We can share the Gospel with Daphne pilgrims, priests, and priestesses going to and from her temple. Their souls are parched like sandy waves on a desert landscape."

"Not a bad idea! God's truth is joyful music to ears."

"We can teach faith to the faithless ones and offer hope to the hopelessly lost." I concluded.

The following days which soon turned into months, Barnabas and

I spent our daylight hours making tents as well as joyfully sharing the Gospel at the city's southern gate. After work, we'd spend our nights teaching in Jewish neighborhoods.

Sleep was a rare companion for us in that metropolis. Our pre-dawn hours were spent on bended knees, seeking the Lord's guidance on spiritual issues. We wanted to be led by prayer and the Holy Spirit, not by pride and arrogance. Sleepless, prayerful nights provided us with heavenly direction and divine counsel on urban issues.

~~

The church in Antioch experienced tremendous growth in the summer of my forty-four[th] year. It had become even larger than the church in Jerusalem; furthermore, Antioch's church had more Gentile than Jewish members.

Unbelievable events were occurring within the churches. Antioch's congregations let the Holy Spirit choose who should lead them, not the status or wealth of would-be leaders. Antioch's churches were blessed with servant elders and devoted staff members. They helped move church members' faith from inactive to reactive to proactive.

Barnabas and I usually worshipped at Manaen's house church along with hundreds of others. His abode was two blocks form the Forum and easy for visitors to find.

We joyfully anticipated every worship service with our culturally diverse congregation. A worship service would run out of space once it exceeded two hundred and twenty-five people. When this occurred, new churches were established throughout the city.

Our congregation and church staff had an international makeup. Lucius, a Cyrenian presided over the church's outreach ministry. A black man from Africa named Simeon, led our music ministry. A Greek Gentile named Titus, a partner and fellow worker in Christ, oversaw all administrative duties. Manaen, Jewish brethren, managed our finances. Barnabas and I usually taught the worship services in the capacious courtyard. We all taught small groups throughout the week.

"The Way has created a community that incorporates all races, tribes, and nationalities," Simeon thankfully declared one summer Sabbath afternoon to the church staff as we ate a quick lunch between services.

"Our integrative actions have inspired racial harmony, and our racial harmony has inspired integrative actions," said Titus.

"You're right, no race feels superior in the Antioch church; every race is admired for its unique qualities," Simeon said before pouring everyone a cup of green tea. "Our congregation realizes every nationality and race is part of God's family. Also, our Heavenly Father created all of us in His image and loves us all the same!"

"Yes. The church has changed our pronouns from singular to plural, our action from egocentric to altruistic, our relationships from solitary to communal, and our emotions from hate to love," Barnabas added.

"Congregations are busting at the seams all over the city. At least thirty house churches have sprouted just from Manaen's original congregation," chimed in Lucius, while scratching a flea bite atop his bald head.

"It's amazing the variety of worshippers we have; Jewish businesswomen, Bedouin herdsmen, Persian merchants, prostitutes, jesters, politicians, soothsayers, farmers, star-readers, shopkeepers, battered slaves, snake charmers, perfume mixers, camel drivers, tax collectors, Apollo priests, Daphne priestesses, and Roman soldiers. Just about any occupation one could imagine attends our worship services," declared Simeon.

"This morning in the marketplace I heard a term for the first time to describe all of us. It seems The Way has become such a force in the city that non-believing Antiochenes have nicknamed us, *Christianois*." I announced.

"I like it! It's got a rhythmic tune," Simeon proclaimed.

"I just heard that term walking through the Forum on the way here! What does it mean?" Lucius asked.

"The compellation is of Hellenistic origin. It's common practice for Greeks to reference groups by a name. The Messiah's name in Greek is *Christos* and the Greek term for 'belonging to' is *ianus*, hence *Christianois*," Manaen translated.

"It seems we are now a distinct and separate sect from Judaism, maybe even a spiritual and political force within Antioch," said Titus with a laugh. Within weeks, even the local Roman officials were referring to us as Christians.

Chapter Forty-One
A Time of Giving

"Plenty has made me poor."
Ovid

Barnabas and I had been teaching together in Antioch for several months. On our twelfth Sabbath together Simeon began the sunset service as usual. He led us in several songs of praise. Then, something unusual occurred during our third worship song. A small group of Jerusalemite believers unexpectedly entered Manaen's courtyard.

There were frequent correspondences between the Jerusalem and Antioch church, but we had never received a letter regarding this visit. The mother church in Jerusalem had an endless thirst for news regarding its Syrian daughter, the Antioch church. We thought our guests were merely Jewish visitors quenching their longing for congregational anecdotes.

One of our visitors, Agabus, strolled to the front of the congregation. We instantly sensed he had some ominous news. Agabus solemnly asked Barnabas, "May I address the congregation?" Aware of Agabus' eminence, Barnabas nodded his head yes. Agabus was a Jewish Christian gifted in prophecy.

"I've been showed by the Spirit that there is going to be a great famine. It will spread over the entire Roman Empire. The grain from Egypt will become rare," Agabus prophesied to us. "There will be no harvesting in the fields of Judea and Egypt. Crops will wither in the ground, and parched soil will bear no grain." Agabus then stood silent before the congregation.

"God has just spoken to us through His servant, Agabus. As a church, may we act on this prophecy!" Barnabas encouraged, breaking the congregational silence.

"The poor, Jewish Christians in Jerusalem will be hit the hardest!" I informed.

"Yes, the believers in Jerusalem will struggle more than anyone. Jerusalem's synagogues are already full of disdain for The Way. If rations are distributed in the Holy City, our fellow believers will be pushed to the back of the line," agreed Barnabas.

"Barnabas and Paul are right. There are a lot of poor believers in Jerusalem. Many followers have lost their jobs because of religious discrimination. They will be the first in the city to experience starvation," Agabus declared, his commanding voice filling the room. "Please, remember your brothers and sisters in Jerusalem. We will need your help because of meager harvests over the coming seasons."

"We must help our Christian brethren in Jerusalem: the poor, unemployed, slaves, orphans, and widows. The shortage will force grain prices beyond their means. They will starve to death unless we offer aid!" Manaen averred.

"We should spend the next several weeks collecting funds for the church in Jerusalem," Titus suggested.

"We would be grateful for any action taken by the Antioch church." Agabus said, "Forgive our intrusion regarding this matter during your worship services, but since we just arrived in Antioch it seemed the best time and way to inform you. We wish to celebrate the Sabbath day with you! Please continue your service."

Barnabas asked me to give an impromptu sermon on charity and donating to a relief fund. The exhortation was embraced by all, even though our Jewish congregational members were financially stressed from reaching deep into their pockets for weekly church tithes and monthly synagogue taxes. The Gentile members who were just learning to tithe grasped the importance of helping others in dire need. However, the concept of reaching beyond their own community to help people in another nation was foreign to them.

Before the benediction, Simeon stood up and offered, "Everyone has seen how Jewish non-believers shun Jewish Christians in Antioch. When the famine occurs in Jerusalem, our Christian brethren will be completely ostracized. I recommend we establish a Jerusalem Church Collection, as suggested by Titus, today!"

The Holy Spirit spoke to the congregation and the proposal was unanimously approved. When we passed our tithing basket for the Jerusalem Church Collection, everyone gave from the wealthy merchants to poverty-stricken slaves. All gave of their earnings or possessions to help Jerusalem's saints.

After the service and niceties we invited our visitors to stay at our living quarters. On the way back to the southern gate, Agabus said, "Everyone was so charitable! Does their generosity support your ministry here?"

"No, Barnabas and I have worked in our tent shop since my arrival in Antioch. We decided during our journey here from Tarsus to support ourselves, be it here or wherever the Lord may lead us."

"It helps us model a strong work ethic. Plus, we don't want to impose upon others while living and teaching among them," Barnabas added.

"Wise and admirable," Agabus confirmed, walking into our tent shop. He and his companions stayed with us that night and for seven more nights till their departure.

Antiochene Christians tithed extra coins over the following weeks and months. Some believers contributed by selling duplicate household items that weren't being used. Others worked overtime or made extra items to sell for the relief fund. Everyone gave what she or he could afford. All were good stewards during this period of collection for the Jerusalem church.

～～

Barnabas and I continued to teach the Gospel during the remaining summer months. Meanwhile, Antioch's believers continued financially and prayerfully to support the Jerusalem Church Collection. Then, as Agabus predicted, drought hit the entire Roman Empire.

In the summer of that year, the Egyptian farmers' fields were plagued with droughts. This crisis was exacerbated when a heavy flood swept through the southern and eastern Mediterranean areas, just before harvest time. This deluge destroyed the sparse summer wheat crops, fall seedlings, and grain supplies in Egyptian storehouses.

Nearly two-thirds of the Roman Empire relied on Egypt for wheat. Famine swept across the Roman world by mid-September. The poor and underprivileged across the Empire were starving. Most families struggled to buy a weekly loaf of bread.

In early October we began receiving reports that the Jerusalem church's congregants were surviving on crumbs. The local elders chose Barnabas and me to deliver the collection to Jerusalem. What an honor it was, being chosen by the Antioch church to deliver and present our relief fund.

Barnabas hand-picked four burly, Gentile men who had just became believers to accompany us. He chose these men for protection, but more importantly as living proof of the Holy Spirit's work among Antioch's Gentiles. Also, they were young men Barnabas was mentoring.

Our relief group left Antioch the second week of October amidst prayers and God's protective hand. We carried the relief fund by foot to Seleucia, then by coastal vessel to Caesarea, and once again by foot up to Jerusalem.

We had a few minor confrontations during the journey, but nothing major. God safely facilitated our nine-day journey to the Holy City. We arrived in the City of David during the Sabbath's evening synagogue services.

With discretion and without attracting much attention, we went directly to the Jerusalem church's central congregational service. It was held at Barnabas' cousin Mary's house; the same house where believers had gathered several years ago to pray for Peter, who had a miraculous escape from prison during their prayer meeting. Her home was large and employed many servants.

Jerusalemite believers like Agabus couldn't believe their eyes as they thankfully and joyfully greeted us. Our travel fatigue evaporated upon handing the collection over to the church elders and congregation.

～～

We gave the congregation the monetary gifts, then fellowshipped with them for a long time. The church leaders asked Barnabas, "Can we privately meet with Saul and you?"

"By all means!" Barnabas replied.

"Let's go over to my house. It's only a few blocks from here," said James, the half-brother of Jesus and head elder of the Jerusalem church, as we left Mary's estate.

"We are looking forward to meeting with you, for we have worthy words to share with the leaders of the mother church," I stated walking down a narrow alley.

"What are you going to tell them?" Barnabas whispered in my ear.

"I'm going to set before them the Gospel that we preach among the Gentiles," I whispered before entering James' residence.

Our private meeting was with men of impeccable character and faith, Jerusalem's church elders. Among them were Peter and John, Jesus' youngest apostle. The elders chose Barnabas to be our spokesperson.

"Once again, we would like to thank the Antiochene believers for their act of charity," James shared, sitting down on a black wool rug.

"Is this the kind of work the Holy Spirit is doing in Antioch?" Peter inquired before roaming about the one-room bungalow.

"Yes! This gift is evidence of the Holy Spirit's work in Antioch, among the Jews and especially among Gentiles," Barnabas responded while sitting down beside James.

"Gentiles? Interesting!" James muttered before motioning for everyone to sit down.

"Gentiles have fervently responded to the Gospel! Saul's teaching of the Gospel has broad appeal among all races in Antioch. You commissioned me to investigate the Gentile ministry in Antioch, but it is Saul's calling to teach the Gospel unto Gentiles. People there call him the Gentile Apostle!" Barnabas informed.

"Salvation is for all souls, Jews and Gentiles," I avowed, offering a Christological insight.

"Jesus did embrace all races during his earthly ministry," John reminded the other elders. The Holy Spirit was at work in our meeting, eliminating all distrust, misinterpretations, and conflicts.

"Thousands of Gentiles have accepted the Lord as their Savior in Antioch. Furthermore, racial division and strife in our young church is diminutive. I would like for the Jerusalem church leaders to acknowledge as well as decree that the Gospel is for all races Jews and Gentiles!" I said.

"This is unorthodox. Share with us what you are teaching the Gentiles," James requested.

I spent the next twenty minutes presenting the Gospel that I preached among the Gentiles. "My ministry has been ordained by the Lord," I concluded amidst a quiet room. "Do you think I'm running or have run my race in vain regarding the Lord's ministry among the Gentiles?" My voice broke the long silence.

"No. I think you should continue your ministry among the Gentiles in Antioch and areas beyond Syria, since it has been sanctioned by the Lord. Meanwhile, I will continue to focus on our Jewish brethren," Peter declared.

"So, everyone agrees? For Yahweh, who was at work in the ministry of Peter as an apostle to the Jews, was also at work in my ministry as an apostle to the Gentiles," I summarized Peter's remarks for verification.

After what seemed like several minutes of silence. James acknowledged, "For God, who was at work in the ministry of Peter as an apostle to the

Jews, was also at work in your ministry as an apostle to the Gentiles. Go to the Gentiles, and we'll go to the Jews."

"Yes," John said, then validated our accord by trading right sandals with Barnabas.

"It seems we all acknowledge the Lord and Holy Spirit are at work in your apostolic calling," affirmed Peter. Then James, Peter, and John, those reputed to be pillars, gave Barnabas and me the right hand of fellowship.

"Alleluia!" Barnabas and I exclaimed.

"Saul, forgive us for doubting your calling. The Lord gave you this commission several years ago, but we've been slow to open our ears and hearts to it. Since our last conversation, the Lord has shown me that the gift of the Holy Spirit has been poured out on the Gentiles," Peter said.

"Barnabas told me of your vision. The Lord can change anyone's direction, evident in the way He has altered our paths," I remarked with a chortle.

"He sure can!" Peter chuckled as Barnabas stood up to leave, since it was getting late.

"Before you leave, I'd like to ask you one other favor. Will you continue to remember the poor?" James queried.

"It's the very thing I'm eager to do." I responded. "May we never forget the plight of the poor, nor fail to respond to the pleas of orphans and widows. May we be wise stewards of our earthly blessings and funds."

"It's as Solomon said, 'Whoever loves money never has money enough; whoever loves wealth is never satisfied with his income.'" Barnabas said.

"Jesus told us, 'It is easier for a camel to go through the eye of a needle than for a rich man to enter the Kingdom of God,'" John quoted before embracing us farewell.

"Yes, God doesn't want us to be greedy for money but eager to serve," Peter informed.

"The Lord summarized this topic when he said, 'Do not store up for yourselves treasures on earth, where moth and rust destroy, and where thieves break in and steal. But store up for yourselves treasures in heaven, where moth and rust do not destroy, and where thieves do not break in and steal. For where your treasure is, there your heart will be also,'" James said, standing up to embrace us goodbye.

"May your teaching enable believers to focus on the ultimate treasure," Peter prayed after all the elders and I stood up.

"Yes, Christ," James agreed, embracing us. "We'd like for you to return to Antioch and convey our thanks. Please continue your mission work among all the races and helping the poor. May your efforts create a spiritual awakening across Asia Minor and the Orient."

"Just as you are grateful for the Antioch church's gifts, we feel blessed by the Jerusalem church's acceptance of our Gentile ministry," affirmed Barnabas.

"God be with you!" James said as he opened the front door.

"And with you also!" Barnabas and I bade, walking out the door where our four Gentile companions were patiently waiting.

Barnabas gave our cohorts a tour of the city. Jerusalem's skyline had changed since my last visit over seven years ago. The Holy Temple was nearly completed; Herod's Palace wall had been expanded; and the Roman army built a moat around the Fortress of Antonia.

We spent that evening with Barnabas' first cousin, Mary, and her son, John Mark. John Mark, now a young man, repeatedly begged throughout the night, "Please, let me join you on your trip back to Antioch and lands beyond. I want to serve the Lord!"

Chapter Forty-Two
A Time for a Change

"The Spirit of the Lord will come upon you in power
and you will be changed into a different person."
The prophet, Samuel

The next morning at first light Barnabas and I went to the Temple Marketplace. We were inside a friend's bakery shop waiting for fresh bread to be pulled out of the oven, when a large crowd gathered outside. Several caravans of pilgrims had just arrived in the city; furthermore, they had sniffed out the odor of baking yeast.

The baker stepped outside his shop and said, "I will feed your stomachs for free, if you let Paul feed your souls with the Gospel."

"Okay!" Everyone shouted with glee.

"Paul, why don't you preach your sermon on the four S's." Barnabas suggested before I exited the bakery shop.

I squeezed through the crowd, then jumped atop a fountain wall and said, "Fellow Jerusalemites and visitors, lend me your souls. I come to worship God, not humanity. Humanity has a tendency to worship itself and this bemuses our being. We need to acknowledge the transgressions in our lives and sin's lure, because they intoxicate our souls.

"We have a sacred, righteous God! And, just like an honorable judge has the responsibility to sentence guilty criminals, so must Jehovah judge us for the offenses we've committed. If God didn't punish us for our sins, He wouldn't be holy!"

"You have finally come to your senses!" A synagogue elder yelled, while passing by.

"Since we have a righteous God, some animal or person has to pay the ransom for our disobedience. We used to sacrifice lambs and turtledoves for our transgressions, but now there's no need to do this. Jehovah sent a substitute to bare everyone's sins!

"God sent His only Son, Jesus Christ, to earth as a human infant. At the age of thirty, Jesus embarked upon a three-year ministry of teaching God's truth. At the age of thirty-three, God poured out His wrath on His heavenly Son. Jesus bore all of humanity's sins, when he was nailed to a Roman cross, in this very city twelve years ago. His sacrificial death was a substitute for the transgressions of all nations, races and generations. That one sacrifice satisfied God's requirement for sin's payment."

"And we may nail you to a cross!" Several zealots shouted, joining the crowd.

"Since that day, no Jew or Gentile has needed to make an animal sacrifice. We have been forgiven, and now we can have the gift of salvation. All you have to do is believe in Jehovah's Son, Jesus, and you will have eternal life in Heaven. Plus, we now have direct access to God through Jesus. The Lord is now present everywhere, not just in the Holy Temple's Holy of Holies."

"Blasphemy!" the growing crowd screamed.

I continued to preach and by late morning, the local residents were throwing fruits, vegetables, and stones at us. They barked obscenities at us throughout the afternoon hours. Murderous plots were being set in motion against me by sunset. An air of turmoil blanketed Jerusalem that evening.

We spent a painful night sitting in Mary's kitchen, listening to numerous clashes between believing and non-believing Jews. I had thrown the city back into religious chaos. It was as if time had stood still for seven years. Intolerance and hatred had merely taken a nap.

On our third day in Jerusalem, Barnabas and I felt led to return unto Antioch. We were in Jerusalem for such a short period of time, it didn't seem like we were even there. Fortunately, the Jerusalem Church Collection arrived safety and the council meeting was a success.

Packing that morning, I realized God had taught me another lesson in grace and humility. Furthermore, these virtues became the legs for my spiritual walk through life.

It was approaching late fall, the time of year when sailing on the Mediterranean Sea became a perilous event. We decided to walk the seventeen days back to Syria with our fellow Antiochenes. We had an additional member on the return trip. Mary reluctantly agreed to let John Mark join us.

Our small caravan returned to Antioch on a cold Sabbath night, just hours before a major storm. Our chilled bodies entered Manaen's house just as a courtyard full of warm souls were leaving the evening worship service. We went into Manaen's living room with all who could stay, stoked a fire, and told story after story of the mother church's gratefulness.

~~

We spent the winter in Antioch. The Holy Spirit was at work in the hearts of people through godly instruction. Our church was blessed with outstanding teachers like Lucius, Luke, Manaen, Simeon, and Titus. Luke was a Gentile physician, who had heard the gospel earlier in the fall. He intellectually dissected the truth with his logical, rational, and medical mind. Within days he became a follower of Jesus Christ and his faith had grown like a mustard seed over the months.

In early March, Mother Nature packed her winter attire. On the Ides of March I told Barnabas, while finishing our last tent order, "From weather to time to people, there's one aspect of human life you can count on - things are going to change." I had finally comprehended that change is inevitable. Moreover, change brings opportunity if we allow God to use it in our lives.

"Good point! And without faith, change can cause us to dwell on our fears. Change brings growth and insight when we devotionally embrace its unknown proprieties," Barnabas remarked after helping John Mark load the second of three tents onto a Bedouin clan's cart.

"I've come to realize Jehovah is a God of adventure, growth, and change. It seems the Holy Spirit is preparing us for a change! Don't know when, where, or how, but I'm ready!" I said, making the last stitch on the third cilicium tent.

"Same here! Not sure if the changes will make our lives easier or more difficult, but I warmly welcome changes initiated by God," John Mark agreed, lifting the last tent.

"Even Antioch of Syria has changed! For decades, it was the most immoral city in the Roman Empire. The city cherished its vile behavior, ranging from ritual prostitution to taking human life for entertainment. The Orontes River's ethical depravity no longer overshadows the Tiber River,"

Barnabas claimed as they placed the third tent on the cart. Then the three of us departed our tent shop to witness outside Antioch's Coliseum.

"God has blessed Antioch with a moral metamorphosis," I remarked to Barnabas and John Mark as thousands of people brushed past us on their way to the Antioch Open, an annual four-day wrestling event featuring the region's finest athletes.

"We have seen the unchangeable change, the immoral pursue morality, the impatient have patience, the indecisive turn decisive, the insecure find security, the disconnected become interconnected, and the intolerant become tolerant," Barnabas remarked.

"Even though Antioch is our home congregation and base of operation, I think the breath of Heaven is blowing us elsewhere!" I suggested to Barnabas before we started teaching beside the Coliseum's main gate.

"Paul, I love you, brother. You're like the wind that moves forward to subsist." Barnabas joked while orchestrating the noisy crowd and missionary passion in his heart. "The Holy Spirit is the fountainhead of change. Tonight at Manaen's church service, we'll ask the church leaders to pray about a mission trip for us." He added just before I started sharing the Gospel.

That night, we meet with the elders and teachers before the evening service. We were worshipping the Lord and fasting, when the Holy Spirit said, "Set apart for me Barnabas and Saul for the work to which have I called them."

"Hallelujah!" Barnabas and I shouted with joy, then everyone went into the evening service.

Before the conclusion of that service, Simeon stood up and said, "The Holy Spirit spoke to the church elders and teachers earlier this evening. Barnabas and Saul are to be set apart from the Antiochene church for a specific task, missionary work." Every head in the courtyard turned toward either Barnabas or me.

"What is missionary work?" asked an inquisitive teenager.

"Missionary work is when one shares the Gospel and works of Christ with those who don't know him," replied Simeon.

Barnabas stood up and said, "Saul and I feel blessed to be chosen and called to do God's work. The Holy Spirit has been preparing both of us for a change over the last couple weeks. We are grateful for the directional light God has shined down upon our earthly paths."

"What will be your strategy?" Alcina, a strong-minded Roman

centurion, inquired as he stood by the rear gate. He knew two of Satan's generals on the spiritual battlefield are fear and confusion.

"Saul and I are going to visit frontiers, where people have never heard the Gospel. We'll reach out and teach the Gospel to all who will listen, then help new believers establish churches. We'll stay with these new congregations to nourish and instruct them till they are able to stand on their own feet. Then, we'll move to another city and start all over again," Barnabas explained.

"It seems like our congregation is finally able to stand on its own two feet," Manaen joked, filling the courtyard with laughter.

"At last!" Barnabas remarked with jocularity, continuing the mirth. Then he added seriously, "Saul and I will hold ourselves accountable to the Lord as well as this church. The Holy Spirit's calling will forever change us. May this change make us more Christlike as we rely on God's grace and mercy."

"We pray it will! And don't comprise the doctrine of Truth! For you are God's ambassadors, set apart to feed hungry souls!" Titus exclaimed.

～～

Barnabas and I left Manaen's abode, not long after the evening service, to pack. I told Barnabas on the way back to our tent shop, "Years ago, God revealed this direction to me. Unfortunately, it has taken me eleven years to find the path. Thank you for helping me discover it!"

"Plants, like character, take time to blossom once the seed is planted! God was cultivating you for this work during your days in Damascus, the Arabian Desert, Jerusalem, and Tarsus. He also was using the Antiochene church to nourish your character and godly gifts."

"I like your positive view. Speaking of character, I've been observing and admiring yours. You take your cues from heaven, not from what others wish of you," I responded in an encouraging tone. Barnabas was rubbing off on me.

"Thank you. Good character leads to change. Also, character doesn't come from conforming to worldly ways, but from living a godly life and giving praises to God. People follow leaders, like you, who have character," my best friend declared, then added, "Which brings me to the character of another."

"Anyone I know?"

"Yes, and I have a favor to ask of you regarding this individual."

"Ask away."

"I would like to bring my young cousin along with us on this mission trip," Barnabas expressed after we turned onto an empty thoroughfare.

I suppressed my initial response, supplementing the street's silence, then shouted, "John Mark?"

"Yes! The threads of ministry are being woven into the tapestry of his life," Barnabas assured me with a wide smile.

"He barely made the journey from Jerusalem to Antioch!"

"Mostly because of the beating he encountered outside of Gardara."

"I don't know. Sometimes, he acts like a little child."

"It's like Jesus said, 'I tell you the truth, unless you change and become like little children, you will never enter kingdom of Heaven. Therefore, whoever humbles himself like this child is the greatest in the kingdom of Heaven.'"

"Maybe, I'm too harsh on him because of his age."

"Please, look at him as a young man, not an impetuous adolescent," offered Barnabas.

"What would you have him do?"

"John Mark can oversee our travel details, food arrangements, and lodging. He can help us with baptisms and handle our documents."

"Missionary apprentice?"

"You got it! His recent logic to join us has been so persuasive, I now fear offending God more than my trepidations of taking him," Barnabas declared as we strolled past the lifeless marketplace.

"He seems a little immature."

"John Mark has physically and mentally matured a lot over the last couple of months."

"What about his spiritual maturity?"

"The Jerusalem church has been worshipping at his mother's house for nearly fifteen years. Peter is the preacher there. John Mark is like a sponge during worship services."

"Peter always spoke highly of John Mark, while I was staying with him," I thought aloud.

"He still does. Peter baptized John Mark and looks upon him as a son. John Mark personally beheld Jesus' crucifixion, resurrection, and ascension. His firsthand accounts of these miraculous events would offer valuable insights. So, what do you think?"

"Fine, as long as he can handle the rigors and demands of the trip," I agreed before entering our tent shop.

"Alleluia!" Barnabas yelled, patting me on the back as we stepped inside the tent shop. On our last night in Antioch, the last day of May, we spent packing for our long journey. We were leaving in the morning for our first mission trip and hoping to avoid being ambushed.

EVENTS IN PAUL'S LIFE	APPROX. TIMES EVENTSOCCURED	APPROX. AGE WHEN EVENTS CONCLUDED
Born unto and raised by Jewish Parents in Tarsus	Spring 1 AD - Summer 14 AD	1 - 13 years old
Goes to Jerusalem, studies under Gamaliel, attorney in Jerusalem	Summer 14 AD - Summer 22 AD	13 - 21 years old
Returns to Tarsus, his hometown, worked as a Rabbi and tentmaker	Summer 22 AD - Summer 33 AD	21 - 32 years old
Returns to Jerusalem to investigate then persecute followers of Jesus	Fall 33 AD - Spring 35 AD	33 - 34 years old
Conversion on the road to Damascus	Spring 35 AD	34 years old
His religious sojourn in Arabia Desert	Spring 35 AD - Spring 38 AD	34 - 37 years old
Returns to Damascus then travels to Jerusalem	Spring 38 AD - Spring 38 AD	37 years old
Leaves Jerusalem and returns to Tarsus. Then the Silent Years.	Spring 38 AD - Winter 44 AD	37 - 43 years old
Reunites with Barnabas in Antioch and returns Jerusalem	Spring 45 AD - Spring 46 AD	42- 45 years old
1st Mission Trip (goes with Barnabas)	Spring 46 AD - Fall 48 AD	45 - 47 years old
Wrote Book of Galatians (from Antioch)	Fall 49 AD	48 years old

Return to Antioch/part of Jerusalem Council & returns with council letter	Fall 48 AD - Spring 50 AD	48 - 49 years old
2nd Mission Trip: wrote I and II Thessalonians	Spring 50 AD - Summer 52 AD	49 - 51 years old
3rd Mission Trip: wrote I and II Corinthians & Romans	Spring 53 AD - Spring 57 AD	51 - 56 years old
Returns to Jerusalem then is arrested and trialed	Spring 57 AD	56 years old
Caesarea Imprisonment and witnessing to Gentile leaders	Summer 57 AD - Fall 59 AD	56 - 58 years old
Voyage to Rome including storm and shipwreck	Fall 59 AD - Spring 60 AD	59 years old
1st Roman imprisonment wrote: Ephesians, Philippians, Colossians, Philemon	Spring 60 AD - Spring 62 AD	59 - 61 years old
Freed from prison, wrote 1st Timothy & Titus, 4th mission trip	Spring 62 AD - Spring 67 AD	61 - 66 years old
2nd Roman imprisonment wrote: 2nd Timothy	Spring 67AD - Summer 67 AD	66 years old
Death	Summer 67 AD	66 years old

GRATITUDE

I would like to thank my family; Rachel, Kristopher, and Wendy Tustin for their patience and understanding while I deprived them of our time together to write this novel. Their love gave me the foundation and support I needed to write this review of Paul's life. Also, like to thank my parents, Vicki and Carl Tustin for their love and guidance.

Also, I would to thank the follow sources for inspiration, while writing this book: *Holy Bible*, John Pollock's *The Apostle*, Charles Swindoll's *Paul*, Horatio B. Hackett's *Commentary on Acts*, John Polhill's *Acts*, Max Anders' *Commentary of Galatians, Ephesians, Philippians, and Colossians*, Shepherds Notes (Books) on the New Testament and Paul's Life, John MacArthur's *1 &2 Thessalonians*, John F. Walvoord, Roy B. Zuck, and Dallas Seminary Faculty's *New Testament Bible Knowledge Commentary*, Gene Getz's *Paul Living for the Call of Christ*, Nelson's *New Illustrated Bible Dictionary*.

William Barclay's *The Letters to the Corinthians*, J Vernon McGee's *First and Second Corinthians*, Ivor J. Davidson's *The Birth of the Church*, Sholem Asch's *The Apostle* and Robert Picirilli's *Paul the Apostle*, A.W. Tozer's *The Pursuit of God*, John B. Polhill's *Paul and his Letters*, and Randy Alcorn's *Heaven*, Elisabeth Elliott's *Suffering is not for Nothing*, *and* Wayne Sneed the Director of Orphanos Foundation, Todd Burpo's and Lynn Vincent's *Heaven is for Real*.

Also, James M Freeman's *Manners & Customs of the Bible*, Rich Warren's *The Purpose Driven Life*, Woodrow Kroll's *Book of Romans*, Douglas J. Moo's *Encountering the Book of Romans*, Community Bible Study on Ephesians, Colleen McCullough's *The First Man in Rome*, Anne Rice's *Christ the Lord Out of Egypt*, John MacArthur's *Twelve Ordinary Men*, Jim Cymbala-Pastor of the Brooklyn Tabernacle, Don Piper's and Cecil Murphey's *90 minutes in Heaven*, and stories of Ronnie Mohundro.

Plus, F. F. Bruce's *Paul; Apostle of the Heart Set Free*, Ken Blanchard's and Phil Hodges' *Lead Like Jesus (book 2)*, Sam Shaw - pastor of Orchard

Fellowship, Ronnie Stephens -pastor and missionary, Adrian Rodger - pastor of Bellevue Baptist Church, Howard Clark –pastor, Chuck Herring – pastor of Collierville First Baptist Church, Carter Conlon – pastor of Times Square Church, Jim Holland – pastor of St. Patrick Presbyterian Church, K Love radio station, life of Paul, and the Holy Spirit.

A special acknowledgement to my son, Kristopher Tustin, for his creative ideas on action scenes in Paul's life. Also, I'd like to recognize Vicki Tustin, Virginia Mohundro, and Dr. Dennis Hensley for editing this work and being a strong encourager. Thanks to Wendy Tustin for inspiring ideas to let the pages flow like a mountain stream. Also, thanks for the jocularity and ideas from my good friends, Tom Hall and Larry Dormois. Finally, endless gratitude for Rachel Tustin for putting humor in this book and my life.

May the truths in this novel take up residence in your heart, mind, and soul, May every generation find inspiration in the following pages. Along with the numerous missionaries who have influenced my life through their service, words, and faith in the Lord.

CPSIA information can be obtained at www.ICGtesting.com
Printed in the USA
BVOW041730190513

321117BV00001B/56/P

9 781477 263013